Secrets Under the Mesa

by
Nicki Huntsman Smith

NHS MARKETING, LLC

Chapter 1

On the news this morning, I saw a story about a homeless man who had been tossed into a garbage truck while taking a nap in a dumpster. The driver heard the man's screams coming from the back of the truck en route to his next stop. Fortunately, he hadn't activated the compacting mechanism while the homeless man was still in the belly of the beast. Emergency personnel extricated the fellow from the truck along with hundreds of pounds of the detritus we humans generate in abundance.

A Channel 8 news team arrived at the scene after the man had been taken to a local hospital. They filmed the garbage truck with its back door open and its contents spilling out onto the tidy street while a dainty blonde reported from the garbage sidelines. The homeless man was fortunate to have suffered only a fractured hip as well as minor contusions and abrasions. More details of his condition would be reported later on in the newscast, she informed that small percentage of Dallas-Ft. Worth viewers who happened to be watching Channel 8 at 5:30 in the morning. She managed to hide any revulsion at the stench which doubtlessly surrounded her, although I'd bet once the camera stopped rolling she crinkled that perfect nose in distaste. My HD television conveyed such detail that I imagined cartoon squiggles drawn in the air above the pile.

The symbolism here is so visceral even a child could grasp it. But what's really interesting about the news story has nothing to do with the 'disposable humans' metaphor, nor is it the obvious commentary on society's handling of indigents and 'those less fortunate'. The *really* interesting thing is that in the far left corner of the screen, approximately thirty feet or so from the garbage truck, the cameraman had inadvertently filmed something that had no relevance to the current news story at all.

It held no significance for anyone but me and a small group of others; at least in the short term. No one outside of that exclusive group would have recognized what they were seeing, if they'd been attentive enough to have noticed it in the first place. And frankly, considering the observational skills of most people, I'd be very surprised if that were the case.

What I'd seen in that three seconds of unfocused film footage sent me scurrying to the kitchen for the bottle of Mylanta. The shadowy figure caught by the camera in the pre-dawn gloom wasn't human. Oh, it would have appeared human from a distance. They have adapted very well to our culture. They wear clothing and move so similarly to us that the vast majority of our oblivious society wouldn't notice anything unusual. They've even learned to vocalize in a fashion, mimicking the cadence and inflection of our speech but not quite formulating actual words. If you heard one speak, it would sound like an animated conversation from another room where you couldn't quite make out the words.

And still, seeing the figure caught on the perimeter of a local news story wasn't the MOST interesting thing – I'd seen them before, after all. The most interesting thing was that the creature had been in the city. . .the glitzy uptown area of Dallas, to be exact.

The invasion had begun.

I scrambled to the kitchen and gulped down a couple healthy swallows of the magical, upset-tummy-settling elixir to which I'd recently developed an addiction. Hey, it could be worse; at least I wasn't hopped up on drugs or shooting Jack Daniels for breakfast. What I had seen in the last six months had changed my life irrevocably and not in a good way; thus the excess stomach acid, insomnia, horrendous nightmares on the occasions when I was able to sleep and the persistent muscle tic in my left eyelid.

I stood in the kitchen considering my next move. Finally I reached for my cell phone, scrolled down my contacts list and found the number I was looking for.

"Benny, it's Josh," I said as soon as I heard the gruff voice on the other end.

"Why the hell are you calling so early, buttwipe?"

Ben was a big teddy bear. One with claws and fangs and a really bad temper during his occasional bouts of righteous indignation, but his heart was very much proportionate to the rest of him. Two hundred and sixty pounds of mostly muscle and only a tiny bit of blubber (he had a weakness for maple donuts) made him the biggest teddy bear I'd ever been lucky enough to call my friend.

"They're in the city," I said. Vocalizing this fact somehow crystallized the reality of it...a reality I wanted to deny.

The stunned silence on the other end of the phone assured me I had Ben's full attention. As a guy who was rarely at a loss for words (often ones of an expletive nature), this spoke volumes and actually made me feel better. Sharing this disturbing knowledge with another person seemed to diminish my own burden – slightly. I was also relieved that he hadn't dismissed it as typical journalist drama. As a feature writer for the Dallas Morning News, I occasionally indulged in artistic license. I wasn't a street reporter any more after all, so I was allowed some leeway.

However, this situation needed no colorful verbiage or titillating innuendo to hook anyone. Ben and I both understood that their presence in the city did not bode well for anyone.

"How do you know?" he said finally, clear voiced and fully awake now.

"I saw one on a local news story just now. It was in uptown on Pearl Street near the Arts District. The cameraman inadvertently caught it on some video they were shooting about a garbage truck incident."

"You're absolutely positive it was one of them?"

"Yeah, I'm sure."

"Shit," he said. "I'll be over in a few." Those were the words I was hoping to hear. Two reasonably intelligent people working on this problem were better than one, but three or four would be better still.

I picked up the phone again and called Abby.

"Abs, it's me, Josh." I could expect a modicum of graciousness from my former girlfriend despite the early hour – knee jerk politeness was a side effect of being raised in South Carolina. On only one occasion had I witnessed Abigail Brooke Montgomery behaving less than ladylike in the nine years I'd known her, and that was after Ben had plied her with Patrón shots at the Ghost Bar in Dallas. Until that night the worst four-letter word I'd heard her utter was 'dang'. *'Josh, you make me so dang mad sometimes.' 'Dang it, I have to get a root canal.' 'That dang boss of mine grabbed my behind today.'* Ben had practically peed his pants at the steady stream of foul language our gentle, southern-bred doll spewed that night at the bar. She never really forgave him for the subsequent two-day hangover.

"Joshua, what's wrong?" Sweet Abby. Her voice was as lovely as ever and even though I knew I'd awakened her, it just wasn't in her nature to be annoyed.

"They're in the city, Abs. I saw one on TV just now. It was caught in the background of a local news story in uptown."

"Are you sure? Why do you think it was one of them?"

"It turned its head and I caught a glimpse of the eyeshine," I said.

Again, speaking the words out loud to another human being lessened my anxiety. I was calmer now and my stomach was starting to settle. Spreading the misery amongst my friends was apparently every bit as curative as the Mylanta.

"Oh, Lord help us," Abby whispered. This wasn't just an expression of dismay. My Southern Baptist friend was speaking directly to God at that moment. And what could it hurt? We were going to need all the help we could get.

"Let me throw on some clothes and I'll be over as soon as I can."

"Thanks, Abby. Be safe, babe." I set the phone down and cursed myself for the little slip. Abby hadn't officially been my 'babe' for the last two years. The breakup hadn't been my idea, of course. Good god, she was the perfect woman . . . drop-dead gorgeous, long auburn hair, hazel green eyes and a wicked sense of humor that broke through that southern decorum at the most unexpected times. I still pined for her, and of course everyone but Abby realized this. Of course, I'd always known she was out of my league. I'm no Marty Feldman, but Abby could have her choice of society's crème de la crème, which included not just decent looking guys, but hunks who pulled down six figures, drove BMWs and vacationed in Cypress. And that's how I mollified myself after the breakup – she probably always knew she could do better and finally wised up. That was the balm I applied to my broken heart and wounded pride, and it contained a big dose of denial. The truth is Abby didn't really want *that* guy. She just wanted something I couldn't give her. Hello intimacy issues, I'm your BFF, Joshua Hawkins.

There was one more phone call I needed to make. Dylan might already be awake at this hour since his schedule at the 24 hour animal clinic was erratic and demanding.

My best friend also happened to be the greatest guy I know. Dylan (christened by his free-spirited, peace activist parents as 'Dylan Mandella Saretsky') had opened his practice shortly after completing four years of post grad veterinary school. Operating in one of the lowest income neighborhoods in south Dallas where he offered discounted services (oftentimes free) resulted in countless healthy, happy pets which otherwise would suffer or be euthanized.

"Dylan, were you up?" I could never tell with him. He always sounded happy to answer my calls no matter what time it was or whether he had fifty other more important things to do than talk to me.

"Yeah, buddy. I'm at the clinic. A Chihuahua got sat on by a fat lady. Seriously, you can't make this stuff up. Broke both his back legs, poor little guy."

"Is he okay?"

"Yeah, he'll be fine as long as Mrs. Jackson starts checking her Lazy Boy before plopping her fat ass down. What's up, Josh?"

I was fairly certain Dylan preferred the

company of animals over humans most of the time, with the exception of our close-knit little group. Abby and Ben adored him as much as I did. If it weren't for the fact that Dylan was gay, I'd have been a little worried about Abby falling for him. I mean, I know she's going to find another guy someday – maybe even get married, but I couldn't bear it if it were to my best friend. I know this makes me a selfish, horrible person, but when I introduced Abby to Dylan after we'd been dating a few weeks, I felt profound gratitude concerning my best friend's sexual preference. And before you judge me, know this: if Matthew McConaughey had a better looking, younger brother with the same Texas drawl, you'd have Dylan.

"We got problems," I said and repeated the story for the third time in the last fifteen minutes.

"This is bad, Josh. Really, really bad."

"I know."

"I'm just about finished. Candace comes in at 6:00. I'll leave as soon as she gets here." Dylan's business partner was the female version of himself – pretty, altruistic and a player for the other team. Me as well as all other hetero males with whom Candace came into contact couldn't help but find that last part deeply dismaying.

"Okay, buddy, see ya soon." I set the phone down on the counter and started a fresh pot of coffee. It was only 5:30 on a Saturday morning and my spidey sense told me it would be a very long day.

Under different circumstances, I'd be feeling pretty good about sitting in my living room, surrounded by the three people I loved most in the world, with the exception of my parents, of course, who were safely out of the fray and living in Florida.

The information network on which I'd been working diligently for the last six months would impress even the Wayne Madsens of the world. Hell, my living room could pass for a tiny slice of NORAD. All the electronics and hardware represented a small fortune and had wiped out my savings and every bit of credit I could wring from Citibank, Capital One, and the very nice lady at Frost Bank who had approved my small business loan. Hopefully, I'll be around long enough to pay for it all.

As a writer and a journalist, I could access information most people didn't realize was available. As a moderately talented hacker, the information I dug up got a lot more interesting. And disturbing.

Dylan had stopped to buy breakfast on his way to my apartment. Despite the circumstances, Ben looked downright euphoric, sitting in my best chair with a cup of French roast in one hand and a maple donut in the other. The man knew how to compartmentalize, so the prospect of mankind's imminent demise was tucked into a neat mental cubbyhole at the moment, which enabled him to focus on the nirvana that was maple donuts.

"So, Joshua. What do we do now?" Abby looked pensive, as any normal, non-maple donut addict would. We all dealt with the terrifying knowledge we possessed in different ways, but we had agreed months ago that the information would not be shared with anyone outside of our group. It was simply too dangerous. If we let it be known that we suspected members of our own government were plotting against us – possibly allying themselves with an intelligent non-human species whose agenda appeared counterintuitive to the welfare of mankind – we might as well check ourselves into Guantanamo Bay right now. Or a psych ward.

Don't think I don't realize how crazy this sounds. A day doesn't go by that I don't, on some level, wish to be blissfully ignorant of what was happening. For whatever reason – fate, divine intervention, bad luck, I happened to be in the right place at the right time to witness the events that led to this point.

Chapter 2

Six months ago, on a magnificent April day in north Texas, I'd been up early surfing the net, looking for ideas for my next feature article, when I stumbled across a blog about a mysterious small town in New Mexico. I found the web design fairly amateurish but the content was entertaining, so I kept reading "The Mysteries at Dulce." The gist of the blog alleged the existence of a massive, underground biogenetic laboratory run by no less than our government in alliance with (wait for it...) extraterrestrials. In addition to the laboratory, the blog claimed that a secret U.S. military base resided there as well. Both had been built in a vast subterranean complex somewhere below the outskirts of the sleepy town of Dulce. According to the blog, this base housed all manner of curious flying crafts which were, at the least, nothing our government admitted to knowing about and even more likely, had originated somewhere other than our planet. Or perhaps had been built on Earth, by Earthlings, utilizing alien technology.

I'd heard these kinds of stories before, of course. With the explosion of accessible information courtesy of the internet, fringe groups and conspiracy theorists ran amuck these days – the Dulce story was the stuff of wet dreams for those guys. But what caught my attention was a three-line paragraph near the end of the blog:

"Local resident, Joseph McCullough, who resides near the town of Dulce, contacted one of our members with claims of having seen alien aircraft in the night skies on numerous occasions as well having had several encounters with mysterious 'men in black' types. On one such encounter, he alleged the presence of an entity which appeared human but was (according to Mr. McCullough) most definitely not. When we attempted to contact Mr. Mc-

Cullough again in an effort to obtain more details of his encounter, we were unable to locate him." The blog was dated from March of 2009 – more than two years ago.

That was when I started to get an uneasy feeling in my gut. I hadn't seen my uncle in more than twenty years. My mom's younger brother was the rebel of the family. He'd moved away from Texas in his early twenties and lived the life of a nomad for some time before settling down in New Mexico with his lovely Native American bride. Uncle Joe was, in the estimation of my twelve-year old self, the coolest member of the family.

I had no doubt that the Joseph McCullough mentioned in the article was my uncle. He'd always had a fascination with alien abductions and UFO sightings and on one occasion, showed me a number of photographs he'd taken from various locations: Groom Lake, Roswell, Southern California – mostly the Southwest U.S . from what I remember – which contained suspicious-looking flying objects and light anomalies in the night sky. Honestly, at the time I wasn't impressed. I was just a kid, after all, and my interests were limited to sports, skateboards and recently, a fascination with the opposite sex. Crazy stuff aside, I still thought Uncle Joe was cool. He was a few years younger than my mother, had long hair which he had grown out after a four-year stint in the Air Force and which he kept pulled back in a ponytail. He could also play the guitar, a skill which eluded me despite months of practice and the conviction that it would magically open female doors for me.

The last time I saw him was in the early nineties when he'd brought his fiancée to Dallas to meet the family. It was love at first sight for me and probably had been for him as well. Alameda, a brown-skinned beauty with doe eyes and perfect white teeth, inspired my first attempt at poetry, in which I attempted to describe her exotic beauty. I'm ashamed to say that the rest of the family did not share my enthusiasm. A non-white had never married into our family before and they weren't prepared to embrace the idea at the time. This was never spelled out to me as a kid and for a long time, I didn't understand why we never saw Uncle Joe or his wife after that. On a few occasions over the next two decades, my mother attempted to contact him. I'm fairly certain she'd had regrets about not only her behavior, but that of the family as well – but the damage had been done. The ties had been severed and the last I'd heard Uncle Joe and Alameda were still living in northern New Mexico in a mobile home somewhere in the desert.

It seemed that somewhere was in the vicinity of Dulce and after embarking on an internet information-gathering mission for the next hour, I'd been convinced I had my next story idea. The pleasing kicker – it would require a road trip. I'd called Ben, whose work schedule as a part-time fitness trainer and nightclub 'security presence' (the high-end joints where he worked disdained the word 'bouncer'), was the most flexible. He was delighted at the prospect. "Fuck, yeah!" were his exact words, I believe. The quality I most loved about my beefy friend was his sense of adventure and his dedication to experiencing all things new and different. At first glance, people assumed Ben was the typical 'all brawn and no brain's type', but anyone who talked to him for more than five minutes realized there was a lot going on behind upstairs. He'd dropped out of the University of Texas our junior year to do a four year stint in the military, but that hadn't stopped him from continuing his education. He was the only bouncer I knew who could quote Socrates, recite Shakespeare and intelligently debate the legal ramifications of Marbury v. Madison.

A quick call to my editor sealed the deal and we left two days later, our bags crammed into the trunk of my Honda Accord and a Coleman cooler full of ice, lunchmeat, Cokes and beer in the backseat.

Looking back now at the chain of events – the seemingly random circumstances which placed us squarely in the middle of this maelstrom – began with an innocuous road trip to visit a long-lost uncle and, as a sidebar, hunt some UFOs. The intriguing combination of these diverse elements had convinced my editor to approve the idea on the spot: a human interest story dealing with racial and social prejudice as it applied to family dynamics on a backdrop of alien abductions and livestock mutilations. He was downright giddy to the extent that he'd approved $200 per day in expenses – double the going rate. That meant Egg McMuffins for breakfast, bologna sandwiches for lunch topped off by an extravagant meal at Denny's for our evening repast. Many a road trip during our wild youths had been successfully executed on much less.

The 13-hour drive from Dallas to Dulce went quickly. Ben had loaded up his iPod with road trip-worthy selections and when we got tired of bellowing along with Van Morrison and The Eagles, we planned our itinerary for the remainder of our trip in northern New Mexico. Much depended on locating my uncle and frankly, I didn't think the odds were good. Worst case, we figured we'd talk to a few of the locals and see if they could point us in the direction of any

UFO hotspots.

We arrived at the Best Western on Highway 64 in Dulce at about 9:00 pm, checked into our room and after a cursory scan for 'McCullough, Joseph' in the white pages of the obligatory phone book (which resulted in nothing) we headed over for a quick dinner at the restaurant next door. Bonus: the hotel, which was located on the Jicarilla Apache Reservation nestled at the foot of the Southern Rocky Mountains, offered some nice scenery as well as an evening's entertainment in the form of the smoky but decent-sized Wild Horse Casino – which I hoped would provide opportunities for information gathering from and about the locals. With a population of only 2500, I hoped Dulce would prove typical of most small towns where everybody knows everybody.

With a couple of watery bourbon and Cokes in hand, we stood at one of the blackjack tables, watching the action. All the seats were taken and the casino was hopping, which was perfect. I figured someone in this place would know or have heard of Joe McCullough. The first few attempts resulted in no information and seemed to arouse mild suspicion. An intoxicated chubby guy got outright hostile and demanded to know if we were the Feds. Before he started swinging, Ben smoothly maneuvered me out of the fray like a border collie herding an errant sheep. As I surveyed the patrons through the haze of cigarette smoke, I got the distinct sense that a wagon-circling was occurring here. I was just contemplating how difficult it might prove to get information from the residents of Dulce when a tipsy middle-aged woman standing next to me 'accidentally' brushed her breasts against my arm. I decided she might be open to conversation and therefore a good candidate on which to try my luck again.

"Hi, I'm Joshua," I said with my most disarming of smiles. Despite the heavy mascara, she was attractive in a faded beauty kind of way, and more importantly she seemed delighted to make my acquaintance.

"A pleasure to meet you, Josh-yoo-wuh,"

she replied with the careful pronunciation of a drunk. "I'm Loretta," she said, extending her hand in a way that presented a hand-kissing opportunity. I could tell she was disappointed when I shook it then returned it unkissed.

"Are you from around here?" I asked.

"As a matter of fact, I've lived here for fifteen years, which in Dulce time is closer to fifty." Her smile was lovely, with only a hint of lechery. "And as another matter of fact, my house is only five minutes from here."

I imagined a Groucho Marx eyebrow waggling which almost made me laugh out loud, so I decided to cut to the chase before Loretta's libido got out of hand.

"I wonder if you know a man by the name of Joseph McCullough? He's my uncle and I'm trying to find him."

Disappointment turned down the corners of her mouth, evoked by either my uncle's name or the realization that I wouldn't be going home with her. Perhaps a bit of both.

She shook it off quickly though and I

could see the mental gears turning for a few seconds before she answered.

"Joe McCullough...yep, I know him. Well, know *of* him, I should say. Never met him personally though. He's one of those UFO guys. I used to see him at the Waterhole Café every now and then but not recently. He lives out in the foothills somewhere – he and his woman although I don't remember seeing her for a couple of years, now that I think about it."

Elation battled with a sense of disappointment – it seemed a tiny flame of my adolescent crush still burned in some forgotten corner. I forged ahead.

"So, no chance you'd have an address or maybe know the general vicinity in the foothills?" I asked.

"Darlin', if you keep looking at me with those baby blues, I'll tell you anything you want to hear."

I had to admire her tenacity. When I responded with nothing more than a tight smile, she sighed and said, "No, I don't have a clue. But I know someone who might. See that bartender over there?" She pointed to a dark-skinned man pouring drinks at the bar. "That's Charlie. He knows everybody in this town. I bet he can help you."

I thanked her and turned to Ben, who was looking quite amused by the dialogue.

"Shit, Josh. That's what you call a sure thing," he said as we walked toward the bar.

"Shut up, Benny."

"She might have a few miles on her but I bet that little cougar is a wildcat in bed."

I elbowed him sharply in the belly just as we reached the bar.

"What can I get you gentlemen?" Charlie's long black hair was pulled back in a sleek ponytail. His Native American features gave very little indication of his age. He could be 35 or 50.

"Charlie, right?" I extended my hand. "I'm Josh and this is my friend, Ben."

"Pleasure to meet you both." His pleasant demeanor belied the guarded look which appeared at the use of his name by someone he'd never met.

"I hope you can help me. I'm trying to locate my uncle. His name is Joseph Mc-

Cullough. Our family had a falling out with him years ago and I'm trying to reconnect."

Charlie's eyes gave away nothing. He glanced from my face to Ben's and back again. Something told me a stonewalling was about to commence.

"Sorry, can't help you. Can I get you boys a drink?"

I sighed inwardly, then tried again.

"I understand you know everyone in town. I was really hoping you could help me. I know my uncle was into a lot of weird stuff and I have some concerns about his safety."

A flicker behind the eyes told me I'd hit a nerve. I pushed the advantage. "Look, I know you don't know me from Adam, but all I want is to find my uncle and make sure he's okay. I'll be happy to show you identification. If he ever mentioned his sister and her family, you'll know I'm telling the truth." I pulled out my wallet and displayed my Texas driver's license. He gave it a cursory glance and I sensed a slight change in his demeanor.

"What makes you think he's in trouble?"

Good, we were making progress. At least I had an acknowledgement of my uncle's existence. I decided to tell Charlie about the UFO blog and the investigator's failure to make contact with my uncle afterward. I told him that my family was desperately trying to get in touch with him (a slight exaggeration) but refrained from telling him I was a journalist. I sensed that tidbit would cement the wall firmly back in place.

"I'll see what I can do. Do you have a card? I'll contact you tomorrow."

Clever fellow, damn him. The last thing I wanted to do was give him my business card with "The Dallas Morning News" in bold black letters printed above my name and cell phone number.

"I'm in between jobs right now," I lied. "But let me write down my number. We're staying at the Best Western on Jacarilla." I scribbled the digits on a cocktail napkin. He stared at it for a few seconds then quickly scanned the crowd before sliding it off the counter and into his pocket.

"Okay, if you'll excuse me, gentlemen. I have to get back to work." His turned back was our dismissal.

Ben and I ambled through the casino, asking random patrons about my uncle, but to no avail. Most reactions seemed genuine: *Nope, don't know the guy...Never heard of him...*, but I got the distinct impression from a few people that they knew more than they were willing to share. I felt more uneasy by the minute. Something was going on here and I had no clue what it was.

After playing a few slots and losing twenty bucks each at the blackjack tables, we decided to call it a night. We pulled into the parking lot of the Best Western after midnight. Between the long drive and the frustrating evening at the casino, we were wiped out mentally and physically.

Otherwise, we would have noticed the thugs before they jumped us.

Four guys in ski masks came at us from behind as we started walking toward our room. Wisely, three of the guys took on my burly friend at once, which I might have found insulting if I'd had time to ponder it. At any rate if they hadn't, the result would have been very different.

The fourth guy grabbed my arms from behind and before my tired brain could grasp what was happening, he got in a few good kidney punches then slammed me to the asphalt. He followed up with a couple of well-placed kicks to the ribs while my face was pressed painfully into the rough surface of the parking lot. I could hear Ben struggling and cursing, and another voice which wasn't Ben's, cry out in pain. Good. Hopefully, he was having better luck then me.

The sole of a boot pressed on the back of my neck, pinning me to the ground. My assailant barked a muffled warning through his ski mask.

"Leave it alone, asshole, or you'll end up in the desert somewhere under a foot of New Mexico top soil." He kicked my sore ribs a final time for emphasis.

The boot was removed the next moment and I heard the sound of fading footsteps which were followed seconds later by more boot-on-asphalt noises as Ben's attackers departed as well.

"Goddam chicken shits!" Benny growled in fury. Groaning, I rolled over on my back so I could see him. He sat on the ground about twenty feet from me, rubbing the back of his head.

"You okay, buddy?" He'd just realized I was still horizontal.

"Yeah, I think so," I said. "I'll probably pee blood for a couple of days though."

Ben struggled to get himself up and came to my side.

"Anything broken?" he asked as he grabbed my arm and pulled me up.

"No, doesn't feel like." I touched my ribs tenderly. They would be sore for days. "Nothing permanently damaged except my pride. Are you okay, Benny?" It was difficult to imagine even three guys successfully inflicting much damage.

"Fuckers got me in a choke hold then took some shots, but nothing major. I got in a good dick kick to one of the bastards. Goddam, I hate cowards."

I appreciated the sentiment but honestly, when one considered the size of my friend, the 3-1 ratio wasn't that inequitable.

We scanned the parking lot one last time before stumbling to our room and sliding the deadbolt firmly in place. After we'd both showered and I'd removed the remnants of the parking lot from the side of my face, we crawled into our respective beds and stared at the ceiling.

"Josh, what the hell was that about?"

"I don't know but I'm sure it has something to do with all the questions we were asking at the casino. Did you hear what that guy said to me?" He hadn't, being too distracted with self-preservation at the time. I recapped my assailant's warning.

"I think your uncle is into some shit."

"I think you're right." I'd had some time during the shower to contemplate my next move. I couldn't ask my friend to further involve himself in such a dangerous situation, but I had no intention of turning back. I may not be a badass but I also have a problem with strangers telling me what I can and can't do – especially when they're chicken shit thugs in ski masks.

"Benny, I want you to go home. I'll pay for a bus ticket back to Dallas. I'm staying here.

I'm going to find out what the hell is going on and whether my uncle is dead or alive." My voice didn't sound nearly as confident as I'd hoped.

After a few seconds, Ben said, "You know what you can do with your bus ticket, buddy?" I turned my head sideways to see him grinning. I smiled back and gave him a slight nod. There was nothing else to be said on the subject.

I didn't realize I'd been holding my breath until just then, but knowing Ben would have my back in the coming hours allowed me to drift off to sleep.

###

The next morning at around 9 am, we were wolfing down scrambled eggs and bacon at the Water Hole Café when my cell phone rang. A glance at the caller ID showed an unfamiliar area code. I suspected 505 was a local number in Dulce, New Mexico.

"Hello," I answered.

"Meet me on J-2 Road half a mile south of the river in one hour," a male voice said.

"Who is this?" No answer. He'd already

hung up. It could have been Charlie from the casino or it could have been one of the thugs from last night. Maybe Charlie wasn't a good guy – maybe he was the one who sent us the painful warning. Hell, maybe it was my uncle.

We used the GPS on my iPhone to pull up a map of the local area. I estimated it would take about fifteen minutes to drive the six miles which would put us half a mile south of the Blanco River. We had plenty of time to finish breakfast.

"So, what's the plan, Kimosabe?" Ben asked, gesturing to the buxom waitress to top off his coffee cup and eyeballing her backside when she left.

I gazed out one of the diner's large windows, watching the traffic drive by on the two-lane highway. The craggy, stunted flat peaks of the Archuleta Mesa stood impassively in the background. So many questions ran through my mind, but I didn't feel compelled to share them just then. I'd gotten up earlier than Ben that morning and hit my laptop with a vengeance, looking for information on the area and its underlying mythology. If I'd had a week I couldn't have read through it all, and if I gave credence to even a fraction of the allegations, Ben and I were in way over our heads.

"We go meet the guy and see what he has to say," I replied. I got a cocked eyebrow in response.

"Yeah, I know, Ben. Not much of a plan, especially if it turns out to be just more of the same from last night, in which case it's actually a very bad plan. But I have to go. If there's a chance this will lead me to Joe, I need to do it. You know you don't have to come with me."

"You keep talking like that and I'll rub the other side of your ugly mug into the pavement. Then you'll be symmetrical."

I sighed, feeling very responsible and very guilty for dragging him into this. We'd had only the sketchiest of plans when we left Dallas and my so-called research prior to leaving had been superficial at best. Not for a moment did I believe we were heading into anything dangerous – why would I? I mean, *aliens,* for God's sake. Who takes this stuff seriously?

I was still skeptical after delving a bit more into the local folklore that morning. I couldn't believe that our government was in cahoots with extraterrestrial beings and conducted unspeakable experiments deep within the mountain – the same mountain outside the diner window. I hadn't found one shred of plausible evidence to corroborate such assertions. Sure, there were a number of so-called eyewitness accounts from people who had worked inside the alleged massive seven-level underground compound. The abominations and atrocities they described – the womb-like vats containing floating alien-human hybrids, the human-animal biogenetic experiments which yielded half-human half-octopus creatures which sported eight legs, the sedated human captives who were awaiting their turn in the lab – it all sounded like a cheesy science fiction novel.

I refused to buy into it.

I'd shared all this with Ben before breakfast and we shared the same skepticism. But something was going on here and after the beating we took last night, it seemed that someone wanted to keep that something under wraps.

We finished breakfast and hit the road. Dulce resided at an elevation of 6800 feet, so it was chilly that April morning. We both wore lightweight jackets which were all we'd brought. When you think of New Mexico, you think hot and dry; quite true in the lower elevations but not here. The small, largely Native American town had been built in the foothills of the Rocky Mountains just a few miles south of the Colorado border.

"Hey, Josh, if we find that dude with the extra legs, we should recruit him as the new goalie for the Dallas Burn," Ben said as he watched the terrain out the window.

"They're not even called the Burn anymore, idiot." I laughed at the mental image.

"No shit? What's their new name?" One more interesting fact about my friend: he loathed professional sports. In every other way, he was a guy's guy, but Ben hated the greed evident on every level, from the ridiculous salaries of the players to the cost of a beer and a hot dog at The Ballpark. He truly believed that Jerry Jones, the owner of the Dallas Cowboys, was the spawn of Satan.

"FC Dallas or something stupid like that. I don't keep up with soccer."

Football and baseball were my sports. Unfortunately for me, my other best friend, Dylan, wasn't a fan either. Abby was a die-hard though. Some of our best times had been spent curled up in front of the TV watching Tony Romo scramble for a first down or indulging in those pricey hot dogs and beer at a Rangers game. The poignancy of that memory caught me by surprise.

"So, what's going on with Abby lately? I haven't seen her in a couple of weeks," Ben asked with an air of insouciance. He knew exactly what memories the sports talk had evoked.

I glanced over to see him staring out the windshield. We'd been friends since middle school. I wasn't just an open book to Ben – I was a well-loved classic that he'd read and re-read continually for two decades.

"Not much, I don't think. I talked to

her last week and she mentioned being stressed at work. I guess April is a busy month at city hall." Abby had earned her position as Deputy Chief of Staff to Mayor Skinner on her own merits but it hadn't hurt that she was gorgeous, a fact which was underscored by the mayor's inability to keep his paws away from her perfect backside. Abby just shrugged it off as typical male behavior, but I could gleefully squash his pumpkin head with one lethal swing of my caveman's club.

"Hmmph. That fucking Skinner better keep his hands to himself or I will be forced to kick his suit-wearing, speech-giving, wife-cheating ass." Ben meant it too and he wouldn't care if it cost him jail time. And of course I'd be sitting right there next to him while we discussed the finer points of chivalry as it applied to twenty-first century American culture.

The perky, female voice of my Garmin GPS unit informed us we were almost at our destination, which was exactly in the middle of nowhere. Parked about 50 yards ahead was a Chevy pickup, so ancient its original color was indiscernible. As we got closer, I could see one person sitting in the driver's seat. Unless they were hunkered down on the floorboard or in the truck's bed, nobody else occupied the vehicle.

I slowed the Honda and turned onto the side road, pulling to a stop behind the pickup. The driver's door opened and out came Charlie from the casino. Instant relief, although perhaps unwarranted. He very well could have been the one to send the thugs. I rolled my window down as he walked towards us.

"Follow me," he said without ceremony, then headed back to his truck.

"Wait a minute. Where are you taking us?" I asked his backside.

"You wanted to see Joe," he said in lieu of an explanation as he slammed the truck door shut. The engine started a second later and he took off down the road.

We followed.

"I'm sure you've already thought of this, but what if we're heading into a trap?" Ben asked in the same tone he might ask about the weather forecast.

"Yeah, that occurred to me. Did you bring your knuckles?"

"Of course, and I have my switchblade in my boot," he said with a small, predatory smile. I suspect he was actually hoping for an altercation which might exonerate him of last night's ass-kicking. I wish I felt as calm as he seemed to be. The only weapon I had was a Swiss Army knife, another example of poor planning.

Well, I might be bringing a knife to a gunfight, but I also had 260 pounds of piss and vinegar sitting in the passenger seat.

We followed Charlie's pickup for a couple of miles on the dirt road, passing several dilapidated, ramshackle houses. On the Jicarillo Apache Nation Reservation, poverty was a way of life. We drove past another shack where a dark-skinned woman with white braids stared at us from the shade of a rickety porch. A scrawny mutt, mostly rib bones and fur, emerged from under the house to bark a warning at us.

After another mile of stark desert and little else, a structure came into view. As we got closer, I could see it was a mobile home squatting on precarious cinder blocks and nestled in a small grove of scraggly piñon pines. What appeared to be a water cistern and a propane tank sat off to the right of the home. Everything looked weathered, worn and rusty except for a modern satellite dish positioned in a small clearing to the left – anachronistic and probably half the size of the dwelling. The power lines, which had skirted the dirt road the entire way, ended their journey here. Beyond the mobile home, the vast and lonely desert stretched to the horizon, unblemished by any further evidence of humanity.

Charlie sprang from his truck and headed for the wrought iron steps at the front door, motioning for us to follow. We did, but not before a cursory check of our meager weapons stash. The bartender rapped his knuckles on the door as we approached from behind.

I found myself holding my breath. Moments later, the door opened a few inches and the face of a man appeared. His long brown hair was streaked with gray and his face was worn and lined. The blue eyes seemed lighter and had lost much of their fire, but I'd know that face anywhere, despite the ravages of time.

I grinned like the twelve-year old I suddenly felt myself to be. Joe smiled in return.

"Joshua. It's so good to see you. Come in, come in." Charlie stepped aside so we could enter. As soon as we were inside, Joe enveloped me in a fierce bear hug.

"My God, look at you! You're a grown man! What are you, thirty?" His voice had acquired a raspy quality over the last two decades but otherwise, he sounded exactly the same.

"I'm thirty-two. It's been a long time, Joe." It didn't feel right to insert the familial 'uncle'. We were both men now.

"How's your mom?" I could tell the question caused him some discomfort. He and his sister had been very close before the rift.

"She's good. She and Dad are living in Vero Beach now."

"Florida? Hmmmm." He pondered a moment. "Yeah, that's good." Something in his tone told me he wasn't referring to the temperate climate.

"You boys come on in and sit down. Can I get you something to drink? Coffee? Beer?"

"I'll take a beer," Ben chimed in. I glanced at my watch and looked at him with raised brows. He shrugged.

"Nothing for me, thanks," I said as we took a seat on the worn sofa. Charlie followed Joe into the tiny kitchen and I could hear them talking quietly. Then the bartender left abruptly with a curt nod in our direction.

"Thanks, Charlie," I offered, again to his backside. It seemed that during our brief acquaintance, I'd seen more of it than the front.

Joe handed the beer to Ben and sat on the edge of an ancient recliner. I was able to study him more thoroughly now, as he did me. His demeanor was cautious but warm; his sharp eyes took in every detail and I doubted they missed a thing. The lines etched at the corners of his eyes implied sorrow somehow, but I wasn't ready to ask about Alameda. Something told me he wasn't ready either, so we made small talk instead. It took half an hour to catch him up on all the family news.

Finally, I decided it was time to discuss the matters which had brought us to this tiny trailer in the middle of nowhere. I explained my initial motivation for the trip – my job at the newspaper and the feature story I intended to write. The warmth in his smile vanished and his eyes assumed a wary expression. As quickly as I could, I detailed our experience at the casino and the subsequent beating in the hotel parking lot. The last bit of news provoked an angry grunt but no surprise as he examined my face.

"Soft tissue meets asphalt. Asphalt wins," I joked, trying to lighten the mood. "So now it seems this might be about more than just a feature story for my paper. Obviously, there's something going on here, Joe. I'm hoping you'll tell me what."

He leaned back in the recliner and shifted his gaze from us to the panoramic desert outside the living room window. The moments ticked by. I noticed an ambient whirring of machinery now that the conversation had lulled. A computer perhaps? Possibly more than one. The silence had become awkward by the time he finally spoke.

"Joshua, involving you in this is not a decision I take lightly. And by telling you what's going on, what I've witnessed, the experiences I've had over the years, will most definitely involve you. That involvement comes at a very high price. Your life could be in danger. And the life of your friend, here." He glanced at Ben.

"Joshua's friend can take care of himself," Ben replied. The steely look he gave my uncle seemed to have the desired effect. Joe nodded. A silent message had been sent and received.

"I understand, Joe. We're willing to accept that," I said with a confidence that was mostly genuine. "Can I ask you something first though?"

He nodded.

"Where's Alameda?"

"She died two years ago," he said, staring down at clenched fists, as if those hands had somehow failed him, had somehow been too weak or too slow to save his beloved wife.

"Was she ill. . .an accident?"

"She was murdered," he said. Simple words for such an enormity. "Murdered because of me, because of what I was digging up. It was the last of a series of warnings that I didn't heed. What an arrogant bastard, I was. I believed that truth should prevail, at whatever cost. I knew I was risking my own neck but I was so consumed with finding all the answers, I didn't stop and think about protecting my wife – at least not as much as I should have."

He sat, deflated and small, gazing out at the arid landscape.

"Joe, you need to tell me what happened. If we're getting into dangerous stuff, we need to know what it is. What happened to her? What the hell is going on?"

His gaze locked with mine and he said simply, "The end of the world. That's what's going on, Joshua."

Chapter 3

For the next three hours, I discovered what my uncle had been doing for all these years.

Rumors of increased UFO activity had taken him from southern California to New Mexico, where he'd met Alameda. She'd been waitressing at a restaurant in Santa Fe and he'd just spent the last few weeks in the Roswell area, investigating UFO sightings and doing some carpentry work for a local business man. He'd been on his way to Los Alamos when he met her. It must have been around that time that he'd brought her to Dallas. They'd only known each other for a month, something I hadn't realized at the time. For the next few years, they lived the romantic lives of gypsies.

Traveling about the country, gravitating to areas where UFO sightings and rumors of extraterrestrial activity and other weird phenomenon abounded. They picked up the occasional odd jobs when they could find them and existed as much on love and excitement as they did on their meager earnings. Fortunately, Joe was skilled at carpentry and could find work fairly easily along the way.

He'd found in Alameda a kindred spirit. In addition to sharing an interest in the same crazy stuff, she'd contributed to the mix her extensive knowledge of Native American folklore. At the time, it wasn't common knowledge that most of the indigenous population of North America believed that at various points in our history, the earth had received visitors from beyond our solar system. Joe informed us that evidence of these beliefs could be found in a myriad of places: petroglyphs carved into ancient rocks in the Hopi regions of the Southwest which depict ant-like figures and are a representation of a benevolent non-human race that aided humans during the destruction of the First World (the time before the great flood), ancient Hopi villages which had been built to line up identically to the stars in Orion's Belt, and perhaps most importantly, the legend of the Kachinas which factor largely in Native American culture and are depicted wearing masks (breathing apparatus?) and are believed to be messengers between this world and the next.

"Eventually, Alameda wearied of the lifestyle," Joe continued. "She wanted to go back to her home state of New Mexico and plant some roots, maybe start a family. I guess that was about twelve years ago. We decided on this area as a compromise. It was beginning to be a hotspot for activity and it was fairly close to Alameda's family. We'd saved enough money to put down a deposit on the Four Seasons here." He waved his arm to indicate the tiny dwelling. "She got a job at a diner in town and I was hired by a local tour operator as a fishing and hiking guide. I've come to know this area better than most," he said with a look significant look. "That's one of the reasons

I was able to notice things that most people overlooked."

"Like what?" Ben asked, an edge to his voice. Joe glanced at the empty beer in Ben's hand and fetched him another before answering.

"Like the two thousand-acre ranch north of the river that has a ridiculously small ratio of livestock to acreage and where armed guards are occasionally positioned at the entrance," Joe replied. "Like the six-foot metal porthole positioned on the Archuleta Mesa and which serves no conceivable purpose. Like the two ventilation shafts I found at the top of the mesa and which have since been camouflaged in such a way that I wasn't able to find them again. Like the house on the outskirts of Edith, Colorado, where nobody apparently lives but where at various times of the year a parade of white panel vans can be seen coming and going."

Ben wasn't impressed. Joe continued anyway.

"I'd been watching the activity in this area for more than a decade. I'd seen a lot of really weird stuff – flashing orbs in the night sky which seem to originate from and return to the mesa and black helicopters that had no business being here, among other things. I'd heard a lot of weird stuff too." He indicated the room which was the source of the mechanical sounds. "The transmissions started March 29th of 2009."

After basic training, my uncle's four years of service in the Air Force had been exclusively in the field of electronics. His specialty was radio electronics and it seemed his interest in that field hadn't ended with his honorable discharge.

"Come here," he said as he walked into the room and flipped on a light switch. I noticed his movements seemed labored and I wondered suddenly about his health. He was still a relatively young man; I estimated he must be in his late-forties, but he moved like he was much older.

Tables and desks stacked with electronic equipment filled the tiny room. I could identify two computer monitors and several types of radio equipment but the other devices weren't familiar. I wondered briefly how my uncle had managed to pay for all this high-tech stuff – surely his job as a tour guide didn't pay that well.

"You know about my background in radio?" Joe asked me. I nodded. "I'd spend an hour or so each night doing my usual thing, scanning the frequencies, listening in on anything that might pertain to my investigations. I was in communication with several other AROs – amateur radio operators – who would tip me off if they'd heard anything out of the ordinary. One of them mentioned an anomalous sound he'd heard on an SSB earlier in the day. That's 'single sideband'. It means the quality isn't as good as FM but it can travel longer distances," he offered after seeing the blank looks on our faces.

"I dialed it in and listened for at least half an hour before I got anything. Lots of noise and static but after a while I realized there was a distinct regularity to the noise...it was Morse code, sort of. The transmission length took so long that most AROs or anyone else listening in would have just heard static and an occasional banging sound

– like a rock hitting another rock interspersed with scraping sounds. Dot, dash, dot, see? After about three hours of monitoring, I had my message."

I realized I was holding my breath.

"It said, 'Dulce Base lost. No evac. Initiate clean sweep.' That was it. I got the same message four times during the three hours I was listening. Then after that, nothing but air."

"So what did it mean, Joe? You think these rumors of a secret underground base are true?" I asked, still finding it impossible to believe such a crazy story.

"Joshua, there's nothing I'm more certain about. Hopefully you'll agree after I've told you the rest."

He continued, "I listened to that same SSB frequency for the next two nights. The second night the message was transmitted twice and the third night, only once. After that, I never heard it again. I figure whoever was transmitting that message was dead by then. I also figured that I wasn't the only person who heard it because on that fourth day, we were overrun with government and black op types. Whatever Clean Sweep was, it was happening then. There was a bogus announcement on the radio about a chemical spill in the area and the residents were told to stay in their homes. Local businesses and schools were strong-armed into closing so people wouldn't be out and about and risk seeing whatever it was we weren't supposed to see. Of course there was no chemical spill and I spent that day conducting my own covert investigation.

"Alameda wasn't happy about that either, I assure you. She seemed to realize much sooner than I just how dangerous the situation was becoming, but of course I just kept plowing ahead, arrogant and reckless in my need to know the truth." His face, which had been animated, shifted into an expression of infinite sadness.

When he didn't continue, I prompted him as gently as possible. "What did you see that day?"

"I saw a lot of weird shit, Joshua," he replied after a moment. "I had to be really careful, so I couldn't get as close to things as I wanted to, but I got close enough to get a few photos. Black helicopters descended on the area. They weren't just over the mesa either. They were everywhere."

He opened a file drawer, removed a folder and laid it open on the small desk. Inside were photographs depicting exactly what he'd just described. The helicopters dotted the sky like a swarm of titanic black locusts.

"Here's a shot of the caravan of SUVs that went through town on their way to the ranch." He pointed to another photo which showed at least a dozen black Suburbans with dark-tinted windows. It seemed these government types were very fond of black.

"So what's at the ranch?" I asked. I hadn't quite made the connection.

"Essentially, it's a train terminal. It may serve other purposes which I can only speculate about. We believe there is an extensive underground tube system which connects the ranch not only to Dulce Base, but to Los Alamos and Area 51. Possibly other locations too. We believe the house in Edith is a smaller version of the same but probably with just one tube going to Dulce

Base. This is most likely where the workers enter and exit although there may be other locations as well."

"Trains? Like a subway system?" Ben asked.

"Similar, but most likely one that utilizes magnetics and pneumatics. Imagine frictionless vacuum chambers like they have at drive-thru banks except much bigger and much faster."

"Joe, that technology is years away," I said. The look he shot me was mild disdain, as if I'd just broken wind.

"The technology our government possesses, much of which is extraterrestrial in origin, is forty or fifty years ahead of that of the private sector. Trust me. The train system is nothing compared to the other stuff they have that they're not sharing with the rest of the world. Anyway, that was the first time I saw one of them."

"Them what? An alien, you mean?" I asked.

"You could say that. They're certainly part extraterrestrial but we believe them to be a type of hybrid – part human, part alien.

Genetic engineering isn't science fiction. At least it isn't in there," he motioned in the direction of the mesa. "There's a lot that isn't clear but one of the things we're certain about is that our government, or perhaps some 'off the books' government agency has been working in an underground base which was built in the Archuleta Mesa in the 80's. We've found extensive reports of seismic activity which occurred in this area from 1983 to 1988 and which cannot be attributed to any natural phenomenon. Ever heard of the Subterrene?"

We both shook our heads.

"Omni Magazine ran a story about it in the early 80's. It's a nuclear powered, tunnel-boring machine developed at Los Alamos. The machine burrows through underground rock, heating it to magma, then the molten rock cools after the Subterrene moves on. The result is a glaze-lined tube in the rock. That's how the train system was built. It's funny that after Omni came out with that article, there were never any additional news stories about the machine. The impact of such technology should have been huge – the industrial applications are limitless, yet it just fell off the radar."

"That's how the base was built?" Ben asked.

"No, the base was largely already built, in terms of underground boring at least, when the government types found it. They had to outfit it, obviously, but the cavernous, underground structure had already been built – probably tens of thousands of years ago, by life forms the Hopi tribe call 'ant people' or 'kachinas' and which the ancient Sumerians called the 'Annunaki'."

"We're talking ancient astronauts, right?" Ben said. "I've read *Chariots of the Gods*."

"Exactly," Joe replied. "A benevolent, extraterrestrial race is believed to have landed on our planet at the beginning of human origins and essentially jump-started our rapid advancement from hunter-gatherers to pyramid builders. That type of development should have taken millennia but instead it happened, in evolutionary terms, almost overnight thanks to our friendly, intergalactic neighbors."

"So these aliens are still here, living underground?" I tried to keep the skepticism out of my voice without much success.

Joe picked up on my tone, but continued, unoffended.

"No," he said. "The ETs left a long time ago. Exactly when is anyone's guess. We believe some of the UFO sightings seen today are just fly-by checkups. You know, making sure we haven't annihilated ourselves. But in addition to the knowledge and guidance they gave us, they left something else behind.

"Their DNA." He paused to let it sink in.

I thought about the implications. "Are you telling me that these creatures you keep referring to that are here now, are alien clones of some sort?"

"Not clones," he said. "We think those particular experiments hit a brick wall. They're hybrids. Part alien, part human and perhaps part something else."

Ben and I exchanged a look.

"Yeah, I know. It's pretty hard to swallow. If I hadn't seem them with my own eyes, heard other eyewitness accounts of them which corroborated what I'd seen, conducted my own research for years, I'd probably feel what you're feeling now too." He stepped out of gadget central and back into the living room. We followed.

"So is that what the 'grays' are that I've read about on the internet? Or the 'reptilians'?" I asked, smiling.

Joe rolled his eyes.

"No, there are no grays and there are no reptilians. Those stories, along with a ton of other bullshit, are just part of the government's misinformation campaign. What better way to cloud the waters than to pump a ton of garbage into it. Pretty clever, really. It's a technique that's been in use since the Roswell crash. Hell, maybe even earlier. Anyway, most of the crap you've read on the internet started with some very well-placed propaganda planted by the Men in Black. Then others just picked it up and ran with it. The misinformation grew exponentially. People love scary stories and conspiracy theories. So much misinformation has been mixed in with the tiniest bits of truth that it's virtually impossible to discern what's real and what isn't. Their plan worked brilliantly."

"So, what about the Roswell crash?" Ben asked. "Was it a hoax or did a UFO really take a header into the desert?"

"A crash occurred but we believe it was a UAV – an unmanned aerial vehicle of extraterrestrial origin. We don't believe there were any ETs on board and it was most likely just our friendly neighbors checking up on us. We have no idea what caused the crash but we do know it happened. We also know the government took the vehicle and reverse engineered it and that's what most of the supposed UFO sightings are today – our own military testing machines that were built utilizing alien technology."

If Joe had told us he'd been leading a secret double life as Batman, he'd be witnessing the same expression on my face that he was seeing now, which was duplicated on Ben's. He paused for a long moment, struggling with something.

"Look," Joe said. "You don't have to take my word for it. I hadn't planned on showing you the videos, but if things go down as I think they might, it won't matter much in the end anyway. You're already in danger because you've been in contact with me but what you're about to witness puts you in the big leagues. I hope I'm doing the right thing."

He walked to the corner of the living room and pulled up a section of ancient shag carpet which had been cut out in a neat, twelve-inch square. Below it was a section of plywood in the same dimensions with a hole in the center. Joe pulled it up too. Underneath was a small compartment.

He removed a gray metal box with a combination lock and quickly dialed in the appropriate numbers. He gave us an appraising look before he opened the lid. Ben and I craned our necks to see what was inside. A cursory inspection showed a large wad of cash, a small caliber handgun and a stack of CDs or DVDs. He removed the one from the top which had been marked with a black Sharpie. It said, '3rd quarter 2007'. He walked over to the small TV sitting on top of a Sony DVD player and inserted the disc.

"This is some of the first video I got. Up until that point, everything is on still photos." He pressed the play button.

The video quality was surprisingly good.

"This was taken outside the ranch. I'd gotten a tip from one of my contacts about some activity, so I parked my car a couple of miles away from the entrance and hiked the rest of the way. I hunkered down in a cluster of scrub brush and waited. After six long hours of nothing, I finally hit pay dirt. One of the Suburbans started to approach the guard building which is just inside the twelve foot gate. It's electrified, by the way. The entire fence line is. Anyway, the SUV pulled up to the gate and it slid open. That's when I started filming." He nodded at the screen.

The building was a tiny structure, probably only ten feet square. The tall, metal gate slid slowly from left to right and the Suburban drove through. There appeared to be two men in the front seat, but that was all I could see. The vehicle continued driving toward the camera. Before it had built up much speed, a longhorn steer meandered into the middle of the road and stopped. It watched the approaching vehicle without much interest or indication that it might get out of the way. Of course the Suburban was forced to stop and several blasts of the car horn had no effect.

Both front seat doors opened and two men emerged. They looked like your typical government types with their nondescript suits and short haircuts. They walked toward the steer with waving arms, yelling and hooting, trying to scare off the steer which was standing in the middle of the road at a 90 degree angle. Its head had been turned to look at the vehicle, but when the men started playing matador, it turned toward the camera with a blasé expression which seemed to say, 'Get a load of these dicks.' I laughed out loud and saw that Joe and Ben were smiling too.

What happened next wasn't so amusing.

The back seat door on the driver's side opened and out stepped an abomination.

It was dressed exactly as the two men

but that was where any similarities ended. It was thin to the point of emaciation. The wind was blowing and its clothes pressed against arms and legs that looked skeletal under the fabric. The camera zoomed in on the creature, showing more detail. The appendages which extended from the sleeves couldn't be called hands – they seemed almost tentacular in nature, although I did count five squiggly digits. The feet were similar to the hands in the same way our hands and feet compare. No shoes on this planet would fit the aberrant wriggling things on which the creature stood.

The head was a nightmare. Huge black eyes covered half its face and every few seconds a translucent covering slid over them, like a fleshy camera lens opening and closing. Where a human nose might be were two small slits which flexed slightly, like fish gills. The mouth was circular, open and full of spear tips – dozens of them. From the camera's perspective, no ears could be seen and there was no hair, just a covering of grayish-green flesh.

That was when I experienced a paradigm

shift of epic proportion. Monsters were real. They might not live in your closet or under your bed, but they existed. And not just in books or movies, but in the real world. I was seeing one in the flesh and I had never been so terrified in my life. Not in the way that I might be terrified of a charging rhinoceros or a striking cobra, and not because of how fucking hideous the thing was, but because every molecule in its bastardized anatomy was unnatural – nature hadn't created this monstrosity. Humanity had.

And the fuckers had dressed it in a goddam Brooks Brothers suit.

A few seconds later, the steer wandered off camera and both humans and monster returned to the inside of the vehicle. Car doors slammed and the camera panned from left to right as it drove by. Shortly after, Joe pressed the stop button on the remote.

"We think that was one of the first successful experiments," he said. "It's anyone's guess what combination of terrestrial and extraterrestrial DNA was used to create that.

"There's more."

For the next thirty minutes he showed us a variety of footage on DVDs dated from 2007 through 2009. They'd been filmed covertly, like the first, but while some were not as crisp and clear, others were painfully so. All had been filmed in remote, unpopulated areas and somehow conveyed a sense that the creatures were getting their first taste of the great outdoors. The beings varied in appearance but all contained an element of humanness to some degree. I felt complete and utter revulsion. Species don't interbreed for good reason and here were numerous examples of why it shouldn't happen. I'm not religious – hell, I'm not even spiritual, but I do believe in some kind of higher power, and these things were nothing any benevolent, omnipotent being would have created.

Only mankind could be so lacking in wisdom and foresight as to father such monstrosities.

"This is one from what we call the Omega Group. They didn't seem to change much after this. At least in no way we could discern," Joe said. He inserted another DVD.

I glanced at Ben, who looked shell-shocked. I imagine I did too.

The scene had been filmed in the desert, as were all the previous ones. The vantage appeared to be from high up this time and the shadows were long – late afternoon, early evening perhaps. Pinion trees, junipers, cactus and scrub brush dominated the view.

"Watch the right side."

Two men appeared (the prevalent theme, apparently) wearing hiking attire. Behind them, another hybrid followed wearing similar clothing. It was by far more human-looking than anything we'd seen up to that point. I might not have even noticed at first that it wasn't human if I hadn't been focused on it. It wore khaki shorts which revealed normal-looking legs, albeit smooth and possibly hairless. Normal arms extended from the short sleeved shirt and were attached to hands that also seemed typically human. It wore a hat and I could see no hair or hairline below it. The face was slightly shadowed by the hat, but I could discern a nose and mouth – a mouth which seemed wide by human standards. I suddenly had the thought that I never wanted to see what was inside that mouth.

The group began walking toward the camera and suddenly the scene went black for a moment. When it came back on, it was dusk.

"I had to scramble for a better hiding spot," Joe explained.

The group was standing on what looked like the edge of a cliff. I assumed Joe had been on the mesa when he'd filmed this. The hybrid glanced toward the camera and suddenly its eyes came into view. They glowed, like an animal caught in the headlights of a car. I had the sense that it was scanning the area and I worried irrationally for Joe's safety, as if the action were happening at that moment. My respect for my uncle increased about a million percent. He'd placed himself in a dangerous situation and still managed to continue filming this creature which may or may not have been aware of his presence.

Suddenly, the creature grabbed one of the men and tossed him off the cliff. It seemed effortless, as if the man weighed nothing. The other man made a move for his belt where a handgun was holstered, but the creature moved faster and in a split second, he went over the cliff as well.

My mouth dropped open as I looked at my uncle.

"Holy shit," Ben said.

The scene went black again. My uncle stared at the blank television. He paused a few moments before he spoke.

"I had to turn the camera off and take cover at that point. I was pretty sure I wasn't going to make it off that mountain alive. I didn't move a muscle for the next two hours. Just about peed my pants too, but I was worried that thing might be able to smell it. Finally, I took a chance and poked my head out. It was gone.

"Shortly after I got the radio transmissions. We believe the creatures took over Dulce Base and killed the humans – their creators, as it were. Ironic, huh? I'm sure many innocent people were killed in that mess but I just can't help but feel that we had it coming. Humans, I mean. When we start playing God, the inevitable fallout is bound to bite us in the ass. Anyway, then Clean Sweep happened. We believe the operation was a worst case scenario to exterminate anything left alive underground.

"But it didn't work, because I've seen them since." His words hung in the air – noxious and unpalatable.

"So those things are still out there?" Ben asked.

"Yes, they are. We don't know what they're up to, but they've been spotted in the vicinity a number of times in the last year. Even more frequently lately."

"Do the government boys know?" I asked.

"We're not sure. They might have contained the situation at Dulce Base and replaced the human staff, or they might just be monitoring the situation covertly from a safe distance. We just don't know."

He took a deep breath before he continued.

"Alameda was heavily involved in my investigations up until that first video from 2007. When she saw the thing on the road at the ranch, it affected her on a deep level. Her belief system was firmly cemented in the Hopi legends of benevolent, altruistic beings which helped her people come out of the caves. They're considered gods, you know. And for her to see the twisted, repulsive offense to humanity which we had created from their 'essence', it disturbed her to the point that she wanted nothing else to do with this. She backed completely away from it all and tried to get me to do the same. You can see how well that worked." The wry tone was at odds with the mask of sadness he wore.

"It was in late 2008 when the warnings started. To this day, I will never forgive myself for underestimating the threat."

"What warnings?" I asked, reminded of the thugs in the parking lot.

"Phone calls and emails to start, the gist of which was to stop my investigations. I think that whoever was sending them had learned of my videos. I'd only shown them to a select few but obviously I had a leak somewhere. Anyway, then they slashed the tires on my truck and when that didn't stop me, they slashed the tires on Alameda's car when she was working late one night. That scared me for sure, but it still didn't stop me. All this was going on during the time of the transmissions and Clean Sweep, so you could say I was a bit preoccupied and also my male ego wouldn't allow me to be scared off."

I thought of my own reaction to the beating Ben and I took in the hotel parking lot. It had been meant as a warning, but I took it as a challenge.

"I'd contacted the guys from that investigative blog you found, and told them a little of what I'd discovered. I figured it was time to get the news out there.

"A week later, Alameda didn't come home from work." Joe's hands were curled into tight fists.

"Her body was found in her car the next day, out on a side road near the mesa. The medical examiner was never able to determine cause of death. Of course, the state police grilled me for the next few weeks, but they finally decided I wasn't their guy. The case pretty much ended at that point. No leads, no witnesses, no known cause of death. It was a dead-end investigation.

"But, I knew who did it. Not specifically, but I knew it had something to do with Dulce Base. I also knew that if I didn't back off, I'd be next. That's why the blog guys couldn't find me. I didn't want to be found. I still don't, which is why Charlie wouldn't give you any information without checking with me first."

"Have you stopped investigating?" Ben asked.

"No, but I'm extremely careful about how I do it and who I discuss my findings with. I just don't know who I can trust." He gave us a pointed look.

"Joe, something has been bothering me." I said after a moment. "You keep saying we. *We* believe, *we* think. Are you working with someone?" That, along with the expensive equipment in the other room had struck me as curious. My uncle's face became a mask.

"There are some things I'm not able to discuss with you. That's one of them." I was reminded of the stonewalling we received from Charlie and knew that any further questions would be pointless. I didn't like it, though. If I was placing myself and my friend in the middle of something dangerous, I had a right to know as much as he could tell me, but now wasn't the time to push it.

"So Joe, other than the threat from these creatures locally, I'm not seeing the big 'end of the world' thing." Ben said.

Good point, I thought. I'd just witnessed some extremely disturbing events and heard some very troubling news, but I wasn't making the leap to an apocalyptic scenario.

"I mean, do they breed? Are they reproducing?"

Joe replied, "Breeding in the traditional sense seems unlikely. Kind of like why mules are sterile – they're the offspring of two different species. Hell, we don't know if these things even have genitalia.

That's something that's never been documented. But we do know the sightings have increased in the last few months. More sightings probably mean more hybrids. Are they being cloned? Created in a lab? Are they doing it themselves or are they back in cahoots with humans again? We don't know.

"What we do know is that more people have gone missing locally. Unprecedented numbers in the five surrounding counties closest to the mesa. Men, women, and children equally – no bias or preference. The big question is what are they doing with them?"

He let that sink in for a few moments before adding, "The other, much bigger question is: *what do they want?* From us and our planet, I mean. The way I see it, there's only room for one sheriff in town. Humans have been at the top of the food chain for millennia. No species on can match our brain power, our cognitive ability, our rapid advancement – until now. Hell, we can't even get along with each other, why would anyone think we could get along with a similar species which is at least of equal intelligence or more likely superior? Remember how strong that thing was? Throwing those two guys off the cliff was effortless. Obviously, they're much stronger than we are. It's not a leap to assume they're smarter too. And that means we've got a real fucking problem."

"Even so," I said, "If they're contained in this area and some facet of the government knows they're still out there, it doesn't seem to be an end-of-human-life-on-the-planet situation. There are seven billion of us. Why would they be so hell-bent on killing us all and how could they possibly do it?"

"Because that's what they were made to do, Joshua. We believe these genetic experiments – this manipulation of life – was intended to accomplish something specific. Our government, or people within our government, wanted to create the perfect biological killing machine. Other governments have attempted this using genetic engineering, but they didn't have what we had – the extraterrestrial DNA. That gave us the edge. What's out there now," he gestured to the desert, "is smart and strong, and genetically programmed to do one thing and do it with ruthless efficiency: kill humans. And we created it! How's that for a kick in the ass?

"As for your other question...do you know how easy it would be to wipe out entire populations? A handful of dumbass terrorists can wreak havoc with a small suitcase of anthrax or a vanload of dirty bombs. Imagine a small group of the smartest people on the planet, and imagine them sitting together in a room, figuring out ways to kill off the human race. It wouldn't be too difficult, theoretically. Now imagine if that group of brainiacs also happened to be psychopaths. They aren't distracted by typical human emotions such as compassion, empathy, pity. They just want to kill people because it's what they were made to do.

"That's what I believe these hybrids are – serial killers on steroids with one overriding goal: kill us all."

Joe sat back in his chair looking deflated

and tired. Ben studied him for a moment then glanced at me with a raised eyebrow. I can read him almost as well as he can read me and right then his expression clearly said, *I think we're in some deep shit.*

I nodded in agreement.

###

We spent another hour or so going back over various aspects of Joe's story, getting clarification on certain points and questioning the validity of others. Besides the nagging issue of the identity of my uncle's mysterious partner or partners, I was also dubious of our government's seeming lack of concern. Joe thought they'd simply bugged out. He said the normal comings and goings at the house in Edith and the ranch had stopped. I found it impossible to believe that they would bail on such an expensive and important project. More importantly, I couldn't accept the idea that they would leave innocent American civilians exposed to such a dire threat. Our government is supposed to protect its citizens. That's one of the things our tax dollars pay for, right? Joe contended the project had been so deeply blacklisted that most government officials had no knowledge of it. That it was not approved by any senate committee and that the money to pay for it had not been siphoned from the 100 billion general CIA budget as most black projects are for reasons of accountability. He believed there was a nebulous line item in an unrelated bill which was pushed through the house by a handful of key legislators, in the same way *Aurora* program was approved when the military retired the SR-71 spy plane and needed a replacement.

He believed the project had been kept so secret and so few government officials were involved that when it blew up in their faces, they chose to walk away from the fallout. If it had gone well, they would have basked in the glory, but when it failed so horrendously, they just washed their hands of it. And not only that, they would use whatever means necessary to make sure those hands stayed clean. In other words, there would be no going public with what we knew or the same people who had killed Alameda might set their sights on us too. We'd gotten the tiniest taste of this in the parking lot the night before.

If our government officials cared more about plausible deniability and covering their asses than the safety of the people they were sworn to represent, and if they were willing to overlook or even order the murder of innocent people to protect their dirty little secrets, we were essentially on our own in dealing with these creatures.

I don't know which monsters I found more terrifying – the hybrids or their human conspirators.

We were wrapping things up with Joe and had discussed some sketchy plans for the upcoming weeks when he took a deep breath and said, "There's something else you should know." His expression told me there was more bad news coming. "I'm sick. I'd been feeling tired for a month or so and finally went to the doctor in January. I have melanoma – stage three. I probably won't make it another year, so whatever we're going to do, we need to do it fast. Otherwise, you boys are on your own."

I had just gotten my uncle back in my life and the thought of losing him so soon felt like I'd won the lottery then promptly lost the winning ticket.

Ben mumbled his condolences (he was terrible at that kind of stuff) while I walked over to Joe and hugged him. I sensed that making a big deal out of the news was not what he wanted, so instead I said, "I think I'll have that beer now."

"I think I'll join you."

His grin showed no trace of self-pity. I think he must have made peace with it a long time ago.

###

A few hours later we were gassing up the Honda at a Chevron station ten miles outside of Dulce for our drive home to Dallas. Ben was on window washing duty and I was pumping the gas when a car pulled in. It was an older Nissan with as much Bondo as metal, a bad paint job and homemade window tinting that looked like grayish bubble wrap glued to the interior glass. What caught my eye was the erratic way it was being driven. I wondered if perhaps a student driver was behind the wheel, but I couldn't see the occupant through the shoddy tint job.

The car came to a jerky stop at the gas pump farthest from ours. We'd been the only other customers at the Chevron prior to its arrival. Ben had noticed it as well, but he continued his window washing task after a brief look at me to acknowledge the oddness of it. We shifted into heightened security mode. The pummeling we'd endured in the hotel parking lot was still fresh on our minds. Minutes ticked by and still nobody got out of the car. Something strange was going on, and in the area surrounding Dulce, that something might be hazardous to our health.

I topped off the tank and replaced the nozzle on the pump, continuing to covertly watch the Nissan as the pump spit out the receipt. Ben leaned against our car like he was in no hurry to get on the road.

Still, the Nissan's occupants remained hidden.

"I get the impression they're waiting for us to leave," I said in a low voice, my back to the Nissan.

"Yeah, me too. Let's go take a piss and buy some Slim Jims. Maybe that will get them moving and we can watch from inside."

I nodded in agreement and we walked toward the Chevron's mini-market. Once inside, I made a show of being interested in the products displayed along the front windows. Ben really did go to the bathroom. The counter guy studied me with mild interest for a few moments, then yawned and picked up the comic book he'd been reading.

While Ben was still in the bathroom, the driver's door of the Nissan opened. What stepped out was similar to the creature we'd seen in Joe's video – the one that threw two people off a cliff. To anyone who hadn't seen one before, it appeared human. Exceptionally observant types might sense something about this person was a bit off, but even they would be hard pressed to pinpoint exactly why.

I realized instantly what I was seeing, what it was capable of and just how isolated and vulnerable we were in this small building surrounded by empty desert.

"Shit," I breathed. I remembered its show of strength in the video – there wasn't a damn thing I could do but watch. The counter guy still had his nose in the comic book, oblivious to the fact that something distinctly non-human was 50 feet away. I toyed with the idea of alerting him and getting him to lock the door, but decided that might arouse the creature's suspicion. Pretending I didn't know what it was and hoping it would simply get gas and be on its way seemed like the safest option.

It wore similar clothing to what we'd seen in the video except the pants were long and the shirt had long sleeves. A ball cap covered its head and no hair stuck out from underneath. Bald, just like in the video, I thought. Aviator sunglasses covered much of its face. I was so focused on the creature that I barely registered Ben as he came up beside me.

"Fuck me," he muttered.

"Exactly," I said. Just then it turned its head in our direction. I walked down the aisle as if I'd spotted something in the mini market I couldn't live without. Ben grabbed a magazine off the rack next to the window and appeared to be fascinated by the latest Hollywood gossip in People Magazine. The lighting in the place made us clearly visible from outside. I thought again of how isolated the Chevron station was. There was absolutely nothing else in the immediate vicinity – no residences or other businesses. The tagline from the movie 'Alien' popped into my head: *In space, no one can hear you scream...*which worked equally well for this section of the New Mexico desert. I doubted comic book guy would be much use in a fight. We had no guns. Our pathetic weaponry consisted of Ben's switchblade, his brass knuckles and my pocket knife. If the hybrid decided we posed a threat, or was just feeling froggy and had the urge to kill a few humans, I didn't like our odds. We'd seen this creature or one of its brethren toss a two hundred pound man off a cliff as effortlessly as a smoker flicking a cigarette butt out a car window. Even Ben didn't possess that kind of strength.

And what if it had weapons of its own? I kept thinking about the teeth that might reside in that wide mouth.

I risked a quick glance out the window again and saw it had turned its attention back to the gas pump.

Whew.

Ben strolled up to me. "I think it's about to leave," he said. "You think we should try to follow?"

I pondered the idea and decided it would be too risky. What if it led us directly into a hive of its brothers and sisters? I told Ben as much.

"Dude, you think there might be hybrid chicks? What are we waiting for?"

"Don't be a dick. You know what I mean. There's not much along this stretch of highway. We're too vulnerable. Remember what one of those things did to the guys in the video?" This took some of the edge off his cockiness.

"We'll make a note of the sighting with the GPS unit. The information might be useful later, but right now I don't think there's much we can do except live to tell the tale."

Ben nodded, for once in agreement to act with caution.

The creature was getting back into the Nissan with movements that were quick and confident. Just as it began to shut the car door, its head turned toward the mini market again. The hat did a good job of keeping the face in shadow, but we could see the corners of the mouth pull up in a macabre caricature of a smile – a mockery of that human expression which generally conveys good will, friendliness, happiness.

This depraved version was the smile of a November jack-o-lantern; rotting, putrid, baleful.

Then the creature was gone.

I turned to Ben. His mouth was open but for once, no glib remark was forthcoming.

Chapter 4

Now, six months later, I looked at these friends gathered in my living room. I remembered the night shortly after our return when Ben and I sat in the same places we sat now, and told them what we'd discovered in New Mexico. It was a testament to the depth of our friendships and the intense respect we all shared, that Dylan and Abby never displayed an ounce of skepticism. If they had secretly harbored doubts about our tale or our sanity, they were believers after watching the videos. Just as Ben and I had been.

I looked at the three of them now and pondered the morning's event that had brought us together: I'd just happened to be up at 5:00 am and just happened to be watching that particular news channel so that I'd just happen to catch a glimpse of the hybrid. I had seen one in Dallas, no doubt.

Now, what the hell were we going to do about it?

Ben crammed another maple donut in his mouth and said, "We should get a trailer full of industrial strength Raid – the canister kind that you bomb a house with – pop the tops, throw them into their underground hive and plug all the holes. Roaches go in but they don't come out. Piece of cake."

Abby watched the donut disappear with the dismay of a rubbernecker viewing a ten-car pileup, then asked, "Have you found out how far they've spread? Other areas, other states?" She gestured to my computers set up on one side of the living room.

I'd been conducting my own research since our return from Dulce, using Joe's information as a starting point. What he'd shown us and told us that day in his home had only been the tip of the iceberg. I'd been back to Dulce twice since our first trip, meeting with Joe and scouting the area. As a former tour guide, Joe knew the area like the back of his hand and now, I knew it better than most residents. With my research skills added to his radio knowledge and considerable talent for covert investigating, we made a fairly good team. I'd begun to suspect his military training had not been limited to electronics and because he refused to elaborate when pressed, it only raised my suspicions. If he'd had spy training in the military, he wasn't going to discuss it with me.

"I've been getting an unusual number of hits on my site from the Mount Shasta area in California, but I haven't been able to confirm any actual sightings. I hacked into the local law enforcement data bases and found nothing to corroborate the posts. There are so many crackpots out there who post on these UFO forums; needle meet haystack. I think the government bogies are still running their misinformation campaign too, which makes it even more difficult."

Shortly after our return from Dulce, I'd

set up a website called, 'Have-You-Seen-An-Alien.com'. I'd manipulated Google's algorithms to expedite my ranking so my website would be on the first page of a search for a number of relevant phrases. I'd used a discussion forum format and encouraged people to post about their ET sightings and experiences. I figured we should utilize as many eyes out there as possible. I was deluged with stories about 'the grays', UFOs and mysterious spacecraft, alien abductions, and other stuff which required a massive dose of reality suspension to take seriously. After the first hundred implausible posts, I'd started to get disgusted. Then I realized how crazy our story would sound to others and decided to keep my mind open to all possibilities, no matter how incredible they might seem.

After wading through hundreds of posts each month, nothing surfaced about our hybrids. And that made sense, since the hybrids didn't appear as the typical alien creatures found in books and movies. They looked a lot like us which actually made them more terrifying. What's scarier, the hairy, fanged easily identifiable monster in the closet or the evil twin sleeping in the next bed?

"Did you call Joe about the Dallas sighting?" Dylan wanted to know.

"I thought I'd give him until mid-morning before I call. He's been sounding really tired lately and I don't want to call too early and wake him up." The cancer seemed to be progressing on schedule, and I doubted he'd be around in another six months. I tried not to think about that too much. We'd become close and communicated almost daily. I couldn't bear the thought of losing him so soon.

"Well, I say we take a little drive over to Pearl Street," Ben said.

"Definitely," Dylan agreed.

"And what if we run into one?" Abby asked. "What do we do? Grab it and hog tie it, then call the Alien Police to come pick it up?"

Ben spewed maple donut particles all over my coffee table.

I laughed and said, "Abby has a point,

guys. We need a plan."

A loud knock at the front door of my apartment interrupted the conversation.

I frowned, wondering who it could be at this early hour, as I put my hand on the doorknob and started to press my eye to the peephole.

Something made me stop.

An internal alarm sounded in my brain – perhaps some danger-sensing ability leftover from our ancient ancestors, or maybe my subconscious mind had picked up a warning sign that it failed to share with its cognitive cousin. At any rate, I removed my hand from the doorknob and stepped away from the door, just as the peephole exploded. Bullets blew a five-inch hole in the wood before embedding themselves in the opposite wall.

I was standing there in a daze, gawking like an idiot when Ben jumped from his chair and pulled me down on the floor just as more bullets shattered the front window. A shower of broken glass peppered our backs. Dylan and Abby hit the ground too.

Ben yelled, "Stay down!" a half second before more bullets annihilated the living room windows in an explosion of glass. A few hit Mini NORAD, shattering a CPU screen and causing unknown damage to some of the other electronic hardware for which I still owed considerable sums.

The bullets stopped. We waited on the floor for another few minutes before standing up. Ben now held a .38 automatic, two-hand style like the cops do on TV. It had magically appeared in his hands at some point during the action. I knew he owned one and had mentioned taking the concealed handgun permit course, but he really looked like a pro just then. He crept to the side of the front window and slid an eyeball to the edge of the remaining glass.

"It's clear," he said. Then he repeated the procedure at the other set of demolished windows. "Clear."

We took a moment to check each other for damage. Other than a few cuts from broken glass on my forearms, we all seemed to have emerged from the assault intact and unharmed.

"What the fuck, Josh?" Dylan asked. He had his arm around Abby who appeared remarkably calm. Most women would have been reduced to hysterics after a violent attack like that, but not Abby. I was beginning to think she was made of sterner stuff than me.

"I think someone is trying to send us a message," I said, annoyed by the quaver in my voice. "What are the odds that this was a random act? Somebody must know about our involvement. I wonder if it was the same assholes from Dulce?"

"I don't know," Ben replied. "But the next time, I'll be ready for them." No quaver there, damn it. I felt like Don Knotts to his Clint Eastwood.

I conducted a cursory examination of my computers. The damage looked extensive, but until I ran diagnostics on everything, I wouldn't know. My heart sank. If we lived through the next few months, I would have to take a second job.

Police sirens in the distance now. This day was getting better by the minute.

###

The next few hours were filled with police reports, cleaning up broken glass and supervising the replacement of the windows. Fortunately, I'd found a company that agreed to send a crew over later that morning.

The police had proven more difficult than the window repairs. I didn't live in south Dallas after all – drive-by shootings weren't common in this white collar area. Initially, just two officers arrived, and after they'd confirmed that the shooters were long gone, the grilling began. Squad cars carrying backup officers came next and were followed by a nondescript sedan bearing plainclothes detectives. We stuck with the same story no matter how many times and how many different law enforcement officials asked the questions.

Did you see the shooters? No. We were too busy crouching on the floor avoiding gunfire.

What were your friends doing here? We'd met at my apartment and had planned to go to breakfast together.

Why so early? What kind of question is

that? We're early risers, I guess. And we really love breakfast foods.

Who would want to harm you? I have no idea.

Do you think you were the target or could the target have been one of your friends? How would I know? To my knowledge, none of us has any enemies. But you might want to do a cavity search on the big one there.

(Middle finger from Ben.)

Are you or your friends involved in any illegal activities? Absolutely not. We're all law-abiding citizens. Still, that cavity search might not be a bad idea. He's got a shifty look about him, don't you think?

And so on and so on for the next two hours.

Finally, the fine representatives of the Dallas PD were finished and left en masse, with the parting threat of more questions to follow as reports were written and found lacking. Shortly after, Ben and Abby also left to run some errands but planned to return within a couple of hours, at which point we would venture down to the arts district of Dallas. Dylan stayed behind with me.

I watched him as he made a fresh pot of coffee in my kitchen. I could tell that methodical brain of his, which had aced pre-med classes, was contemplating thoughts more complex than scooping coffee. I remained silent. Finally, after we sat down at the kitchen table with steaming cups, he spoke.

"Josh, I've never doubted anything you've told me. You know that right?" I nodded. "The problem is I wonder if you've underestimated the situation."

"Well, no shit, Dylan. Obviously I have. That's how I almost got myself killed a couple of hours ago. My friends too."

"I don't mean what happened this morning, per se. I mean the bigger picture."

"You mean the bigger picture of not just alien hybrids trying to kill off our species, but the fact that people in high places apparently want us to stay out of it?"

"No, the even bigger picture." He gazed out the kitchen window at the fall colors in the neighboring park. That view was the main reason I'd leased the apartment. Dallas wasn't known for breathtaking scenery or interesting topography – flat and extensively developed were the predominant themes here. But a lovely little manicured park resided next to my complex and from the kitchen window I could watch children play, leaves change from green to orange and neighbors walk their dogs in the dusky, golden light of early evening. I did some of my best writing in the spot where Dylan sat now.

"Elaborate, please."

"We know the alien hybrids exist. We've watched the videos numerous times. You and Ben saw one at the gas station on that first trip. Joe has confirmed recent sightings in Arizona and now we believe they're here. We don't know their agenda; we just assume they mean us harm, as evidenced by what happened in the video on the mesa. We also assume there is a group of powerful people in the government who are responsible for the creation of these hybrids and are even now aware they're loose."

He paused a moment before continuing.

"Do we really believe these government people didn't plan this all along? Doesn't it seem a bit far-fetched that they'd lose control of their multi-billion dollar project and then just write it off to experience?"

I had a feeling that whatever Dylan was about to say would send me to the Mylanta cabinet.

"What if that was their plan all along? Develop the technology, create the hybrids and then step back and let their protégé do their dirty work?"

"What dirty work?" I asked. "We believe the hybrids were created as part of a weapons program to create the perfect killing machine. One that was smarter and stronger than our enemies. One that would look human on the battlefield but could out shoot, out run and out last any human adversary. I'm not following you, Dylan."

"What happened twenty thousand years ago, Josh? Remember the ancient astronaut theory? It's always made sense to me. The DNA jumpstart we allegedly got from extraterrestrials gave Homo sapiens the edge over Cro-Magnon man. We developed farming, we built cities, we advanced so rapidly and in such a superior manner that Cro-Magnon died out. He couldn't compete. It could have been a case of natural selection – the best, brightest, strongest and fastest always prevail in nature. But it wasn't a fair competition because we had an advantage given to us by the extraterrestrials. This had nothing to do with nature. They jacked around with our DNA, plugged in an extra gene or two, or maybe just activated some that were dormant, who knows? But they did something to us that gave us an edge. Homo sapiens prevailed, Cro-Magnon died out. And it wasn't because nature had determined we were the better species, but because we cheated.

"We became extraterrestrial ourselves. We were the first hybrids." He let that sink in before continuing.

"Part earthling, part something else. Now we, the hybrids, have created another, supposedly better hybrid. It's like a mailman suddenly deciding to perform brain surgery. We're out of our league. The extraterrestrials are capable of space travel. They are unquestionably vastly superior to us in evolutionary terms. Yet we have the balls to think we can do what they did? The arrogance of the people responsible for this is astounding."

I couldn't deny any of his logic, but I still wasn't clear on where he was going.

"What do you suppose would happen if the ETs found out what we'd done? Do you think they'd be happy about it? Something tells me no. We don't know why they did whatever it was they did to our DNA, but let's assume it was for altruistic reasons. We must seem like children to them, or even pets maybe."

I smiled at that. It made me think of a Jack Handey quote: *I wish outer space guys would conquer the Earth and make people their pets, because I'd like to have one of those little beds with my name on it.*

"You're thinking of the Jack Handey thing, aren't you?" Dylan smiled. "Anyway, I imagine it would be like parents dealing with naughty children. We might be in for a very bad scolding. Or, let's say their motivation wasn't so magnanimous. Maybe they engineered us to be a slave race. Or a food source. Good grief, there are seven billion of us fuckers on this planet. If 'human' is on their menu, we'd be quite the smorgasbord."

I couldn't help it. The writer in me found the idea hilarious. I imagined Goliathan tables covered with platters of braised human in delicate wine sauces. Ben could feed a family of aliens all by himself.

We have to worry about natural disasters, asteroids hitting the planet, nuclear war, global warming, solar flares and EMPs. Now we also have to worry about aliens devouring us at some massive intergalactic feast?

"So, what you're saying, Dylan, is that not only do we have to contend with the hybrids who want to kill us, the government traitors who also want to kill us if they can't keep us out of their business, now we might be dealing with some pissed ETs coming back to earth and either spanking us or eating us? This situation just gets better and better."

"Yeah, but that isn't all. There might be another concern. Maybe the assholes that started all this were after more than just putting down insurgences in Afghanistan or Iraq. Maybe they're looking at a much bigger picture too.""What, like world domination?" I smiled.

Dylan cocked an eyebrow. "Consider history, my friend. You think it's that far-fetched?"

I realized it wasn't. A flood of would-be world conquerors ran through my head: Ghengis Khan, Alexander the Great, Napoleon, the Romans, Hitler. An inner circle within the tangled web of scientists, politicians and military people involved with Dulce Base whose ultimate goal was to control the world, starting with their own country. It's happened countless times in history. Just because there was a science fiction edge this time around didn't make it any less plausible.

"Fuck, Dylan. That would explain Operation Clean Sweep. They sicced the hybrids on the people they wanted out of the picture, staged an uprising, then sent in the military as part of the emergency protocol to finish off the rest of them."

"Maybe. It seems reasonable, doesn't it?"

"Yeah, unfortunately it makes more sense than anything else. And if that's the case, there might be more hybrids than we've been thinking. If they knew Clean Sweep was coming and had time to hunker down somewhere, it could be that very few or perhaps none of the hybrids were killed."

I remembered the creature at the Chevron station outside of Dulce – thought of that horrific smile and what it conveyed and wondered how many more had been crammed in that Nissan. How many more were holed up somewhere, safe and sound...waiting for the opportunity to unleash their killing urges? How many more were infiltrating my city even now?

I headed for the Mylanta cupboard.

"One thing at a time though, buddy," Dylan replied. "We should probably just focus on the here and now – the immediate threat that we know about."

"I think that's an excellent idea," I said, looking out the window at the park below. I watched a woman in a black track suit walking her dog. It was some kind of foo foo breed...a shih tzu or poodle. Dylan followed my gaze and confirmed my theory.

"It's a shih tzu. They're cute and friendly but prone to renal dysplasia and respiratory problems. A good choice for an apartment dweller though," he shot me a pointed look. I smiled, and watched the woman and her dog. At that moment, she glanced in our direction. She was wearing dark sunglasses which covered a large portion of her face, but despite that, something about her seemed very familiar – and not familiar within the context of the park. I studied the shih tzu, realizing it was not one of the canine regulars.

"What is it?" Dylan asked.

"Son of a bitch," I said.

"Who is she, Josh?"

"Remember the woman from the casino that I told you and Abby about? The one who was hitting on me but who finally directed us to the bartender for information about Joe? I'm 90 percent sure that's her. What in the hell is she doing here?"

Dylan studied her for a few seconds then said with a frown, "I'm guessing she's spying on you."

My bay window was tinted to improve energy efficiency during the long, hot Texas summers, but I'm sure she could make out two figures on the other side of the glass.

I jumped out of my chair.

"What are you going to do?" Dylan asked, following me into the living room.

"I'm going to have a conversation with that woman," I smiled in a way that made Dylan visibly nervous. I'd been beaten up, shot at and almost killed in my own home. I was at the breaking point, and this woman was going to give me some answers.

I bolted out the front door and flew down the concrete steps of my apartment complex with Dylan on my heels. The quickest way to the park was through the gated swimming pool area, then down a sidewalk that ran between two other apartment buildings. The sidewalk connected with a paved walking path that led to the park.

She'd been close enough to my building for me to recognize her, but we had to go about a city block in the opposite direction to gain access to the park. Still, it took two minutes tops to get there. We slowed to a halt on the spot where she'd been. Even in late October, the grass was still green but the trees were losing their leaves and there weren't many places she could be hiding. She was nowhere in sight.

I detected a faint fragrance and lifted my nose up in the air like a bloodhound. They say the olfactory receptors have the ability to trigger memories more poignantly than any of our other senses. The scent of that perfume placed me squarely back in the casino in Dulce, New Mexico.

I was right.

Just then, we heard a car door slam on the far side of the park. We sprinted in that direction but were too late. The black sedan (again with the black!) was driving away at an accelerated speed and was already too far away to make out the numbers on the license plate. We stood at the curb of the residential street and watched it disappear around a corner.

"That was her, Dylan," I said, breathing heavily after our sprint. "I recognized her perfume."

Dylan didn't question me. He just nodded in silent commiseration. We'd had an opportunity to get some answers and blown it.

We walked back to the place she'd been when we spotted her. I wanted to stand where she'd been and see what she had seen. From that vantage, the second story bay window of my apartment wasn't opaque. I could make out the back of my kitchen chairs and a round object on the wall, which I knew to be the tacky rooster clock my mom had given me for Christmas two years ago.

Next to the bay window was the recently replaced smaller window of my living room. The one which was located directly above mini NORAD. How interesting that the larger window had not been targeted by our assailants this morning. Was it possible that our attackers had known precisely where my electronics were? Had they known all the human occupants were in the living room and not in the kitchen? The intact bay window implied some kind of advance or covert knowledge.

Just one more mystery to add to my burgeoning list of Shit I Don't Know.

###

We'd been back in my apartment only a few minutes when Ben returned. I brought him up to speed on our female friend in the park.

"Damn, Josh. I knew that broad had the hots for you but I can't believe she followed you all the way back here," he said with an evil leer.

"Fuck you," I said. I noticed he looked thicker, somehow; a condition I did not attribute to fast-acting maple donuts. He wore a military-looking flak jacket – the kind without sleeves and about a million pockets. I had no doubt as to the nature of the 'errands' my burly friend had been doing.

"Gotta be prepared for anything. This ain't no snipe hunt, you know. So, are we ready to head downtown?" he asked.

"Yeah, I suppose," I replied. "Where's Abby?"

"Isn't she here?"

"No," I said, as my stomach plummeted a few floors. "She left at the same time you did. She hasn't been back."

Three hands dug cell phones out of pockets. No missed calls. But even as we scanned the screens, a text message appeared on all of them at the same moment.

We have your friend. Her continued health is dependent upon the ceasing of all activities by your group. Involving the authorities would be ill advised.

That was it. No additional texts, and the number from which it had originated had been blocked.

The bastards had my girl.

Dylan sat down abruptly in a kitchen chair. Ben looked as angry as I've ever seen him. I suddenly felt the need to throw up. Whatever my face looked like at that moment seemed to have a galvanizing effect on my friends.

"We're getting her back, Josh," Ben said, his voice calm and menacing.

"Absofuckinglutely," Dylan agreed in that overly soothing tone he uses on injured animals.

I wish I could say this made me feel better, but it didn't. I knew the three of us were all willing to put our lives on the line for Abby. It wasn't even something that needed to be vocalized. But first we had to find her before we could even think about coordinating her rescue.

And how in the hell were we going to do that?

Thoughts of my life with Abby flashed through my mind. Not just the time when we were a couple, but all the great memories before and after too. Abby laughing at some lame joke I told her, Abby at a baseball game with her hair in a ponytail and a mustard smear on her face, Abby helping Dylan at the animal hospital with a stray she'd found on the side of the road, Abby sitting on my sofa with her legs tucked off to one side and tears silently streaming down her face during some chick flick I'd agreed to watch with her. Scene after scene of wonderful memories.

Then I imagined Abby blindfolded and terrified, sitting in the corner of a dark room. Somewhere. Anywhere.

Ben grabbed me by the shoulders, shook me out of my reverie and forced me to look at him.

"Listen to me, Josh," he said. The determination I saw in that face transformed my friend into something unfamiliar – alien almost. I imagined this was a similar visage worn by assassins, snipers, Navy Seals, drug lords, African militants – all those determined to achieve their goal no matter the cost in blood or pain. He had my attention.

"We. Will. Find. Her." The words came slowly and with a funereal cadence. "Those fuckers won't even know what hit them. There is nothing, *nothing* that will stop me. Do you understand?" He shook me again for good measure.

I began to feel the tiniest bit hopeful. I

looked at Dylan and saw a similar expression of determination, but less scary. I took a deep, shaky breath.

"Okay, where do we start?"

"Let's see what you can pull up in her emails," Dylan said.

I glanced at one of my computers – the one used to conduct my slightly illegal activities – and prayed to whatever gods might be listening that it hadn't been damaged by the gunfire.

"Good idea," I said with a surge of renewed energy.

For the next hour, we combed through Abby's emails, both personal and work related. Fortunately, my 'hacking' computer hadn't been damaged. I'm ashamed to admit that it wasn't the first time I'd peeked into her private business. There'd been a time shortly after we'd broken up, when I went slightly insane. If you knew Abby like I do, you'd understand. 'Better to have loved and lost than never to have loved at all' is a load of crap. I say, better to never know what you're missing than to have a few months in heaven and then be cast out. The sense of loss was so intense, so devastating that I wasn't myself for a while. That's the justification for my invasion of Abby's privacy. I only did it once when I thought she'd broken up with me to date some hotshot guy from her office, only to discover my suspicions were unfounded. I felt so disgusted with myself that I never did it again, even when I knew she had other dates with other guys. I'd lost Abby, but I wasn't prepared to lose my self-respect – at least not a second time.

The contents of her inbox contained mundane business correspondence and innocuous personal emails. They all appeared to have been read recently. Her 'deleted' folder was empty, but whether that was the result of Yahoo's random purging process or Abby manually emptying it herself was unknown. The next step was her 'sent' folder and there we hit pay dirt.

A series of emails had been sent and received between Abby and her boss, Mayor Skinner. Nothing unusual about that in itself, but the content raised some red flags.

Skinner was a slimeball. We knew that for a fact. Abby knew it too but contended there was also a noble side to him. She claimed he wanted to bring about positive change that would help the lower income people of Dallas have a better quality of life. He introduced programs to the city council which provided low income housing and raised the city's pay scale for 'grunt jobs' – school cafeteria workers, municipal buildings' janitors, the workers who cleaned the city buses. She considered his efforts noble but I doubted Skinner's motives were truly selfless. There was nothing the mayor did that did not benefit himself in some way.

Skinner's emails to Abby were lascivious but shy of being incriminating – not that Abby would use them against him anyway, which he certainly knew. The euphemisms and innuendos were disgustingly clear to us: he wanted more from Abby than a professional relationship and was willing to risk losing her as a valuable employee if it meant getting her in bed. I didn't realize his sexual aggression had become this blatant.

I wanted to crawl through the CRT and grab him by his throat.

Ben and Dylan hovered behind me in similar states of agitation as we read through them. The most recent email chain contained correspondence from the previous week. We started reading from the bottom up to get the proper chronology.

The subject line contained the words 'information you wanted' and the gist was that Abby had approached Skinner for information on a particular government project which was classified. They both carefully avoided specifics and the content was essentially a cat and mouse game. Skinner had information Abby wanted and Abby was willing to jump through hoops to get it.

Abby referenced something called 'DB' and the 'group responsible'.

Skinner responded with 'I have three names. Our agreement will need to be adjusted as a result.'

Abby's response was short: 'Why?'

The smugness fairly oozed from his response: 'Because these are names everyone will recognize. Meet me at the A at 11:00. The number is 703.' Abby's last response had been sent at 9:30 that morning: 'I'll be there.'

We had a lead.

It was now 2:00 pm. Maybe she was still at 'the A', whatever that was. We figured the number 703 indicated a suite number or perhaps a hotel room. We checked hotels first. Skinner had expensive tastes, so we Googled 5 star hotels in Dallas and the Adolphus appeared as the second non-sponsored listing.

Bingo.

I clicked on the map, printed it out then clicked back to the window where Abby's emails were. I intended to print out the email chain as well as save a screen shot. As I placed my fingers on the appropriate command keys, the entire page went blank.

The next moment, the blank screen was replaced with the generic Yahoo index page. I closed that window, opened a new one and repeated the hacking process, but no luck. There was simply no longer an email account assigned to abby_montgomery@yahoo.com.

Someone had deleted it right before our eyes in real time.

It was unsettling to know that our adversaries – the people responsible for abducting Abby and perhaps the attempt on my life this morning – were on the other end of that virtual connection.

We took Dylan's Explorer so Ben could sit in the backseat with me and demonstrate proper weapons handling. He'd brought a SIG 9mm for my use. He also carried a Glock and a Browning High Power 9mm – the handgun of choice for SWAT and FBI types. I knew his fascination with guns hadn't ended with his stint in the military. I'd accompanied him to the shooting range on a few occasions, so I wasn't completely unfamiliar with these lethal toys, but a quick refresher couldn't hurt. Ben spent enough time at the range to be on a first name basis with all the employees. His bullet patterns on the targets awarded him a semi-celebrity status there.

It was a comforting thought at the moment.

We decided not to use the valet service for obvious reasons and parked in a remote lot towards the back of the hotel. Walking towards the building, I imagined how we must look to those hotel employees and guests who happened to notice us.

I'd like to think we resembled some bad-ass vigilante types as we walked three abreast, switching to slow motion so all the nuances of our grim expressions could be adequately conveyed. In my mind, I heard the theme song to Tombstone as Val Kilmer, Kurt Russell and the other two guys whose names I can never remember, march towards the OK Corral. In reality, we looked less intimidating. Except for Ben, of course, who even if he were sipping tea with his pinky finger pointed heavenward and nibbling on tiny, crustless sandwiches, would still look dangerous.

We located the back entrance, a less grand version than the front foyer. Security cameras were positioned at the door and at various points down the luxuriously carpeted hallways. Nothing we could do about that. We tried to look like we belonged in the elegant surroundings as we stood in front of the elevators, anticipating the flash of the green 'up' button. Finally, one of the cages rumbled to a stop at the ground floor.

The doors slid open to reveal none other than the mayor himself.

Fortunately for us and unfortunately for him, he was alone. His eyes opened wide in alarm. He recognized me as Abby's former boyfriend whom he'd met on a couple of social occasions. He glanced at Dylan then at Ben as that clever brain, the brain which had gotten him elected to a position of power in one of the largest cities in the United States, weighed its options. He gave Dylan a cursory appraisal then took in Ben's size and cold demeanor.

That seemed to be the turning point.

Skinner's calculating expression changed suddenly to one of resignation. That was when I noticed his disheveled state. He looked like he'd been on a bender. His dark gray suit was wrinkled, his red power necktie hung askew, the normally perfect salt and pepper hair poked out in all directions and his left eye was swelling shut.

We stepped in, blocking any attempts at escape. Dylan pressed the 7th floor button and the doors slid shut behind us with a quiet mechanical swoosh that managed to ratchet up the intimidation factor even further. Skinner backed up as far as he could in the small space and raised his manicured hands, palms up and fingers splayed, in a motion which had been used to calm boisterous crowds and overzealous reporters. It had no power within the confines of the elevator and these particular constituents were in no mood to simmer down.

"Where is she?" I asked.

"Honest to god, I don't know!" he stammered. The mayor's self-assured, refined voice had been replaced by the screechy vocal quality of a high school girl. Interesting. I'd never seen him less than perfectly composed and while I allowed myself a few seconds of schadenfreude, the next moment it came crashing home that the people responsible for his current condition might also be Abby's captors.

"Here's how this is going to play out," Ben said as he glanced up at the sequentially lighting floor numbers. "We're going to get off this elevator at the seventh floor. If there is anyone about, you're going to act like we're your best friends. Then we're going to room 703 and you're going to let us in. At that point, you will tell us exactly what has transpired. You got all that, big fella?"

Skinner's head bobbed.

"Excellent. If you get any silly thoughts about causing a scene or trying to get someone to help you, I must tell you that I will inflict an enormous amount of physical damage on your person before anyone is able to come to your aid. I work very fast," Ben grinned and winked, like a salesman sealing the deal. "If you're a good boy and do what you're told, you just might get out of this with your testicles intact. You're in complete control of how this will go. I'm hoping, for your sake, that you make the right decision."

Ben slid his hand from the pocket of his jacket, revealing his brass knuckles. Skinner's eyes followed the movement.

"I got it, I got it!" he squealed. The man was very close to hysteria and something told me a hefty portion of that had nothing to do with us.

The elevator came to a halt at the seventh floor and the gleaming doors slid open. A well-groomed older couple stood in the hall, their faces set in small, pleasant smiles befitting the greeting of fellow guests in a luxury hotel. They noticed Skinner's condition simultaneously, and if it had been under different circumstances, the cartoon-like transition from bland congeniality to wide-eyed alarm would have been comical. I threw my arm around Skinner's shoulders and smiled at the couple.

"Bar fight," I said. "One of these days he'll learn not to hit on other guys' wives."

The man nodded slowly. The woman's eyes narrowed, then dawning recognition appeared on her face.

"Isn't that the mayor?" she asked, suspicion changing to morbid fascination.

Dylan piped in then, charm set on overdrive and heavy on the Texas drawl. I've seen him go into what I call his 'aw-shucks-good-ol-boy' mode many times during our friendship, and I've never once seen it fail at whatever it was meant to achieve.

Fortunately for the world, Dylan only used his powers for good.

"Ma'am, he gets that all the time," he said, stepping out of the elevator and into the hallway, drawing the couples' gaze toward him and away from Skinner. "They say everyone has a double and our buddy here is a dead ringer for the mayor. You ever heard of a doppelganger?"

Ben and I ushered Skinner out of the elevator and down the hallway as Dylan continued chatting. I hazarded a glance back and confirmed that the couple was securely under his spell. They weren't even looking in our direction but gazing at him like he was a movie star. I couldn't help but smile. I vowed to never be jealous of Dylan's charm and good genes again.

"Key card," Ben said to Skinner, who fished it out of his jacket pocket with a shaky hand.

Ben swiped it and opened the door. I pushed Skinner inside. Dylan caught the door behind us before it swung shut.

"Sit," I said to Skinner, pointing to the bed which was messy but had not been turned down. Skinner did as he was told. His eye looked worse by the minute but he got no sympathy from us.

We surrounded him like a quiet but determined lynch mob.

"Let's try this again," I said. "Where is she?"

"I'm telling you, I don't know. I was here in the room when she arrived at about eleven this morning. Right after she came in, there was a knock at the door. I assumed it was room service with my, uh, order." He glanced at a tray on the desk which contained a bowl of chocolate covered strawberries, a bottle of champagne floating in a bucket of ice water and two crystal glasses. Seeing this and knowing what he'd had planned for Abby made my stomach twist into knots and my hands curl into fists.

Dylan gave me a light pat on the back.

Focus.

"It was my order, but the guy who brought the tray in wasn't a hotel employee, I don't think. I opened the door to let him in and two other guys came in right behind. Big guys, all of them. They took Abby and beat the crap out of me when I tried to protect her." His voice was querulous now – a little boy who'd been denied his favorite toy. "I must have passed out because I had just come to and was leaving when you saw me in the elevator."

Something in Skinner's demeanor told me he was telling the truth, but that he knew more than he was saying.

"Who were the guys, Skinner?" Ben asked, crossing his arms over his chest. The mayor's eyes darted down to the brass knuckles displayed on top of a large bicep.

"I don't know who the guys were! I'm telling you, I don't know what the hell is going on!"

"I think what my friend is asking is, who did the guys work for? Who hired them to take Abby? What were you sticking your dirty fingers into?"

Again, the sly, calculating look as the mayor analyzed his situation. He did know something – I could see it on his face – and he was mentally working out the odds for his best chance of survival. Who to piss off? He seemed to come to the conclusion that the guys in front of him, who undoubtedly planned painful retaliation for withholding information, were the more pressing threat.

He started talking.

Abby had approached him for information on a top secret military base in New Mexico. He said she wanted to know anything he could find out about it and, most importantly, she was interested in the people who were behind it – the top dogs, the ones who called the shots. Being mayor of a large city didn't open doors for him in terms of security clearance on federal projects, but he knew people – people who owed him a favor or two. That's how it works in politics, he said. No newsflash there. He made some calls, sent some emails and had been able to get three names for her along with a few details about the base. Names that even those who only casually dabbled in politics would most likely know. Those names were the bait with which he'd lured her to his hotel room. He bluntly admitted an intense infatuation with our Abby – one that had endured much longer than his usual indiscretions and which seemed to intensify the longer she deflected his advances. When she came to him about the base, he'd made it his mission to get the leverage necessary to force their relationship to the next level.

At this point in Skinner's narrative, I felt hands on my shoulders, gently pushing me down into a chair by the bed. Then Dylan moved to stand slightly in front of me in case I decided to act on the murderous urges that he knew may, at any point, override my self-control. Skinner was so wrapped up in thoughts of Abby that he seemed completely unaware of just how tenuous was his continued enjoyment of non-fractured body parts. He went on to explain that Abby had agreed to meet him and he'd felt certain that she knew this would be a quid pro quo arrangement. He said she'd known what would be expected in return. He stated this defiantly, as if he considered his transparency to be honorable in some way. I shook my head in amazement. I suppose there was some kind of sliding scale for sleazebags like Skinner. If he was telling the truth, and his body language implied as much, Abby knew she'd made a deal with the devil.

"So, what exactly was the information you planned on trading to our friend in return for sexual favors?" Ben asked, his voice deceptively friendly. I knew that tone. Dylan may have his hands full keeping us both off the mayor.

"That is information I will not share with you. It's for Abby alone. And besides, it's classified."

Skinner seemed to think that would suffice.

With the swiftness of a much smaller

man, Ben delivered a backhanded blow to Skinner's face, causing his head to whip to the side and almost knocking him off the bed.

"The next time, I'll use the other one," Ben said, holding up the hand with the brass knuckles.

As it turns out, Skinner had no stomach for torture, and talked nonstop for the next ten minutes. I hoped the man never got elected to higher office where he would be privy to critical national security information. Between his inability to withstand a beating and his susceptibility to beautiful women, our country's secrets wouldn't stay secure for long.

###

Back in Dylan's Explorer, my mind raced. The information Skinner had given us was interesting and potentially explosive if it went public, but it didn't get us one step closer to finding Abby. I felt myself edging toward the mental abyss again. She could be anywhere...maybe she wasn't even in the city. Maybe they'd transported her to some remote location in Mexico or Guatemala. The thought of her scared, alone and at the mercy of ruthless strangers made my stomach churn.

"What was she doing?" Dylan said to nobody in particular. "What did she hope to find out?"

"Answers," I replied. "She wanted to get answers, since I'd obviously failed so miserably in that regard. And maybe leverage. If we knew the people who are behind all this, maybe she thought we could use it against them – pressure them to find a way to stop these monsters. She was trying to stop the abductions. The thought of all those people – the children, the moms and dads, the old folks being plucked off the face of the earth and never seen again – made her crazy and reckless. So she decided to get information that could help put an end to it."

Silence followed as we pondered Abby's actions. She had been willing to go much further than her personal ethics should have allowed.

"Are we certain that the people Skinner told us about are even behind Abby's abduction?" Dylan mused out loud as we pulled out of the hotel parking lot.

"Who else makes sense?" I asked. "Red flags must have been raised when Skinner gathered the information. They must have connected Abby through him and back to us. They knew we knew something, right? They must have connected the dots."

"We know someone knows that we know something," Dylan said. "But we actually don't know if it's the same people that Skinner gave up. Hell, there could be any number of people mixed up in this."

"Obviously, I'll end our investigations if Abby's life is at stake," I said, defeated. "I need to call Joe and tell him what's going on. He'll have to stop too. If they know about us, they must know about him."

I pulled my phone out of my pocket just as it rang. The incoming number displayed as 'private'. I answered, my heart pounding.

"Joshua, we know where she is, and I can tell you how to get her," a female voice, soft and husky. I closed my eyes and pictured myself back in the casino at Dulce. I recognized that voice.

"Loretta!"

I could hear the smile in her reply. "That name is as good as any. Listen carefully."

She explained in detail where to find Abby and the necessary actions and precautions we must take in order to extricate her safely. I scribbled down an address.

"Who are you? Who are you working for? Why are you helping us?" I demanded when she was finished.

"Oh, Joshua. Don't push it. I'm taking a huge chance doing this favor for you. You're welcome."

The connection ended.

I relayed the details of the conversation to the guys, which made Ben's face light up like he'd just been given a lifetime supply of maple donuts. The rescue mission would incorporate many of his favorite things: danger, feats of physical prowess and the rescuing of damsels in distress.

"How do we know this isn't some kind of trap?" Dylan asked. Of course that thought had occurred to me for a nanosecond, but I'd quashed it like the pesky insect it was.

We'd been presented an opportunity to get Abby back and no matter what our odds of success, I intended to take the chance. Dylan knew this too, but as the Professor to Ben's Skipper and my Gilligan, it was his job to think things through a bit further than we did.

"Doesn't matter," Ben growled. He wanted to rescue Abby, of course, but he also didn't want anyone to thwart his field trip. I smiled and nodded. Dylan was smiling too. After many years of friendship, we all understood our roles within the group. We'd just been presented with an extraordinary gift and we intended to make the most of it – no matter the cost.

Chapter 5

If there'd been a video documentary made of our rescue mission, it would have looked like some of the footage you see on the Discovery or History Channel filmed by the helmet camera of a Navy SEAL or a DEA agent, but without any of the finesse, skill or cool moves those guys have. Ben played the part well, of course, but let's face it – the closest Dylan and I got to being badass types was an occasional game of football at the park or at a bar deflecting unwanted advances toward Abby.

The address Loretta had given us was a rural location north of the city and close to the town of Pilot Point. Sprawling horse ranches and large homes dominated the landscape on both sides of State Highway

377. Lake Ray Roberts offered residents beautiful views to the west and the gently sloping terrain was honeycombed with farm to market roads in all other directions. It was a little slice of rural Texas heaven but within commuting distance to the city. There was money here and it manifested in the way money does in such settings – with huge tracts of acreage surrounded by neat white fencing, large homes that didn't push the envelope into opulence, and shiny, tricked out pickup trucks that individually probably cost more than the gross national product of a small African country.

I wasn't told the name of the person who owned the property where Abby was being held, but I'd been given an idea of what to expect in terms of hired muscle as well as a rough outline of the lay of the land. The rest we had to figure out for ourselves. During the drive, I'd gathered information on my laptop and we formulated a plan utilizing the tips Loretta had suggested.

Still, it was thin.

As we pulled off the state highway and

onto a side road, the butterflies which had been lazily flitting about in my stomach turned into manic kamikazes. I thought of all those classically cheesy lines from every action movie I'd ever seen: 'Yippee-kiyay motherfucker!', 'Hasta la vista, baby!' and of course, 'Go ahead...make my day!' I was merely a wannabe badass but maybe today I would graduate to the real thing.

We parked in a grove of pecan trees off the side road, twenty yards away from the graveled driveway which led to Abby. We'd been advised that motion detectors were placed at the entrance to the driveway, so we took the scenic route towards the house. The homeowners, whoever they were, had let nature have some leeway here. There was no shortage of cover as we scrambled and skulked through the saplings and brush which circled the perimeter of the property. Twenty minutes and several thorny scrapes later, we made it through to a manicured lawn. The house sat prominently in the center of at least a two acre square of neatly trimmed grass. A large swimming pool, covered now in late

October, consumed a large section of land to our right and a white gazebo sat to our left.

We were looking at what must be the back of the house, a country Victorian boasting a large wraparound porch. Rural Texans loved this particular style. The obligatory pots of ferns hung at perfectly spaced intervals and a glider near the steps inspired thoughts of sipping iced tea on a warm summer evening.

The type of people who would abduct and threaten the life of another person shouldn't be living in a place as lovely as this. The bucolic setting conflicted with the image of Abby imprisoned inside; perhaps bound or hurt and certainly frightened.

What had been going through her mind these past few hours?

The anger I felt at this thought worked as a pesticide to the noxious butterflies jetting about in my stomach. It's interesting how acute anger overrides everything, like a bottle of black ink spilled on a page of lesser emotions. It blotted out all else and gave me the focus necessary to get the job done. I flicked the safety off the loaner SIG and held it with both hands like I'd been taught.

Ben gave us the signal to approach the house. We spread out so we'd be coming from different directions as we traversed the lawn. Dylan arrived first at the door we'd selected for our entrance. It appeared to be a secondary door of some sort; not the primary back door which most likely led to a kitchen and where the odds of human occupants would be greater. He stood off to one side, between the door and a window. He'd refused to carry a handgun for the same reasons many people won't wear fur – it was against his moral code. He had, however, brought something that might prove just as useful and much less permanent in terms of destructive power: a tranquilizer gun which he'd brought from the animal clinic that morning. It looked similar to a handgun and he wielded it like a pro. Ben checked the handle on the door and found it unlocked.

So far, so good.

We crept in and found ourselves standing in a medium sized room which was a combination pantry and laundry room. Cans of peaches and jars of spaghetti sauce stood sentry on a wall of shelves to the left and a state-of-the-art washer and dryer, both currently in operation, hummed and whirled to our right. The inner door which led to the rest of the house was closed. We took a moment to regroup in this strangely comforting room which smelled of Downy and cinnamon. The contradiction between the sensory and the cerebral was a bit distracting. I marveled again at the hominess of the kidnappers' hideout. I hoped that Abby wasn't being held at gunpoint by the Brady Bunch because I would really hate to have to shoot Mike and Carol.

With a 'get ready' nod, Ben turned the interior door handle and opened it a crack to peer through. He opened it further then stepped into the next room – his two-fisted grip on the Glock seemed as natural as a pro golfer holding a nine iron. He motioned us in with a jerk of his head.

The kitchen was even more inviting than the pantry. Golden oak cabinetry, granite countertops and shiny stainless steel appliances created an ambiance of coziness despite the large size of the room. According to the lighted dot on the coffee pot by the sink, the machine was on and the carafe looked half full. Somebody liked their coffee with cream and sugar judging by the half and half container and the empty sugar packets left by the sink.

Abby liked her coffee that way. She also loved to drink it late in the afternoon during the fall and winter months, just like now. I wouldn't allow myself to hope that her captors were treating her with kindness. I knew that kind of thinking might impact my reaction time and possibly get one of us killed.

We crept through the kitchen into the adjacent living room. A staircase, bisected by a landing, led to the upstairs. Muffled voices, conducted through the stairwell, could be heard from above – but first we needed to clear the downstairs.

One room after another proved empty until I opened an inconspicuous door off a hallway which ran behind the kitchen and beside the stairwell. I don't know who was more surprised – me or the guy who was sitting on the toilet with his pants around his ankles and the sports page spread between his hairy hands. His eyes flew wide in alarm and he reached for his gun which was lying on the vanity countertop next to the sink.

Instinct kicked in at that point – the second time in one day that my hypothalamus would save my life. I clocked him with the butt end of my SIG. Fortunately for him, the wall was close to the commode and rather than falling onto the floor, his unconscious body simply collapsed against it – his slicked-back dark hair incongruous with the winsome daisy motif of the wallpaper. The newspaper fluttered to the carpeted floor.

Ben came up behind me, assessed the situation and gave me a hefty pat on the back. I'd like to think his expression conveyed admiration, but I'm certain there was a healthy dose of surprise mixed in as well.

The rest of the downstairs offered no additional excitement. It was time to head up.

The stairs were also carpeted and the sounds of our ascension were muffled. Ben took lead and we scaled the steps to the upstairs hallway. Just as we reached the top, a door opened and a man emerged. His eyes were lowered to the doorknob that he was closing but he glanced up as it clicked shut. He was similar to Sports Page Guy downstairs, but with less hair product and more muscle.

Ben's Glock flew up at the same time the man's hand went to a shoulder holster, but before either could take a shot, a faint pneumatic sound came from behind us and a dart magically materialized, protruding from the man's belly. Whatever was in Dylan's tranquilizer gun worked with lightning speed – the man crumpled to the floor even as he continued to fumble for his weapon. Within seconds, he was passed out on a homey braided rug.

Ben turned to face Dylan with a mixture of amazement and exasperation. This was twice now he'd been denied the lead role in a confrontation and it was clearly piss-ing him off. Dylan grinned, pleased with having defused a life-threatening situation with no bloodshed and little effort.

We continued down the hallway. There were five closed doors, two on each side and one at the opposite end of the stairs. We started with the room where the gunman had just left.

No human occupants here. It appeared to be a small guest bedroom containing two twin beds with frilly Laura Ashley comforters (I know this only because Abby loves that stuff), a chest of drawers and a mirrored dresser with a small television on top. A black leather duffel bag lay on one of the beds, unzipped and open to reveal a cache of lethal objects, discordant with the pink tea rose bedding. Ben ferreted through it, stuffing a few items into the pockets of his jacket.

Door number two was more of the same – more of the frilly bedding in a room that felt unused.

Door number three was the one at the end of the hall opposite the stairs. We steeled ourselves for a third time and

Ben turned the knob. It was locked. He pantomimed the movement of turning a key and pointed to Sleeping Beauty on the floor. I covered the distance and rifled through the man's pockets. A bi-fold leather wallet was wedged next to a set of house keys. I stuck the wallet in my own pocket to peruse later and handed the keys to Ben. He studied the doorknob then selected one out of the dozen or so on the ring and slid it into the deadbolt opening with a tiny clink of metal.

It fit. Ben opened the door.

The room was large and airy with late afternoon daylight filtering in through a wall of windows on the opposite end. Below the windows was a large sofa on which my uncle was lying. Abby was tending to him. Nobody else was in the room.

I ran to Abby and wrapped her in a fierce hug. I'm happy to say she returned the hug with equal enthusiasm. I stopped short of kissing her because we were just friends after all, but it took herculean self-control not to. I let Abby go and turned my attention to my uncle.

Joe managed a smile. His presence here was surprising but his appearance was shocking. His complexion was gray and he'd lost even more weight. The battle with cancer was a war of attrition and my uncle was losing.

"What's the situation?" Dylan asked. Ben had retreated back to the hallway and I could see him drag the unconscious man into the second bedroom.

Joe sat up on the sofa with some effort. "There are two goons that we know of but I think there's a third person giving orders," he said.

"What happened to you? How long have you been here?"

"Since this morning. They got me at home in Dulce...woke me up in the middle of the night, tied me up and threw me in the back of a panel van. By the time I got here, it was daylight. I didn't even know where 'here' was until they brought Abby in."

"You must be Joe," Dylan extended his hand to my uncle. "I hate to rush this reunion but I think we need to get the hell out of here quickly."

Ben was closing the door of the room where he'd stashed the unconscious man as we ushered Joe and Abby out into the hall. "How long until that tranquilizer wears off?" he asked Dylan.

"As long as he has nothing else in his system to counteract the effects, I'd say at least an hour."

"We may not have that long then," Ben replied as he held up a bottle of pills. "Found 'em in his pocket and there were more in the bag."

"Let's get going then," I said.

No more than five or six minutes had elapsed since we'd been upstairs but I was worrying about Hairy Hands in the bathroom below.

We filed downstairs. At the landing, Ben said, "You guys go on. I gotta get something," then trotted back up, taking the stairs two at a time. We reached the living room, with me in the front and Dylan bringing up the rear. I stuck my head around the banister to check Hairy's door. It was still shut. Good.

I motioned Abby and Joe through to the

kitchen. I went through the pantry first and opened the door to the backyard, noting how low the sun now hung in the sky. It must be close to five o'clock. Twelve hours had elapsed since I'd seen the news this morning and thus the beginning of what had proved to be the longest day of my life.

And it wasn't over yet.

Abby helped Joe down the steps, followed by Dylan. My head was turned back to watch them when I heard the unmistakable sound of a rifle bolt being drawn. It came from behind me – from the direction we needed to go. I turned slowly to face whatever had made that sound. I'd tucked my SIG down the back of my pants but I knew there was no way I could reach it before a rifle bullet would reach me. The others looked up at the sound and saw our adversary a split second before I did. She was emerging from behind the gazebo, but could have been stepping out of a magazine ad for fashionable Western clothing, high end shampoo or any other product where they use breathtakingly beautiful people as models. She wielded the rifle as if it were an extension of her slender body and there was no mistaking the cold, calculating look in the lovely eyes.

"I was the first place winner at the Texas State Rifle Association's 2009 sharp shooting competition. Just so you know." Her voice was low and menacing with just a hint of a Demi Moore rasp. I also thought I detected the barest suggestion of an accent – eastern European perhaps?

"Put your weapons on the ground – now. And don't think about doing something stupid. I will shoot you without hesitation." This was directed at Dylan who was making a tentative move to raise his tranquilizer gun. Instead he laid it on the ground at the same time I removed my weapon and placed it at my feet.

"What did you do to the men?" she demanded.

"They're not dead or even seriously injured," I replied.

"Too bad," she said with an indelicate snort. "I was hoping someone would save me the trouble."

"Who are you?" I asked. Perhaps not the best approach but I figured as long as she was talking, she wasn't shooting. Things were more complicated than I'd imagined.

And I have a very good imagination.

With a sly expression, she said, "Now, Joshua Hawkins, whatever would I gain from telling you who I am?"

"Well, since you obviously know who I am, it would just be the polite thing to do,"

"Next you'll be asking me where to find the nest," she said with a smirk.

"Nest? What nest?"

"Don't be coy, Joshua. You know what I'm referring to...the place where our genetic cousins are, of course."

"Oh, so you work for the assholes that created them?" I asked.

Another snort. As lovely as the woman was physically, she inspired no prurient thoughts.

"Hardly, and that's all you get from me." She motioned with the rifle toward the door through which we'd exited moments before. "Back into the house, all of you."

I was in the process of turning away from

her, when I saw a flash of movement from behind the gazebo. The problem with a rifle is it requires two hands to hold and shoot properly and thus impedes one's agility. She heard Ben's rapid footsteps but couldn't spin around fast enough to draw a bead on him. He grabbed the rifle from her hands and in a rapid follow-up motion, smashed the butt of it against her head. She was tough though; it took a follow up punch to the jaw to get her to drop to the ground like a beautiful sack of flour.

"Let's get the hell out of here," Ben said in his grumpy voice. Tangling with a girl was not the kind of action he'd been hoping for.

Chapter 6

At Dylan's house, southeast of Dallas in the rural area of Seagoville, we sat around the kitchen table, wolfing down Taco Bell pseudo food and drinking cold Budweisers from Dylan's garage fridge. Night had finally fallen, bringing an end to a day that felt more like a month.

Animals were everywhere.

At last count, Dylan's menagerie consisted of a German Shepherd with hip dysplasia, a Himalayan with a missing eye (Dylan had ignored my suggestion of a pirate kitty eye patch), a dachshund wearing a doggy diaper, a Jack Russell terrier who was just as fast on three legs as most dogs were on four, an iguana who'd been left in a box outside the clinic, and Monty the pit bull. Despite Dylan's assurances of his gentle nature, Monty always made me a bit nervous – his jaws were massive. The latest addition since my last visit was a sweet twelve-year old golden retriever named Trixie whose geriatric owners had recently passed away. The brown eyes gazed up at me from my lap where she'd strategically placed her head in hopes of a dropped morsel.

You'd think with all those animals, the place would smell like the monkey house at a zoo, but it didn't. Dylan was an immaculate housekeeper and even though a faint smell of disinfectant always lingered in the air, it wasn't unpleasant. I associated that smell with my best friend and the motley crew of pet rejects who owed their lives and happiness to his big heart.

Joe's color looked better and he smiled around a mouthful of tacos at the zingers and clever repartee.

"Josh, admit it," Ben said with an evil grin, "you got a boner when that broad had a gun on you. Nothin' sexier than a hot chick holding a firearm"

"I'll admit it only if you admit to sphincter puckering when that dude came out of the upstairs bedroom."

"Fuck that noise," Ben replied. "If Robin Hood over here hadn't shot that damn dart gun," a quick punch to Dylan's arm, "Upstairs Dude would have been toast."

"Too bad your reaction time is so slow, big guy," Dylan returned the arm punch. "Your dinosaur brain is so busy managing all that brawn it doesn't have enough RAM for awesome Ninja moves." Dylan scooted his chair back and assumed the classic crane pose from *Karate Kid*.

"Yeah, you're a real Ninja," Ben said. "Oh wait, you could be the next gay super hero: Ninja Dart Man. Look! Up in the sky! It's a bird, it's a plane! No, it's Ninja Dart Man and that pink cape is *fabulous*!" Ben could do a flaming gay guy better than anyone. We howled with laughter – Dylan most of all.

An hour later, the levity had faded and fatigue began to set in. I decided it was time to get down to business.

"So, let's go over what we know. One, Skinner was digging for information about

Dulce and may have tripped some wires in his search. Two, the people who kidnapped Abby and Joe may be affiliated with the high level names he gave us, or they may not. It does seem likely though. Three, Loretta, may represent a third party. If so, who? What is their angle? Why would they help us? Four, the hybrids are in Dallas which indicates they're making their move, whatever that entails. Do the other groups know this? Are the hybrids acting autonomously or are they affiliated with humans in any way?

"Have I missed anything?"

"Who do we think the hot broad in Pilot Point was?" Ben asked. "If the hired muscle was on her hit list and if they worked for the crooked feds, do we assume she's not affiliated with the crooked feds? Is there another group operating behind the scenes?"

The tiny molehill of facts we did know was dwarfed by the mountain of what we didn't know.

"Maybe it's time we went public with this," Abby said. "I think we're in way over our heads."

"I don't think that's such a great idea," Dylan replied. He took a deep breath and his expression conveyed a mixture of shame and relief as he spilled his guts.

After my phone call to him early that morning about the news story on TV, he'd made another phone call before he left. It was to someone he knew who worked for Reuters. He'd had the same thought Abby had just expressed – we were in over our heads and needed to go public. He hadn't given details or any of our names; just the highlights. He was met with skepticism, but his friend had promised to delve into the matter. Hours later on the drive back from Pilot Point, he'd received a text from his friend's cell phone which he showed us now: *Try that again and even more of your friends will disappear.*

"You tried to go public without telling us?" I asked.

Dylan nodded, unhappy. "Yes, which may have gotten Abby kidnapped and probably worse for my friend."

"So all afternoon we were thinking it had something to do with Skinner's political connections, but now it appears there are people in the media who want to keep the lid on this thing," Ben said, shaking his head in mild disgust.

If I hadn't been so angry with Dylan at that moment, I'd have felt sorry for him. He looked like a whipped puppy.

"That doesn't explain why I'm here," Joe said. "If Dylan made that call early this morning, I was already hogtied in the back of that van heading for Dallas."

Good point. We sat in silence for a few moments, digesting the new information.

"The lesson someone wants us to learn is we can't go to the media and we can't go to the government for help. What about the police?" "Police are the government," Ben said. "Anything relayed to the police will get back to the wrong people."

All heads nodded in unison.

"Why didn't the kidnappers just kill Abby and Joe?" I asked. "Why bother with the kidnapping business at all?"

"Maybe they wanted to interrogate them first," Dylan suggested.

"But if that's true, what could they learn

that they don't already know? And why did the super model want to kill the kidnappers? Abby and Joe, those guys never said anything to you? Didn't question you?" Both shook their heads. We'd already been over this.

"Nothing significant," Joe replied. "They were just hired muscle. I did get the impression they were waiting for something though, either new orders or maybe someone higher up on the food chain."

"Maybe the kidnappers weren't affiliated with the government people at all. Maybe they just wanted to get their hands on the technology, or even the hybrids themselves. Can you imagine how much this little science project would be worth to China or Russia?" Dylan mused.

When I considered the scope of what we were involved in, I decided I was too exhausted to allow my head to explode. There would be time for that tomorrow.

Reading my thoughts, Dylan said, "Joe and Abby can have the two guest bedrooms and Josh, you and Ben can have the sofa and the recliner."

Great. I knew who'd be sleeping in the recliner.

###

I was having one of my recurring dreams – the one where I'm at an airport trying to find my gate – when I was roused by a wet nose nuzzling my hand. I'm not one of those people who takes a few minutes to shake off the cobwebs of sleep. I was instantly awake and remembered that I was in Dylan's living room. Ben snored on the sofa. It looked darker in the house than it should have. No soft glow from the porch light penetrated the gloom and the bathroom light in the foyer, which I'd intentionally left on with the door cracked, was dark.

My internal alarms were clamoring. Trixie whimpered. She knew something was wrong too. I pressed the backlight button on my watch: 3:07 am – the witching hour. We'd had approximately five hours of sleep and still needed more. It was the time of night when people were home from the bars but not up for work yet. I'd always heard that the hour between 3:00 and 4:00

am was the best window in which to conduct covert operations. All the good little boys and girls were sound asleep in their beds making it easier for the bad ones to commit their nefarious deeds unnoticed.

I slipped on my shoes and crept over to the sofa to wake Ben.

"Something's wrong. The electricity is out," I whispered.

The power was off and there'd been no storms which meant that somebody had cut it. Dylan's house had been built in the 50's making it easy for someone to tamper with the electricity. The archaic metal monstrosity of a breaker box was attached to an exterior wall in the backyard because that's how houses were built during more innocent times – sabotaging it would be a cake walk for anyone so inclined. The double whammy was the semi-rural location of the house which was the primary reason Dylan had purchased it five years ago. Originally, it had been a farm house sitting in the middle of a hundred acres, but much of the land and been parceled off decades ago. When Dylan bought it, it came with twenty acres, most of which had been fallow for years other than Dylan's huge fenced-in backyard and the vegetable garden.

The nearest neighbor was at least a half mile down the road.

I heard a soft throaty rumble from the kitchen. Enough starlight came through the window to illuminate Monty, the pit bull. His paws were on the window sill and he looked out into the backyard. Monty was no longer the dog to be nervous around; he was the dog you wanted in your house when people who meant you harm skulked in your backyard.

"I'm going to wake up the others," I whispered and trotted upstairs, with Trixie hot on my heels.

Within two minutes, we were all clustered in the dark kitchen. Monty's growls had intensified.

"The way I see it, we have two choices," Ben whispered. "We try to make a run for it to the car or we sit right here and let them come to us." The Glock was back in his hand and the Browning was tucked into the waistband of his jeans. "And there's no guarantee that they haven't jacked with the car too. I think we should stay right here, set up an armed perimeter in the living room and pick them off as they come in." When we considered how exposed we'd be on a dash to the car – a car which might not even function, it really was a no-brainer.

We decided to stay.

The item that Ben had run back upstairs to get at the kidnappers' house was the duffel bag. After going through its contents earlier in the evening, I felt certain that Upstairs Dude was going to be mighty pissed that we'd taken it – it contained an impressive assortment of weaponry. Joe knew his way around guns but Abby needed a quick lesson.

Ben selected a small .38 Special snubnose for her, saying it was the perfect choice for a woman despite the nasty recoil. Of the two remaining guns, Joe picked a Walther P99 semi-automatic and deftly loaded the magazine he'd located in the bag. Ben nodded with approval then handed me the remaining weapon – a

Glock similar to his which would serve as a backup to my Sig. I stuck it into the back waistband of my jeans after ruling out the frontal area in the vicinity of my penis.

We set up our perimeter in the living room per Ben's instructions. Joe was stationed next to the front window; Ben stood sentinel at the back window. Dylan was positioned behind the sofa with his dart gun pointed toward the kitchen. Monty stood beside him, still growling even though he'd been forced to relinquish his post at the kitchen window. I was at the other end of the sofa with my Sig pointed toward the front door which also allowed me to cover the stairs in case the bastards decided to come through an upstairs window. Abby crouched on the floor between us. I was surprised to feel a sense of relative calm. No manic butterflies and no acid reflux despite the imminent danger. We were all together, we were sufficiently armed and we had a certain strategic advantage by being in a familiar setting. It was the best we could possibly do given what we had to work with. I didn't hate our odds at that moment, which just goes to show how a little bit of cockiness can come back and bite you in the ass.

Monty's growls suddenly changed in tone from *'I'm not sure I like this'* to *'someone is about to make the biggest mistake of their life.'* His intense focus was on the darkened kitchen. Just then, we heard the rattling of a door handle. Dylan had locked the door leading to a covered carport but it only took a second for a muzzled gun to render the lock useless. If we'd been asleep, I doubt it would have woken anyone.

The door creaked open, emitting a soft thump when it hit the kitchen cabinets.

In a soft whisper, Dylan said: "Go, Monty."

Eighty pounds of muscle, claws and teeth bolted into the kitchen before the last syllable was spoken.

After that, chaos.

A few seconds after Monty took off for the kitchen, glass shattered at both of the windows near Ben and Joe. The intruders assumed we would be sleeping and therefore vulnerable, so didn't bother with much caution as they stuck their hands through the broken panes searching for the lock. Joe reacted with the swiftness of a younger, healthier man. He shot three times in rapid succession through the broken pane. Grunts of pain filtered through the shattered opening.

They'd just learned we were awake and ready for them.

Ben's window adversary received similar treatment. Four rounds through the hole in the glass stopped further ingress.

My attention remained focused on the front door, and despite the intense distractions surrounding me, I managed to stay focused. My mind registered sounds of struggling and growls coming from the kitchen, and I was aware that Dylan had left his position by the sofa. With my peripheral vision, I could see that Abby had moved from the floor to take his place. At that moment, the front door crashed open with an explosion of splintered wood.

I've always considered myself somewhat of a moderate in terms of aggression; whether in foreign affairs, invasion of other countries or testosterone-driven bar fights. Most of the time, brute force isn't necessary and situations can be handled without moving armies, dropping bombs or knocking out teeth. That mindset went out the window the moment the men came through the front door. They weren't here to have a tea party, after all. They were using extreme violence to gain entry into a private residence in the dead of night. They weren't officers of the law or teenagers on a lark. They were here to do bad things to people I cared about.

And for that reason, I didn't hesitate when I shot them.

Their eyes didn't have time to adjust which gave me a distinct advantage. I'm no sharp shooter, but at a distance of fifteen feet, my aim is decent enough. I shot five times and both men crumpled to the entryway floor. If I said I felt remorseful, I'd be lying. I was euphoric right then – at least until I looked at Abby's shocked face. Even in the gloom, I could see that her eyes were wide and she was looking at me with a mixture of shock and something that might have been revulsion.

More shots came from the kitchen. I noticed that Ben had moved from his post at the window and must be in the fray alongside Dylan and Monty. The sounds were a cacophony of grunts, growls, bodies slamming against appliances and cabinetry, items being broken and the soft thud of fists making contact with flesh and bone. I was sorely tempted to throw my hat in the ring but I knew I needed to stay at my post. The front door was a gaping maw of blackness through which anyone or anything could easily gain entry. Abby moved to cover the window that Ben had relinquished and I could see her small form squatting off to the side, careful to keep her face away from the glass. She'd been paying attention during the rushed and impromptu lesson.

The sounds from the kitchen came to abrupt stop with a loud thud, which sounded like a body making contact with linoleum.

Ben shouted, "Kitchen's clear!"

I took my eyes off the foyer in the

process of standing up as Ben came back into the living room. Just then, two shots whizzed past from behind me, so close that one of them grazed my bicep. The burning pain was instantaneous. A second later, a body fell down the stairs and landed alongside its compadres on the foyer floor. Joe had just covered my ass even though he'd come awfully damn close to killing me in the process.

The next few minutes went by without incident and we gathered together in the living room once more.

Finally, Ben said, "We need to get the electricity back on." Dylan nodded and motioned for Ben to follow as they went back through the kitchen and out the carport door to the backyard. In another minute, the lights came on – a weak offering since most of them were still switched off.

But it was adequate enough to illuminate the gruesome fallout of the attack.

We were still on high alert, but as a group we began to survey the damage, starting in the foyer. Three bodies. Men dressed in black clothing wearing black gloves. They all appeared dead. Dylan squatted down and held his fingers against their carotid arteries, one after another. A quick shake of his head each time confirmed our suspicions. Joe stood behind me with his hand on my shoulder, squeezing gently, as I gazed down at the carnage.

I guess he thought I might feel horrified about what I'd done. Don't get me wrong – it wasn't something I took lightly. Still, there was no rush of self-loathing or mental hand wringing. They'd brought this party to us. We hadn't gone looking for trouble.

Joe stayed by the front door as the rest of us ventured into the kitchen. We were careful not to turn on any room-flooding lights. We didn't know if there were more bad guys outside watching for a clear shot through the windows. Dylan turned on the stove light which cast an eerie glow on the scene. Two human bodies, dressed just like the ones in the foyer, were sprawled on the kitchen floor. Beside them, lay Monty.

Dylan checked the humans first. One dead, the other unconscious with a dart protruding from his chest. Next, he knelt beside Monty.

Dylan had adopted the pit bull four years ago after he'd been rescued during a raid in Waxahachie. The home owners had been conducting illegal dog fights and Monty was one of the few animals with treatable injuries. The odds of being adopted with his history were slim though. That's when Dylan had stepped in, tending to his physical wounds as well as the psychological and behavioral ones.

The brown eyes opened and the stump of a tail lifted and fell a few times as he gazed up at his beloved human. An expanding puddle of blood surrounded him.

"Flashlight," Dylan said.

I grabbed one from a kitchen drawer and focused the beam on Monty. The bullet wound was dead center of his chest. It didn't take an expert to notice the rhythmic nature of the blood flow. He would bleed to death in moments and there was nothing we could do to stop it.

Of course, Dylan knew this before anyone. He sat down on the floor beside him and stroked his head. Monty licked his hand.

"Good dog, Monty. Good boy. You did a good job." Dylan's voice was steady and calm.

Abby put her hand on Dylan's shoulder, tears streaming down her face. A tight knot formed in my throat.

Monty's eyelids began to close. Dylan continued speaking soft praises to his canine friend until it was over. When he lifted his face finally, the anguish I saw was almost more than I could bear.

"Joe, still clear out there?" I managed to say.

"Yep, no movement."

"Let's take care of him," I said to Dylan.

Ben ran upstairs to get some towels and we wrapped Monty in a soft cocoon. I helped Dylan carry him out through the carport as Ben and Abby kept watch.

"The garden," Dylan said.

We buried Monty at the far end of Dylan's vegetable garden, next to a crepe myrtle bush and under an ancient oak tree. Even at night, I could see that it was a lovely spot. The moon hung full and heavy and the clear sky allowed the stars to shine with an intensity we didn't experience in the city.

I tried to help Dylan with the digging but he seemed to need the physical exertion and pushed me away. Finally it was done and I pulled my friend toward me in a fierce hug. I felt him choke a couple of times against my shoulder. A wave of guilt washed over me then. I had done this. I meddled in things which people didn't want meddled into and my blind determination to get to the bottom of what was happening in Dulce had led to the abduction of Abby and Joe.

And now this. If it weren't for me, Joe would be in his home, Abby would not have put herself at the mercy of a scumbag like Skinner, we wouldn't have had to take human lives (the moral and legal ramifications of which would come crashing down on us at some point soon) and Monty would still be alive.

It was all my fault.

Finally, we headed back to the house.

Four bodies had to be dealt with and

the fifth living assailant would be an even greater challenge.

"We're not calling the police," Ben said, as we entered the kitchen. "Not yet. First we're going to question this dickhead." He punctuated the statement with a kick to the unconscious man's ribs, eliciting a groan. The tranquilizer was wearing off.

The man looked younger than the other assailants we'd encountered that day. His skin was pasty and his hair was a greasy, nondescript blond. You wouldn't look twice at this guy if you passed him on the street.

Pasty Boy's eyes fluttered open when Ben clicked handcuffs onto his wrists, another offering from the duffel bag. Lying on his side on the floor, the first thing he saw was a forest of legs surrounding him. His gaze traveled upward to hostile faces.

"Oh, fuck," he muttered and closed his eyes.

Ben kicked him in the ribs again and received a satisfying squeal of pain for the effort.

"Wake up, dickhead. You got some

splainin' to do."

"Fuck you," the man replied with a groan.

Ben kicked him again, harder this time. Pasty Boy howled.

I smiled. There was something distinctly unlikeable about this guy and I had a lot of pent up frustration.

"No, you're the one who's fucked, asshole. You're going to tell us everything you know. Starting now." Ben emphasized the 'now' with another kick, this time to the groin. He gave his victim a few minutes to work through the groin pain before pulling him to his feet and shoving him into a kitchen chair.

The man was getting more lucid by the second. I could see intelligence in those pale eyes; a sly, shifty intelligence that told me we'd need to handle this jerk carefully if we wanted to get the truth from him.

"Who do you work for?" I asked him. The pale gaze shifted from Ben to me. I saw fear in those eyes but also defiance. We'd see how long that lasted.

"I work for the Keebler elves. We heard

the recipe for Milanos was here and we came to steal it."

Ben backhanded him. The blonde head snapped to the side and blood trickled out of his mouth. He spat a disgusting wad of red-tinged sputum onto Dylan's floor.

This minor act seemed to flip a switch in the section of my brain that processes rage. Dylan's house had been immaculate when we arrived earlier that evening. Now glass, broken doors, blood and bodies littered his home all because of this little fucker and his cohorts. Dylan's home, which had been a sanctuary for injured, abused and unwanted animals like Monty – and this creep thought he could spit on the floor? Not in this lifetime, pal.

I squatted down so my eyes were level with his pale blue ones. I studied him at my leisure, my head cocked to one side. The seconds ticked by and I could tell he was becoming unnerved. Whatever expression showed on my face, it seemed to undermine his confidence more so than getting kicked and smacked around by Ben. Still, he kept his mouth shut as he fidgeted in his chair, doing his best to avoid making eye contact with me.

Joe came into the kitchen. "Nothing else going on out there," he said. "I did a recon of the perimeter."

My eyes never left the face of Pasty Boy as Ben recounted the events of the last 20 minutes, informing Joe that the only survivor was sitting right here. That prompted a flash of panic on the bland face.

When I spoke, it was in a soft, matter-of-fact tone.

"You get one chance to talk. After that, no matter how much you scream, beg for mercy or cry for your mama, it won't matter because the window will already have closed. But right now, that window is open. I strongly suggest you take advantage of this opportunity because I can tell you it would be in your best interest to do so."

"You think you're scaring me?" Pasty Boy blustered. I could see the bravado beginning to slip.

I smiled and said, "Yeah, I think so. Because you realize that we're not going to go easy on you. You realize that you have pushed us past the limit of normal behavior. You thought at first that we were a group of schmucks...pushovers...pussies. And now, as you look at us, as you look at me," I held his face between my hands so he was forced to look into my eyes, "you know that we are capable of committing atrocities above and beyond what we could ever have imagined before all this began. And you know that I will take my time with you because there is something in my eyes that tells you I will enjoy hurting you. And you know what? You're absolutely right."

My smile broadened. I couldn't help it. I was enjoying this.

Two seconds later, he started talking.

He knew little about his employers other than they were government and they paid very well. He suspected a prominent senator was involved because a name he recognized had been inadvertently spoken in his presence. The guy who'd committed this faux pas fell off the face of the earth soon after. The senator's name was one Skinner had given up – a step in the right direction.

"So, what do you know about Dulce, New Mexico?" I asked. The recognition was instantaneous.

"I've been there a few times. Now that you mention it, I think I ran into you and your goon there a few months back." The little prick had the nerve to smile.

Ben squatted down and looked him squarely in the eyes. "You must have been the little fucker I kicked in the nuts. I hope you don't have plans to reproduce because I'm pretty sure your swimmers are seriously impaired by now."

The smile disappeared.

Ben stood and took a step back. The next moment a bullet came through the kitchen window and lodged in pasty boy's temple.

"On the ground!" Ben yelled for the second time in 24 hours. We stayed low for the next couple of minutes as blood oozed down the side of our captive's head. His eyes were half open and the spark of life that all living creatures possess was clearly gone.

"Joe, I think your perimeter sweep was a

bit lacking," Ben said from the floor.

Joe shrugged. "I didn't beat the bushes. This was a sniper's bullet. My guess is he was 50 yards or so due south in that line of trees.

"Somebody didn't want him talking, but why just this guy? Why not us?" Dylan said.

"Maybe we were next," Abby replied in a horrified whisper.

We were still hunkered down on the floor when my cell phone rang. I pulled it out of my pocket and saw the incoming number was blocked.

"Hello, Joshua," Loretta didn't wait for a greeting. "Sorry for the window, but it couldn't be helped. We couldn't let that cockroach live. The rest of you are safe for the time being. Please make sure everyone is out of the house in exactly one hour. I'm sending a cleanup crew."

"Loretta, what the hell?" I yelled into the phone, but it was already dead air.

I relayed the conversation to the group. We stood, staying clear of the window. By the time we got ourselves cleaned up, the sky was beginning to lighten.

Dylan decided the animals would be coming with us, so we put the iguana and the cat in small carriers and set them in the back of his SUV. The dogs were used to road trips to the clinic and their tongues lolled happily at the prospect of a ride. Daisy the dachshund sat in Abby's lap sporting a fresh doggy diaper. She seemed perfectly content to let the other dogs jockey for best window position in the back.

"Clinic first?" I asked Dylan as we pulled away from his house. We were crammed into the Explorer like a bunch of furry and fleshy sardines.

"Yep. I'll board them there until this settles down. They won't like it but at least they'll be safe."

The drive to the clinic was quiet. Everyone seemed to be working through the emotional fallout of their actions. Some of us had taken human lives. Had those jerks deserved it? Of course. At the moment I didn't feel remorse for the killing I'd done, but maybe that would surface in time.

Or maybe not.

It had been exactly twenty-four hours

since I'd seen the hybrid on the local news story. My brain struggled to absorb the preponderance of events during that time period – the significance of individual threads and the horrific, half-formed tapestry they were surely weaving, vague and nebulous, like those pictures you have to look at with unfocused eyes to identify the pattern.

We pulled into the empty parking lot of Dylan's clinic around 6:00 that Sunday morning. Humans and animals spilled out of the cramped SUV like too many clowns from a tiny car. Dylan herded us into the clinic and I headed for the break room to make coffee. Soon everyone joined me, drawn by the smell of fresh coffee.

Ben was the only one who seemed perky, as he rooted through the cupboards, looking for something to eat. I decided it was time for my speech – a speech I'd been working on in my head for the last hour.

"Okay, here's the thing." I said in a reasonable voice. "I can't keep putting you guys in harm's way. I can't stand the thought of anything happening to any of you and I already feel responsible for every horrible thing that's happened to us today. I won't allow it to continue. I won't allow you to be drawn into something so dangerous. This is my battle, not yours. I know Joe wants to stick with it because this is also his battle. But, the rest of you need to put your own safety first. I'm afraid I have to insist. As of this moment, you're released from active duty. I want you all to hole up somewhere safe, at least for the next few days."

Ben arched an eyebrow and said, "Go fuck yourself, Hawkins. I can't speak for anyone else, but I ain't going anywhere. So stick that in your pipe and smoke it."

"Joshua, how can you think we'd back off now?" Abby looked like she might punch me. "What do you think we are...a bunch of pussies?"

If she was angry enough to drop the P-bomb while sober, she was definitely angry enough to punch me.

Before I could respond, Dylan spoke.

"This isn't just your problem, Josh. Or

Joe's either. It never has been. People have died – have been dying for quite some time and probably in more gruesome and horrendous ways than we can even imagine. A great many more people could die in the future. Your intentions are noble but also selfish. You want to save yourself the guilt and anguish you'd feel if something happened to one of us. I get that. But we're not children...we know what we're getting ourselves into. We understand the danger. We're also not the type of people who can turn our backs, especially when there's so much at stake. You should know that.

"Now, let's pretend this conversation never happened."

I looked at Joe who shrugged.

"Now that *that* steamy bowl of crap is taken care of, I propose a leisurely drive over to Pearl Street for a little reconnoitering. After a quick stop at Dunkin Donuts first," Ben said.

Chapter 7

The streets of Dallas were free of traffic. The church-goers weren't venturing out this early, but of course the donut shops were open. After breakfast, Ben bought an extra half dozen maple donuts to go, 'just in case.' I don't know what that meant, but when it comes to Ben and maple donuts, the fewer questions asked, the better.

All we had to go on was where the hybrid had last been seen, so we figured we'd start there then work our way outward in ever-expanding concentric circles. We carried our small arsenal in backpacks borrowed from Dylan's house and in Abby's oversized handbag. Just tourists out for an early morning stroll in the city.

But we were tourists loaded for bear. Or

technically, alien hybrids.

We split up into two teams: Joe, Ben and Abby on one team, Dylan and I on another, staying in touch via cell phone. After an hour, we'd covered a lot of ground but had seen nothing unusual.

My phone rang again but this time it wasn't a call from Abby.

"Mr. Hawkins?" a businesslike female voice asked immediately.

"Yes, who is this?"

"This is Detective Monica Trevino from the Dallas PD. I was one of the officers at your apartment yesterday morning."

"Oh, okay. What can I do for you, Detective?" I remembered the petite, stern female officer who'd asked me about a million questions while her male partner stood a few feet away, silent and bored. "I have some follow-up questions I need to ask. Can I meet you in an hour? I'll be happy to come to your home."

"Uh, didn't we already cover everything?" I asked, annoyed.

"No, we didn't," was the curt reply. "I have some additional questions."

"So fire away." I was getting exasperated.

"Not over the phone. This is important, Mr. Hawkins. I'll be happy to meet you anywhere you'd like. Somewhere private would be best."

Interesting. Something told me she was concerned about more than just my broken windows.

"I'll meet you at my apartment in two hours. That's the best I can do."

"That will be fine. I'll see you then."

The line went dead.

Dylan shot me a look of curiosity so I relayed the conversation as we walked. We were speculating on what the detective wanted when we realized we'd gravitated to the spot where the news story had taken place the previous morning.

The garbage residue could be seen and smelled on the section of Pearl Street where the truck had dumped its load. At that moment, a man emerged from a nearby boutique with a water hose snaking behind him. He squeezed the nozzle and began spraying down the slime. As an employee or owner of the shop, perhaps he'd seen something unusual the day before?

As I walked up to him, I noted the fine laugh lines around his dark eyes – eyes that seemed intelligent and friendly. His salt and pepper hair was covered by a Dallas Cowboys ball cap.

"Hey, how're you doing?" I asked.

"Doing pretty good. How about yourself?" he replied. His voice was deep and had a pleasing tone, but the accent was definitely not Texan.

"I was wondering if you've seen anything unusual around here in the last day or so?"

"You mean besides the guy in the garbage truck?" he replied in a wry tone.

"Yeah, I saw that on the news yesterday. Crazy, huh?"

"Indeed."

"Actually, I was wondering if you'd noticed anything else – maybe around the same time all that happened yesterday. I hope that man is going to be okay."

He continued spraying without taking his eyes off the street. I noticed his smile had faded.

"He should be fine, thanks to all the publicity. Our city fathers want to make a good showing, after all. He's probably sipping on single malt scotch and getting sponge baths from bonny nurses." The accent became stronger the more he talked.

I noticed he didn't answer my question.

"Hey, your accent is great," Dylan spoke up. "You probably get that a lot, I bet. Ireland?" A grin and nod confirmed it as the man shifted focus from me to Dylan. He seemed to be loosening up a bit.

"So were you around when all that happened?" I asked.

"Yep, I have a flat above the shop. I'm an early riser."

"Did you happen to see anything else strange?" I asked again, knowing I was belaboring the point. "I see lots of strange things here, mister. Living in the city isn't like the suburbs. No matter how nice all this is," he waved a hand to indicate the buildings and streets.

"Uh, right. I don't mean strange in that respect, really."

"Well, perhaps if you told me what you think I might have seen, I could be more helpful. Are you a cop or something? Wait, let me guess. A reporter?" If he'd said 'cockroach' instead, I doubt he could have injected more loathing.

I took a leap of faith.

"I'm Joshua Hawkins and this is Dylan Saretsky. This is going to sound crazy but we have reason to believe there is…an element…that has entered the city which may not be what it appears to be. They appear human from a distance, but they're not."

He turned the hose off and looked into my eyes.

"Look, you don't know me from Adam, but please know that we're the good guys here. We've been through a lot of shit recently as a result of those things, and we're just trying to get some answers and maybe save some lives."

Even to my own ears it sounded lame and melodramatic. I couldn't get a read on the guy. He just continued to study me and then Dylan in turn as he pondered a response. With every second that ticked by, we ventured further into socially awkward territory.

Finally, he spoke. "Let's go inside," he said, then turned his back and began dragging the hose back inside the shop.

After an exchange of raised eyebrows, we followed.

"Turn the deadbolt behind you there," the man said as he coiled up the hose and disappeared through a door at the back of the small store.

The inventory was an interesting and eclectic mix of décor type items and touristy stuff with a dominant Celtic theme – a tiny Irish mecca in the middle of downtown Dallas. The man returned and motioned to us from a second door. We followed him up the narrow staircase that lay on the other side.

The loft apartment was polar opposite of the shop below. No kitschy four leaf clovers or Celtic crosses here. The vaulted ceiling and absence of any interior walls was typical of urban lofts and the décor was ultra-modern. Sleek, contemporary and functional. Somehow, this didn't fit with my initial impression of the shopkeeper, who was now standing before us with his hands on his hips and an appraising look on his face.

"I'm Ian Connolly. You boys want some coffee?" he asked and headed towards the kitchen, which could easily have made the cover of Modern Home magazine.

"Sure, Ian," I replied. "Cream and sugar, if you don't mind."

"Same here," Dylan said.

"Get settled over there on the sofa and I'll be with you shortly."

We were enjoying the view from the broad expanse of windows that overlooked the urban setting below, when he returned carrying a loaded tray. I figured this little chunk of real estate must have cost a small fortune.

"So, you know about the grogoch," he said without preamble as he took a sip of coffee, leaned back in his leather chair and waited for our reaction.

"What's a grogoch?" Dylan and I asked in unison.

"That's what I call it since I don't know what the hell it is," Ian replied with a tight smile. "A grogoch is a mythical Irish creature – half man, half spirit. It has the power of invisibility and can be malevolent or benign, depending on whether it fancies you. I saw it for the first time several weeks ago and twice since then. Don't know what to make of it and don't know what can be done about it. I'm hoping you boys can enlighten me."

"Where exactly did you see it? What was it doing? Did it know you'd seen it?"

I had about a million more questions I wanted to ask. Here we had a situation where a 'civilian' had been in contact with a hybrid, multiple times, and had lived to tell the tale. This fellow could be a goldmine of information.

"Tit for tat, right boys?" he replied. "I'll tell you something about the grogoch and then you can tell me something. Sound reasonable?"

We nodded.

"Okay, the first time I saw it, I was going for breakfast. It was quite early – probably around six or so, and I'd cut down a wee alley which is a shortcut to the diner." He removed the ball cap and ran a hand through his hair. "I saw a man come out of a building on the left, about thirty feet ahead of me. Something about him seemed odd, but I can't say why I thought that. From a distance, he looked normal. He wore clothes like you might see a tourist wearing...chinos, a baggy tee-shirt and a fisherman's hat. You know, the canvas type that covers the head, ears and half the face? Anyway, something about him just wasn't quite right. When you live in the city, you see indigents. Oftentimes they're mentally ill and behave strangely. This wasn't like that. The mannerisms just seemed...well, alien, for lack of a better word. Anyway, it saw me about five seconds after I'd seen it. I couldn't make out too much detail on the face but got the impression it didn't like being seen. Something about it was just so creepy. I stopped and looked at it for a couple of seconds while it did the same to me.

"It smiled then...a smile that seemed to take up the entire lower portion of its face. Like a jack-o-lantern except with a lot more teeth. I don't mind admitting that the hair on the back of my neck stood up. At that moment I wondered if I would make it out of the alley alive, but it just turned and scurried off in the other direction. It moved like a human, but it was damn quick. After I was certain it was gone, I checked my britches to see if I'd wet myself. Fortunately, the nether regions were still dry but I'd lost my appetite for breakfast and headed home.

"And that was my first experience with the grogoch," he said then paused a moment before continuing. "Now, I'm assuming you boys know a lot more about this creature than I do. Let's have it."

And so we shared the Reader's Digest condensed version of the past six months.

Maybe that was reckless since we didn't know a damn thing about this guy, but I thought it might be worth the gamble. He accepted it all rather calmly except for a low whistle when I got to the part about the hybrid tossing people off a cliff.

"So, they were created in a laboratory, just like anthrax and the atom bomb," he mused. "I'd be more disgusted with our race if we weren't also capable of such immense good. We're just like children, aren't we? Piddling about in our mum's kitchen or our dad's workshop."

Dylan nodded in agreement.

"You've seen it more than once though," I prompted. "What were the other experiences like? Was it in the same area? Does it only come out in the early morning?"

"Well, here's the interesting part. The next time I saw it, it was dusk, probably around seven. I was out for an evening stroll and passed it on the opposite side of the street. There were very few people out and about. Its clothes were similar as before. The hat was different but still covered a good portion of its face. That time, I'm not sure that it saw me. But the last time, which was yesterday morning during the time of the garbage truck incident, I think it saw me before I saw it. I'd been distracted by the activity and when I looked up across the street, it was just standing there. None of the emergency personnel had arrived yet, so there weren't many people around. I got the impression it had been watching me. This time, it smiled again and it also nodded at me – like people do when they're acknowledging someone they recognize. I was not happy at the prospect of the grogoch wanting to make friends."

"Have you contacted the police or told anyone else about it?" Dylan asked.

"No, and I can't really explain why I haven't, to be honest," Ian replied. "I know I should have and had actually picked up the phone to dial 911 when I got back home after that first sighting, but something told me not to. Perhaps that was an unknowingly wise decision, I realize now."

I nodded, "Yes, I agree."

Just then, my cell phone rang. The display showed an incoming call from Ben. We'd been so caught up in Ian's story that I'd completely forgotten about the rest of our group out there roaming the streets of Dallas.

"Hey, Ben. What's…" but before I could get out the rest of my sentence, he interrupted me in a rush.

"Where the fuck are you guys? We have it surrounded! Get your asses over here.

We're on an alley off Pearl, near McKinney. HURRY!"

"They have it cornered!" I yelled at Dylan, then grabbed my backpack and ran to the door. We flew down the stairs, through the shop and as I fumbled with the lock on the front door of the shop, Ian spoke.

"I should come with you. It already knows me, sort of."

We were out the door when I answered, "It's dangerous, Ian. You really don't want to get involved in this."

"I'm already involved. You people have weapons of some sort, yes? All I have is this." He pulled a tiny canister of pepper spray from his pocket, the kind that attaches to a keychain. It seemed so absurdly innocuous, I laughed out loud.

"Your decision," I answered and we took off down the street.

We rounded the corner of Pearl at a dead run. Thankfully, the only other people out on the streets of Dallas at that hour were a couple of scruffy looking homeless types. Otherwise, our behavior would certainly have aroused suspicion. The first alley off

Pearl was empty in both directions. We raced to the next one and there, twenty yards away, were Ben, Abby and Joe standing in a semi-circle pointing a variety of weapons at a hybrid. Its back was against the brick building and its long hands were open and held at chest height in an 'I give up' posture. I couldn't believe what I was seeing. I scrutinized the hybrid as we slowed our pace and approached the odd gathering.

The reality that we'd actually captured one, or nearly so it seemed, filled me with awe. And dread.

"What the fuck do we do now?" Ben demanded of no one in particular. "And who the fuck is that?" He indicated Ian.

We stood about fifteen feet from the creature. Its demeanor appeared surprisingly calm, although I say 'surprisingly' with absolutely no frame of reference. Maybe these things were used to being at gunpoint on a regular basis. How the hell would I know what would surprise them? The fact that they were part human didn't predispose them to normal human behavior, whatever the hell that might be.

"This is Ian. Introductions later."

From this relatively close distance, the non-human traits, although subtle, were more evident. It was average height; probably somewhere between five foot ten to six feet tall. The eyes were mostly pupil, surrounded by a thin ring of a lighter color, green perhaps, and very little white area. Its nose was perfectly normal looking – the mad scientists got that part right at least. Its hands, which were still held up in a vaguely defensive gesture, also seemed normal but on the large side.

The mouth was a different story. It made me think of Heath Ledger as the Joker in one of the Batman films – but achieved by a genetic mutation rather than Hollywood makeup. It literally stretched from one side of the face to the other and was, thankfully, not smiling. Not for the first time, I found myself wondering about the teeth inside.

"I think it's trying to tell us something," Abby said, her expression a mixture of fascination and horror.

The creature moved the tips of its fingers

and began to vocalize. As we'd seen in one of Joe's videos, it seemed to be attempting human speech but apparently lacked the necessary equipment to actually formulate words, whether vocal cords or some other critical speech component. Maybe something was wired differently in its brain, but all it could do was simulate the vocal musicality of human speech but without words. It seemed to be repeating the same three syllables in conjunction with the humanlike and somehow familiar movements of the fingertips.

The mental image of a computer keyboard flashed in my mind. The fingertip movements seemed to mime typing on a keyboard. With that thought, my brain connected the dots. The three syllables could be formulating the word 'com-put-er'. Putting the fingertip motion together with the mushy vocalization, I felt certain that's what the hybrid was trying to convey.

"He wants a computer!" I said. "He's trying to communicate with us! He wants to communicate!"

All five fully human mouths opened in wonder as the hybrid nodded a confirmation. It allowed just the corners of its very long, very unsettling mouth, to turn up the tiniest bit. And then it did something that almost every human on the planet would understand – it slowly shifted one of its hands from the typing pantomime to a 'thumbs up' position.

The breakthrough experience was on a level the trainers at the San Francisco zoo must have felt when they taught sign language to Koko the gorilla. However, if the evidence Joe and I had compiled was to be believed, *we* were the gorillas in this scenario and the hybrid took the role of superior species. This thought took the edge off my jubilation and was followed by another which quashed it completely: these things killed humans.

"I have a laptop in my loft," Ian said in a quiet voice. I glanced at him and could see he was keeping a safe distance from the Grogoch. "Shall I fetch it?"

Dylan responded, "I don't like being out in the open like this. Ian, is there any way you'd consider allowing us, and this," he gestured toward the hybrid, "in your home? Providing we can get it there, of course."

He glanced at me and back again to Dylan. "Okay," he said after a long moment. "I can't believe I'm doing this. I must be fekking crazy. If that thing kills all of us, I'm going to be very pissed. You've been warned."

"Just remember what we've seen these things do to people. I don't know why this one seems so friendly but we can't trust it," I said.

That had a sobering effect after the near giddy reaction to the communication breakthrough. The hybrid shook its head in what seemed like a gesture of sadness or remorse. I wasn't buying it though. That thing could be Jack the Ripper as far as I was concerned. I glanced at Joe and knew he was having similar thoughts by the narrow-eyed, suspicious expression on his face. One of these things might have killed Alameda. If not one of them, then certainly the people who were responsible for creating them.

"Okay, here's the plan. Ian, is it?" Ben asked the Irishman who nodded in response. "You take point since we're following you. "You," he gestured to the hybrid with his Glock. "You follow ten feet behind him. You got that, ugly motherfucker?"

The hybrid blinked once, slowly, then repeated the thumbs-up gesture which had served him well a few moments ago.

Ben continued, "The rest of us will fan out behind and beside it. Keep your weapons concealed but easy to get to. If that thing tries anything stupid, blow its fucking head off."

I remembered how quickly those things move but I figured it couldn't get to all of us before somebody managed to pump a few bullets into it.

"Let's move out."

The walk back to Ian's loft seemed to take much longer than it actually did. We made it without any glitches other than being stared at by a grubby man on the opposite side of the street. I was grateful that it was Sunday morning and the area was nearly deserted.

We trudged through Ian's shop and up the stairs to his loft. The hybrid moved with the gracefulness of a large, predatory cat – fluid, confident and always alert. The cat analogy did nothing to improve my confidence in our ability to handle this thing. This creature's DNA was probably more similar to ours than any other species on the planet, yet I felt less of a sense of kinship with it than I might a dog or cat. Hell, even Dylan's iguana seemed less alien to me than the hybrid.

Once inside the apartment, Ian indicated a desk in a corner which contained a laptop computer. The hybrid understood and promptly seated itself in the chair in front of the computer. Its back faced us and we could see the monitor clearly.

The long, nimble fingers danced across the keyboard. The words it wrote, if they were to be believed, would change our perception of everything.

"Mean you no danger. No hurt. Want to discover location to remain unrestrained. Imploring civilian humans no impede this venture."

We finished reading the text and looked at each other with raised brows.

"Are you alone or are there others?" I asked.

The hybrid pondered this for a few seconds before his fingers responded with lightning speed.

"Others some. No many."

"Like exactly how many? Can you count, big boy? Do you know numbers?" Ben asked.

It turned its head to study Ben as he spoke. I could tell the unblinking gaze of those huge, mostly black eyes had an unnerving effect on him, but he tried to cover it.

"Numbers yes. Three like this one." The hybrid tapped its chest.

Interesting. The concept of 'me' must not be in the hybrid's lexicon, perhaps as a result of being grown in a lab next to other glass jars full of identical siblings.

"There are three of you hybrids that escaped from Dulce Base?" Joe asked.

The hybrid swiveled around the other direction to stare at Joe. I don't know if it was thinking about Joe's words or studying the human who spoke them, but I swear I saw a flicker of recognition on its face when it looked at my uncle.

"Escape yes. Three like this one." The chest tap again.

Then everyone began talking at once.

The hybrid's gaze shifted from one human to another under the onslaught of the rapid fire questioning. Its fingers remained off the keyboard and I got the impression it was being overwhelmed. Who knew what mental process the creature went through to understand us and in turn formulate a response? Yes, they were part human but they were most definitely part something else and we had no idea how those 'something elses' normally communicated. I raised my voice above the din.

"People, people! One at a time."

Abby spoke quickly, "Why are you killing humans? What do you want from us? Why are you taking children?" That had the effect of an ice water dousing on the group. The hybrid looked at Abby and tilted its head slightly to the side as she spoke her last question.

"Children is small human?"

"Yes, damn it! Children are small humans," Abby said. "They're innocent and pose no danger to your kind or anyone else."

The hybrid typed a response. *"Knowledge of children zero. No interaction. View children* (it gestured to its eyes) *one example. Human boss restrain far away from this one all time. Human boss restrain human others."*

"Why are humans being restrained? What's happening at the base?"

"This one escape at extermination time. Boss humans harm others. Soldiers harm human others and others like this one. Many hurt. This one escape. Three like this one escape."

"So, you don't know what's going on at the base now? Did anyone survive? Did any of your kind survive besides you and two others?" Joe asked.

There was enough human in this creature to be able to convey hesitation – a very human quality. I could see it. It didn't want to answer the question and it took a few seconds before the fingers began to fly over the keyboard.

"Yes, many survive no harm. No hurt. Few humans and many like this one (chest tap) *but also no like this one."*

It was clear the hybrid was struggling with an abstract concept that was difficult to express. 'No like this one' told me there was still a mixed bag of mutant monsters inside the Archuleta Mesa.

"Others look like this one. Only outside. Inside is harm. Desire harm and hurt to humans."

I exchanged a look with Joe. Just as Joe suspected, hybrids had been engineered for the purpose of killing humans – alien mercenaries who would be ruthless, tireless and superior to humans in combat situations.

"You're not like those? Those who desire to hurt humans?" Dylan asked.

"No. Not this one. This one arrive after those others. This one no cause harm. No hurt. Desire to remain unrestrained."

"But these others that want to hurt h

umans...they look like you?" Joe asked the hybrid and then pointed to its chest so it would understand the concept of 'you'.

"Yes, others look like this one only on outside. Inside is harm." It looked up at the ceiling in a human-like way that indicated it was concentrating. After a few seconds, it typed again. *"Others is rotten inside. Desire to hurt. Desire to harm. This one is healthy inside. Desire to remain unrestrained. Desire to be good. Good to humans."*

"Is it possible there are two Omega Groups? One good, one bad?" I mused out loud.

Joe shrugged then asked, "Do you know how many of the bad others are left?"

"After extermination knowledge of others is zero."

"Do you know how many bad others there were before the extermination?"

Again, the hybrid hesitated before responding. I couldn't tell if it was thinking or was reluctant to share the information.

"Many bad others before extermination."

"Give us a number," Ben said.

The hybrid turned around to look directly at Ben again, hesitating. Was it stalling or did it find Ben fascinating for some reason? Finally, the fingers went back to the keyboard.

"Many bad others. Large number. One three six. Before extermination. Knowledge of numbers after extermination is zero. Many? Few? Knowledge is zero."

It turned completely around in the chair and watched our reaction. It might have realized this information would not be well received.

Holy mother of God. One hundred and thirty six of those things that wanted to kill every human they could find.

"Do you have a name?" Abby asked after a moment.

The hybrid looked puzzled.

She continued, "Humans have names that we call each other and know each other by. I'm Abby, this is Joe, Ben, Dylan, Josh and Ian. These are names. Do you have a name too?"

The hybrid nodded slowly and turned back to the computer.

"Name is Two Seven." It looked at Abby as

if for approval, it's long mouth twitching at the corners.

Please don't let it smile, I thought.

The creature appeared pleased to have been asked the question and I suddenly felt a pang of empathy. It seemed to realize that showing pleasure by smiling would evoke a negative reaction – and what's more inherently human than smiling?

Dylan spoke up. "I don't like that name. It's not even a name really – it's just a number. How about we call you Grogoch? Or Grog for short?"

The twitching mouth indicated its pleasure even before the typing began.

"Yes. Grog this one." (Chest tap.)

"Okay, enough with this bullshit," Ben said. "What the fuck are you doing here?" He indicated the area outside Ian's window.

"Sanctuary." Just the one word, which Grog seemed to feel explained everything.

He swiveled around and faced us again with an air of finality. He even crossed his arms in a manner that indicated his work here was done. Then he stood up and began walking toward the door.

"Whoa, whoa, whoa, there cowboy! Where the hell do you think you're going?" Ben made a move to block the hybrid, raising his Glock to chest level.

Grog's movement happened so quickly nobody even saw it. One moment Ben held the gun and the next, the hybrid held it. He wasn't pointing it as Ben had done – he simply dangled it from his long fingers, trophy-like. The corners of the mouth twitched as he handed the gun back to Ben, barrel first.

"Sonofabitch," Ben said.

The hybrid's smile widened as he opened the door of Ian's apartment. The next second, he was gone.

###

Thirty minutes later I was back at my apartment, alone except for Joe, who rested in the spare bedroom. We all needed showers, fresh clothes and a nap.

Plus, I had an appointment with Detective Trevino.

I made a pot of coffee and opened the newly replaced windows, letting some cool October air chase away the stuffiness. I sat at the kitchen table looking down at the park, struggling to remember what day of the week it was. We'd crammed a lifetime into the last thirty-six hours it seemed – it didn't seem possible to still be Sunday. I would be expected at work the next day and knew I'd have to call in with a fictitious case of the flu.

If we survived the next few days, weeks, months...I would have one hell of a story for my newspaper, assuming that this mess would become public knowledge at some point in the near future. And how could it not? The hybrids had migrated to a big city – or some of them had at least. Ian had discovered one, so I could assume others had as well. If the so-called 'good' hybrids were on the move, it stood to reason that the 'bad' ones were too.

That was a terrifying thought.

Not knowing what had happened during Clean Sweep and how many of those things had escaped weighed on my mind, along with a million other worries. I'd just begun to slip into a mental quagmire of who-what-when-where-how and most importantly why, when a knock at the door startled me back into the here and now.

"Come in, Detective," I said as I opened the door which still had a temporary plywood patch job. Her demeanor seemed calm but I sensed an underlying nervousness.

"Would you like some coffee?"

"Sure. Black, thanks."

"So what can I do for you?" I motioned for her to sit at the kitchen table and sat down across from her. "Do you have any leads in my case?"

"I have some suspicions – let's put it that way," she said in a tight voice. When she didn't continue, I began to get annoyed.

"And...?"

She took a deep breath before answering. "I received a somewhat disconcerting phone call yesterday after I left here. It was from the captain – my boss, that is – telling me, essentially, not to pursue the investigation of your shooting. When I asked why, I was shut down. When I tried again to get an answer, I was threatened. My job, that is. I've been with the department for 19 years, right out of college. I've never had anything like this happen to me. It really pisses me off but I'm not in a position to jeopardize my job. I'm a single mom and I have bills to pay. In this economy, who knows how long it would take to find another job?" She took a sip of coffee as she studied my reaction.

"Why in the world do you suppose your captain wouldn't want you to investigate the case?" I was careful to keep my poker face in place.

"Well, I thought you might have an insight to that," she replied as she set her cup down on the table, leaned forward and looked unblinkingly into my eyes.

I imagined Detective Trevino was an excellent interrogator. I squirmed a bit under her scrutiny…I couldn't help it. Those intense dark eyes looked directly into my soul.

"I don't know why you'd think that," I said, sounding half-hearted and lame even to myself.

She blinked one time in response as if to say 'bullshit', then continued to stare while waiting for another response that was closer to the truth. I decided the best defense was a good offense.

"You're the detective…didn't you say you have some suspects? What do you think is going on?"

A flash of frustration slipped out from behind the interrogator mask when she replied. "I think the order to shut down the investigation came from the mayor's office. That's one of the things I think. Isn't your friend, Abigail Montgomery, on the mayor's staff?" She didn't wait for a response since she didn't need one. "I also think you know exactly who tried to kill you yesterday morning. The question is: why are you stonewalling me? Why did you have your friend make a call to her boss to get the investigation dropped?"

My genuinely surprised expression seemed to catch her off guard.

"Abby didn't call her boss. They're not on the best of terms right now," (that was the understatement of the year), "and I know for a fact she wouldn't have done that."

"How do you know? It seems the most

logical thing in the world to have your friend pull some strings for you. The big question is why would you do so? And the answer to that is because you already know who shot up your apartment and tried to kill you. And for whatever reason, you don't want to get the police involved, which means you must have something to hide. And when people try to hide things in situations like this, it's usually because they've done something illegal."

As I considered the events of the last thirty six hours, I tried to return her level gaze but with no success. Illegal? Yes, you could say that. Let's see...we'd committed a number of crimes including breaking and entering, assault with a deadly weapon, and, oh yeah, murder. Sure, it was self-defense, but that didn't change the fact that human beings were dead because we'd killed them. I glanced out the window, just to be looking anywhere but into Detective Trevino's soul-stealing, all-knowing eyes.

When I didn't answer, she retreated back into her chair and sighed heavily.

"It doesn't matter anyway, since I'm off

SECRETS UNDER THE MESA

the case. I just have a problem being manipulated and stonewalled. It really rubs me the wrong way, know what I mean?"

"I can imagine."

"I'll tell you something else that's strange," she continued, "I got an anonymous phone call this morning, from someone telling me to 'help you' and to 'trust you', which is exactly the opposite of what my instincts are telling me to do right now. Weird, huh?"

Interesting. Had Loretta or one of her cohorts been the mystery caller?

I shrugged my shoulders and avoided those laser eyes.

"I tried to have the call traced, but no luck. The really interesting part of the conversation was when she told me to get my hands on a piece of local news footage from yesterday morning."

Uh oh, I thought. The detective smiled when she saw my reaction.

"I see you already know about this. I haven't had a chance to track it down yet – perhaps you could enlighten me so I don't waste my time going through hours of local news video."

I returned her speculative gaze with one of my own. Unlike Detective Trevino's instincts, mine told me this woman could be trusted. It would be a huge risk bringing someone else into this, but the payoff could be enormous. She'd have access to information and resources that could save time and possibly lives.

"Channel 8, five-thirty yesterday morning. That's all I'm going to tell you," I said.

"Come on, Hawkins, save me some time. What was in the news story?"

"That's all I'm saying for now, Detective. After you've watched the video, call me. We'll go from there." I stood up. "Detective, just be careful. And your mystery caller was right...you can trust me. I'm not the bad guy, I promise."

I escorted her back to the patched front door. Before she left, she turned back to face me one more time.

"Just what am I getting myself into?"

"The smart thing would be to stay out of it. That's what I'd do if I were you. But something tells me that's not in your nature. Good luck, Detective. And remember, just be careful. Everyone may not be who or what they seem."

I shut the door before any more questions could be asked.

###

After Detective Trevino left, I puttered on my computers for a while, running diagnostics and determining how much damage had been done during yesterday's shooting. Overall, it wasn't too bad. I'd need to replace one CRT screen and a recently purchased external hard drive had taken a gut shot, but hardly any information had been stored on it, so the loss wasn't catastrophic. It could have been much worse. Not just in terms of Mini NORAD, but my friends as well. I contemplated the seemingly astronomical odds of all five of us surviving the recent events relatively unscathed – the shooting at my apartment, Abby's kidnapping and the subsequent rescue, the night attack at Dylan's house. In hindsight, it seemed improbable that we'd prevailed against armed and ruthless people who meant us harm. Except for Joe and Ben, collectively we had nothing in the way of combat or even self defense skills, yet we beat them...every time. Were we really that lucky or did we have a guardian angel looking out for us?

And with that thought, I pondered Detective Trevino's mystery caller. Had it been Loretta? She seemed the most likely candidate unless, of course, there were other players who were also concerned about either our well-being or our mission to root out the truth and end the abductions of innocents. There were two groups we knew about: the government assholes who had concocted this brilliant scheme to create the perfect killing machine and who were utterly determined to keep it under wraps, and the mysterious shadow group to which Loretta belonged. What was their agenda? Loretta pointed us in the direction of Joe when we'd first arrived in Dulce. She had supplied us with the location of Abby and her kidnappers. Lastly, she had arranged for some sort of clean-up operation at Dylan's house which may just save us some serious prison time. We'd taken a huge risk by trusting her in this regard, but for some reason, I hadn't hesitated.

I heard Joe stirring in the second bedroom and hoped he'd been able to get some sleep. As my mind drifted back six months ago to that day at his trailer, a thought popped into my head. He'd mentioned someone or perhaps some*ones* he'd been in cahoots with and from whom, I suspected, he'd received financial help in his endeavors. This person or people wanted him to get to the truth. Why? Who were they? Could they be Loretta's group or were we now dealing with a third organization? Joe refused to give us any information about them. Maybe he didn't know much himself or maybe he was just being stubborn. Or perhaps he'd been threatened. Whatever his reasons for holding out, I decided the time had come for some answers.

"Hey, Josh," he said as he came into the living room, rubbing his eyes. "How long was I out for?"

"Not long. Maybe an hour. Longer

would have been better," I replied as I noticed his pallor and the dark circles under his eyes. "Joe, I think it's time we had a talk about who you were working with in Dulce. I know you said you wouldn't talk about him, or is it them?" I fished, without much finesse or subtlety. "But things have changed now. My friends are putting their lives on the line. If you have any information that might help, we need to know about it."

"Can't do it, Josh. I made a promise," he said abruptly. He seemed to think that would be the end of it. I loved my uncle, but I loved my friends too. It wasn't right that he should withhold information that could help us. The more I thought about it, the angrier I became.

"Really? A promise? Don't you think circumstances have progressed to the point that you should re-think your priorities? We could have been killed multiple times in the last thirty six hours. Abby could have been killed. Do you think putting your integrity, if that's what this is about, before the lives of my friends is the honorable thing?"

I had worked myself into a nice froth which was mostly genuine. I saw the conflict playing out on his face. Finally, he sat down on the sofa with an air of resignation.

"You're right. You're absolutely right. It's just that when I make a promise, I keep it. My word is everything to me, Josh, because it's pretty much all I have left.

"I'll tell you all I know, Josh, but it isn't a whole helluva lot. I was waist deep in this obsession of mine when I was contacted by a man. He came to the house one afternoon when Alameda wasn't home. He said he knew what I was involved with and wanted to help. He offered to pay for whatever equipment I needed since he knew I wasn't in a position to buy it myself. When I asked him what his angle was – why he wanted to help me, he just said that he and others were concerned about the direction our government was going, and that any information I could give them which might illuminate any nefarious activity would be helpful for the greater good of our country."

He spoke that last part as if by rote and since 'nefarious' was not a word Joe used on a regular basis, I suspected this was a near verbatim retelling of the conversation. I also knew that as a patriot, those words would have been quite effective on my uncle.

"When I agreed, he made me take an oath that I would never tell anyone else about him or his group. I didn't take that oath lightly. I never do when I give my word. After that, an envelope of cash came in the mail with a note attached. *'This should cover any initial expenses. In return, we'll expect regular reports. Once you're set up, we'll contact you again with further instructions. Fight the good fight, Mr. McCullough.'* And that's exactly what I did. I bought everything I needed and submitted video reports to a post office box in Los Alamos per their instructions.

"So you have no idea who these people are? Did you continue to have contact from them?"

"Every now and then I'd get a phone call with tips on locations where I might get some good video, which made me wonder if they had a mole feeding them information and then passed it along to me. I got sucked into the deal when they dangled the carrot of virtually unlimited resources and by believing I might be helping to expose and possibly put an end to the atrocities that were going on down there. Having that money to buy all the equipment I'd needed was just more than I could resist. And as you've seen, it took me to a much higher level in my investigations."

"Which is exactly what they wanted," I mulled. "The big question is why did they need *you*? If they had an insider and monetary resources, why involve you?"

"That's something I've wondered about myself and I suspect it's because they wanted others to help expose what was going on at Dulce. Maybe they didn't want to have their cover blown. And they definitely wanted this stuff to get out there because they instructed me to contact the website guys. They seemed to be pushing for a big, public exposé but wanted to orchestrate it from behind the scenes. I suspect they had other investigators just like me positioned all over the southwest, collecting data and evidence of the base and the activities there. I can't prove that, but it's a strong hunch.

"When I contacted the website guys and then Alameda was killed shortly after, that was it. I cut ties with them. I offered to send them all the equipment their money had bought and told them I was washing my hands of it all, but I never heard back from them."

The modus operandi of Joe's mystery group seemed similar to Loretta's.

"Did you ever meet anyone from the group other than the man who came to your house?"

Joe pondered this for a few seconds before answering. "Not officially. I would get the impression sometimes that a woman standing in line next to me at the grocery store or a guy getting gas at the next pump over seemed to study me more intently than a casual observer might. Know what I mean? And who knows if they were people from the same group? Hell, they could be

SECRETS UNDER THE MESA

spies from the government or even spies from other governments. I don't believe for one second that other countries aren't aware, at least to some degree, of what has been going on at Dulce. And then, there's the private sector aspect." "What do you mean?" I asked.

"Don't you imagine just about every defense contractor on the planet would like to have this technology? Think about private security companies...and I'm not talking about the ones who install alarm systems in your house. I mean the ones who hire ex-Navy seals to protect people and high risk assets. They would love to get their hands on this hybrid technology and build stronger, more ruthless mercenaries to do their bidding. Then there's the terrorist element. Can you imagine what extremist groups would do with some of these hybrid killing machines?"

I thought about Grog. Despite how alien he was in many ways, there was a humanness to him that couldn't be denied. I pictured him being used by his creators and wondered again just who the monsters were in this scenario.

That line of thinking made me switch gears to the incredible experience at Ian's loft. We'd made contact with a hybrid and had survived. Everything we'd assumed up to that point was now in question. Could there actually be hybrids who didn't want to rip us to shreds? If so, could they help us in some way? Would they? If our plan involved somehow eradicating the so-called 'bad' hybrids, would Grog be willing to assist in the demise of his own kindred? It seemed unlikely. Who knew if we would ever even have contact with the seemingly benevolent hybrid again, let alone convince him to help.

"It's overwhelming, isn't it?" Joe said, studying me with a knowing expression.

"Yes, it is. I don't know what the hell to do about any of this. Should we just walk away, Joe? While everyone is still alive?"

"I don't think that's an option, Josh. I think we're in too deep for that. Too many people know about us. The only reason I think we're still alive is because they're not sure exactly what we know and what we plan on doing with that information. I strongly suspect their goal at Dylan's house was to contain and question us. Too bad we had other ideas."

"What's to stop us from going public with everything we know?"

"We'd be discredited and ridiculed first; then when that settles down, we'd probably be quietly escorted to a cold dark cell and never see the light of day again. I'm sure they'd send a bigger crew this time. Or, they might just kill us all." He said the last part with an air of indifference. Death was just around the corner for him no matter how this all played out.

My cell phone rang, startling both of us. The number wasn't blocked, so it must not be Loretta. Too bad. I was ready to have a throw down with my little mystery friend.

"Hello?"

"It's Monica Trevino, Mr. Hawkins. I just watched the video." A pause.

"And what did you make of it, Detective?"

"What the fuck is that thing?" she demanded.

"The answer is not something to be discussed over the phone, Monica," I said, feeling the time for formal titles had passed. "You need to think long and hard about whether you really want that answer because just knowing about this could put you in danger."

Silence on the other end.

"You mentioned being a single mom. Do you really want to get involved? Remember what my apartment looked like yesterday morning?"

"Did that happen just because you know about these things?"

"No. But it's a slippery slope. And that's really all I can say right now."

"Just answer this: are they dangerous?" she asked.

I hesitated only a second before answering. "Absofuckinglutely."

When she replied a few seconds later, her voice was terse. "I'll get back to you." And she was gone.

Prompted by Joe's questioning expression, I relayed my previous conversation with Detective Trevino. He wasn't pleased.

"Josh, we agreed. Nobody else gets brought into this. You and Dylan already broke that rule with the Irishman today. Now you want to get the cops involved? You have no idea who she might tell and what the backlash to us would be. Not to mention, putting her in danger." I knew he was angry and I couldn't explain why my instinct had been to trust both of these people on the spur of the moment, but it was done and couldn't be undone. We might never have contact with either of them again after what they had seen.

"Cop, not cops. Besides, I didn't tell her anything, really. Somebody else tipped her off about the news story. I just saved her some time in finding which one. And I may never hear from her again anyway."

He sighed in exasperation. "Well, if you do and if something bad happens to her or her family as a result, just remember it's on your head. Can you handle that kind of guilt?"

I thought of Alameda then and knew what Joe was alluding to. He'd been wearing that guilt like a hair shirt for a long time. I already felt badly about bringing my friends into this and I hoped nobody else would suffer because of their affiliation with me. But when I thought about the bigger picture and the human lives already touched in such a horrendous way, I felt some minor justification. People were going to get hurt one way or another. It was just a matter of who, how soon and how many.

I headed for the kitchen and the Mylanta cabinet.

Chapter 8

We decided to meet up for dinner at Abby's place. The house was the perfect reflection of the owner...lovely, understated. If I wasn't such an idiot, I might have been living here with the woman of my dreams.

Dylan and Ben were already there and everyone gathered in the kitchen, as usual. The aroma wafting through the house wasn't identifiable and I wondered, with some minor trepidation, what Abby had decided to prepare for dinner. Southern girls of a certain demographic were expected to not only look beautiful and display impeccable manners, they were also expected to be fabulous cooks...at least according to Abby. The tragedy of this archaic paradigm to which she subscribed was that she truly believed she *was* a wonderful cook, when in fact nothing could be further from the truth. Of course nobody would consider bursting her bubble because, more than anything, she loved being a gracious hostess and cooking for her guests. It continually amazed me that despite countless hours in her kitchen, she never seemed to improve. It was a mystery and one which would be perpetuated shortly, I noted as I lifted the lid off a large, bubbling pot on the stove. Judging by the smell, I wondered if the large chunks floating in the brownish primordial ooze might in fact be decaying body parts.

"Irish stew!" Abby exclaimed happily when she saw what I was doing. "I got the idea from Ian, you know, because he's Irish. I've never cooked it before but I found a recipe online that looked great. Of course I had to tweak it a bit. I never follow a recipe exactly...that's what makes it fun! I think it's going to be wonderful!"

I hadn't seen her so animated in days. I didn't care how disgusting her Irish stew was – I was going to eat a huge bowl and pretend to love every bite. I couldn't avoid the pointed looks I got from Ben and Dylan, who were only too familiar with Abby's shortcomings in the kitchen. We had an understanding though...we would never be the ones to tell her the truth.

"It looks and smells delicious, Abs," I said. In an ocean of white lies, that was a whopper. I noticed Ben's eye roll but it was quickly followed by an indulgent smile. Joe had picked up on the vibe and when he smelled the aroma escaping from the pot, his eyes widened in alarm.

Dylan grinned and gave Abby a shoulder squeeze and a kiss on the cheek. "Thanks for cooking, sweetie."

"Oh, it's no trouble," she replied, just as the doorbell rang. We were all there, so I couldn't imagine who it could be. "Oh, I hope it's okay – I invited Ian too. I figured after what he'd been through with us today, he deserved a place at our table."

I couldn't fault her logic and the only person who seemed less than thrilled with this news was Joe, no doubt due to his attitude about bringing strangers into our midst.

Ian had been in the trenches with us today – trial by fire, so to speak. I figured he had earned the right to be there.

"I didn't know whether to bring wine or whiskey, so I brought both," Ian said with a big smile as he followed Abby into the kitchen holding up bottles in both hands. He'd gone to some effort with his appearance, I'd noticed, which put my jealousy radar on high alert. There was no denying he was a decent looking fellow, although well into his forties. And his exotic accent made me hate him slightly. Chicks love accents, damn him.

"Good man," Ben said, snatching a bottle. "MacAllen 18...niiice." He clapped Ian on the back.

"Glasses are in the bar," Abby indicated the small room off the kitchen. "We're eating in the dining room tonight, so everyone get a drink, pick your place and grab a bowl."

Fortunately, Abby had also heated up some store-bought rolls which I slathered with butter and used to bribe my pallet into tolerating the rest of the dinner. Those of us in the know watched the newbies eat their first bite of stew with evil delight. Despite his attempts to cover it, I could tell by Ian's expression that he hadn't been prepared for the culinary scourge that was Abby's cooking. I felt all warm and fuzzy inside as he swallowed each bite with a grimace.

"A toast!" Ben said with a wide grin, holding up his glass. "To Abby and the lovely dinner she has prepared for us tonight." He gave Ian a pointed look which said, *'You will act like you love this crap or I will kick your ass.'* Ian nodded in understanding which made me hate him and his cool accent slightly less.

There was an enthusiastic round of 'here-heres' and we all got down to the business of ingesting the meal. It was fuel after all.

"So, Ian, where in Ireland are you from?" Abby asked.

"A small town called Kilwoghan. It's east of Dublin near the river. Beautiful little place but not much to do there other than drink and fish and drink," he said with a wink. "That's what we Irishmen are known for, right?"

"And how long have you been here in the states?" Joe's question was interrogation, not polite small talk.

"About ten years, actually. I've never regretted the move for a second. I love my home town but I love living here more. The friendly people, the fast pace, the energy. It was the right move for me even though I'd never set foot in this country before I packed up my life and came here."

"Really? Just out of the blue you decided to move to a place you'd never been before?" Joe asked.

Before Ian had time to answer, Abby piped in. "So, your shop is lovely," she said with a disapproving glance at Joe. He'd broken one of her cardinal rules: he'd been rude to a guest. "Do you enjoy living in the city?"

Ian swallowed with some minor difficulty before answering. "I do. There's a lot to be said for a bucolic lifestyle but give me the energy of a big city any day. Maybe when I'm old and gray...well grayer, I'll retire to the country, but for now I'm quite happy where I am."

"You must do pretty damn good in that shop of yours to pay for all that real estate," Joe said.

This time, it wasn't just Abby who gave him the death look.

"Joe, come on," I said.

Ian seemed nonplussed and his smile was relaxed when he answered. "Actually, the shop doesn't do that well. It's more of a hobby business – it does just enough to pay for itself but not much more. When I left Ireland, I'd just sold my software company. I had a few nickers in my pocket and a respectable portfolio and wanted to start somewhere fresh. I put most of my belongings in storage and did a bit of exploring. I visited New York, Chicago, Miami and Los Angeles before coming to Dallas. After a few days of seeing the sights, I decided this was the place for me. Been here ever since."

Joe responded with an unimpressed grunt. I hadn't been around my uncle enough since we'd reconnected to know if he was always this suspicious of strangers or if he was targeting Ian in particular. Either way, I was embarrassed. I guess some of Abby's manners had rubbed off on me.

"Who needs another drink?" I asked to cover Joe's rudeness. All glasses were raised simultaneously. Soon, the conversation turned to our experience with the hybrid, even though the brief reprieve from such heavy matters had been pleasant while it lasted.

"I wonder what the hell it was doing in downtown Dallas," Ben said, voicing the question we all shared.

Ian shrugged. "Not a clue. I'm just glad to have other people to talk to about it. I was beginning to think I'd lost my mind."

"Did you report the sightings?" Ben asked. He hadn't been present during Ian's initial telling of the story.

"No. I never told anyone. I have to admit, I was afraid of getting the reputation of one of those crazy UFO types. You know, those people who see flying saucers and Bigfoot."

Of course he'd have no way of knowing

Joe's past, so the insult was unintentional. Joe's dark expression told me that didn't matter...the damage had been done.

"I'd really love to hear more about everyone's experiences with these things," Ian continued. "It appears I'm in the middle of this whether I'd like to be or not. I figure the more I know the better."

Despite Joe's obvious misgivings, I took the next ten minutes to tell a slightly more detailed version of what we'd already told him at his loft. Out of respect for Joe, I left out any references to his mysterious benefactors, although I doubt that scored many points with my uncle.

"So, let me get this straight," Ian said, polite but clearly skeptical. "Extraterrestrials visited our planet and left their DNA lying around so we could find it and use it to create these creatures which are half human and half alien? Why would they do that? *How* would they do that? DNA doesn't stay viable for that long, does it?"

"Who knows if they intended to," I replied. "Maybe they didn't worry about leaving their DNA because they never thought we'd be advanced enough to do anything with it.

"We're also not entirely sure there isn't some other element in the mix. The scientists cooked up a lot of combinations down in those labs – we've seen the proof on at least one occasion."

Ian raised his eyebrows in surprise just as Joe kicked me squarely in the shin. Apparently this was not a subject to be shared with the new kid. Before Ian could demand details of these mutants and how we'd managed to see them, I answered one of his other questions.

"DNA can remain viable for millennia if stored properly. Remember the movie *'Jurassic Park'* where dinosaur DNA had been sealed and preserved in amber? Yeah, yeah, I know it was just a movie, but the theory wasn't that far off the mark. Something similar could have happened with the ETs. Scientists have managed to harvest enough DNA from ancient Egyptian mummies to run all kinds of tests. Who knows how they got the extraterrestrial DNA but the evidence that they did is overwhelming."

"What were the ETs doing here in the first place? Why didn't they just take over our planet? Why keep us humans around? If they have the technology to get here, they certainly could wipe our race off the planet and do whatever they pleased with it."

"There's evidence to indicate that the so-called 'ancient astronauts' were here long before humans. In fact, Sumerian tablets tell the story of how the Annunaki actually created our race. The theory is, when they first arrived we were nothing more than mouth-breathing bipedals – completely unsuitable for the tasks they needed us to perform for them. So they gave us a small dose of their own DNA to kick start our evolution and thus become more useful to them. Many believe this is the so-called 'missing link'. In an evolutionary nano-second, we went from grunting, fucking, defecating hairy beasts to an intelligent species, proficient in mathematics, astronomy and architecture. We even developed a written language practically overnight, in evolutionary terms. This wasn't a case of macroevolution – those kinds of advancements just don't happen that quickly nor do they happen on that scale. We are nothing like anything else on earth in terms of consciousness, our thought process and our ability to learn and advance. Even intelligent creatures like dolphins and chimpanzees haven't advanced in any significant way in the eleven million years they've existed. We have the ETs to thank for our big brains, not God, which is precisely the reason virtually all ancient religions allude to a divine creator or creators which came from the heavens and sparked human life as we know it on this planet." "I'm guessing there are no biblical fundamentalists in this group," Ian said with a smile.

I glanced at Abby before responding. "I was never a big church-goer, but after all I've discovered on my own and with the help of Joe, I think you could say I no longer subscribe to the doctrines or dogma of structured religion. But I try to be respectful of those who do."

I sneaked another glance at Abby who

looked distinctly uncomfortable. It must be difficult to remain a proper southern Baptist considering everything we'd discovered over the last six months, and I knew she'd been struggling recently. Some people, and Abby might have been one of them, needed that faith-based, heaven and hell, 'Jesus is the answer' philosophy that Christianity provided. Believing in a God, being convinced that prayers might actually make a difference in the outcome of a given situation and having faith that Jesus was your golden ticket to the kingdom of heaven was vital to the sanity and happiness of many. So, in that regard it served a purpose – just not one that I needed in my life.

"Okay, so the ETs tampered with our DNA and created humans. For what reason?" Ian took a small sip of wine. I noticed he hadn't touched the scotch, which was fine with Ben.

"There are several theories but the most logical seems to be the slave race hypothesis. Our planet is chock full of minerals which in many cases, such as gold, take as much muscle as technology to extricate. If the ETs had the ability to create a species which was intelligent enough to follow instructions and dexterous enough to do the physical labor, why wouldn't they do so and save themselves a lot of work?"

"Okay, now you're losing me. Why would the aliens want our gold? Surely the monetary system of these little green men isn't the same as ours, but you're saying they came to our planet to steal our money?" Ian no longer bothered to contain his skepticism. If I hadn't been doing extensive research into this stuff for the last six months, I'd have felt the same way.

"Are you familiar with the properties of gold, Ian?"

"Only in terms of investment when the stock market takes a dive," he replied with a smile.

"It's a near perfect conductor of electricity as well as heat. It's not affected by air, moisture or most other corrosive agents. It's extremely pliable and can be used in an infinite number of applications. Currently, we use it as a protective coating on many artificial satellites for its reflective ability of not only visible light but infrared, which means it helps to keep those satellites from burning up. One gram can be beaten into a sheet of one square meter so it's very lightweight – a real bonus for space travel. It performs critical functions in computers, communications equipment, jet engines and tons of other commercial products. Its isotope even has medicinal benefits and is used in some cancer treatments. Next to water, it's clearly one of our planet's greatest resources. And many experts who subscribe to this whacky ancient astronaut stuff believe that gold is the reason they came to our planet in the first place."

Ian raised his eyebrows. "Interesting."

"This theory wasn't fabricated out of thin air," I continued. "The evidence is everywhere that our species' light-year jump in technology was enhanced by extraterrestrials: the Nazca lines in Peru, the megalithic structures scattered all over the planet, the pyramids, Machu Picchu, and my personal favorite, the ancient structures at Puma Punku in Tiahuanaco in South America – much older than the pyramids, and even with the advanced technology we now have, we can't figure out how in the hell they were made. There's evidence of machining on the stonework – lines that are so perfectly straight and holes which have been drilled so precisely and to the exact same depth every time – so utterly flawless that they simply could not have been made utilizing the technology of the time, which by the way, was probably during the Stone Age. And do you know what kind of stones these lines and holes were cut into? Granite and diorite...the two hardest rocks on the planet and which would have required diamond-tipped stone cutting tools to carve. Bronze tools may not have even existed yet and even if they had, they would have been useless in cutting these rocks. It's universally agreed that even the Andeans of a much later period couldn't have done this, and that was a 2500 years ago.

"So, many of the experts who subscribe to this theory of how humans accomplished such amazing feats also believe that gold was what brought the ETs to our planet in the first place. I'm sure you've heard of the Sumerians, Ian?"

He nodded.

"Those smart little monkeys popped onto the charts at least 8500 years ago, possibly longer, with highly sophisticated irrigation systems and widespread, extremely organized agriculture. In no time, they'd built magnificent cities, an advanced system of government and most importantly, a written language. Their little clay tablets tell all about the Annunaki – advanced, god-like beings which came from the heavens, created our race (read as 'genetically engineered') approximately 50,000 years ago, then stayed around to mentor the new, improved *homo sapiens* ...giving us vital technological tidbits along the way. The grunt work of mining, which they expected in return, was seemingly not resented by the Sumerians. The Annunaki weren't cruel slave drivers, but patrons and teachers. They were venerated as leaders, not gods, and were not worshiped as such."

I paused. Ian's expression was unreadable now."Okay, all I'm saying is the evidence is there – the Annunaki did visit out planet and the documentation of that is irrefutable. The fact that the scientific evidence leads to extraterrestrials is why the proof is not embraced by mainstream science. Most of those guys are more worried about their reputation than sounding too 'out there'."

An uncomfortable silence followed my long-winded, Aliens 101 lecture.

"Well, this is certainly interesting stuff," Ian said with a tight smile. He had a pretty good poker face but it had begun to crack around the edges.

"Whether you buy into all this or not doesn't really matter," I continued. "Frankly, some days I'm not even sure I do myself, but what I do know is these hybrids are real and they are the result of genetic splicing and dicing using a combination of our DNA and that of the extraterrestrials. There's no denying that, right, Ian?"

He contemplated for a few seconds before answering. "Why does it have to be extraterrestrial DNA? Maybe Grog is actually just a human with a few genes moved around a bit?"

I had no intention of sharing some of the more sensitive information Joe had gotten in his investigations, but I felt it was safe to speak in generalities. "Could be, but the evidence indicates otherwise." "Okay, if you say so," Ian replied. "No matter what Grog and his buddies are, the big question is – what's to be done about them?"

We'd been cleaning up after dinner as the conversation continued. Now, sitting in Abby's comfortable living room with the warm ambiance of a couple of lamps and some candle light, we settled in with our drinks.

"What's to be done about them is directly dependent on what they're doing in the city. I got the impression that our new BFF, Grog, isn't alone. Is he there with his cronies or is there a faction of the so-called 'bad' hybrids at large in Dallas?"

"And how much of what he told us do we believe?" Ben piped in.

"Exactly," Joe replied.

"I got the feeling he was being truthful," said Abby. "I know, I know. There's nothing to base that on other than my own instincts, but that's how I feel."Dylan disappeared for a few seconds and returned with his laptop. He turned the screen so we could all see the headline which read, *'12 Missing Persons in DFW over Weekend.'* And the subtitle which read, *'Unprecedented number represents a cross section of Dallas and Ft. Worth residents. Police are withholding details.'*

Ben let out a slow whistle. Dylan typed furiously for a few seconds then held the screen up again. I recognized the news blog as one of the fringe type sites that I'd been frequenting over the last six months. If any of these sites could be considered reputable, this was one of them. The splashy top story headline read, *'What's Happening to the People of Dallas? Missing Persons Statistics Go Thru Roof.'*

"Is it a coincidence that we find a hybrid here and suddenly people are going missing?" Joe growled. "You can believe that thing if you want, but I don't. This is exactly what happened in New Mexico and now it's happening here. Don't forget that the ultimate goal of these creatures is to kill. It's what they were designed to do and nothing I've seen indicates otherwise. And I've seen a helluva lot more than any of you."

"You're right, Joe," I replied. "You're our expert, no doubt. But I think there's certainly a possibility that what Grog told us is true. And if it is, who better to help us find and eradicate the bad hybrids than a hybrid?"

"You're taking a leap of faith, Josh," said Ben. "A, we may never see our little buddy again. B, why would he help us even if we do find him? And C, maybe he's lying and there are no 'good' and 'bad' hybrids...just hybrids, and their ultimate goal is what we've assumed all along...to kill humans."

The words hung in the air for a few minutes, unanswered.

Finally, Abby shook her head. She believed our new hybrid friend was one of the good guys. I could see it on her face.

As usual, I was on the fence. When in the presence of Grog, he'd seemed so compelling that I'd been inclined to take everything he'd told us at face value, but how accurate was my intuition with a creature not fully human? All of my journalistic experience in coaxing honesty and candor from my subjects had been with people – as in one hundred percent human people. Why would I assume that the hybrids would function and interact the same way we do? Maybe they had some built-in bullshit cloaking device.

"It seems to me the next step is to try to make contact with the hybrid again," Dylan said finally. "I'm also thinking it may be time to get the authorities involved."

"You get the authorities involved and they'll shut us down faster than you can say fuck-my-life," Ben replied. "We don't know who at the DPD or local government has their fingers in the Dulce pie. It's not a stretch to assume they have moles at any number of law enforcement and government agencies. If we go running to them now they'll either laugh in our faces or worse, haul our asses off to jail on some trumped up charge. Remember what these people, whoever they are, did to the mayor? If they'll beat the shit out

Made in United States
Orlando, FL
03 February 2025

Chapter 9

My cell phone rang at an indecent hour the next morning. For a few seconds, I was disoriented by mounds of lavender pansies and frilly lace, but soon remembered where I was. The no-nonsense female voice on the other end of the phone served as a splash of cold water.

"Hello, Monica. I was kind of hoping I wouldn't hear from you."

"I was up all night. I took my daughter to my parents' house early this morning. She's not in school yet, so it won't be a problem for her to be away from home for a few days."

I sighed. The benefit of having someone with her resources on our team was a boon but knowing I would be putting another person in danger got the old stomach juices squirting again.

"Okay, let's meet for breakfast."

An hour later as I backed my Accord out of the driveway, I noticed Abby's next door neighbor stood on her front porch watching with obvious disapproval. Gladys Kravitz had just witnessed overnight male visitors taking their leave of Abby's house in the wee hours of the morning...two male visitors, in fact – even more scandalous. The corners of her old-lady mouth were turned down in a caricature of condemnation. Abby stood in the driveway watching us leave, demurely wrapped in a fluffy pink robe and holding a steaming cup of coffee – hardly the picture of carnal decadence. As we started down the residential street I saw that Gladys had actually walked out onto her lawn to get a better look at Abby's visitors. I glanced back at Abby just in time to see her giving the finger to the old broad.

We'd all come a long way in the last 48 hours, but Abby perhaps more than the rest of us. The conflicting thoughts I had about the changes wrought to her psyche by what she'd recently been through – the battering to her morals and ethics, the assaults to her deeply felt personal philosophies – couldn't wipe the huge grin off my face at the sight of Gladys Kravitz's gaping pie hole.

###

By the time I got to the diner, I was running a few minutes late. I was greeted by an annoyed expression and a pointed look at her watch.

"Sorry, sorry," I said. "I got here as soon as I could."

"I have a lot on the line here, Josh. I want some answers."

Dark circles marred the otherwise flawless mocha skin, but did little to lessen the overall beauty. I realized with a start that Monica Trevino was quite attractive. The no-nonsense, blazer-wearing policewoman demeanor worked well in downplaying her good looks, but in a snug University of Texas tee shirt and faded jeans, they surfaced loud and clear, despite the absence of makeup and messy ponytail. I guessed her age at mid-forties but from ten feet away, she could have passed for a grad student.

"Okay, but remember what I told you yesterday," I replied. "Simply knowing what we know could get you in trouble. People have been threatened, kidnapped, beaten, and God-knows what else as a result of what's happening. Do you really want to put yourself in that situation?"

The level, unblinking gaze was answer enough, but she responded anyway.

"I wouldn't be here if I didn't. I'm a cop, Josh. For most of us – the good ones at least – it's a calling. Like a nurse or a fireman or a teacher or a minister. It's what I've wanted to be ever since I was a kid. My whole life, I knew with every fiber of my being that I wanted to help people. And to me, being a cop was the most effective, immediate way to do that.

"So putting my own safety or well-being before that of others is practically impossible for me. I'm not trying to come across as a hero, I just want you to understand why I'm here. If lives are in danger, as you say, I can't turn my back on that. No matter what."

I nodded. "Okay, then," I said, then took the next twenty minutes to tell her exactly what was going on.

It helped that she'd seen the news footage. Otherwise, she'd have laughed in my face. As it turned out, she seemed to buy everything I was selling. By the time I finished, the professional cop mask was gone. Horror had taken up residence on her features and I got the sense that Monica Trevino would never look at her world exactly the same again. "Okay, so what's the plan? When do we hit the base?" she asked as casually as she might have asked what time the football game started.

Her questions prompted another of those paradigm shifts which seemed to be happening frequently these days. I tried to cover my surprised reaction, but it was too late.

"You hadn't planned on wiping out their base of operations? How the hell do you think we can stop these things if not at the source?"

"Well, just wait a minute. We don't even

know if there is anyone or anything left at the base after Clean Sweep."

"Bullshit. Operation Clean Sweep would have been a 'bio eradication' effort. Kill the people, or in this case the hybrids and any humans unfortunate enough to be left behind, but preserve the billions of dollars' worth of equipment. Think 'neutron bomb' on a small, localized application. The mesa provided the perfect location for this type of operation. The base is surrounded by miles and miles of desert as well as millions of tons of rock and earth, not to mention man-made fortifications. There would have been no casualties outside of the base itself. My theory is it didn't work on the hybrids...just the poor human shmucks that were left inside. Whatever other ingredients the hybrids have mixed in with their DNA must have provided enough protection against the bio eradication tools used during the operation. That's why they're still around, invading our city and abducting our citizens. They're sending out scouts as evidenced by the encounter you had at the gas station outside of Dulce and the one you cornered in Dallas – your new buddy. By the way, I'm not buying the 'good hybrids, bad hybrids' for one second. The bulk of them are still nestled in their little hive at the base – why would they leave? It provides everything they need. They're probably self-replicating even now in an effort to bolster their army.

"Which brings me back to my original question: when do we hit the base?"

The brown eyes bored into mine with the ferocity of a lioness. There was no denying her logic. If we were serious about putting an end to the abductions, gathering evidence to expose them and their human creators AND stop their alleged plan to take over our world, we'd be making another road trip to Dulce.

###

"She's right," Ben said before I'd even finished recapping my conversation with the detective. I wasn't surprised by his knee-jerk reaction to the idea of storming the castle. As cerebral as my friend is, ultimately he's a man of action and over-talking things makes him testy.

"I'm thinking it may come to that but I don't think we're there yet," I replied as I placed the Mylanta bottle back in my kitchen cabinet. I really should start buying the stuff in bulk at Costco.

Monday afternoon in North Texas, just a few days before trick-or-treaters would swarm the streets like costumed locusts, had decided to be glorious. I usually got a ton of the little candy-grubbing beggars at my apartment which I attributed to the concentration of residents. Kids aren't stupid and had figured out the logistics. They could probably quadruple their candy revenues by hitting an apartment complex versus a sprawling neighborhood with only single-family residences.

Coincidently, this was the same concept which articulated what Monica was proposing: hit the area with the greatest concentration of hybrids. Take the bulk of them out in one fell swoop. Document the process and present it to John Q. Public on such a grand scale that there could be no wriggling out of it by the people responsible.

Piece of cake...IF we had a platoon of Navy SEALs.

"And just how the hell do we get in there, Ben?"

"We enlist the help of the hybrid, obviously. If we can't find him again, then we put feelers out about the base. We need schematics and building plans and a lot more information than we have now."

I thought of Joe's group and the possibility that they'd had an insider feeding them information which was then passed along to Joe. If that were the case and he/she had been inside at the time of Operation Clean Sweep, they'd be no help to us now. Still, it might be an avenue worth pursuing if we weren't able to find Grog and convince him to help us.

As it turned out, we didn't have to approach Joe's former benefactors. The following day while Abby and I were in Dallas beating the bushes for our favorite hybrid, he approached us from behind on a quiet side street and calmly tapped me on the shoulder. Startled, I swung around to find the unsettling visage of Grog before me, the corners of his mouth working furiously to keep from breaking into a huge grin. His amusement was evident and I was struck again by the humanness of such a response. Who doesn't laugh their ass off when they sneak up behind someone and scare the beejesus out of them? None of my friends, that's for sure.

"Holy shit, Grog, you scared the crap out of me!"

He lifted the long palms of his hands skyward and shrugged, body language which said, "Sorry, didn't mean to!" Nevertheless, his mouth still twitched and I detected not a shred of remorse.

"We need to talk," I said, still peeved about almost wetting my pants in front of Abby.

I pulled an electronic tablet from my backpack and handed it to the hybrid. It was time to get down to business. I noticed a secluded bricked-in area ten yards down the street, which turned out to be an enclosure for a stairwell leading to a second floor. Perfect. I indicated that Grog should sit on the steps to have his hands free to type. He nodded in complete understanding and sat on the second to the bottom step, awaiting further instruction.

I suddenly realized that I had no idea how I should begin. At the same time, it also occurred to me that what we wanted of him seemed a bit like fratricide.

Maybe more than just a bit.

"Grog, we need your help," Abby said, seeing my hesitation.

She squatted down next to the hybrid and placed her hand on his sleeve – the act of someone reaching out to connect with someone else on a personal level. A human instinct, and as Grog glanced down at her hand, then back up to her face, I could see him respond to it. She had his full attention, and he appeared to be pleased at being approached in such a friendly manner. It made me wonder what his human creators and captors had subjected him to. Detached scientists and military types probably didn't make for warm and fuzzy social interaction. If what Grog had told us about escaping the base to find sanctuary was true, it must have been pretty damn bad for him there.

"We want to stop the bad ones from hurting more people. We think some of them are here in Dallas now, killing people. Do you know anything about that?" Abby's charm was as effective on alien hybrids as it was on everyone else. Grog seemed content just gazing into her eyes and it took him a second before he registered what she'd said. With obvious effort, he began to type.

"Knowledge of bad others is zero. Grog viewed missing humans on television and know some bad ones are here. Others like Grog fear the bad ones. They desire to hurt humans and others like this one." Chest tap.

His ability to communicate had improved since yesterday and I wondered how he'd managed it. Had he spent the last 24 hours in front of a television, soaking up language and whatever else he could glean from news, sitcoms and Keeping Up with the Kardashians?

"Have you seen them? Do they look different from you? Hell, for that matter, how different do any of you look? Are you all identical?"

Grog nodded slowly and began to type again.

"Good and bad ones look little different. Very similar."

Not good news.

"How do you tell the good ones from the bad ones, Grog? How do you know which is which?" Abby asked.

The hybrid pondered his response and after a few seconds one of his long fingers tapped his temple. Our blank expressions must have conveyed a lack of understanding, so he began to type again.

"All others like Grog and bad ones too talk with brains. Not like humans with mouth."

It took a few seconds for that to sink in.

"You mean you communicate telepathically with each other?" I asked.

He nodded slowly. Perhaps 'telepathically' was a new word to him but he seemed to grasp the concept.

"Yes. Grog and others send thoughts with our brains but only to each other. Humans don't hear."

Fascinating. I had no idea if this valuable

bit of information would have positive or negative implications for what we wanted to accomplish. I'd need some time to think about it. It did explain the hybrids' inability to vocalize. They didn't need vocal cords to communicate with their own kind.

"Grog, do you hear the thoughts of the others now? Even the bad ones?" Abby asked. He hesitated a few seconds before responding while he stared dreamily at her face. Finally, his fingers moved again.

"No. Grog can put up wall and others can put up wall. Sometimes strong thoughts come through wall. Grog likes quiet."

"If you try to send thoughts to the others, the bad others, will they get them? Even if they're far away?"

"Yes. If Grog sends strong thoughts the bad others will get them. Distance has zero importance."

"And if you put your wall down, you will get all their thoughts? The good ones and the bad ones?"

"Yes but Grog likes quiet. Keeps wall up."

The hybrid allowed the shadow of a smile...the barest stretching at the corners of his mouth.

"So you identify the bad ones from the good ones by thoughts?" I asked.

He nodded again.

"Yes. Bad ones thoughts are rotten. All thoughts are to hurt humans. Grog puts up wall so rotten thoughts don't come through. Grog likes humans now." He looked significantly at Abby. *"Desire to be friends with humans."*

Long, shy fingers touched Abby's arm. It's a testament to her kind heart and self-control that she not only didn't flinch, but grasped his hand with hers and squeezed it gently. I have no idea if the hybrids have tear ducts, but I swear Grog's eyes got misty. I felt like I was watching the Lifetime channel in the Twilight Zone.

"I'm so glad you feel that way. We want to be friends with you too." Her smile was dazzling.

Suddenly the dreamy expression vanished and the hybrid's eyes widened in what I could only interpret as alarm. He swiveled his head around to survey the street in both directions. Instinctively,

Abby and I did the same. There was nothing significant – just a few business types walking to and fro. It was late morning on a Tuesday in the downtown district of a large city. Nothing stood out as anomalous as far as I could tell, but the hybrid's demeanor indicated danger.

"What is it, Grog?"

"Must leave now. Bad ones are near," he typed frantically then tossed me the tablet with the grace and quickness of an NFL quarterback. Was he afraid of what they would do to him or to us? Or both?

He dashed up the stairs and motioned for us to follow him into the building. Holding the door open, his hand moved in a frantic 'hurry up' gesture. It was a moment of truth for me. Could we really trust him or was the good guy act just that...an act? Abby and I exchanged pointed looks. I could see in her eyes that she trusted him. In mute agreement, we darted up the stairs – a climb that felt more like a leap of faith.

The heavy industrial door slammed shut behind us. We stood in a huge room which had perhaps been a call center at some point in the last decade or so, but was now devoid of office furniture. Weak sunlight filtered through the grime-coated windows and skylights.

The hybrid stood just inside the door with his eyes closed and his body tense with concentration. What were those telepathic messages revealing? Was he receiving or sending as well?

"Grog, what's going on? Are the bad ones chasing you?"

He responded with the merest shake of his head and held up a long finger – universal body language for *'shut the fuck up I'm trying to think.'*

Abby watched the hybrid with the patience of a person who has never interrupted anyone in their life. The only indication that she was afraid was when she slipped her hand into mine. My heart did a back flip.

Muffled footsteps came from the street below, the noises floating through a broken window. There were no voices – only the footsteps which sounded closer every second. Grog's strange eyes flew open and before I had a chance to feel even more alarmed, he grabbed our arms and broke into a fluid run, causing me to drop my backpack and dragging us along before I could retrieve it. That leap of faith we'd taken by coming up the stairs had just turned into an Evel Knieval vault across the Grand Canyon as we headed into the dark maze of hallways.

Visibility was worse in the interior of the building, but random fluorescent overhead lights still worked in some of the corridors which provided a sporadic and barely adequate light source. Grog placed a long finger vertically to his wide mouth – *'hush now...'*

The sounds of our pursuers echoed down the corridor from the room we'd just exited. Immediately, we were on the move again, dashing down a dark side corridor. I could tell Grog's night vision was superior to ours as he navigated us through hallways where I could barely see a foot in front of me.

If our pursuers were still on our tail, I could no longer hear them.

Finally, the hybrid pulled us into a room off a narrow corridor. A vague light source from the end of the corridor barely illuminated a medium sized break room. A small table and plastic chairs were scattered about and there was some cabinetry with a sink against one wall. Grog shut the door soundlessly and motioned for us to squat down on the floor below the level of the square glass opening in the door. I could barely see in the gloom. The hybrid repeated the *hush* gesture as he squatted next to us by the door. We were inches from each other in the dark and the sound of our breathing – mine and Abby's at least – seemed unnaturally loud in the oppressive silence.

Grog's hushing gesture became frantic. Did he want us to stop breathing?

The answer was yes. The hybrid placed one long hand over each of our faces, pinched our noses shut and covered our mouths.

We heard movement right outside the door...the barest hint of stealthy footsteps on carpet. Grog didn't need to suffocate us

– I'd have been holding my breath in terror anyway.

The seconds ticked by. Pressure blossomed in my lungs from lack of oxygen. At the moment I thought my body would defy my brain and demand a breath, Grog removed his hands from our faces. He glided to the cabinetry and began opening drawers and cupboards, rifling through the contents in utter silence. Finally, he motioned to us. He held two long knives and a large serving fork, gesturing for us to take them. *'Weapons.'*

The knives were long and wide but not sharp...probably bought at Walmart for the purpose of slicing employee birthday cake. I made Abby take the giant fork as well as one of the knives. Holding them up in each hand, she looked like a Lilliputian at Gulliver's dinner table. I thought longingly of the guns in my backpack and cursed my clumsiness for dropping it. Instead of the Sig and Glock, I'd be protecting Abby with barbecue implements.

Grog opened a lower cabinet door and gestured to Abby. It was pitch black inside and possibly full of spiders, but she nodded and scrambled in. Before he shut the cabinet door, he placed a long finger on that wide mouth again.

The hybrid turned to me and indicated another cabinet door. I shook my head. No way was I going to hide like a coward. Grog placed his hand on my shoulder and squeezed, motioning again to the dark opening. *"I really must insist,"* the friendly squeeze said, but it hurt like hell. Our hybrid was even stronger than I had imagined. I crawled inside, wedging my body into a tight space that was barely large enough to accommodate me. The cabinet door shut soundlessly behind me.

What happened next is fuzzy since I couldn't see a damn thing. I'd been sitting in the pitch blackness for what seemed like an hour but was probably closer to fifteen minutes when I heard the break room door open. Immediately after, there were sounds of a struggle which must have turned into a life or death brawl judging by the escalating crashing noises. I continued to squat in the cupboard for another few moments, trying to convince myself that I'd be useless in a fight with any hybrids, good or bad. Finally, I couldn't stand it any longer. You have to live with the choices you make in life, and I decided I couldn't live with myself knowing I'd chosen to hide in a cupboard rather than fight to protect the woman I loved. Besides, if Grog couldn't hold his own against our assailants and they decided to conduct a more thorough search of the room, Abby and I'd be dead anyway.

Might as well come out swinging.

Which is exactly what I did, although with much less grace and skill than my hybrid counterpart. There were three figures in the dark room. I was able to identify Grog by his clothing. The other two were identical in size and stature. Grog was engaged in hand to hand combat with them and seemed to be losing ground. My loud exit from the cupboard drew the attention of the other. It swiveled to face me in a rapid blur of movement. With nothing more than a dull butcher knife in hand, I faced the stuff nightmares are made of.

Its smile practically split the human-like face open. Even in the gloom, I could see dozens of sharp teeth in that grinning mouth which literally stretched from ear to ear. If it hadn't been for that fleeting second the hybrid took to enjoy the prospect of killing me, I'd have been dead. The minor delay was all I needed to thrust the knife into its torso. I could feel the blade pierce flesh, but I must have missed any vital organs because it retaliated with a pissed-off backhand motion that sent me flying against a wall. I almost blacked out, but managed another stab with the knife when it came at me again.

Miraculously, I must have done some damage with the first stab because the creature moved slower now. It hadn't been quick enough to block the second knife thrust which split the skin on its forearm wide open, but was no death blow.

The macabre grin vanished. It grabbed me by my throat with one hand while the other hand pinned my wrist and knife against the wall. It began to squeeze my throat, the force of those long fingers a steel vise on my windpipe. Within seconds, I saw black spots in my vision.

This was it, then. The whole 'life flashing before your eyes' thing didn't happen – I just felt terribly sad that I'd let Abby down. Again.

As I was slipping into unconsciousness, I felt the vise grip relax. I forced huge, ragged breaths of air into my lungs.

The hybrid still stood in front of me, but its bloodthirsty expression had changed to one of surprise. It collapsed to the floor, graceful and fluid even in death. Standing behind it was Abby, the knife and giant fork still in her hands. My Lilliputian had just killed a monster, and even in the gloom, I could see her tight, satisfied smile.

Grog and the second creature still struggled near the door. I took four quick steps and thrust my knife into what I hoped was a kidney. The hybrid swiveled around with the blinding speed of a cobra and duplicated the backhand gesture used by the first one. My head slammed against a table on the way down to the floor.

My puny assault hadn't been in vain

though. The distraction allowed Grog to get a choke hold on it from behind. Both hybrids appeared equally strong but Grog now had the advantage. He held on until the creature's struggles weakened and slowed. A long minute later, he released the choke hold, grabbed the other hybrid's head with both hands and twisted it rapidly to the right. For the rest of my life, however long or short that might be, I'll never forget the snapping sound of the spinal cord, like a brittle tree branch thrust against a knee.

Grog had executed the movement like a trained killer.

"Is he dead?" I whispered.

The quick nod was visible in the dark.

"Are there any more?" Abby asked.

Another nod. No more monsters for now, thankfully.

"Grog, are you okay?"

The hybrid shrugged his shoulders noncommittally then gestured that we should leave. Back in the call center room, I could see bruises already spreading on the hybrid's face and one eye beginning to swell shut. I imagined I'd have a nice purple ring around my own throat very soon.

I retrieved the tablet from my backpack where it had been dropped during our flight, and handed it to Grog. He sat down at a dusty metal desk and waited for my questions.

"Grog, are you seriously injured? Did the bad one hurt you?" Abby asked, placing her hand on his shoulder.

"No, just small pain," he typed, offering a ghost of a smile. *"Bigger pain in here."* He pointed to his chest. Had the fight injured some vital organ or done more damage than was visible?

"You didn't want to kill your brother, did you?" Abby asked in a soft voice. Of course she'd understood immediately what 'bigger pain in here' meant. Grog was hurting emotionally because of what he'd done.

He shook his head, dejected.

"He wanted to kill you...and us too, Grog. You did the right thing. You did what you had to do."

"Grog understands. But still not happy. Was something the bad ones would do. Not Grog. Grog is better. Should be better."

It seemed our hybrid possessed a personal moral code. He wasn't upset about murdering his own kind – he was disappointed that he'd had to lower himself to the base level of 'killer'.

"We all do things we don't want to do...things that make us feel bad about ourselves. We have an expression for this: The lesser of two evils. It means in a situation where we have only a few choices, and all of those choices are terrible, we pick the one that isn't quite as bad as the others. It's just part of life, Grog. Welcome to humanity." She gave him her best smile. It had the same knee-weakening effect on him that it did on me.

"I will remember this. Thank you, Abby friend."

"Grog, there are a lot of questions that need answering if we're going to put an end to the killing. Are you willing to answer them for me now?" I asked.

He studied me for a moment, pondering my question, then with the irresistible pull of a magnet to steel, his gaze glided back to Abby.

He nodded.

For the next hour, I got more information than I'd been able to gather during the previous six months. I began to think we actually might have a chance.

Chapter 10

"*You killed a hybrid*? Holy freaking shit, Abby!" Ben's admiration was visible in the rear view mirror. We'd picked him up on the way back from uptown. Abby's weak smile was less exuberant.

Josh had already wounded him. I stabbed him from behind, after all. It wasn't terribly noble."

"Good grief, Abby, it wasn't a fair fight to begin with! Those things have super human strength and speed. I'm just so damn impressed...with both of you guys!"

There was a healthy dose of jealousy in Ben's tone. He was the best fighter of all of us, yet he kept getting denied opportunities to kick ass.

"I wasn't that impressive, Ben. Trust me.

Abby was magnificent, of course."

Another weak smile. She hadn't reconciled herself to taking a life, even in self-defense and despite the life not being entirely human.

"Where to?" Ben asked. "I wouldn't say no to a Dunkin Donuts pumpkin muffin right about now.

"What, no maple donuts?" I teased.

"Blasphemer! Of course there will be maple donuts. Maple donuts are a given, like fries with a burger, or salsa with chips. They don't need to be mentioned because they are inherent to any and all trips to any and all donut shops."

We selected a table in the corner of the jarringly bright donut shop, away from the other patrons.

"Now, the burning question is this: do I eat the maple donut first as an appetizer to the pumpkin muffin or should it be saved for last, therefore allowing the anticipation to enhance the orgasmic deliciousness of the world's most perfect food?"

The smirk said he was joking, but the glassy eyes as he stared at the donut implied otherwise.

"You're putting way too much thought into this, Benny," I said.

Abby watched with a mixture of fascination and disgust as he tore into the donut. Apparently, the decision had been made.

"So, where are we with your cop friend?" Ben asked between mouthfuls. "Was she able to find anything out about the base?"

"I haven't heard back yet. I'm expecting her call any time. I'm still second guessing myself about involving her. She has a kid."

"It's too late now, Josh. You did everything you could to discourage her from getting involved. It was her choice," said Abby, still watching Ben but not really seeing him now.

This, from a softie like Abby, surprised me. It was just one more indication of how the recent events had changed us; for the better or worse remained to be seen.

As if on cue, my phone rang. I expected to see Monica's name on the caller ID but it was a number I didn't recognize.

"Hello?"

"Hello, Josh. It's Ian. I thought I'd check

in with you guys. I tried calling Abby, but she didn't answer. Is everything okay?"

I held the phone up so Abby and Ben could hear the conversation. Abby scrolled through her phone and confirmed a missed call with a nod of her head.

"How'd you get my number, Ian? I don't remember giving it to you."

Abby winced at my rudeness, which made me smile. She'd just killed an evil hybrid but still fretted over telephone manners.

"Dylan gave it to me," Ian replied after a slight hesitation. "Is it not cool to call you? I'm sorry if I'm being presumptuous. I just figured we're all kind of in this together. There's nobody else I can talk to about this stuff."

"No, it's alright," I said. He had a point. "Anything weird happen in your area this morning? Did you see any…uh, activity?" There was no point in alarming any eavesdropping donut customers with verbiage like 'alien hybrids' or 'extraterrestrial serial killers'.

"I did see something this morning, but

I was pretty far away, so I can't be sure. It almost looked like two of them walking, rather hurriedly, down near Greenwood Cemetery on McKinney. I was out strolling before I opened up the shop."

"Well, funny you should mention that. Abby and I encountered them this morning as well as our new friend," I replied. "It's hard to talk about now, but let's just say it didn't end well for the duo."

Dead silence on the other end of the phone. I thought for a moment that the call had been dropped.

"Ian...you still there?"

"Yes, yes. Still here. What are you saying, Josh? Did you kill them?" His voice had taken on a choked quality.

"Affirmative. It was them or us, know what I mean?"

"What about Grog?"

"Well, thanks, Ian. Abby and I are just fine."

"Sorry, Josh. I just assumed you were okay since you answered your phone. Is Abby alright?"

"Yeah, she's fine. So is Grog. We can give

you the details later."

"Uh, okay, Josh. Listen, can I get together with you guys this evening? How about I buy you all dinner? Let's say 8:00 at Fearings on McKinney. It's in the Ritz-Carlton. Does that work for you?"

I'd heard of Fearings and knew Abby had been wanting to go there. It was one of the trendiest restaurants in Dallas. Abby nodded. Ben gave a thumbs-up sign.

"Yeah, that's great Ian. I'll tell Joe and Dylan."

"Excellent!" The lilting confidence was back. "Let's meet in the bar for cocktails at seven. See you all then." The call ended.

"I need to get home, Josh. I have to figure out what I'm wearing."

The prospect of getting all dolled up and going to a fancy restaurant put a spark in Abby's eyes that I hadn't seen in a long time, and for that reason, I didn't mind being out-classed by Ian.

I called Dylan and Joe on the way to drop Abby and Ben off at their homes. Joe declined. His excuse of not feeling well could be legitimate, but I thought it also likely that he was making a statement about accepting free dinners from Ian. The reaction I got from Dylan was polar opposite, and eerily similar to Abby's.

"Oooooh, Fearings! I've been dying to go there. I wonder how he got reservations? They book up a month in advance. Josh, no offense, but don't wear your corduroy sport coat, okay? The lavender shirt I bought you for Christmas last year with your black and purple striped tie and a pair of dark gray slacks. And tell Ben to wear the pumpkin shirt with the dark brown slacks. I know he won't wear a tie."

"You got that right," Ben grumbled from the back seat when I relayed the conversation. Dylan had always asserted that Ben's aversion to having anything tight around his neck was residual emotion from a past life experience. He was convinced that Ben had died by hanging in at least a few former incarnations. Once, we spent an entire evening speculating about the crimes Ben might have committed. We decided he'd been everything from a horse thief to a Salem witch. He almost punched me over the witch thing. There was no way he'd ever been a chick in ANY life, but shortly after, he developed a fascination with the Salem witch trials and read everything on the subject he could get his hands on.

Just to mess with him, anytime I come across witch figurines, I buy them, then leave them where I know he'll find them. The funny thing is, they disappear and he never mentions them. He might be throwing them away, but something tells me his growing collection is locked away where nobody can find it.

###

When I got back to my apartment, I found Joe sitting on the sofa watching television. His color looked good and he was laughing at a sitcom.

"What's up, Joe? Feeling any better?"

"Not horrible, not great. Anything interesting happen today?"

I sat down in my recliner, suddenly exhausted. I hadn't yet told Joe about the day's events. Describing our hybrid-killing adventured needed to be done in person, not over the phone. He was on his feet, whooping and cheering by the end of the conversation.

"Josh, this is huge! As impressive as those things are, now we know they can be killed, and actually easier than we thought. Man, I just can't believe that Abby. If you have half a brain, you'll get that girl back. She's a keeper – and not just because she's pretty. Pretty girls are a dime a dozen. She reminds me of Alameda in a lot of ways...beautiful and ballsy." His sigh was wistful but thoughts of his absent wife didn't diminish his exuberance.

"Yeah, I know, Joe. I'm working on it," I gave him a tired smile.

"So, you all still going out to dinner with that Ian guy?"

"Yeah, Abby and Dylan are pretty excited. It's a fancy place and I figure we could all use the distraction. Are you sure you don't want to go?"

"Yep, I'm sure. I have some stuff I want to work on tonight. I talked to your cop friend when she came by earlier. Got me thinking along some new lines on how we might approach this thing."

"Monica came by? What the hell...she was supposed to call."

"She said she preferred to discuss anything 'of a delicate nature' in person..her words. Anyway, don't ask me about it because she wants to explain it all to you herself. I gave her my word," he added.

"Why the hell is she talking to you about this stuff anyway? She doesn't know you. Why would she just spill her guts to a stranger who just happened to be in my apartment when I wasn't home? Pretty sloppy for a cop, if you ask me."

"Funny you should ask...I had the same thought and asked her directly." His smile was indulgent. "She's done her homework on all of us. Probably did extensive background checks before she opted in to this mess. She knew exactly who I was the second I opened the front door. Knew about my military record, knew about the UFO stuff, knew about Alameda, knew that I'd been living in New Mexico for the last couple of decades. Hell, she probably knew what I ate for breakfast and whether I had a bowel movement this morning."

I laughed. I couldn't blame the detective. If mini NORAD had been functioning better, I'd have done the same thing.

"She said she would drop by in the morning around eight. Said to tell you to 'have the coffee ready and make damn sure it wasn't that flavored shit. The stronger the better.'" Joe chuckled to himself as I watched, bemused. Did my uncle have a crush on the woman?

"Does she know about the cancer?"

"Yep. Guess it came up on some medical or hospital records. You know what was cool? She didn't go all sad-faced and mushy about it. Just told me life sucks and then you die. Said she hoped I surprised the bastards who gave me that six-month death sentence and that I would stick around another ten years just to spite them."

He was more relaxed and cheerful than I'd ever seen him. I suddenly wished I hadn't accepted Ian's dinner invitation. At that moment, nothing would please me more than to hang out with my uncle. Maybe order a pizza, watch a football game and forget that alien creatures were trying to kill us.

I toyed with the idea of canceling, but then remembered how beautiful Abby looked when she was all dressed up, and that she'd mentioned thinking Ian was a bit 'dashing' after meeting him the first time.

No way in hell was I missing this dinner.

###

"Pretty fucking fancy place, Ian. I hope you don't think I'm gonna put out on the first date just because you're buying me a $50 dollar rib eye and plying me with twenty-year old scotch." Ben took a sip of the amber liquid and sighed happily. "Although, if a dude was ever gonna get into my pants, this would be the way to do it."

Abby and I exchanged a knowing glance then waited for Dylan's reaction.

He wore that lazy, slow smile we knew to be the precursor of verbal throw down.

"Trust me, Ben. Nobody from our team would even try it. Your hetero vibe is pungent and stinky to us. It smells like a pair of gym shorts that's been used for an entire basketball season then left in a locker for a month. We wouldn't waste a good steak on such a lost cause."

Ben looked genuinely hurt. "Seriously? You guys don't find me attractive?"

"Benny, you're smokin' hot. We can see that. But why bother trying to climb Mount Everest in a blizzard when there's a hot toddy, a roaring fire and a cute guy with a photo of Liza Minelli next to the condom in his wallet back at the ski lodge?"

The analogy was a bit dodgy but we busted out laughing anyway. Dinner had been sublime and the conversation quite enjoyable. I had to admit, Ian was a gracious host and his self-deprecating humor kept him just this side of insufferable.

"So, Ian, tell us an Irish folk story," Abby asked.

"If you want an Irish folk story, my bonny lass, then you shall have one."

Okay, I might have to hate him again.

Abby clapped her hands. Ian's accent became more pronounced as he launched into his narrative.

"Well, you'd have heard of our faeries, of course. Sometimes we call them 'the little people' and even though we revere them and treat them with the utmost respect, they sometimes play tricks on us, or even worse, pilfer our wee babes and leave one of their own sickly faerie children in its place. We call them 'changlings'." He paused for a moment and took a casual sip of wine, an old actor's ploy to build the suspense.

"One bonny spring day, a fisherman's wife was going about her chores at home. She'd flung open the windows and doors so as to catch the fine breeze coming off the River Shannon. As she was churning her butter, she looked up to see an old woman walk, brazen as you like, through the front door. The old woman then hobbled directly to the cradle where the wife's wee babe was sleeping. The wife was shocked at seeing the stranger in her house, but the old crone cooed and smiled so that the woman knew she meant her infant no ill will. The wife turned her back for a brief moment to check on the butter and when she turned back around, the crone had vanished. She thought it odd but then soon forgot about it, as often happens in such stories."

Ian gave Abby a wink.

"Well, from that day on, the babe would do nothing but cry and fret and waste away before the eyes of the fisherman and his wife. It was about a week later when the wife thought to tell her husband about the old crone. 'That's nae our bairn, that's one of the faerie folk! Our bairn's been stolen!' the fisherman exclaimed. He grabbed the crying babe who was now all withered and wizened, ran to the neighboring ravine and tossed the infant into the swirling water...much to his wife's horror, as you can imagine. 'Do nae fret, wife!' he said. 'Watch wha' happens now!' As soon as the babe touched the water, it changed into a little gray manikin, swam to shore and in a blustery rage, scurried off in the opposite direction on his short, bowed legs. When the fisherman and his wife ran home, they found their infant son had been returned and slept soundly in his cradle."

Ian bowed his head in acceptance of the spontaneous applause which came from our table as well as one nearby.

Yes, I was officially back to hating him.

"How about the grogoch story? You know, the one that made you think of our friend? Please tell us about it," Abby asked with such a sweet expression that resistance was futile.

"Of course, my dear," Ian replied. "The grogoch is a delightful creature, half human and half faerie. Legend has it they originally came from Scotland, but we Irish claim them as our own since most good and benevolent creatures tend to gravitate to our bonny island, whilst all the foul and wicked ones prefer the company of the Scots."

Another wink for Abby.

"They seem to be predominant in the Donegal area, which is a hop, skip and a jump from my hometown of Kilbarry. They're short in stature and covered from head to toe in red fur and are not known for personal hygiene, if you take my meaning. What makes them especially interesting is their ability to become invisible. It's said they only allow trusted humans to observe them and oftentimes will become attached to a specific human, and in return for nothing more than a pitcher of cream, will help with the harvesting and planting of the crops. No wonder they're well thought of in my country – free labor!"

"Oh, I see now why you came up with that, um, nickname," Abby said as she exchanged a pointed look with Ian. He nodded.

"So, my turn now," he continued. "What happened this morning?" The congenial, gracious host had vanished. In his place was a grim-faced stranger.

I explained in a quiet voice and rather broad terms what had happened at the building. Ian's response was low-key. None of us wanted to alarm the nearby patrons.

"So, what next?" he asked.

"We have some plans in the works," I replied, swallowing the last of the scotch in my glass. "Nothing concrete yet, but a pretty good idea of what we want to accomplish and a working theory on how to do it."

"And that would be…?" Ian pressed.

"Eradication," I replied simply.

"You mean the ones that are here in Dallas?"

"No, I mean full eradication. Anything less is just putting a Band-Aid on it...not fully resolving the problem." A man at the next table glanced in our direction with a raised eyebrow. I lowered my voice further. "After what happened this morning, I'm even more convinced that's the only solution. Have you seen the paper today? Seven more people have gone missing in the last twenty four hours. We think they're escalating their plan, whatever *that* might be. Picking off humans seems to be a big part of it though."

Ian appeared thoughtful as he leaned back in his chair. He reached for his pocket and removed a vibrating phone. His face became stony after a glance at the screen.

"Problem, Ian?" Abby asked.

"Damn alarm is going off at the store. I need to head out." He scooted his chair back quickly. "I'm terribly sorry to rush off like this. Dinner has been taken care of so please, take your time and enjoy another round if you'd like. It was a pleasure, my friends. Abby," he lifted her hand and brushed it against his lips. "You are an absolute delight. I hope to see you all again very soon!"

And then he was gone.

After seeing my former girlfriend and soon to be current girlfriend (if all went according to plan) turn into a puddle of goo before my eyes, I resolved to learn that hand-kissing thing.

Chapter 11

My cell phone rang at six-fifteen the next morning.

"Who the fuck is calling me this early?" I growled into the phone.

"Josh, it's Monica. There's something you need to see. Get your ass out of bed and get down to Cedar Springs and Olive. You know where that is?"

"Yeah, it's very close to where I was last night for dinner...which was only a few hours ago."

"Trust me. You'll want to see this. Call me when you're five minutes out and I'll get you through the police tape."

Well, that got my attention.

Forty minutes later I handed Monica one of the two coffees I'd bought on the way.

She held up the police tape for me to duck under. A uniformed cop gave me the stink eye but Monica ignored him. She exuded authority. As a journalist, I was usually treated like crap by most cops, so I let myself bask in the differential treatment.

"So, what happened?" I asked, eyeballing my surroundings. We were in the middle of a long and narrow grassy corridor which was bisected by an urban walking trail. Alongside the trail ran a massive and far-reaching system of power lines. Like perfectly spaced dominoes, the towers meandered up and down the slightly rolling terrain. From our vantage, the symmetry of the identical, imposing man-made structures juxtaposed with the concrete walking path and the still-green Bermuda grass was eerily beautiful in the morning light.

"Bodies. Two of them. How strong is your stomach?"

"Um, actually not very, but I think I'll be okay. Nothing in there but coffee at the moment."

She nodded and motioned for me to follow. As we made our way to one of the towers, the crowd of official types became thicker. Most of them wore badges that read FORENSICS – CITY OF DALLAS but a few white jackets labeled 'ME' told me the medical examiner's people were here as well. I was also surprised to see a few navy blue windbreakers with bright yellow letters stenciled on the backs.

What the hell was the FBI doing here? Surely, this was a local police matter – whatever 'this' was. The agents kept to the perimeter and seemed mostly interested in talking to individuals in the burgeoning crowd. It was almost seven now and people were going to work. The crime scene tape and flashing red lights beckoned, inexorable and thrilling to passersby. What is it about human nature that makes us want to look at horrible things? When I worked the night shift as a rookie reporter, I'd seen enough gore to last me a lifetime. I would never understand the fascination.

We were fifty yards from an electrical tower where much of the bustling activity was focused – the location of the body. The grisly sight was bad enough from that distance and would only get worse the closer we got. I realized that I'd stopped walking only when Monica tugged on my sleeve. My feet started moving again, much to the dismay of my stomach.

It was as gruesome as I'd imagined. A body hung, Christ-like, from the metal girders. The arms had been secured to a cross beam with plastic tie-wraps, the legs dangled five feet from the ground. The head rested against a shoulder at an impossible angle. He was naked. Penis and testicles had been removed, and not with precision – the work of a novice butcher or improper tools. Or both.

This final detail prompted me to stumble several feet away and puke in the grass.

"Hey! This is a crime scene, asshole!" I heard a man bellow. I felt Monica pat my shoulder from behind.

"It's okay, Josh. They've already gone over this spot. Puke till your heart's content."

I stood up, wiping a sleeve across my mouth. "I think I'm finished," I said. "Sorry about that. That kind of stuff is the reason I got out of homicide reporting and into feature writing."

"Yeah, I figured," she replied. "I guess I'm mostly immune these days, but this is pretty awful. And don't feel bad...you're not the only one who puked this morning." She indicated a young uniformed cop near the police tape. Even from here, I could see the green tinge in his complexion.

"The woman was three towers down from the man," Monica continued. "The body has already been removed. Same MO except her genitalia wasn't sliced and diced and instead of a broken neck, she was stabbed with a butcher knife – in her front torso and also her back. The back injury was the fatal one. No signs of sexual assault either."

"So why call me? What makes you think this has anything to do with, uh, our situation?"

"Call it a hunch," she shrugged. "I've been doing this a long time and something just doesn't seem right about this scene. It seems staged, for one thing. And there's something else I can't put my finger on."

"I'm no cop, Monica. I don't know what help I can..." my voice trailed off as her description of the two victims' injuries sunk in. The woman had been stabbed in exactly the same way that Abby and I had killed a hybrid. As I glanced up at the man's broken neck, I remembered in vivid detail the sound the second hybrid's neck made when Grog snapped it.

"Josh? What is it?"

"Oh, shit, Monica. I think I know what this is about," I replied. "We gotta talk, but not here."

She nodded and took off at a brisk pace toward a lone vehicle on the far side of the police tape. Once inside the privacy of her car, I revealed what had happened at the office building yesterday morning.

"So, it's a revenge killing. You took two of theirs, so they took two of ours," she said.

"Yeah, that's what I think. But it may be more than that. Have you heard about all the missing people lately?"

"Of course, Josh. It's all over the department."

"Yeah, but I didn't know if you were involved with that sort of thing. I mean, are you homicide or what? You came to my apartment about a shooting, so I'm a little confused."

She looked annoyed at having to explain herself.

"I'm a floater. I've been trained in several areas – homicide as well as the gang unit and narcotics. When someone goes on vacation or calls in sick or there's an increase in crime in a certain area, they put me in. Make sense?"

"Sorry, Monica. I don't know why I didn't think to ask you before. I've been distracted."

"S'alright."

"So, you won't mention my theory to your cop friends, right?"

She responded only with that level, unblinking gaze.

"Yeah, okay. Sorry again. I just feel this is getting harder and harder to keep a lid on. The fewer people in the loop, the better we can contain it and deal with it."

"And just where are we on that?" she

demanded. "I went by to talk to you about some intel I got my hands on and you weren't home. Your uncle seems to be a good guy, by the way. We could use more like him on our team."

By 'team', I had no idea if she meant our team, her cop team or the fucking armed forces, but it didn't matter. She and Joe had developed a rapport, and I figured it could only be a good thing.

"Yeah, I'm sure you know all about him just like you know all about me and the rest of us."

Silent stare. It seemed to be a favorite in her repertoire.

"Well, where we are might be dependent on whatever it is that you were going to tell me but told my uncle instead," I continued.

"Okay, fair enough," she said finally. "I've made contact with a former worker at the base who is willing to provide a floor plan as well as technical details we'll need to gain access and maneuver throughout the facility." I detected a hint of smugness in that steely demeanor.

I smiled. This, along with what we'd

learned from Grog, just might give us a fighting chance.

"How did you find him?"

"Sneaky cop stuff. Accessed data bases I wasn't supposed to even know about. Got a hit with a military ID and followed the lead to a former low-level employee who had worked at the base for a couple of years. He got laid off during some budget cutbacks. Typical pissed off ex-government employee. He was making $40 bucks an hour to clean toilets and mop floors and is bitter now because he can't find a job in the private sector doing the same thing for the same wage."

"How do you know this guy is legit?"

"I just do. I interviewed him in person. He's legit."

"He's local?" I said, surprised. That seemed coincidental.

"Yep. Lives in a crap apartment down in south Oak Cliff. The kind of neighborhood where you put on your Kevlar before you go in. It's all he can afford now that he's not making insane wages for a mindless job any idiot could do. God, I love our government. Bunch of fucking, power hungry bastards. Every last one of them."

She and I were in agreement on that point.

"So, how difficult was it finding this guy? In the cyber world, I mean?" Hacking interested me.

Her eyes slid away from mine. My heart sink.

"Oh, fuck, Monica. You had somebody else do the hack? Somebody else *knows*?"

"I didn't have a choice, Josh. I'm pretty good with computers but I'm not that good. I needed help. Don't worry about it. I've known Aaron for a long time and he owes me big time. I saved his ass, literally, on more than one occasion. And he didn't know what he was looking for, exactly. I gave him just enough information to find the guy."

"He knows about the base?"

"Of course he knows about the base. That's not top secret shit, Josh. Anyone who Googles 'alien astronauts' will pull up something about Dulce."

"Okay, so you didn't get the floor plan

when you interviewed him?"

"No, he has to draw it. I know, I know," she said when she saw my expression. "But it's the best he could do. Security going in and out of that place was thorough. Body scans at the main entrance, retina scans to get into the high-security areas down on the sixth and seventh levels. Even if he could have gotten his hands on schematics, he wouldn't have gotten out the door with them. They weren't allowed to bring anything into the base except themselves. Couldn't even bring a sack lunch to work. Of course, there are always ways to beat the system, but our guy wasn't ambitious or motivated enough to try. Maybe others were."

"So you think he can accurately depict the layout? What was his security clearance? Did he have access to all levels?"

She smiled. "That's the beauty. It seems the janitors were moved frequently to various levels for unknown reasons. Maybe to keep them from getting too familiar with anyone or anything. At any rate, he says he knows it and can draw it. He needed a day to get it done. Oh, and two thousand bucks. Where do I submit my expense report?"

###

Joe was making breakfast when I arrived back at my apartment. He seemed to be in a particularly cheerful mood.

"So, what do you think? Pretty good little detective, huh? Finding that guy from the base is a real bonus." Joe said with a smile.

"Yep. Of course I'm worried too though. The fewer people who know what we have in mind, the better."

"Oh, you mean that hacker kid? Don't worry. Monica told me he'd be able to cover his tracks completely. Nobody will even know that he was in whatever database he hacked into. Something about unrestricted proxy servers and a buggy wind fence something-or-other. You probably know what that means." He waved me towards the kitchen table and brought me a plate heaped with scrambled eggs and bacon. "Salsa's already on the table. I'll bring you some toast. Get started on those eggs before they get cold."

He saw my slightly bemused expression and interpreted it correctly.

"Yeah, I woke up feeling especially good today. I don't know how to explain it and I don't expect it to last, but I'm gonna make the most of it...that's for damn sure." He sat down with a second loaded plate and dug in with a vengeance.

"A buggy Wingate server," I said between mouthfuls. "Older Wingate servers are vulnerable to a bug that allows anyone on the internet to have unfettered access to Telnet. The hacker gets into a non-updated server and can do anything he wants without anyone knowing he's there. If they track him at all, they'd track him to a proxy server. Voila. Dead end. That's pretty old school though. Hopefully nobody has found a way to track from the proxy server back to the hacker. IT is growing at a ridiculous rate...I can't keep up with it all and I'm pretty good. Let's hope Monica's friend is better."

"So," Joe shifted in his chair, bored with the finer points of internet hacking, "those two bodies they found on the electrical towers. Pretty gruesome, huh?"

I nodded, appetite gone. I poured myself another cup of coffee and gazed out the kitchen window as I thought about the innocent people who had paid for our crimes against the hybrids. There was no question we'd been sent a message. How many more would die before we could stop them?

"Have they been identified yet?"

"No, not yet. Monica said they'd found some tattoos on the man that would be helpful, and there was a cell phone left near the woman's body. She figured it would be a simple matter to identify them, especially with all the missing persons' cases. Concerned citizens are jumping the gun and reporting people missing before the 24 hour period, so she figures they'll get a lead sooner rather than later."

"Well, let's hope those hybrid bastards didn't pick decent people to string up. Hopefully, they're just a couple of druggies or losers they found on the street and not good, honest folks."

"People are people, Joe. Nobody deserved what happened to those two. I don't care if they're druggies or thieves or anything else. If you'd seen them, you'd agree." Joe looked skeptical. "If you say so, Josh. Still, you can't deny that some lowlife drug dealer or worthless, hooker-beating pimp wouldn't be a better victim than a productive, honest member of society. Right?"

I shook my head. "Nobody deserved that, Joe. We treat convicted murderers, rapists and pedophiles in a humane fashion because as a society, we have to rise above the lowly, base emotions of the individuals. I don't care if that guy had just sold a thousand dollars' worth of heroin to a high school kid, I wouldn't want to see him end up like that. Does that make sense?"

Joe looked at me steadily for a few seconds before he replied. "What if that drug dealer had just raped and murdered Abby? Can you honestly tell me you wouldn't enjoy seeing him crucified and strung up on a pole with his dick sliced off?"

I sighed. "Okay, you got me on that. Still, I don't like the concept of a different set of rules applying to different people based on their 'usefulness' to society. It's wrong."

"It's not so much about usefulness as destructiveness. If they did bad things, now they can no longer do those bad things. That's what's great about being a simple, not overly cerebral guy like me, Josh. If those people had to die, I just hope that in some small way they had it coming. That's all I'm saying. Otherwise, this situation would be more tragic than it already is." He followed my gaze out the kitchen window to the park below.

I had to admit, he had a point. I found myself hoping that the naked, brutalized people on the towers had been child abusers or animal torturers. It would make it easier for me to deal with the guilt. And not just for me, but for Abby, who would feel responsible no matter how I packaged the news.

When my cell phone rang, I hoped it wasn't Abby.

"Hello, Joshua." Loretta's tone was pleasant but businesslike.

"Hello, Loretta. I bet I know what you're calling about."

"I suspect you do. I had you pegged for a very bright young man from the moment we first met."

"Yeah, right. I could be a fucking super nova if you'd be a little more forthcoming with your information. I take it you've heard about the two victims found on the electrical towers off Cedar Springs?"

A heavy sigh. "Yes. What a mess. So you know who was behind it?" Her tone was noncommittal but a sudden instinct told me she was fishing. I decided to give her a taste of the crap she'd been spoon feeding me for the last few days.

"Of course. Don't you?"

"Don't be an ass, Joshua. Of course we know 'who' is responsible. We're just confused about the 'why'. Something must have precipitated this event and we need to know what that might have been. The situation seems to be escalating more rapidly than can be contained. I've helped you, after all. If you know something about this, please share with the class."

"Quid pro quo, Clarice," I replied. "I know exactly what precipitated this event and I will tell you if you tell me a little about yourself and this group you're associated with."

"No way, Joshua. Take it off the table and get to a question I can answer so we're not wasting any more time here." Something in her voice told me if I wasn't careful, I would find myself minus one helpful albeit mysterious ally.

"Damn it, Loretta. You suck at this quid pro quo stuff. Okay, what are we up against here? The hybrids are in the city. God knows where else they've spread. People are going missing and people are getting killed. We want to stop it. What are the odds we'll be successful at putting an end to it if we target ground zero?"

She replied promptly. "Honestly, Joshua, the odds are against you... I won't sugar coat it. However, they're not astronomical. Did you ever see the first Rocky movie? I think it's a good analogy for the situation."

"Great. That's extremely useful."

She continued, ignoring my sarcasm. "Still, you could do it. Never underestimate human inventiveness and determination. It's what we're known for."

"You're a veritable fount of helpfulness, Loretta."

"I know you're frustrated, Joshua. But my hands are tied. The perimeters within which I must operate in order to help you at all are specific and narrow. On that subject I can't say more, but I can say this: you are on the right track. The nature of most creatures, human or otherwise, is to stay within their comfort zone – with a few notable exceptions, of course. Tactically, what you're proposing is the only viable option if you want to stop the killings."

"Then why won't you help us?" I demanded, fed up with the one-sidedness of the situation. "Clearly, you have a sophisticated operation of some sort. Your 'clean up' crew was Johnny-on-the-spot at Dylan's house. You have inside information and you know a helluva lot more than we do. Why not help?"

Her tone was gentle but firm. "Because that's not an option, Joshua. It's not the directive of our group to become involved in that capacity. Please just appreciate the help that I am able to give you – be a good boy and I'll keep you on speed dial. Now, back to the reason I called. What precipitated the murders?"

If I could have climbed through the phone, I would have happily strangled her. Since that wasn't an option, I shared the details of yesterday's adventure.

"Oh, my," she said when I'd finished. I was about to ask her another question but she cut me off.

"I have to go. I'm not sure how this will impact the dynamic of the situation but all I can say is, if you weren't being as careful as possible before, now would be the time to begin. Goodbye, Joshua. I'll be in touch."

I placed the phone on the table and relayed Loretta's part of the conversation to Joe. When I finished, we both fell silent and gazed out the window at the park below.

I felt strangely elated. The task ahead might be herculean, but if Rocky could beat the odds, then maybe so could we.

Chapter 12

"Josh, I got a call from my guy. The one in Oak Cliff," Monica said when I answered her call a few hours later. "He's finished with the project."

"That's great! Are you going to pick it up now? You want me to come with you?" I was anxious to get my hands on those schematics. Grog had been a huge help but there was still a language barrier which had caused some frustration during our conversation at the office building. Having a diagram of the base's layout made by someone who'd had access to most or perhaps all of the facility would be invaluable.

"Yes, I was going to suggest that. Safety in numbers, right? I'll be at your apartment in fifteen minutes. Joe can come too, if he wants," she added.

I smiled.

We met her down in the parking lot. Joe had taken extra care with his appearance, I'd noted. His long hair was pulled neatly back in a ponytail, and I thought I smelled cologne.

"We need to stop at an ATM so I can get the cash for this guy," I told Monica from the back seat. I'd worry about my debt situation later if I managed to survive long enough.

"Don't worry about it. I covered it," she replied. "We have petty cash at the department for things like CI payments and whatnot. No worries."

"We don't want you getting in trouble, Monica," Joe replied. "Are you sure that's a good idea?"

"Trust me," she said. "It's no problem." She patted his hand and gave him a rare smile.

I suddenly felt like an interloper. Just how long had Monica been at my apartment with Joe yesterday and what exactly had transpired?

The scenery outside the window of Monica's Nissan became bleaker by the minute. We'd exited off the freeway onto Sylvan, then turned right on Colorado. The neighborhood was even more seedy and grim than the one surrounding Dylan's clinic.

We parked on the street next to a dilapidated apartment building. A small child, perhaps four years old, sat on the cracked sidewalk playing with a toy truck. His clothing was tattered and inadequate for the cool day. He watched with huge, calm eyes as we exited the car.

"Hey, Labron. Where's your mama?" Monica asked the little boy in a gentle voice.

"She got company. Tol' me to play outside." The brown eyes were wise beyond their years. I imagined they had seen more than any four-year old had a right to.

Monica shook her head, disgusted. "Well, you stay close to the door. Don't go too near the street, okay?"

"Okay. You goin' to that white guy's house again?"

"Yep."

"He's home. He gave me a sucker yesterday."

"Well, that's probably okay, but don't be taking candy from people you don't know. Especially if they want you to get in their car. You remember that, okay?"

"Yeah, I know, I know. I won't," he promised.

Monica reached into her back pocket and pulled out some bills.

"Tell your mama a cop lady gave this to you, so it was okay to take it. Tell her I said to buy you a winter coat with it. Will you do that?"

The child's head bobbed, excited.

"Now, put that in your pocket and give it to your mama as soon as her company leaves, okay?"

"Okay, cop lady!" He smiled.

Monica knocked three times on the paint-chipped door of apartment 6A. It opened just wide enough to allow a pair of close-set eyes and a bulbous, red-veined nose to appear in the gap. The door shut again and we heard the sound of the chain sliding off its runner. The door opened wider this time, and we stepped into the darkened room.

"How about some light?" Monica said to the man skulking in the gloom.

"Okay, okay. It's only my money we're wasting turning on all the lights," the man grumbled, clicking on an ancient table lamp with a stained shade.

The room and the man looked better in the dark. His reddish hair was greasy and thin, and I doubted the t-shirt had seen the inside of a washing machine for some time. The smell was bad too – stinky feet and body odor mingled with rotting garbage to create a stomach-churning miasma in the cramped space. I watched an enormous cockroach crawl across the wall near the tiny kitchen as the man offered us a seat on the sofa.

Thankfully, Monica declined for all of us.

"We don't have time for a social visit, Mr. Doyle. These are my associates, Mr. Hawkins and Mr. McCullough. May we see the drawings?" She managed to sound professional instead of rude.

"Yeah, yeah. Got 'em right here." He

pulled out a large, pristine drawing pad and set it on a rickety coffee table in front of the sofa. "You got the money?"

His close-set eyes gave him a rodent-like appearance. I superimposed twitching whiskers on his face at the sight of the envelope Monica withdrew from her jacket.

"It's all there, of course."

Her level expression stopped the man from rifling through the bills. He folded the envelope instead and stuffed it down a grimy jeans pocket.

Grubby hands clapped together suddenly in a gesture of excitement. Now that the sordid issue of compensation had been handled, he seemed eager to show us what the Dallas PD's petty cash had bought.

He sat down on the sofa and peeled back the cover of the drawing pad.

"I've done it by levels, of course. This first page here is the hub. It's the main level. You can see it's laid out like a wheel with spokes. These corridors," he pointed at the spoke sections of the drawing, "go to all different areas, and these elevators," the grubby finger tapped at some square boxes drawn inside the main circle of the wheel, "go down to all the other levels."

The drawing wasn't too bad, actually. He'd gone to some trouble to make it neat and reasonably detailed.

"This corridor here leads to the train station."

"The train station?" Monica prodded.

"Yeah, although it ain't like any train you've ever seen. That's how most of us lower level people come and go at the base. I always came from Edith, just north of the border in Colorado, but I know some came from the ranch."

"What about the high level people? Where do they come from?" I asked.

"Well, you gotta understand. People don't talk to each other much. And they sure as hell don't talk to us janitors. I overhead one of the scientists say something about Los Alamos, so I think there's a train that connects base to that place, but I can't say for sure cuz I've never seen it. I've only ridden the train from Edith to Dulce. That thing goes fast too. I think it's a Maglev...you know, magnetic levitation like they have in Japan. I read about it in a magazine. One time I estimated about how many miles the trip was and based on how long the ride was, I figure that train must go about 600 miles per hour. I know it's crazy," he said when he saw Monica's expression. "I don't know how they do it, but they got stuff down there that we don't have up here."

"Please continue, Mr. Doyle."

"Okay, this is where all the power to operate the rest of the facility comes through. Electromagnetic generators are what they use. Most of that stuff takes up this area," he pointed to a pie-shaped area roughly one quarter of the circular hub. "The computer stuff is in this area," the finger moved to encompass half of the hub. "And this part is the security section. There's an entire room filled from floor to ceiling with TV screens showing different areas of the base...inside and out. They usually turn 'em all off when we're in there cleaning. Don't want us dumb janitors to see any of their secret stuff."

His look conveyed the bitterness of a man who'd worked at menial jobs his entire life but who probably possessed above average intelligence.

"This is the floor I usually worked on. I'm most familiar with it but, like I told the detective here, they moved us around pretty regularly. I think they were afraid if we stayed in one area long enough, we'd start figuring out what they were up to or how their fancy electronic stuff worked."

I noticed Joe studying the man rather than the drawing. "You feel okay about sharing this information with strangers, buddy? Didn't those Feds make you sign some kind of confidentiality contract?" he asked.

The man lit up, a thrift store Christmas tree.

"Fuck, yeah, they made me sign one. Made me sign my life away. Said they'd do all kinds of terrible things to me and my family if I ever breathed a word about the base or anything I'd seen there. But guess what? I don't *have* a family anymore and I don't give a rat's ass what they do to me. You call this a life? You think I'd be upset if it all ended tomorrow?" he gestured broadly at the bleak surroundings. "Besides," he continued, quieter now, "I'm leaving as soon as we're done. I'm taking my two grand and leaving town. I'm not telling anyone where I'm going and I'm gonna live off the grid. Those fuckers will never be able to find me anyway." His grin revealed a dental hygienist's nightmare.

"Now," he said, turning the page with a flourish, "this is Level 2." The drawing was similar to the first in its circular shape and spoke-like corridors. "This half is mostly offices for the scientists and head honchos, plus sleeping quarters for military guys. The other half here is the food and maintenance area. That's where the cafeteria is and where all the supplies are kept for maintenance and repairs of the facility. Nuts, bolts and screwdrivers, ya know? Nothing weird in there that I've ever seen. That's a bit further down."

With the last sentence, his eyes widened for dramatic effect as he turned the page.

"Levels 3 and 4 are mostly labs and the infirmary is here." He pointed to an area on the third level. "Nothing special about it. It's just a regular infirmary for people who get sick or hurt...at least as far as I could tell. Levels 3 and 4 are where all the scientists work. I figure they're scientists 'cuz they all wear those prissy white coats. See this?" He pointed to a large rectangular diagram on Level 4. "This is like the CDC in here. I never cleaned that area but I talked to one of the guys who does. Said they make him wear one of those suits when he does it. Everybody else is wearing those suits too. I figure they're making anthrax or Ebola. Some kind of shit that's contagious because you have to go through all these checkpoints and jump through hoops just to go in and out. Lots of shit goes on in the labs on both levels but they didn't let me get too close to anything. They always had a grunt with an AK47 up my ass every time I was in there cleaning. Lots of computers and science equipment but I sure as hell couldn't tell you what any of it was for. Science was never my *forte*," he sneered, then turned the page.

"Okay, Level 5. I only been in a few times but I can tell you, I go back there all the time in my nightmares. There are things in there that don't belong on God's good earth. They keep most of the fish tanks covered with tarps whenever we're in there cleaning, but the last time I was in there, one of the tarps slipped a bit and what I saw floatin' inside was something out of a horror movie. I didn't get a good look at it 'cuz the scientists freaked out when the tarp slipped and the soldier pushed me outside real fast. But I saw enough to scare the living shit outta me. You ever see that old movie, *The Creature from the Black Lagoon*? That's what it reminded me of."

He paused a moment, letting the image soak in.

"Fish tanks?" I asked.

"Yeah, well, I guess they're not really fish tanks but that's what they kinda look like. Huge rectangular glass cages filled with some kind of liquid. That Lagoon creature was just floating in the stuff. Its face was pressed up against the glass like it wanted out real bad."

So much for getting a good night's sleep tonight.

Joe nodded as if the man's story confirmed his suspicions. "So, this entire area is all laboratories and fish tanks?" he asked Doyle, pointing a finger at the circular diagram that was Level 5.

"Yes. Not all are fish tanks, some cages are just cages. Like glass or metal but without liquid in them. There are eight different labs on this level. See the wedges?" he pointed to the sectioned areas of the wheel. "A few of them I never went in, but I been in most of 'em. Pretty fucking creepy, that's for sure."

He turned the page. "Now, here's where it gets even weirder."

The diagram was no longer circular in appearance but rather took up the entire page and was shaded around the edge. The detail wasn't as good as on the previous pages and the floor plan was a simple rectangle within a rectangle.

"I was only on Level 6 one time. I had to fill in for a guy who got pneumonia. Or at least that's what they told me. Level 6 had their own cleaning staff and they didn't associate with the rest of us. I think they were told not to. They have their own supplies and kitchen down there for..." he paused, "the people who live and work there."

"What do you mean, Mr. Doyle? Scientists? Military personnel?" I asked.

He shook his head.

"No. Just people," he said as the corners of his mouth turned down, oddly childlike. "People like you and me. Little ones too. They were kept in cages that ran along the perimeter of the open area here in the middle."

"Were they mistreated?" Joe asked. "Tortured? What were their living conditions like?"

"They didn't seem to be suffering...physically, I mean. They all looked pretty healthy and well-fed. They had cots to sleep on and wore clean hospital clothes. But they were so quiet...I knew something had to be wrong with them. The soldiers moved them from cell to cell so us janitors could get in there and clean the floors and toilets. We'd get one cell clean and then they'd transfer them back into it along with the ones in the next cell that needed cleaning.

And so on. Until all the cells were clean. It took about four hours to finish and the entire time I was working, not one of them uttered a peep. None of them even looked at me, except for a little girl. She watched me through the bars, her eyes were as big as saucers and her pupils were all dilated like she'd been drugged. She didn't say anything, but a tear slid down her cheek from one of those big eyes."

He actually choked on the last word, then withdrew a filthy handkerchief from a back pocket and honked into it.

This wasn't an act. I could see the man was genuinely distressed.

"One tear drop, falls from the others; free. Another tear drop falls down silently. All my pain is held, captured in each one. They glisten like diamonds and sparkle in the sun."

The last thing I would have expected to come from Doyle's pie hole was poetry. I exchanged raised brows with Joe.

"'Cept that little girl's tears will never glisten in the sun. She'll never see the fucking light of day." His voice barely a whisper now.

Suddenly, Doyle shook his head, clearing the remnants of despondency, and after an awkward few moments, resumed.

"I don't know what you crazy fuckers are planning, but I hope to God you get that little girl out of there. All the rest of them too, if anyone is still alive. And I hope you kill as many of those fucking asshole scientists as you can get your hands on. I don't know what they were doing to those people, but I know they were using them for some kind of experiments. They told us janitors that they were all 'criminally insane' and were there for observation.

"Bullshit! You think I'm a dumb fuck? That little girl wasn't any more criminally insane than you or me." He gazed at us all in turn. "You promise me you'll get her. Promise!"

"We promise, Mr. Doyle. If we can save that little girl, we will. You have my word," Joe replied.

"Okay, okay," he said, shifting his attention back to the diagram of Level 6. "This area around the cells? See where I have it shaded? That's all rock. Granite I think, but I ain't no rock exert. It wasn't finished out like the rest of the facility. I don't know why. I guess they didn't need all the high-tech stuff to contain a few drugged up humans."

"What about Level 7?" I asked.

"Well, I gotta be honest with you," he eyed Monica, nervous now. "I never went down to Level 7."

"You told me you had been to all seven levels," she replied, eyes narrowed.

"Well, I thought that's what I needed to say to get the job. Look, I've given you a helluva lot more information than you coulda gotten anywhere else. I been there! I seen that stuff with my own two eyes. This," he gestured to the drawing pad, "is worth more than two grand even without Level 7. And you know it!"

Monica arched an eyebrow, allowed a few moments of squirm time, then finally answered.

"All right, Mr. Doyle. You've done well. I appreciate your time and your efforts." She picked up the pad and held her hand out to shake his, just as a child's screams emanated through the thin apartment walls.

"Cop Lady! Cop Lady!"

The front door crashed in, coming off its hinges in the process.

A gloved hand tossed a metal canister through the opening. One end exploded in a cloud of white smoke as it hit the floor.

"Hold your breath!" Monica bellowed. She crouched to the floor and pulled out her gun. Through the eye-burning smoke, I could see Joe hunch beside her with his gun aimed at the front door opening.

The Sig was in my hands before I'd mentally registered what I was doing. As pressure began to build in my lungs, visibility became non-existent. The sound of gunshots pierced the fog-like gloom, but I had no idea if the shadowy, darting forms I saw were friend or foe.

I became completely disoriented. Carbon dioxide built rapidly in my bloodstream – my lungs demanded a breath, despite whatever noxious chemicals were in that smoke. I could barely make out the doorway by its rectangular shape of slightly brighter smoke. I had to get out of that apartment, even if our assailants were right outside waiting for me. Our bodies' need for oxygen is funny that way ...it doesn't care whether it's convenient or not.

I made a dash for the door and stepped outside. As I took deep breaths of the sweetest air I'd ever breathed, I looked up in time to see a car speed away. A black SUV, of course.

I ran back into the apartment. Monica had opened a window, allowing the smoke to begin clearing. Joe stood next to her, his head thrust through the screen-less opening like a dog on a joyride, taking in lungfuls of air and clearly alive.

Doyle hadn't fared as well.

He lay sprawled across the dirty sofa. As I stepped closer, I could see a round hole above his left eye from which a surprisingly small amount of blood oozed. His eyes were open, the blank stare of a dead man.

The drawing pad was gone.

"Damn it!" Monica said, looking at the empty coffee table.

"Yeah, they got it. Him too."

Monica's dismissive gesture implied she mourned the loss of the drawings more than the artist.

"Let's get out of here before the cops show up," she said.

"Uh, the cops are already here, Monica."

"Yeah, well, nobody needs to know that, do they? Trust me, nobody in this neighborhood will have seen anything. That's just how it works in the projects."

As we left the apartment, I looked back to see Labron peering at us from behind a scraggly tree. Monica noticed him too.

"Cop lady wasn't here, right, Labron? You didn't see me or these other guys, okay?" she called to him.

"Okay! Can I buy some candy with the money?" he hollered back.

"Yes, but only use one dollar for candy, no more. Tell your mama to buy you a coat. When I come back, I better see you wearing it."

"Okay! Bye, cop lady!"

We couldn't get out of there fast enough for me. As we pulled around the corner, I already heard police sirens.

After a half mile of careening around corners, Monica finally slowed to a normal speed. My pulse still raced though, and my eyes burned like hell.

"This does not bode well for your hacker friend, Monica," I said. "If they found Doyle shortly after we did, they probably figured out how we found him in the first place...via your guy."

"Yeah, I'll call him." Monica replied, terse and annoyed.

"I've got a bad feeling about this," Joe said. "They seem to know what we're up to and where we're going even before we do. Makes me wonder just how safe any of us are in our homes right now. Obviously, they know where we all live. Are we just gonna sit back and wait for another attack? We've been damn lucky so far."

"What are you proposing, Joe? We hole up in a hotel somewhere?" I asked. Visions of dollar signs flashed through my mind.

"I don't know, something like that. Maybe a rent house somewhere paid with cash? I think we need to fall off the radar."

"He's right, of course," Monica said. "To

be honest, I don't know how you guys have lasted this long."

She gave Joe a covert wink. He grinned.

"Seriously, though," she continued. "You guys probably need to pack a bag and lay low somewhere while we work out our strategy. If I thought I could trust people at the department, I'd get you a safe house. The problem with that is the paper trail. If there's a leak, they'd find out pretty quickly where you are."

"Yeah, I don't think that's a good idea." I imagined a shifty-eyed DPD clerk on the payroll of our adversaries. "I'll talk to Dylan about his parents' weekend house in Decatur."

"Homeowners' names are public record. You know that, Josh."

"Not these homeowners and this house. Trust me."

###

Monica dropped us off at my apartment. We had plans to meet the rest of our group for dinner at six, which gave us time to clean up and relax for a while.

After showering and putting on some

fresh clothes, Joe and I sat in the living room with a couple of Miller Lites. I flipped on the local five o'clock news.

"...were apparently murdered at a different location and then brought here to be staged in this horrific manner. Police are not speculating on motive at this time and have not released the identity of the two victims yet, pending notification of the families. Reporting live from Dallas, this is Dan Godwin, Fox 4 News."

"I'm guessing Monica knows who the victims are by now," I told Joe as I took a swig of the beer.

"Yeah, that might be what she was in such a hurry about when she left."

"Speak of the devil," I said, glancing down at my ringing cell phone.

"Josh, I have some really bad news."

I don't know what scared me worse: being told there was bad news or hearing the uncharacteristic quaver in her voice.

"What is it, Monica?"

"The vics...we know who they are... I mean were."

"Oh, god, who were they?" With every

fiber of my being, I did not want to hear whatever it was she was about to say.

"John and Margaret Saretsky."

I'd been steeling myself for bad news, but this was worse than bad news. It was devastating news. I pictured Dylan's parents, who we had just been discussing a short while ago. They were two of the kindest, most generous human beings I'd ever known. Gentle-spirited, aging hippies, they'd been like second parents to me all through high school.

A wave of guilt washed over me. I was responsible. Dylan's parents had been brutally murdered and it was my fault. How would I face my best friend? The image of their ravaged bodies flashed through my mind. I jumped up and ran to the bathroom, barely reaching the toilet in time.

Joe stood in the doorway while I finished vomiting mostly beer and bile. Wordlessly, he handed me a damp washcloth.

"Who were they, Josh?"

"Dylan's parents," I whispered through clenched teeth as I fought another surge of nausea.

"Oh my god." His horrified whisper summed it up perfectly. "Does Dylan know yet?"

Oh shit! I called Monica back from the bathroom floor. She confirmed that he had been notified by the police about half an hour earlier.

"I tried to deliver the news myself, Josh, but there were already two detectives en route."

"It's okay, Monica. I need to go. I need to call him."

I tried calling ten times and each time got his voice mail.

"Let's go," I told Joe as I pushed my way out of the bathroom and grabbed my jacket and car keys.

"Where are we going?"

"To his house. I know that's where he'll be. We'll call Abby and Ben on the way.

The next few hours were a hazy blur of the worst kind of anguish and misery I'd ever witnessed. This kind of horror – horror on such an intensely personal level, changes a person irrevocably. Looking into

Dylan's eyes, I knew the person who had been my best friend since grade school was gone forever. In his place was a hollow eyed stranger who wanted nothing but revenge.

And who could blame him?

Chapter 13

By two o'clock in the morning, three cars loaded with people, suitcases, groceries and animals arrived at what would have been John and Margaret's retirement home. Decatur, a semi-rural community north of the Dallas-Ft. Worth metroplex, was a mixed bag of farms and ranches scattered among modest residential neighborhoods. Their house was a roomy, four-bedroom 'shotgun' style home with a large kitchen, an enormous wood-burning fireplace in the den, and sat on twenty acres of land. The reason it would never show up in public records as attached to the Saretskys in any way, was because Dylan's bohemian parents had bartered for it. They'd literally traded a Winnebago, a gas grill and a lump of cash to one of their hippie friends who'd wanted to end his days traveling the country. Dylan had accepted his parents' eccentricities and handshake deals many years ago, but it drove him crazy that they'd never had the house put in their name. Eventually they'd have gotten around to it, but it served our purposes well that they hadn't.

We parked our vehicles on the circular gravel driveway in front of the house. There was a fenced-in backyard for the dogs but the rest of the acreage was open and grassy up to the line of huge oak and pine trees which provided a natural property line.

Once all the animals and supplies had been unloaded and everyone else was getting situated in their rooms, Dylan and I went out back with the dogs. The waning moon hung in a sky of infinite blackness. On a clear night such as this, the stars were breathtaking in their brilliance...so much brighter here than in the city.

Dylan watched the dogs sniff out all the new smells in the backyard. He gazed up at the moon and I could see tears stream down his face. I put my arm around him and thought of a recent, similar night. Losing Monty was bad, but what could compare to this?

"Dylan, this is my fault..." I started to say.

"Josh, do not even start with that shit or I will deck you. You didn't do this – they did, whoever or whatever the fuck *they* are. And we will make them pay. Understood?" His tear-streaked face did nothing to diminish the ferocity of his words or his meaning.

"Oh, yeah, buddy. We certainly will."

We sat on the back porch steps while Dylan's beloved dogs frolicked in the moonlight, blissfully unaware of their master's agony.

Everything was different now. There would be no going back.

Abby emerged through the back door and sat down on the step next to Dylan. She wrapped one arm around him and with the other arm, pulled me into their hug. We rocked back and forth, shedding tears of grief and heartache.

I sent up a silent prayer to a god I wasn't even sure I believed in.

Please don't let anything terrible happen to these people. Please...

In my mind, I heard a cold, mocking response that sounded like Loretta's voice: *Honestly, Joshua, the odds are against you...I won't sugarcoat it.*

Shut up, Loretta. Just shut your stupid mouth.

###

It was a pathetic bunch that gathered around the kitchen table the next morning. Dylan had decided to stay busy, resulting in mountains of fluffy pancakes and heaps of Jimmy Dean sausage – more than enough to feed, if not an army, at least a small would-be militant group. The only person with any appetite was Ben, of course. I found this strangely comforting though – the one constant in all this horror was Ben's love of food. He caught me shaking my head in mild amazement as he speared another stack of pancakes from the platter.

"What, Josh? A man's gotta eat," he whispered, defensive.

Dylan turned from the stove. His face was ravaged by anguish and fatigue, but the sight of the people he loved most in the world evoked a smile.

I knew then he would be okay.

"Look guys, I'll be fine. I have a lot to work through, but I'll be fine. The worst thing you can do is treat me like I'm fragile, or a freak or something. The sooner you get back to treating me normally, the sooner I'll be able to start feeling normal again. Okay?"

He opened the back door to let the dogs in. Trixie, the aging golden retriever, bounded up to me, looking for scraps. Margot, the pirate cat who was curled up on Abby's lap, raised her head to gaze at the dogs with feline disdain.

"Breakfast time, guys. Let's take this circus into the laundry room," Dylan said to the assembled critters. "Daisy, we need to put your diaper on if you're going to be in the house."

Even Margot seemed interested now that breakfast was imminent. She jumped off Abby's lap to follow the dogs. I was so thankful for these sweet animals, knowing they would be crucial to Dylan's emotional and mental well-being in the months ahead.

"Monica called this morning and wants to come out whenever we're at the 'mission discussion' stage," I informed Ben, Abby, and Joe. "Do we give Dylan some time? I just don't think we can wait too long, especially in light of what just happened. I think between the base schematics that Joe and I have up here," I tapped my temple, "and the information Grog gave us, along with his help, we have enough to go forward."

Ben nodded before I could finish.

"But, I just don't know if Dylan is ready."

"Dylan is ready," the man himself said, emerging from the laundry room. "Dylan is more than ready. Trust me."

"Okay, then. I'll call Monica back, and I'll drive to Dallas to leave the signal for Grog to meet me later today – get him started on the first phase."

Before letting our hybrid friend get away last time, Abby and I had worked out a plan to be able to contact him in the future. We would leave a scarf tied to the outside door handle of Ian's shop. If he saw the scarf, at six o'clock of the same day, he would go to the stairwell of the building where we'd met him last time. He'd had no trouble grasping the instructions.

"Here are everyone's shopping lists," Joe said, pulling out sheets of folded notebook paper. "We're officially on the buddy system, understood? Nobody goes anywhere alone. Ever. Is that clear?"

I got a glimpse of how my uncle might have been back in his military days. The ponytail made him look like an aging hippie, but his demeanor was pure former military. Along with Ben's input, we'd put the finishing touches on our plan last night in the bedroom we shared. I felt pretty good about it, despite the odds Loretta had given us. After all, she didn't know the particulars of our plan nor understand the conviction of our group.

What had happened to Dylan's parents further galvanized the resolve we'd already felt. I knew it was a distinct possibility that all of us wouldn't make it through alive. I'd agonized for days over our decision to take on such a monumental challenge...up until the phone call identifying the victims on the towers. I'd had private conversations with everyone in the group, giving them the opportunity to bow out. I'd begged Abby to reconsider, but of course she wouldn't. They were as committed as Dylan and I to putting an end to the atrocities – or die trying.

We didn't know if the Saretskys' murders had been the work of the hybrids themselves or their human associates. Was it a simple case of retaliation or was this the start of a new phase in their plan? Were they sending us a message to back off or was this the beginning of a new, more heinous crime wave? Monica had told us that there were absolutely no leads in the case, so we couldn't count on the police to find the perpetrators. She'd also told us that the missing persons' reports were off the charts. The order had come down from the police chief to keep a tight lid on the numbers, but still some of it leaked to the local networks as evidenced on the morning's broadcasts.

Something had to be done and soon.

"Ben and Abby, you're a team today. Ben, here's the list we discussed. Did you get in touch with your buddy from the shooting range?"

"Affirmative," Ben replied as he scanned the list, then stuck it in his shirt pocket. "Gotta hit the bank first for some dinero. I'm thinking Abby might help in negotiating a better price." He winked at Abby who gave him a crooked smile.

"Josh and I are getting the rest of the stuff. I heard back from my contact this morning. We're supposed to meet their guy at three today." As usual, Joe was not forthcoming regarding his 'contact', but I knew about the items he'd asked for and assumed this was the same group that had outfitted him in the past. It was risky taking help from people we didn't know anything about, but we had no choice.

And they'd promised to deliver everything Joe had requested, no questions asked.

"I'm staying here?" Dylan questioned. "What about the buddy system?"

Abby and I exchanged a look. "We thought you needed some time alone, Dylan. You're welcome to come with us if you want, but I think hanging out with the crew here," I gestured to the furry group lounging around the kitchen, "might be the best thing for you."

"Yeah, I guess you're right. I need to make a lot of phone calls anyway." I knew Dylan would prefer to make the funeral arrangements in private. He wouldn't want us hovering around, giving him pained looks of sympathy and watching his every move for signs of a breakdown.

Ben and Abby pulled out of the gravel drive ahead of us, but we soon lost them. Ben knew only two speeds: breakneck and dead stop.

It was a good hour and a half drive from Decatur to Pearl Street in Dallas. By the time we arrived at Ian's shop, it was almost lunch time. I figured we'd tie the scarf around the door handle, pop in to say hello and explain what it was doing there. We hadn't seen or heard from Ian since dinner the night before last. I remembered his sudden departure from the restaurant that night as we approached the darkened shop.

"That's weird," I said, trying the door just to make sure the CLOSED sign wasn't an oversight. All the lights were off too.

"Hopefully everything's okay. I guess I better try to call him," I muttered. Joe looked like he couldn't care less whether Ian was up in his apartment sleeping in or dead in a ditch somewhere. I scrolled down to my incoming calls to pull up his number. After five rings, I got his voice mail.

'You know what to do.'

I left a message for him to call. We were responsible for drawing him into this mess – I'd hate to add him to our growing list of casualties.

"Let's go next door and see if they know anything," I told Joe, indicating a boutique to the right of Ian's shop. As we opened the door, a bell announced our presence, prompting a buxom, middle-aged woman to scurry over. Half of Walgreen's makeup aisle had been applied to her face.

"What can I help you gentlemen with?

A lacy negligee for your wives? Or girlfriends? Perhaps something a little racier?" she asked with an exaggerated wink of unnatural eyelashes.

"No, no, nothing like that," I replied, embarrassed by the adventurous nature of much of the shop's inventory.

"Oh, then something for one of you gentlemen, perhaps?" A knowing smile was added to the dramatic stage wink.

"We were just hoping you might know the whereabouts of your neighbor next door," Joe offered, amused by my discomfort.

"Oh, the Irish fellow?"

"Yes, Ian Connolly," I replied. "Do you know him?"

A delicate sniff of disapproval. "Well, I've met him, but I can't say that I know him. Not the friendliest guy in the world."

"Really? He seemed quite friendly to us," I replied, surprised. "We just met him a few days ago and thought we'd drop by to say hello, but his shop is closed. Do you know where he might be?"

"No, no idea. He certainly doesn't check

in with us and he comes and goes as he pleases. Not the proper way to run a business if you ask me. It's been that way ever since he opened his shop three weeks ago."

"Three weeks ago? Surely you're mistaken," I blurted, even as a myriad of alarms sounded in my brain.

She raised an amused, penciled eyebrow. "Hardly. I've been in this location for seven years. I know everyone and everything that happens on this block. He's an odd one, that guy. He moved into that space three weeks ago. He lives in the loft apartment above it. The really strange part, he literally moved in overnight. One evening I locked my store and went home, and the next morning when I came to work, there was this fully stocked shop with the sign in place and everything, in a spot that had been vacant for six months. I'm glad they finally leased the space. It helps everyone to have a fully leased building.

"Of course, I immediately went next door to introduce myself and welcome the new tenants. It was just him, no staff or help to run the store. And, like I said, he wasn't overly friendly. He basically pushed me back out the front door once he realized I was just another business owner."

"We got the impression he'd been here for quite some time," Joe continued, shooting me an *'I told you so'* look.

The woman laughed. "You got the wrong impression then. Three weeks to the day, that's it. And if you ask me, he won't be around for much longer. I rarely see any of his customers leave his shop with a shopping bag. He must be as friendly to them as he is to me. Either that or he's the worst salesman on the planet. His shop is closed a lot of the time too, even during normal business hours. It's ridiculous!"

"Do you see any strange activity going on there? Government or perhaps military types going in and out?" Joe asked.

"Funny you mention that! Just yesterday there was a group of business types that went in and stayed for at least an hour. They looked like Secret Service or something – they were all wearing dark suits and sunglasses. Not the type of people you'd see going into a shop like that. And once, about a week ago, I saw a real weirdo go in there. I didn't get a close look at him but his movements struck me as odd. He was wearing one of those Indiana Jones hats and I could tell he was bald underneath that hat. Something about that guy gave me the creeps. I saw him across the street and when he started coming this direction, I prayed he wouldn't come in here. We get enough weirdos as it is, and something was really off about this guy. Anyway, thankfully he went next door. I could hear the Irishman's door ding a few seconds after he walked past. That's how I know he went in there."

"Did he ever happen to tell you where in Ireland he was from?" I asked the woman. An inconsistency in Ian's story, previously ignored or unacknowledged by my conscious mind, chose that moment to surface.

"As a matter of fact he did. When I first went over to introduce myself and found out he wasn't American, I asked where he was from. He said Killwagon in Ireland. I remembered it because it sounded like something Dexter might drive around in. You know, that show on TV about the serial killer who only kills other serial killers? I figured he would drive something called a Killwagon." The woman seemed happy to have remembered this tidbit.

"Kilwoghan..." I corrected. "You've been such a help – thank you so much for talking to us," I said, grabbing Joe's elbow and pulling him towards the door.

Back on the sidewalk, I said to Joe, "Do you remember dinner at Abby's house when Ian said he was from Kilwoghan?"

"Vaguely. I knew it was a name that I didn't recognize like Dublin or Belfast."

"Well, the other night when he treated us to dinner at that fancy restaurant, Abby asked him to tell some stories – Irish folklore, fairy tales and such. During one of them, he mentioned that the legendary grogoch was said to have come from Kilbarry, which was his hometown. Kilbarry, not Kilwoghan as he'd originally told us and apparently that woman too."

"So he's a big stinking fraud," Joe said with obvious satisfaction. "Just as I suspected. I knew something wasn't right about him."

"Yeah, but who the hell is he and what does he want?"

"The million dollar question is why the hell did a hybrid go into his shop?"

Joe was nodding in agreement when I saw quick movement behind him and heard a voice I knew all too.

"Damn, I was hoping this could be avoided, gentlemen. I don't think I'll stand a chance with Abby if I kill you, but c'est la vie."

Ian stood directly behind Joe. Judging by my uncle's expression, there was a gun pressed into his back.

Chapter 14

"Please, no sudden moves. I'd prefer not to kill you out here on the street, but I will if I have to. Let's go inside and have a little talk, shall we?"

Joe was furious to be at the mercy of this man whom he'd disliked all along – and for good reason, as it turned out.

"Slowly, and I mean *slowly* remove your weapons and place them on the counter there," he instructed once we were inside the store. "Now we're going upstairs where we can have some privacy for our chat." He prodded Joe with the gun, which meant I had to do exactly as he said.

At the top of the stairs he said, "It's unlocked, just go in and sit on the sofa. And please don't try anything stupid. I'm quite adept with this thing."

My mind raced as I considered various scenarios to turn the tables on this bastard. I dismissed all of them as I watched the level, confident manner in which he pointed the gun at us.

"Help yourself to the scotch there on the table. It's never too early for a nip of the good stuff, right boys?"

I started to decline then the stirrings of an idea began to formulate. I splashed some of the amber liquid into two heavy crystal glasses which sat on the coffee table in front of the sofa. I feigned defeated resignation as I sat back against the cushions, holding the scotch on my knee.

"So, I'm guessing 'Ian Connolly' isn't your real name," I said as the man sat down in front of us, holding the gun steady at chest level in my direction.

"Indeed not, but it's one I answer to at the moment...among a few others."

I wanted to smash my fist into the teeth of that smug smile.

"What's your game, then? Who do you work for?" I was surprised at the conversational tone Joe managed, considering how much he hated this guy – had hated him before he'd even known he was the enemy.

"I don't think you understand the dynamics of the situation, Mr. McCullough. The person holding the gun gets to ask the questions. Makes sense, yes?" Clearly, 'Ian' was proud of himself at the moment, which gave me some hope. Overconfidence can be a liability.

"Now, the two Omegas that you killed the other day – I must know the details of how you managed that. Surely, you don't expect me to believe that you and the sweet, delectable Abby killed one yourself. What exactly happened? And please, don't exclude even the smallest detail, as I will know...and that would make me upset with you."

I decided to play it straight and told him the detailed version of our fight with the hybrids, or as we would now call them, the Omegas. It seemed fitting to differentiate them from the other hybrids like Grog.

"Where exactly on the creature did Abby's blade pierce? Lower back, upper back, left, right center?"

I started to stand so I could demonstrate the location in question on my own back. "Slowly, Joshua. Too much moving around on your part makes me nervous, and I have a bit of an itchy finger at the moment as it is."

I continued at an exaggeratedly slow speed and pointed to a spot on my own back that was in the region of the right kidney.

"And the exact spot where your knife went in on the first round?"

I pointed to an area of my ribcage on the left side. I'd gone over those events in my mind numerous times since the incident and had come to the conclusion that my first blow must have gotten very lucky and managed to slide in between the Omega's ribs, piercing the lung. It must have been what slowed it down enough for Abby and I to accomplish what we had.

"Hmmmm, so you must have hit the lung. Lucky shot. No doubt that's what saved your life. Do you have any idea how lethal these things are?"

"I think we have a pretty good idea," I replied.

Ian studied me with an amused air. "You think your little encounter with two renegade Omegas has made you an expert on these creatures? I could tell you things that would make your skin crawl," he said with the same theatrical tone he'd used the other night at dinner. Whatever or whoever 'Ian' was, he certainly had the soul of a performer, which gave me an idea. The one character trait that every actor or performer I'd ever encountered in my personal and professional life had in common was narcissism. I would pander to his ego and see what information I could glean.

"You've had contact with these Omegas yourself?" I asked with what I hoped was the right balance of grudging curiosity and admiration.

"Of course," he replied. "Did you ever ask yourself the question, what are these things doing in this particular part of the city? This specific city block?"

I kept the annoyance out of my voice when I answered. "Certainly we have. Grog told us he was here for sanctuary but we've gotten no closer to the reason the Omegas are here."

"Yet now that you suspect I'm not merely an innocuous shopkeeper, you still haven't considered the unlikely coincidence that I am here and they are also here?"

I hadn't given it a thought until that moment. "They're here because of you," I said.

"Bingo!"

"Why, Ian? What are you doing here? Are you their ally? Some kind of human liaison?"

"You're not too far off. Squad leader might be a better term though."

The ramifications of that statement filled me with dread.

"You're saying that you command these killers?"

"Indeed. They don't seem to resent it much, despite the fact that they're superior to their human creators in every way. They just like to kill, and I present them with opportunities in which to do so."

The horrific image of John Saretsky as I'd last seen him flashed through my head.

"You had them kill Dylan's parents." It wasn't a question but a statement.

"It seemed a reasonable response to the murder of two of their brethren," he replied. "As a matter of fact, that phone call I received at the restaurant? It wasn't an alarm at the shop...it was the green light to go forward with the Saretskys. My idea, of course. You seemed so pleased with yourself after killing two Omegas, I couldn't resist the opportunity to take you down a peg or two."

"How many of them do you have?" Joe asked.

Ian's gaze shifted to my uncle. "You mean Omegas? And why should I tell you that, Mr. McCullough?" the Irishman asked.

"Why not? Clearly you have no intention of letting us out of here alive, so why not indulge us? I've got a lot of questions that have been piling up for quite a few years now."

To my amazement, Ian seemed to genuinely consider my uncle's request. "Well, you have a point, I suppose. You're right. Neither of you is getting out of here alive.

And just so you don't get any bad ideas about trying to jump me, you should know you'll both have a bullet in your brain before you make it past the coffee table. Top of my class and all. That's why I was put here."

The narcissist couldn't resist a captive audience. I silently applauded my uncle. At the very least we'd bought ourselves some time and perhaps much more.

"Now then, I'm responsible for ten Omegas at the moment. Originally it was a dozen, but you and the lovely lass saw to that, didn't you?" The mention of Abby put a gleam in his eye.

"What are your plans? Why bring them here?"

"Dallas was chosen as the test city, and it was quite an honor to be selected to lead this inaugural mission."

"Test for what?" I said, intrigued despite the dangerous situation.

"Well, the eventual takeover of the country, of course. And ultimately much more." His smile was more lascivious now than when he'd mentioned Abby.

"The New World Order then? Is that it?" Joe asked, as if he'd suspected it all along.

"Ah, you're familiar with us then? I'm not surprised. Any UFO junkie worth his salt would have heard about us. Our disinformation campaign has worked brilliantly for years – hiding in plain sight behind the cover of outlandish theories and paranoid delusions. Of course, that's not really what we call ourselves, but the concept is accurate. As you probably know, there are currently no extraterrestrials here to whom we can give our allegiance in order to gain world domination as these wild theories suggest. Just their D-N-A." He over articulated the letters and smiled.

"So, you're saying Dallas is the only city the Omegas have infiltrated?" Joe asked.

"Indeed. If all goes well here – and so far it's been remarkably glitch-free thanks to my masterful handling – the next city will be Denver."

"How will you do it? How will you bring about the collapse of our country with just a few Omegas placed in a handful of cities?"

The bright blue eyes slid back to me. I noticed Joe's intentionally belittling phrasing had the desired effect.

"A *few* Omegas are capable of exterminating thousands of humans in a remarkably short time. A *few* is all we need in each city to incite panic, along with the help of some well-placed operatives in local government, law enforcement and key utility companies. You were smart in not going to the police with your concerns, by the way. You wouldn't have gotten much help."

"So, you bring in the Omegas, kill a bunch of humans and then what? You have a city full of panicky people. How does that translate into world domination?"

His confident smile became creepier by the minute.

"Panicky people are easily controlled people," he replied serenely.

"The remaining Omegas are still at the base then?"

"For the moment. Once Dallas is going according to plan, they'll be sent on their way." He studied our reactions for a few seconds before continuing. "It's a pity you won't be able to go forward with your ridiculous idea to storm the base and wipe out the Omega population. Even though the facility has changed hands, so to speak, most of the security measures are still in place. Without the proper credentials you wouldn't have a snowball's chance in hell of getting in there." He glanced at something in the corner of the room. "It would have been fun to watch though. I'd fully intended to tag along but alas, it wasn't meant to be." He waved the barrel of the gun in a small circle, still pointed at my chest.

Ian sat in a chair facing us with his back toward the door, so didn't see it open. It took every fiber of self-control I had to keep my eyes focused on the man before us, while banning the image of Grog to my peripheral vision. I sure as hell hoped Joe was doing the same thing.

As Grog crept up behind Ian, I resumed the question and answer session. "How many years has this plan been in place? Decades, I'm guessing?"

"Oh, yes. The bio-genetics part took many, many years and until recently was a dismal failure. You should see some of the freaks those scientists came up with! Totally useless too, but fascinating to look at. Pity that most of them had to be destroyed – we could have made a fortune off them on the sideshow circuit!"

Grog now stood behind the Irishman. Careful to keep my eyes on Ian's face, I still noticed the slight cocking of Grog's head when Ian spoke the last sentence.

"So you say the base has changed hands. Who's in control of it now? I assume it was run by our government prior to the change?" Ian opened his mouth to respond, but before he could speak a word, Grog grabbed the Irishman's head. In a move identical to the one he'd used on the Omega in the office building, he snapped the neck. The gun fell to the ground and Ian slid sideways in his chair, dead.

The hybrid studied us. His body language seemed anxious and unsure.

"Thank you, Grog. You saved our lives." I stood up, knees trembling. That had been close.

He nodded, happy now. His mouth

twitched and I know he was sparing us the effects of a full-blown smile.

"Well, that was a squeaker," Joe said, walking toward Grog, hand extended. "Thank you. If you hadn't come when you did, we'd have been dead. I owe you a huge debt of gratitude."

Grog stared at the hand for a few seconds before understanding Joe's intent. I suspected he'd seen people shake hands before, but this human courtesy must not have been extended to the hybrids. After a moment, he gripped Joe's hand in his own. There was no smile now. As I watched the exchange, I knew Grog appreciated the gesture and understood its meaning.

I locked the door leading to the stairs. I had no idea who else might show up and we had some business to do before we left.

"Joe, you start in the bedroom and I'll go through this," I gestured to a pricey-looking credenza in the corner of the room – the item Ian had glanced toward when he mentioned the credentials for gaining access to the base. I started at the top, rummaging through all the nooks and crannies, before giving up in disgust after the second time through.

"Damn, I was sure I'd find something in here."

Joe emerged from the bedroom carrying a silver Halliburton case.

"Found an interesting toy in there."

He set the case on the coffee table and flipped open the top. Nestled in a bed of foam rubber, was what looked like a prop weapon from *Dr. Who*. I'm no gun expert, but even I could tell this was no standard production weapon.

"Interesting. Anything that looks like a proximity card or magnetic key card kind of thing?"

"Nope, just this. I'm getting kind of antsy to get out of here Josh. I feel like a sitting duck."

"I know, I know. Me too. I just knew we'd find something in that credenza though. He looked right at it when he was talking about access to the base."

"Maybe there's a hidden compartment. If there's anything that should have its own secret compartment, it'd be the keys to Dulce Base."

"Okay, then you go through it and see if I've missed something."

Joe rooted through all the drawers in exactly the same order as I had – it must be hereditary – and came up with the same, frustrating result.

At that moment, Grog moved from his post by the door toward the credenza. With ease, he lifted the end of the very solid, very heavy desk and moved it three feet from the wall – just enough to reveal the wall safe hidden behind its bulk.

"Did you know about this, Grog?" I asked. Had the hybrid been involved with Ian somehow as his Omega brethren were?

Grog shook his head – a denial, then tapped his right temple with a long finger: *'No, dumbass, I just figured it out.'*

I laughed despite the tenseness of the situation. "Okay, smarty pants, can you get it open?"

The hybrid shrugged his shoulders and shook his head again. It seemed even he had limits.

"Let me try," Joe said. "This looks like a standard hotel type safe – actually pretty low tech for a guy like Ian. Maybe he figured it was just a redundant layer of security and got lazy."

After a few seconds of trying several combinations of numbers, the safe remained closed. We would waste too much time trying to figure out what it might be and in the meantime, anyone or anything could come through that door.

I surveyed the living room and spied what I was looking for.

"Stand back," I said, hefting a twenty pound metal plant stand and smashing it against the electronic keypad.

We got lucky. The small door popped open.

Joe reached in and pulled out two pieces of credit card-sized plastic – one silver and the other blue. Neither contained a photo, just some printed letters and numbers and a magnetic strip on the back.

"Let's get that case and get the hell out of here."

We made good time getting back to my

car and left Pearl Street as soon as traffic would allow. It felt surreal to see Grog sitting in the backseat wearing his seat belt, his hands in a neat fold on his lap. He watched the scenery fly by with an expression that reminded me of a one of Dylan's pets on a joyride.

"You sure there's nothing you need to bring? Clothes, toothbrush? Stuff like that?" I asked his reflection in the rear view mirror.

He shook his head and mimed a keyboarding motion: *'I'll explain later.'* The mystery of Grog's toilette would have to wait. On the way to the car, I had explained that I wanted to him to go with us. He'd agreed instantly with a nod of his head and climbed into the back seat like he'd done it a hundred times already.

If anyone other than Ian's people discovered his body, we'd be in big trouble – the lingerie shop owner would have no trouble identifying us.

###

We had a few hours before our appointment with Joe's contact, so we went shopping for the rest of the items on our list, as we'd originally planned to do before being held at gunpoint by a crazy Irishman. Grog waited in the car while Joe and I went into a Dick's Sporting Goods store. We came back with arms full of shopping bags.

I was glad for tinted windows because no matter how humanlike Grog appeared from a distance, close up he clearly was not. As I studied him in the rearview mirror on the drive back to Decatur, I found myself wondering about his day-to-day life. What did he eat? Did he sleep at night like most people? What were his biological and physiological processes? Did he poop and pee like humans, or did his alien side have a more efficient way of dealing with such issues?

"Do we assume that bastard told his compadres about our eventual plans to get inside the base? If so, they're gonna know we're coming," Joe asked, interrupting my contemplation of Grog's morphology.

"Yeah, I thought of that. If he did, they'll have no idea when and how. Thank goodness we didn't tell him about Grog helping us. They'll think we're going in blind."

Joe's suspicion of Ian had prompted me to promise not to discuss the details of our plan with him. At the fancy dinner, we'd made no mention of our conversation with Grog after we'd killed the Omegas, the valuable information he'd given us, nor the fact that Grog had agreed to help. Whoever these New World Order people were, they would only know that a small group of civilians lacking any special skills or equipment were intent on wreaking havoc on their highly-secure installation and the dangerous Omegas still residing there. They'd probably gotten a good laugh out of it.

"So, we figure the NWO jerks are the ones in control of the base now?" Joe asked.

"That would be my guess. Grog said the humans who were still there after Clean Sweep were a mixture of new and old. NWO must have had people in place there, just as they do everywhere else, it seems. Thinking about a shadow government operating within a black ops project of our own government makes my head spin. We still don't know who all the players are, and we probably never will, unless I can get Loretta alone in a soundproof room sometime. She probably knew about Ian and could have warned us if she'd wanted to."

Joe shrugged. "What's done is done," he replied. "You know where you're going?"

"Yep."

The address Joe had been given was an odd choice considering the gear we hoped to acquire: Bluebonnet Hills Cemetery, located in a sprawling, high-end suburban area. I'd been to this particular cemetery on one sad occasion the previous year, so knew exactly how to get there.

The designated spot within the cemetery grounds was secluded and far from prying eyes. Our contact was already there waiting – a tall, scarecrow of a man wearing corduroys, a plaid shirt and a windbreaker. I hadn't given much thought to what Joe's contact would look like, but I was surprised to see a human swizzle stick sporting L.L. Bean and leaning casually against a silver Land Rover.

I looked at Joe with raised brows.

"I've met him one other time before

when he brought me some stuff. Seemed like an okay guy," he said.

"Yeah, that's what we thought about Ian," I replied.

"No, that's what *you* thought about Ian."

We pulled up behind the SUV and I popped the trunk. Grog had positioned himself on the backseat floorboard, out of sight, as I'd instructed him to do. I had no intention of letting anyone know we were transporting such precious and unusual cargo – not even people who might be considered allies.

"Hello, Joe!" Scarecrow extended a bony hand. "This must be your nephew, Josh!" The hand was thrust at my torso with even more enthusiasm. I shook, surprised by the strength.

"Neil Young – no relation. Pleasure to meet ya, Josh!"

"Neil Young, really? You must get some grief about that," I said.

"Indeed, indeed! And the really sad thing is I can't stand his music! Really, really hate it. Give me a good piano or violin concerto, and I'm a happy camper. I hate all that rock and roll stuff."

The man looked about my age, but I could picture him in the role of a kind, straight-laced fatherly type in one of those black and white sitcoms from the sixties.

"Well, let's get down to business, shall we?" He pulled the Rover's key fob out of a front pants pocket and pressed the hatch button.

Inside was a mercenary's wet dream.

"It's all here," Neil the scarecrow continued. "And, a few extras we thought you might be able to use." He grinned.

I was impressed. The pile of weaponry and electronic equipment would certainly improve our odds of success. I think at last count, we were at one in a million. These shiny playthings probably bumped that up to the same odds as the Cowboys making the playoffs – not good, but not completely out of the realm of possibilities.

"Now, here's the part you're not going to like," Neil said, his tone paradoxically buoyant. "This is a package deal. Where these guys go," he indicated the Rover's cargo, "I go too. No wriggle room on that either, Joe." He administered an affectionate shoulder punch to Joe.

"What the hell, Neil?" my uncle replied. "You know they didn't say a damn word about that yesterday."

"True, true. They told me it might be a sticking point, but I knew I could make you see reason. We've been working with you for quite a while now, Joe. We've given you everything you've ever asked for and then some. We expected very little in return, and that's the case here too. Do you have any idea of the value of these items?"

He could have been *The Price is Right*'s host, chatting with a contestant.

"Not a clue, and it doesn't matter anyway. We've already been burned by someone who we thought was a friendly. Not gonna let that happen again." Joe's face was set in stubborn lines.

My eyes darted back to the treasure trove in the Rover. "So, you're saying they want you to stay with this stuff to protect monetary assets? I thought money was no object to them."

Neil showed the first sign of discomfort,

shifting from one skinny leg to the other. "Well, it's not so much a monetary concern, but rather to make sure they're used properly and for what they're intended. I mean, let's face it – if you decided to chuck it all and retire to Tahiti, you could easily do it with what these trinkets would bring on the black market."

Joe replied, "You know, and they know, exactly how much time I've got left in this world. That would never happen. I'm guessing they're worried we're just gonna screw things up. Is that it?" Joe's anger was beginning to fade. He seemed almost amused now.

"Well, Joe, I'm not going to lie. Some of these devices are quite technical and even though your knowledge is admirable, they felt that the expertise I bring to the table would tip the odds a bit more our way."

"What about the policy of no direct involvement?"

The question hung in the air for a few moments. Neil squirmed, which prompted a satisfied smile on my uncle's face.

"Excellent point, Joe. Excellent point.

The thing is, it's all escalating beyond what we'd projected. Not everyone is in agreement on this decision, but it was ultimately decided we had to take a more proactive role. And frankly, the consequences of that decision may quite well be our undoing." His tone had become less game show host and more Walter Cronkite, a shift which suited him. I suspected we'd just glimpsed the true Neil Young.

"I have no idea what that means and of course you won't explain it, I'm sure," Joe replied, weary now.

"You know how that goes, Joe. I wish I could, but there'd be hell to pay," Neil replied, brightening at the chink in Joe's resolve.

"What's to stop us from just hitting you over the head and taking the stuff?" Joe asked.

"Well, there are safeguards in place, of course, but I just don't see you as that kind of man, Joe. You have too much honor. *'Mine honor is my life; both grow in one; Take honor from me, and my life is done.'* Shakespeare," Neil said without a trace of patronization. He seemed to think it summed the situation up perfectly.

Hell, maybe it did.

Neil had hit a nerve and everyone knew it. Of course we weren't going to jump him – we hadn't devolved that far...yet.

I took a few seconds to ponder my response. The bottom line was we were in danger with or without this guy. If he or his group intended to screw us over, why go to all this trouble? There were much easier ways for people with such resources to keep us quiet. Neil came with the goodies and together they increased our chances of success and hopefully reduced the odds of someone getting killed.

"I say yes," I said.

Joe nodded in resignation. "Yeah, I thought you might."

"Okay, Neil. I hope you brought an overnight bag. You sure as hell better know what you're doing."

Neil's smile was dazzling in its relief. "No problem there, Josh. I'm kind of a tech geek. This stuff is right up my alley, so to speak."

I studied him for a moment, then said, "It's a dangerous alley, Neil. I hope you realize that."

Chapter 15

"Honies, we're home! And we brought company!" I announced as we walked into the Decatur house.

"Who's the skinny dude?" Ben growled. He held what appeared to be a new firearm, which was now pointed at Neil's head.

"He's okay, Ben. We'll explain everything."

Dylan and Abby emerged from the kitchen and introductions were made. Abby engulfed Grog in a bear hug. The expression on his strange features was pure, human delight.

"No shit? *Neil Young*? Your parents must have hated you," Ben said. Neil looked injured but didn't respond. "Okay, let's see what you brought us, Neil Young."

The contents of Neil's Land Rover, plus the gear Joe and I had bought at the sporting goods store, took up much of the floor space in the living room. It looked like Christmas at James Bond's house.

"Well, fuck," Ben said sitting back on the sofa after Neil's brief explanation of what everything was and how it worked. "This means we're gonna have to change things up a bit. Still, I like what I'm seeing. Pretty impressive stuff, Neil Young."

"Um, you can just call me Neil."

"Not a chance, Neil Young buddy," Ben replied.

I felt sorry for the skinny fellow. Ben was like a Doberman with a beef rib in situations like this. Don't ever let on that something has gotten under your skin or there'll be hell to pay for weeks – perhaps longer, depending on his level of boredom.

"Now, surely you realize you're going to tell us all about yourself and the organization you work for. You can't expect us to trust you, not knowing a damn thing about you and where your loyalties lie." Ben continued. His casual tone held an underlying menace.

"Well, you see, it's like I've told Joe – he knows how this works – there's not a whole lot I can tell you folks. I'm sworn to secrecy and all that. Sorry to say, but it's for everyone's good, mine included, that we keep a tight lid on things."

"Yeah, yeah, yeah. I know about your 'arrangement' with Joe, but that dog don't hunt anymore, Neil Young. Today we're going to have a new arrangement and in that new arrangement, you're going to tell us what we want to know or we're going to duct tape you to a chair and leave you to rot here in the boonies while we go off to New Mexico with all your fun toys."

Ben didn't blink an eyelash as he waited for a response.

Neil's Adam's apple bobbed in his skinny throat. My cell phone rang, alleviating some of the tension. Ben glanced at me in annoyance. His goal had been to keep that tension building and crack this skinny nut.

The caller ID showed 'blocked'.

"Hello, Loretta," I said.

"Joshua, hand the phone to Mr. Young. I need to talk to him briefly."

Finally, one of my suspicions was confirmed. Neil Young worked for Loretta, which meant the group who had helped Joe in Dulce, and her group, were one and the same – or at least affiliated. Two tiny pieces of the puzzle snapped together…finally.

"What, he doesn't have his own phone? You guys cutting back on expenses?" I replied.

"If we were, you wouldn't have half a million dollars' worth of equipment at your disposal." I let out a low whistle. She continued, "Mr. Young volunteered for this assignment and as part of the deal, he has severed all ties with us. We'll have no further direct communication with him after this, so there can be no backlash to our group. In case you don't realize it, you should be extremely grateful for his help and his sacrifice."

I handed the phone to Neil.

"Hello? Yes, ma'am. Everything is fine. No problems. What? Are you sure? Okay then. Yes, ma'am. Thank you very much.

You're welcome, ma'am. Goodbye, now." He handed the phone back to me, a bemused look on his face.

"Well, folks, I guess this is your lucky day. Probably mine too," he added with a glance at Ben. "I've been given authorization to release certain information to you people with the understanding that it goes no further. I have your word on that?" He looked at each of us in turn, his eyes gleamed with an intelligence and intensity that had been missing before. Or masked.

At that moment I realized I'd need to reevaluate my initial assessment of Neil Young. I remembered his Shakespeare quote about honor and knew that word carried a great deal of weight with the man.

"You have my word," I said, which was echoed by everyone else in the room. Even Grog, who had been patiently sitting in a chair waiting for instruction, gave a fervent nod.

Neil started to speak but I held up my finger to stop him.

"Monica just texted and she's on her way,

so let's hold off on these revelations until she arrives." I paused. "Also, something significant happened today that we need to tell you about in the meantime," I said, sitting back in one of the cozy recliners. I wondered how often the Saretskys had sat in this chair. Was it John's or Margaret's? People always had their favorite chair, or spot on the sofa in their living rooms, and it seemed important to know in whose chair I sat.

I felt good about Ian's demise. I just wish he could have suffered a bit first.

We took the next fifteen minutes to relay the morning's events. Everyone was duly shocked, except for Ben, who professed to have had a feeling about the Irish bastard all along, and Neil, who hadn't known him but was visibly interested in everything about him, and the information he'd shared before his death.

The knock at the door startled everyone except Grog, who'd probably heard the car five minutes before it arrived.

"It's Monica." Her muffled voice was recognizable. I opened the door and stepped out onto the front porch. I needed to warn her about our two newest additions.

When she entered the living room, her face revealed only the slightest trace of surprise when she looked at Grog. Her years of training served her well.

Introductions were made and it was finally time to get down to business.

"So, Neil, you guys know about this New World Order business?" Joe asked.

"Of course. They've been in existence for a very long time and have placed their people in many areas of government and law enforcement. We have too, but our resources and objectives are of a different nature, so we haven't duplicated their reach, so to speak."

"Please tell us about your organization," I said. "Everyone on this death mission deserves to have answers."

Neil nodded in agreement. "Think of us as sort of a watchdog group. We try not to meddle directly with the natural order of things, but rather we stay on the sidelines and observe, only getting involved when we perceive a serious threat with large scale implications."

"So you see these New World Order people as a serious threat?" Joe asked.

"Yes, always, but certainly much more so now. The roots of the group go all the way back to the birth of our country and beyond. Yes, the Illuminati, as they were known then and to some extent, still are today." He nodded to me when he saw I grasped the implications.

"William Guy Carr's theory that there was a powerful, clandestine organization in existence which was intent on controlling the world wasn't outlandish - because it was true. But it was quickly sensationalized by the NWO itself. They made his research appear to be the delusions of a conspiracy-obsessed nut job – a classic maneuver they used regularly to cloak their activity. Don't try to cover it up, just dress it up a bit to make it sound crazier than it actually is. Then all the reasonable people will throw the baby out with the bath water.

"It's really only been since the early 20th century that their agenda became clear to us." He paused for a moment, observing the intense focus of everyone in the room, then continued with a tight smile.

"A one-world, oligarchy-based government in which the leaders are selected by themselves and from within their own elite, possibly genetically-related class. Similar to the feudal system during the Middle Ages, actually. There is no lower, upper or middle class in this scenario – just rulers and servants. All laws would be globally uniform and enforced by a NWO police force and military; no longer are there nationalistic or regional boundaries, no more countries. Just the One World government leaders and their one billion or so worker bees." Neil paused again, reaching for the glass of water Abby had brought him.

"What do you mean one billion? There are seven billion people now," Abby asked, the horror on her face indicating she already knew the answer.

"Yes, according to Dr. John Coleman, another distinguished man the NWO would have us believe is a nut job, the population will be reduced and limited in a variety of ways. Controlling the number of children families are allowed, targeted manipulation of famine and disease are just a couple methods they'll use – until a more manageable population of one billion is all that remains. These remaining people will be useful to the ruling class for the services and manual labor they provide." He paused again, taking a group pulse on what we'd just heard.

"If you're having trouble swallowing all this, that's because you've been conditioned to be skeptical on the subject," Neil continued again, after noting Monica's arched eyebrow.

"For years, educational and media influences have been manipulated in order to orchestrate skepticism on certain key topics, such as conspiracy. When you hear the term 'conspiracy' or 'conspiracy theories', what type of reaction do you generally have before you've even heard what the conspiracy theory is? Disbelief? Distrust? Exactly. There's a term the CIA uses: *slides*. Slides are conditioned responses triggered by specific keywords. Essentially, they short circuit a person's thinking process under conditions when they would otherwise be inclined to examine the issue or subject intellectually. You hear conspiracy and your knee-jerk reaction is skepticism or even hostility in some cases. Of course, everyone is different and some aren't susceptible to this conditioning, while others are pliable and receptive. Most people, though, are somewhere in the middle. Joe is likely one of the ones on whom this technique didn't work.

"Our group is made up of many people like Joe, because years ago we figured out a method to minimize or neutralize the effects of the brainwashing, similar to how de-programmers work with rescued cult victims.

"But all this is just the tip of the iceberg. The NWO is likely responsible for many global conflicts – Bosnia, the Gulf War, Kosovo – the list goes on and on. In addition to the slide technique, they also use something NWO researcher David Icke calls 'problem, reaction, solution'. First, their strategists create a problem. This usually takes the form of a well-funded and trained opposition force whose job is to stimulate controversy and turmoil with an established political power in the area they wish to control. These opposition forces are usually referred to as freedom fighters or liberators in order to designate them as the good guys – even though they're often criminal types. Then the NWO-controlled media portrays the existing political power as evil and oppressive. Most freedom-loving people jump on the bandwagon, only too happy to support such a noble cause. In this information age, it's easier than ever to garner support using visceral images which depict the atrocities evil tyrants are inflicting on innocent civilians. This is the 'reaction' phase.

"The UN peace keepers then go in, which of course is the 'solution'. These are in fact NWO agents who are now in control of the area. Once in place, they never leave. The idea is to have NWO-controlled troops in all major countries and strategic areas."

He paused to take a sip of water.

"All media outlets are controlled by them?" I asked.

"Not all, but a couple of the big ones are. In the news business, nobody wants to get scooped, so the NWO-controlled news services begin airing coverage of these conflicts, then the other outlets follow suit. Before you know it, it's big news. Bigger than such isolated events might otherwise be if it weren't for the sensationalized coverage. Everyone reacts with outrage, and support is then given to oust the tyrants and replace them with a UN sanctioned temporary government. Or in some cases, the so-called Freedom Fighters take over who, of course, are merely puppets of the NWO.

"This has been going on for many years. They have strongholds now all over the world – the Middle East, Africa, Asia – in addition to much influence in more advanced countries where they simply place their people in positions of power within the existing governments. It's all part of the big build-up to be positioned for the end of the world as we know it, which of course, they will orchestrate."

"And very soon, it would seem," I said.

"Exactly," Neil continued. "As this Ian fellow confirmed, the United States is next. We knew they had agents planted at the Dulce Base all along. We were fortunate to convince one of the workers there to funnel information to us when he was able. He didn't make it through Clean Sweep. Most people who weren't connected to the NWO didn't. Clean Sweep was prompted by NWO agents located in the base, in order to get rid of everyone there who wasn't affiliated with them. They instructed the Omegas to kill certain humans in order to trigger the government's Clean Sweep response protocol.

"The response was intended as a worst case scenario in the event the Omega hybrids rebelled and posed a threat to the human population outside of the base. Everyone who worked there was required to sign a waiver stating they'd been told of the protocol and accepted the consequences that it might, at any point, be initiated. The general consensus was, of course, that it was highly unlikely, and the wages these workers were paid made it worth the gamble.

"The Clean Sweep protocol required that all hybrids, the Omegas and the Zetas, such as Grog, along with everyone and everything else inside the base be exterminated – the wiping clean of the slate, as it were. But of course that's not what happened. The NWO agents orchestrated the Omega's rebellion, then arranged for a secure area for the hybrids and their own people to evacuate to when Clean Sweep began. We think it's a biohazard level 4-type facility where the pathogens used in Clean Sweep couldn't reach them."

"Are these pathogens still dangerous?" Joe asked.

"We don't think so. We think the government used a type of bio weapon which delivers a deadly but short-lived virus. They probably released it through the ventilation system. A bio hazard level 4-type facility would have a separate ventilation system, of course."

"I don't like the sound of 'we don't think so'," I said. "Although you must be fairly certain the pathogens are no longer viable or you wouldn't have volunteered to go with us."

Neil nodded. "You have to remember, there are still Omega hybrids and NWO people there. We doubt they've stayed within the biohazard area this entire time."

"Our government killed its own people," Joe said in disgust. "I'd suspected as much but never wanted to believe it."

"In all fairness, it was for the greater good," Neil replied, his tone reasonable. "The last thing anybody wanted – well except for the NWO – was for the Omegas to escape into the general population. The desire to kill, which had been genetically engineered into them, was a stronger prime directive than anyone thought possible. We have evidence that the government was seriously considering shutting down the program and euthanizing the Omegas just prior to Clean Sweep. Too bad they didn't or we wouldn't be in this situation now."

"So, how did Grog survive? Did they put the Zetas into the biohazard area along with themselves and the Omegas?"

"Unknown," Neil replied. "Until meeting

Grog, we didn't even know there were any left. We assumed only Omegas and NWO members were spared. Perhaps he can answer that himself?"

The hybrid squirmed under the sudden scrutiny.

Abby, seated next to Grog, spoke to him in a gentle voice. "Do you understand what we're talking about, Grog?"

He nodded slowly but also held up his hand and tipped it from side to side. *A little.*

Dylan handed his laptop to Grog.

"Do you understand what Clean Sweep is, Grog?" I asked him.

He began to type.

'One day Grog is told to stay in different room. Others like Grog also but more bad ones. Many more bad ones. Also some humans."

"What happened when they let you out?"

"Many humans dead. Other things dead. Grog and others carried them to outside. Put in big hole. Humans made fire on them."

"They torched the remains in a mass grave," I said.

Grog nodded.

"Is that when you and the others escaped?" Abby asked. Grog shook his head.

"No. Waited three more days. Human bosses talked to Grog and others. Bosses said to hurt humans. Out here. Grog did not desire to hurt humans. Grog and others like Grog went outside and did not come back with bad ones. Came here."

"Hmmmm. It seems the NWO people may not have realized they'd mixed up Zetas with the Omegas," Neil said, thoughtful. "I can't imagine how such a mistake could have been made."

"Neil, surely our government would have determined by now that Clean Sweep was not a complete success," I said. "Why didn't they send in a squad of Navy SEALS wearing biohazard suits to wipe out whatever was left in the base?"

"Because the few people in the government involved with the base and who pulled the stings to make it happen are most certainly NWO higher ups themselves. They simply reported to their peers that Clean Sweep had been a success. End of story as far as everyone but NWO people thought."

"Remember the names Skinner gave us?" Abby said. "Those were some powerful people. They would have the kind of political leverage needed for what we're talking about."

"And now the NWO is using the Omegas to initiate panic and chaos in American cities so they can take over during the ensuing confusion. If I hadn't seen the evidence myself, I'd sure have a hard time believing it," Monica said. "Why use Omegas for this? Why not just use human mercenaries?" I asked.

"Excellent question," Neil said. "We believe the reason is to elevate themselves to the status of 'creator' in the eyes of the population, once the information leaked out that these creatures aren't entirely human. They created these hybrids, therefore they created life. That places them at the very top of the food chain, above average humans, in a god-like position. Theoretically, if they're perceived as such, then it would be easier to gain control of the humans who believe it."

He paused, tilted his head and shifted his attention back to Grog.

"I'm still baffled by the mistake they made in keeping some of the Zetas alive," Neil continued. "Grog, may I ask you some questions?"

The hybrid gave a slow nod.

"Were the Omegas, the bad ones, kept separately from the ones like you – the Zetas?"

"Bad ones kept away from Grog and others. Desire to hurt too much. Always desire to hurt. Grog is Zeta?"

"Yes, we think so. We know there were many failed genetic experiments. We think the Zeta group was viewed as a success except for one flaw: the urge to kill wasn't strong enough – thus the further tweaking which resulted in the Omegas." Neil directed this last bit at us. "The question is whether they were spared from Clean Sweep intentionally or if it was truly a mistake. Visually, they're identical, so I suppose it's not out of the realm of possibilities that it could have been an oversight."

"But if the Omegas were isolated from everyone and everything else," I said, "how could such a mistake have been made when it was time to get those intended to survive to the safe area? If it wasn't a mistake, what was the reason for keeping the Zetas alive? Does it seem realistic that with such tight security, a few hybrids could simply wander away from the base?"

Nobody had the answer. I found myself studying Grog.

"Grog," Neil continued. "What is your prime directive?"

"Not understand."

Did I see a trace of obstinacy on those strange features?

"Do you know what the humans wanted from you?"

Good grief. Why hadn't we thought to ask this question before?

Suddenly, Grog seemed very unhappy.

"Grog," Abby said and placed her hand on his arm. As he gazed into her lovely face, the wide mouth turned down at the corners.

"Grog like human friends. No desire harm

them."

"Did the human bosses want you to hurt humans, Grog?" Neil pressed.

Grog shook his head, his frown deepened. Finally, he began to type again.

"Human bosses tell Grog and others like Grog, Zetas?" He looked at Neil who confirmed the question. *"Human bosses tell Zetas..."* Despite the remarkable improvement in his language skills, he seemed to struggle for the appropriate word now. *"Warn? Human bosses if bad ones Omegas desire disobey."*

"Oh, I get it. Because of the telepathy between the hybrids, the Zetas would be able to pick up on thoughts of mutiny or rebellion. Makes sense," I said. I could tell there was more. "What else, Grog? What else did the human bosses want you to do?"

His sigh was heavy and human-like.

"Human boss tell Grog be nice to human friends. Human friends need trust Grog. Grog tell human boss information."

My heart sank.

"You were supposed to spy on us?"

Grog appeared confused by the question. 'Spy' was not in his vernacular.

"You were instructed to become friends with us, then tell your human boss – was it Ian? – everything we were doing and talking about?"

Grog nodded and looked as miserable as a child caught with a stolen candy bar. *"Spy? Yes Grog no desire to spy. Tell human boss Ian little data. Ian tell Grog many times learn much data but Grog no desire help Ian. Grog not like Ian."* He looked at Abby now, seeking forgiveness.

Her southern manners failed her. She shook her head, disappointed and wordless.

Neil broke the awkward silence. "Grog, did you really escape from the base, or were you and other Zetas part of the team of Omegas that travelled to Dallas with Ian?"

Grog turned away from Abby and nodded. He focused on the keyboard, avoiding eye contact.

"Grog not obey Ian. Grog like human friends and keep friends safe from Ian and Omegas."

As disturbing as the prospect was that Grog had been a spy, he had a point. He had saved our lives on two occasions. But was it enough to prove his loyalty to us? Considering what we were about to embark upon, and how much we'd be relying on Grog's help, could we risk it?

For the next few hours, well into the night, we discussed the events which would occur on what might be the last day of our lives. Strangely enough, the following days before leaving for Dulce, were some of the happiest I'd known. Not because we would soon embark on a dangerous mission, but because later that evening when everyone headed for bed, Abby motioned me to her room and shut the door behind me.

Chapter 16

Our three-vehicle caravan left the sanctuary of the Saretsky's bartered home on a gloomy late October morning. Earlier that morning, Dylan had taken the animals to the clinic where they would be well cared for by Candace and his staff. Neil drove point in his Land Rover, accompanied by

Joe and Monica, who argued about leaving her own vehicle behind, but was eventually overruled. She was a woman who liked to be in control of her surroundings, and relinquishing that control to a stranger went against the grain. They achieved a compromise when Neil agreed to split the driving with her.

The trip to Dulce would take thirteen hours. Ben and Dylan brought up the rear in Dylan's Explorer, and Abby and Grog rode with me in my Accord, sandwiched between the other vehicles.

We'd been at the ranch house for four days without incident, fine tuning our plan and training with our smorgasbord of weaponry. We had so much ammunition on ourselves and in our vehicles that a traffic stop for speeding would prove disastrous. We all agreed to drive the speed limit and obey all traffic laws – a challenge for Ben.

I was especially grateful for the nighttime hours when I hadn't been on watch duty. I'd spent them in Abby's room, in heaven. I was one of those lucky bastards who'd lost the love of his life, then defied the odds by getting her back. Anyone who wanted to take her away from me again would have to pry her from my cold dead hands.

During those days, some of Grog's alien physiology was revealed and partially explained, but much of it still remained sketchy. Yes, he ate food – he seemed to have a particular fondness for peanut butter – but he didn't seem to need much of it. I also assumed his body contained some sort of system for waste removal, but his trips to the bathroom were infrequent. He did sleep but not much. Almost every time I left the bedroom for a glass of water or for my turn at watch duty, I'd see him on the sofa, surfing the internet. The few times that I came up behind him, of which he was surely aware, I saw he was perusing topics such as English grammar, interpersonal communication and even American pop culture. It occurred to me then that Grog was largely self-educated. Had all the other hybrids, Omegas and Zetas, taught themselves our written language? Had they bothered? Or was Grog's desire to assimilate unique? His grasp of English had improved in a remarkably short time, which suggested learning more than simple commands hadn't been encouraged at the base.

Maybe the assholes behind all this didn't want the hybrids to know too much.

At any rate, I finally decided I didn't need to know too much about Grog's physical traits. He'd convinced me of his loyalty and his dedication to our cause, and that was all that mattered in the end. Maybe if we survived the next forty-eight hours, we could kick back with a beer (he'd actually sipped a Miller Lite and seemed to enjoy it) and discuss the finer points of hybrid anatomy.

I know Ben really wanted to ask him about his junk.

After a few hours of driving, we agreed to stop for lunch in Logan, Texas, a bleak, one-horse town just west of Amarillo. We pulled through a Dairy Queen drive-thru and took our greasy bags of artery-clogging fuel to a nearby rest stop. Dilapidated picnic benches beseeched weary travelers to stop for a spell and enjoy the marginal appeal of the lonely West Texas landscape. It was deserted, which mattered more than the ambiance. We made quick work of our steak finger baskets and Hunger Busters. We wanted to get to Dulce before dark.

I decided the restrooms probably hadn't experienced a good cleaning since the Carter administration, and rather than mirrors, above the sinks hung some sort of vaguely reflective metal squares – mirror wannabes which were just adequate enough to reveal the stranger coming up behind me.

The split second of warning the pretend mirror provided gave me sufficient time to dodge the blow that was aimed at my head. I swiveled around, pulling the Glock out of my holster in a fairly fluid motion, but not fluid enough to get a shot off before the Neanderthal came at me again.

He was big, so the uppercut to my jaw knocked me against the graffitied cinder block wall. My head snapped to the right, and in one of those weirdly lucid moments, I learned that *'Bubba has 12 inches'* and

'Darlene B. swallows'.

Fortunately, the big guy overestimated my sense of honor and left himself vulnerable to the vicious side kick I executed to his nut sack. As most men do when kicked in the balls, he went down on his knees. I coldcocked him with the butt of my gun. My hands shook from the residual adrenaline and my jaw hurt like hell, but I sure was happy that it was the goon instead of me lying face down on the urine-soaked concrete.

Before I could take a step, I heard shots fired.

I took a few seconds to edge my face around the opening of the rusty men's room door to survey the situation before I would fling myself into the fray. I'd be no help to anyone dead.

It wasn't as bad as I'd imagined before sticking my nose out the door. Abby, Dylan and Joe squatted next to one of the picnic tables where we'd just finished eating. All three, including Dylan, who'd put aside his aversion to lethal weapons since the murder of his parents, had their guns drawn and pointed toward the parking lot. Ben and Neil crouched behind two gnarled oak trees which were positioned between the picnic table and a shiny red pickup truck in the parking lot. The front windshield of the pickup imploded a second later when a shot from Neil's gun penetrated the safety glass on the driver's side. A groan escaped through the shattered opening. It was then that I noticed Monica fifty yards farther down in the parking lot, handcuffing a man who leaned over the hood of a blue sedan.

On the edge of my peripheral vision, I saw movement in the opposite direction. I swung around in time to witness Grog take on three more assailants, all with weapons drawn, who had just emerged from a late model Cadillac.

The assholes never had a chance.

They were all on the ground within ten seconds. From here, I couldn't tell if they were alive or not, and then realized I didn't much care either way.

The groans from the red pickup had stopped, but Neil and Ben approached in a cautious, low crouch with guns drawn. I made a dash to the picnic table and squatted by Abby.

"There was another one in the men's room," I whispered.

Abby scrutinized my face. I could tell by her expression I had been prettier going into the men's room than I was now.

"Did you kill him?"

"No, but he's out cold." I placed the thug's gun on the weathered boards.

She seemed relieved, but distracted. We watched Ben and Neil search the truck. Their body language told us there was no imminent threat. Monica bullied the stumbling, handcuffed man toward us. Grog left the three men on the ground and walked toward us in that fluid, big cat way. We all met at the pickup.

"The driver is dead," Neil said, sliding his gun into a belt holster. He might have been commenting on the weather.

As it turned out, that one was the only casualty. The three men Grog had dealt with were merely unconscious. That left us with a grand total of five living combatants and the question of what to do about them.

Ultimately, it was decided they would be tied up and placed in the Cadillac. The unlucky dead guy would stay where he was. Neil made an anonymous phone call. It would be left to the living to explain to the state police what had happened at the rest stop.

Several hours later as I watched the arid, unremarkable landscape of New Mexico through the passenger window, I examined our recent, inexplicable luck. Not only regarding this last assault, but the previous ones as well. Did the NWO hire inept thugs or were we just that fortunate?

The rest of the drive passed quietly. It was a tuckered-out group that checked into rooms at a La Quinta Motor Inn five miles outside of Dulce. Even Grog looked droopy-eyed. I realized with dismay that I was first up on watch that night. I was dog tired but deeply thankful we'd made it through another day alive.

Chapter 16

Our three-vehicle caravan left the sanctuary of the Saretskys' bartered home on a gloomy late October morning. Earlier that morning, Dylan had taken the animals to the clinic where they would be well cared for by Candace and his staff. Neil drove point in his Land Rover, accompanied by Joe and Monica, who argued about leaving her own vehicle behind, but was eventually overruled. She was a woman who liked to be in control of her surroundings, and relinquishing that control to a stranger went against the grain. They achieved a compromise when Neil agreed to split the driving with her.

The trip to Dulce would take thirteen hours. Ben and Dylan brought up the rear in Dylan's Explorer, and Abby and Grog rode with me in my Accord, sandwiched between the other vehicles.

We'd been at the ranch house for four days without incident, fine tuning our plan and training with our smorgasbord of weaponry. We had so much ammunition on ourselves and in our vehicles that a traffic stop for speeding would prove disastrous. We all agreed to drive the speed limit and obey all traffic laws – a challenge for Ben.

I was especially grateful for the nighttime hours when I hadn't been on watch duty. I'd spent them in Abby's room, in heaven. I was one of those lucky bastards who'd lost the love of his life, then defied the odds by getting her back. Anyone who wanted to take her away from me again would have to pry her from my cold dead hands.

During those days, some of Grog's alien physiology was revealed and partially explained, but much of it still remained sketchy. Yes, he ate food – he seemed to have a particular fondness for peanut butter – but he didn't seem to need much of it. I also assumed his body contained some sort of system for waste removal, but his trips to the bathroom were infrequent. He did sleep but not much. Almost every time I left the bedroom for a glass of water or for my turn at watch duty, I'd see him on the sofa, surfing the internet. The few times that I came up behind him, of which he was surely aware, I saw he was perusing topics such as English grammar, interpersonal communication and even American pop culture. It occurred to me then that Grog was largely self-educated. Had all the other hybrids, Omegas and Zetas, taught themselves our written language? Had they bothered? Or was Grog's desire to assimilate unique? His grasp of English had improved in a remarkably short time, which suggested learning more than simple commands hadn't been encouraged at the base.

Maybe the assholes behind all this didn't want the hybrids to know too much.

At any rate, I finally decided I didn't need to know too much about Grog's physical traits. He'd convinced me of his loyalty and his dedication to our cause, and that was all that mattered in the end. Maybe if we survived the next forty-eight hours, we could kick back with a beer (he'd actually sipped a Miller Lite and seemed to enjoy it) and discuss the finer points of hybrid anatomy.

I know Ben really wanted to ask him about his junk.

###

After a few hours of driving, we agreed to stop for lunch in Logan, Texas, a bleak, one-horse town just west of Amarillo. We pulled through a Dairy Queen drive-thru and took our greasy bags of artery-clogging fuel to a nearby rest stop. Dilapidated picnic benches beseeched weary travelers to stop for a spell and enjoy the marginal appeal of the lonely West Texas landscape. It was deserted, which mattered more than the ambiance. We made quick work of our steak finger baskets and Hunger Busters. We wanted to get to Dulce before dark.

I decided the restrooms probably hadn't experienced a good cleaning since the Carter administration, and rather than mirrors, above the sinks hung some sort of vaguely reflective metal squares – mirror wannabes which were just adequate enough to reveal the stranger coming up behind me.

The split second of warning the pretend mirror provided gave me sufficient time to dodge the blow that was aimed at my head. I swiveled around, pulling the Glock out of my holster in a fairly fluid motion, but not fluid enough to get a shot off before the Neanderthal came at me again.

He was big, so the uppercut to my jaw knocked me against the graffitied cinder block wall. My head snapped to the right, and in one of those weirdly lucid moments, I learned that 'Bubba has 12 inches' and 'Darlene B. swallows'.

Fortunately, the big guy overestimated my sense of honor and left himself vulnerable to the vicious side kick I executed to his nut sack. As most men do when kicked in the balls, he went down on his knees. I coldcocked him with the butt of my gun. My hands shook from the residual adrenaline and my jaw hurt like hell, but I sure was happy that it was the goon instead of me lying face down on the urine-soaked concrete.

Before I could take a step, I heard shots fired.

I took a few seconds to edge my face around the opening of the rusty men's room door to survey the situation before I would fling myself into the fray. I'd be no help to anyone dead.

It wasn't as bad as I'd imagined before sticking my nose out the door. Abby, Dylan and Joe squatted next to one of the picnic tables where we'd just finished eating. All three, including Dylan, who'd put aside his aversion to lethal weapons since the murder of his parents, had their guns drawn and pointed toward the parking lot. Ben and Neil crouched behind two gnarled oak trees which were positioned between the picnic table and a shiny red pickup truck in the parking lot. The front windshield of the pickup imploded a second later when a shot from Neil's gun penetrated the safety glass on the driver's side. A groan escaped through the shattered opening. It was then that I noticed Monica fifty yards farther down in the parking lot, handcuffing a man who leaned over the hood of a blue sedan.

On the edge of my peripheral vision, I saw movement in the opposite direction. I swung around in time to witness Grog take on three more assailants, all with weapons drawn, who had just emerged from a late model Cadillac.

The assholes never had a chance.

They were all on the ground within ten seconds. From here, I couldn't tell if they were alive or not, and then realized I didn't much care either way.

The groans from the red pickup had stopped, but Neil and Ben approached in a cautious, low crouch with guns drawn. I made a dash to the picnic table and squatted by Abby.

"There was another one in the men's room," I whispered.

Abby scrutinized my face. I could tell by her expression I had been prettier going into the men's room than I was now.

"Did you kill him?"

"No, but he's out cold." I placed the

thug's gun on the weathered boards.

She seemed relieved, but distracted. We watched Ben and Neil search the truck. Their body language told us there was no imminent threat. Monica bullied the stumbling, handcuffed man toward us. Grog left the three men on the ground and walked toward us in that fluid, big cat way. We all met at the pickup.

"The driver is dead," Neil said, sliding his gun into a belt holster. He might have been commenting on the weather.

As it turned out, that one was the only casualty. The three men Grog had dealt with were merely unconscious. That left us with a grand total of five living combatants and the question of what to do about them. Ultimately, it was decided they would be tied up and placed in the Cadillac. The unlucky dead guy would stay where he was. Neil made an anonymous phone call. It would be left to the living to explain to the state police what had happened at the rest stop.

Several hours later as I watched the arid, unremarkable landscape of New Mexico through the passenger window, I examined our recent, inexplicable luck. Not only regarding this last assault, but the previous ones as well. Did the NWO hire inept thugs or were we just that fortunate?

The rest of the drive passed quietly. It was a tuckered-out group that checked into rooms at a La Quinta Motor Inn five miles outside of Dulce. Even Grog looked droopy-eyed. I realized with dismay that I was first up on watch that night. I was dog tired but deeply thankful we'd made it through another day alive

Chapter 17

"I sure hope you can find that mole hole," Ben said to Joe during breakfast the next morning.

We were wedged into a large booth at the Denny's next to the motel. Appetites were healthy, considering we'd soon be making the pilgrimage to the Archuleta Mesa. I think we'd had enough time over the previous days to ponder our mortality and come to terms with it. This had become bigger than ourselves and it felt, at least to me, that once again we were low echelon chess pieces in somebody else's game – a game which could end with the deaths of an inconceivable number of people. It was too much to wrap my brain around, so I chose not to exhaust precious mental energy in this windmill tilting venture. I opted for mental blinders and tunnel vision instead. All that mattered was the mission. Backing out at this point never entered my mind and as far as I knew, nobody else's. Gathered around me were the finest people I've ever known – Grog included, even though we had him stashed at the hotel at the moment, his strangeness being too evident in the bright fluorescent light of the restaurant.

"I'm pretty sure I can, with Grog's help," Joe replied.

The first part of our plan involved finding the mysterious metal disc built into the ground on the top of the mesa. Neil had confirmed Joe's suspicion that a rarely used tunnel with an entrance on top of the mesa existed. His contact at the base had said as much, but Joe had been the only outsider to see it – until now. Grog explained, in his rapidly improving English, that the tunnel was used to allow the hybrids access to the outside on occasion. It was part of the assimilation process. If we could find it and manage to open it from the outside, it would be the easiest way into the base.

Hopefully the electronic code breaker that Neil had brought would get us in. We hoped this entrance might be less secure than trying to walk in the front door. If the security system installed at this remote entrance hadn't been updated in a while, it just might work.

###

Seven people and one alien human hybrid squeezed into two vehicles. Our backpacks, stuffed with an assortment of weaponry and electronics, took up much of the interior space. We navigated the desolate switchbacks which, after miles of rattled teeth and frayed nerves, delivered us to the top of the Archuleta Mesa. Once we crossed the river, we didn't see another motorist.

We pulled off the rutted dirt road in an area thick with tall grass, brush and pinion. The wind buffeted us when we stepped out of the vehicles; the chilly gusts moaned through a scattering of Ponderosa pines in the distance. I imagined a warning in the mournful sound: *Turn back! Leave now*!

Nothing but death awaits you here! Spectral fingers tickled the back of my neck as I shrugged off the sudden sense of foreboding.

Fuck those trees and the trigger happy hairs on the back of my neck. We had a job to do.

After taking a few minutes to scatter tumbleweeds and dead branches on the hood and roof of both Neil's Rover and Dylan's Explorer, we were satisfied with our camouflage job. Unless you were looking for them, they were almost invisible from the road. The rest of the trek would be done on foot.

An hour later, we finally arrived at the same area on top of the mesa where Joe had found the shaft entrance. When we stopped for a breather, having just navigated a treacherous stretch of cacti-infested countryside, Joe informed us we stood very close to the spot where he'd filmed the Omega throwing the humans over the cliff. I recognized the landscape from the video now that Joe had pointed it out.

We were close to the shaft. Grog confirmed it a few seconds later.

The job of spying motion detectors before we tripped them belonged to Neil and Joe, who were at point – electronic trip wires that would sound an alarm somewhere deep in the bowels of the mesa. For this chore, we had two specialized gadgets courtesy of Loretta which would hone in on the motion detectors, utilizing electronic sniffing sensors and minor sorcery. The advanced technology was beyond my pay grade.

Twenty yards later, we found the first one positioned chest high in a scraggly pine tree. Neil's device located it before we got close enough to activate the motion sensor. We stayed put while he skirted the pine and approached it from the rear. Within seconds it was disabled and we continued the march.

We found six more additional devices over the next twenty minutes. That was a good sign. Security would surely be increased closer to the portal. I just hoped we hadn't missed any. The longer we could mask our approach, the better.

"This looks right," Joe said, breathing heavily from the exertion of the hike and the thin mountain air. Grog nodded and then pointed to a clearing fifty yards ahead.

"Be mindful of where you're stepping," Neil said. "Pressure sensors may be buried in the obvious paths. We'll need to approach from the least inviting direction."

It turned out the least inviting direction was situated in a cacti field. A slow and painful hour later, we came upon the Holy Grail and found it remarkably nondescript.

The portal lay in the center of a small clearing, a manmade carbuncle marring the natural beauty of the mesa. The four-foot circular metal cover was positioned on top of three inches of poured concrete. Surrounding the glorified manhole was more of the same inhospitable terrain which had proven challenging to navigate. Cacti needles had already poked through our clothing in places, drawing blood, and some particular nasty nettles covered our legs from the knees down. I discovered it was a mistake to brush them off with my bare hands.

The smiles we exchanged were a mixed bag of exuberance, determination and angst. We had found one of the secret entrances to the mythical Dulce Base, and as far as we knew, hadn't alerted the occupants to our presence. If this had been Groom Lake or Area 51, we wouldn't have gotten within twenty miles of any entrance without being waylaid by a cadre of anonymous soldier types, who would have escorted us back out of the restricted area or shot us on sight.

Dulce Base was now the red-headed stepchild of the secret government base world, and we were counting on lapsed security – only a skeleton crew of NWO types remained, in theory.

We squatted next to the portal cover. Neil shrugged out of his backpack and placed it on the ground beside it. Hinged to the top of the metal disk was a stainless steel plate, six inches long and four inches high. Joe flipped it open. Under the plate was a small digital screen and a mini keyboard. Next to the keyboard were some electronic buttons and a USB outlet. Neil and Joe exchanged big smiles. This had been the weakest link of our plan. No USB outlet would have meant no admittance to the candy store.

Neil plugged in his code breaker.

This particular gadget represented a large percentage of the monetary value of the gear we'd received from Loretta. Despite its unassuming appearance, Neil informed us the technology contained in the thing was new and unique – it was the only such device in existence.

I held my breath while I watched the red, rapidly changing digital numbers scroll across the small screen. This was make-it-or-break-it time. Finally, the LED numbers changed to green and stopped at a fifteen digit number that nobody could have guessed without a magical device such as the one Neil held. He'd just earned his paycheck. If I ever saw Loretta again, I'd tell her to double his salary.

I don't know what everyone else expected, but I imagined the metal hatch would simply lift up after the code had been discovered – perhaps some theatrical fog

SECRETS UNDER THE MESA

would spill out from the opening.

That didn't happen. In fact, nothing happened.

The green LED just blinked at us, rather mockingly, requiring a further sacrifice in order to allow entry. The electronic buttons next the keyboard were labeled with letters that meant nothing to us.

But they did mean something to Grog.

He edged his way through the crouching humans and pressed the buttons in a pattern which worked magic. The hatch lifted open. No eerie mist rolled out from the bowels of the earth, but cool air, tinged with the odor of ammonia and decomposition, wafted over us. Attached to one side of the opening was a metal ladder which seemed to say *'come on down...we've been waiting for you!'*

Grog went first, as planned. His presence if noticed might not draw the attention that ours would.

This would be one of our most vulnerable moments.

A minute later, a low whistle came from below. Teaching Grog to whistle had been one of the highlights of the last few days. Once he'd finally mastered it, we could hear him whistling to himself almost every time he was alone. The thought made me smile.

Five minutes later, we were assembled at the base of the ladder in an empty corridor. The ambient lighting which emanated from the ceiling panels was dim, perhaps half strength of what it might normally produce. It illuminated walls and flooring similar to those of a hospital – colorless and without character. A series of closed doors continued down the left side farther than we could see. To the right, the view was different. Perhaps twenty yards of closed doors, but then the corridor ended in a large open area which appeared brighter than the corridor where we stood.

That was the direction we were headed.

The corridor was one of the spokes that channeled off the circular hub of the first level. We needed to get to the elevators which were located in the main hub. According to the now deceased former janitor, the rooms in this corridor were administrative, meaning they were probably now

SECRETS UNDER THE MESA 455

empty and unused after Clean Sweep.

However, the first level hub was where the security systems were monitored. Our first order of business was to eliminate any threat there first.

It wasn't easy being stealthy in hiking boots, but we did a decent job of it. Even so, Grog placed his finger against that wide mouth: *'please quit sounding like a herd of elephants'*. But we expected humans to be in the hub, not Omegas with their exceptional hearing. Taking out unsuspecting humans would be a cake walk with the firepower we'd brought.

At the end of the corridor, our group split into two teams – each team was poised along either side of the corridor. Monica stuck her face around the corner then gave the 'go ahead' signal. Ben took lead and dashed into the hub, followed by Neil and Monica – our three best marksmen. We believed the security area was to our right and that was the direction they went, quickly out of our line of vision.

The silencers on the guns muffled much of the noise, but to our ears, the gunfire still sounded loud. Six rapid shots fired, then a painfully long minute passed in silence. Finally, Ben appeared from the right and motioned the rest of us into the hub.

Still split into two groups, we began reconnoitering the remaining sections of the hub. My group of Abby, Neil and Grog took the computer room, which required walking past the security area where three dead people lay on the floor – two men and one woman. I glanced at Neil, whose face had lost all similarity to the kindly father in the fifties television show, and now resembled a grim and focused Alec Baldwin from *The Hunt for Red October.* Monica, Joe, Dylan and Ben were twenty yards away on the other side of the hub, approaching the power room.

All three doorways to these areas were open and the security card readers on the right side of all the doorways contained an illuminated green LED button.

Prior to Clean Sweep when the base was fully staffed, these doorways would have been sealed, according to Neil's insider. NWO security was either lazy or overconfident, and that made this part of our job a lot easier.

The computer room was massive and cold. At first, we saw no visible occupants, but when we rounded a corner of eight-foot high servers, we found one.

The shock on his face at seeing three heavily armed militant types and one hybrid was comical. He dropped his clipboard and raised his hands. If he'd stayed in that position, he might have lived through the day. Unfortunately for him, he made a move for the radio attached to his belt.

Neil dispatched him with a double tap to the chest. Alec Baldwin showed no remorse.

We moved on.

Next, we discovered a chubby, middle aged guy huddled under a desk.

"We can see you, doofus," I said. "Come out from under there."

"Did you alert anyone?" Neil asked while the man clambered out from under the desk and raised his hands. We could see he had no radio, but that didn't mean he hadn't hit some sort of panic button.

He shook his head to Neil's question, but his eyes shifted from our faces to the floor.

"How long until someone shows up?" I asked.

"I swear I didn't call anyone!" His voice was high-pitched and trembling.

"How long?" Neil asked.

The man's blustering demeanor visibly crumbled in resignation. "Probably five minutes. Maybe ten. We're terribly understaffed."

Best words I'd heard all day.

"How many?"

"I don't know! Maybe five or six guys. Like I said, we're really understaffed."

"What's your name?" Neil asked the man.

"Morgan. Bill Morgan. I'm just a computer geek. I don't have anything to do with the stuff that goes on in the labs or...anyw here else. I just do computer stuff, I swear!" Panic was setting in, triggered by what he saw in our faces.

"Abby, is the video on?"

"Yes, go ahead."

"Bill, tell us, briefly, what this facility is and what happens here, especially on the lower levels," I said.

Abby held the video camera at face level.

"You're joking, right? They'll kill me!"

"Please, Bill. We don't have much time."

Just out of the camera's range, Neil waved his gun so the man would see it.

"Okay, okay. This is the New Mexico Center for Biogenetic Study. Most people just call it the Mesa or Dulce Base."

"And what kind of work is done here? What is the primary focus?"

The man winced. I imagined that would play well for an audience.

"Mostly, they've been working on combining DNA strands from multiple organisms to create an improved life form."

"Improved in what way?" I prompted.

"In every way. Smarter, stronger, faster than humans."

"And what type of DNA did they mix with the human DNA in order to achieve this 'improved life form'?"

The expression on the man's face begged for deer antlers and headlights. He sighed, resigned.

"Extraterrestrial."

"And did they succeed?"

"Yes."

"Who is in charge of this facility and to what end do they intend to use these 'improved life forms'?"

"They don't tell me everything, you know." A last ditch effort at bravado was immediately quashed by a threatening motion from Neil.

"Okay, okay. We just call them the Bosses. They've promised that everyone who helps with their, uh, endeavor, will be richly rewarded. I'm pretty sure they're all over the world but, like I said, they don't tell us much. I think they're part of a shadow government that wants to control everything...everywhere." He whispered the last part, as if even now he was afraid of what his bosses would do when they found out he'd been kissing and telling.

"Are you familiar with the term New World Order, Bill?"

He nodded. "Yes, that's them, although I don't think that's what they call themselves.

When they recruited me, I really didn't have a choice. That's how they operate."

"And how do they intend to achieve this goal of controlling everything, everywhere?"

His deadpan response played perfectly for the camera.

"By killing everyone who gets in their way."

I gave Abby the signal to turn off the video. We had what we needed for now and the clock was ticking.

"You have access to the lower levels?" I asked the man. Despite the cool temperature in the room, rivulets of sweat cascaded down the sides of his flushed, round cheeks.

"No, just this level and level 2, where the cafeteria is."

For some reason he seemed to think this information might help his chances for survival. Maybe the fact that he hadn't been directly involved with the atrocities being conducted in the lower levels might exonerate him somehow.

"Sorry, Mr. Morgan. You're of no further

help to us then."

Neil put a bullet in his forehead.

Holy shit. When all this was over, I would overhaul my system for assessing people I just met.

Abby closed her eyes for a few seconds. When she opened them again, the look of cold determination startled me. I had just accepted the 'flipping the bird to the neighbors' Abby, and now it seemed she had moved on to 'watching cold-blooded murder and being fine with it' Abby. My heart ached as I realized it was all my doing.

There was nobody left alive in the IT room but us. It was time to get ready for the first wave of resistance.

As we emerged from the computer lab, Ben's team came out of the power room on the other side of the hub. Ben pushed a balding, surly looking man in a white lab coat from behind. The man's hands were cuffed behind his back.

"We got a key," Monica said.

"Excellent. We have company coming though," Neil said, gesturing toward the elevators. "Maybe five or six, if the guy was telling the truth."

"Okay, they'll be coming from Level 7, so which elevator is that?"

We knew ahead of time that the four sets of elevators on opposite sides of the circular hub ran exclusively to certain levels, but we hadn't had time to figure out which went where.

"These over here," Joe said looking at the metal plaque above the elevator closest to the security room.

"Get into position, people!" Ben said. "You," he pushed lab coat guy from behind, "lay flat on your face and don't move a muscle. Got that?"

This man had more gumption than the recently deceased Bill Morgan from IT. He spit at his captor, narrowly missing Ben's face but landing some saliva on his shirt. I knew there would be hell to pay later. Ben helped him get to the floor, probably breaking a few of his teeth in the process.

We had thirty seconds to prepare before a green button lit up over the elevator we now faced.

The metal doors slid open revealing a

small cadre of soldier types – all heavily armed. They reacted quickly to the threat of eight equally armed individuals, fanned out in front of the elevator, in a variety of prone or squatting positions.

We opened fire a split second before they did.

We operated from a position of aggression while theirs was pure defense. Three of them went down, but the remaining three rained a barrage of bullets down on us using fully automatic assault rifles, similar to the XM8s that we used.

They had superior training, but we had the high ground as well as the element of surprise. Aiming for the head and neck area, as we'd trained back in Decatur, did the trick. Within thirty seconds, the entire squad lay on the floor of the elevator.

The ensuing quiet on the heels of all that loud gunfire was unnerving. The elevator door began to slide shut, but a boot lying across the doorway kept it from closing.

Ben stood and approached the elevator.

"Careful, Ben. We could have a possum in there," Neil said.

The warning caused Ben to hesitate slightly before continuing his approach to the elevator – a hesitation which probably saved his life.

One of the soldiers sat up suddenly and fired a rapid series of bullets before his rifle quit working. His legs were pinned beneath two other bodies so he wasn't able to reach a new cartridge.

Ben took him out with a shot to the right eye from thirty feet away.

No other soldiers moved.

Now that the immediate threat had been removed, I did a quick survey of our group. Everyone was alive, but Dylan's face was bleeding. Abby noticed the blood at the same time and sprang into action. She slid the backpack off her shoulder, rummaged through its contents and pulled out our first aid kit.

A bullet had grazed his cheek. It hurt like hell and would probably leave a wicked scar but the wound was not serious. Abby had him cleaned up, disinfected and bandaged within five minutes. As the self-appointed medic of the group, she'd spent much of her time in Decatur practicing field dressings and reading everything she could find on the internet about combat first aid. Hopefully, Dylan's wound would be the only first-hand experience she would get on this mission.

But that didn't seem likely.

We removed the bodies from the elevator and moved them to the security room. Knowing that these men aided and abetted the bad guys didn't make it easier to deal with the carnage we'd wrought. They were all relatively young and all definitely dead. A two way radio attached to the shoulder of one of the soldiers squawked suddenly, then a man's voice said, "Bravo Two, do you copy? What is your status?"

Joe didn't miss a beat. He snatched the radio and responded.

"Roger that, Bravo One. Intruders dispatched."

Nothing but radio silence for a few seconds, then it crackled again.

"Roger, Bravo Two. What is your ETA?"

I could see Joe's mind working furiously, then he responded.

"Unknown. Multiple injuries. We're heading for the infirmary first."

"Roger that, Bravo Two. Report in from Level 3."

"Roger, Bravo One. Over and out," Joe said with a smile and stuck the radio in his backpack. "Hopefully they bought it. If not, they won't find us there anyway. Let's move, people."

"This one here," Ben said in front of the elevator closest to the power room. The metal plaque read 'Level 4'. That's where we were heading next: Level 4 and what we believed to be the biohazard area.

"Make it open, asshole," Ben growled to our prisoner as he removed the handcuffs.

Perhaps the sight of six dead soldiers had softened him up a bit. Without hesitation, he retrieved a key card attached to a chain around his neck and slipped it into the metal reader next to the elevator. Several seconds later, the doors slid open.

The elevator was large and smelled faintly of chemicals. We pressed the solitary button.

When the doors slid open again on Level

4, we pushed our captive out first in case anyone was in the corridor.

"It's clear," he said in a sullen tone. The handcuffs were back on and he was surely wishing to be anywhere else on the planet but here at this moment.

Level 4 was a maze of clinical looking corridors, none of which held interest for us other than the bio hazard area. The silence was eerie and oppressive.

"Why is it so quiet?" Ben asked lab coat guy with a shove to the chest for good measure.

"We've downsized, douchebag," he replied with a sneer.

Ben backhanded him.

"You want to keep that smartass behavior in check, buddy," Joe said. "For your own good."

"Okay, okay. We're operating with minimal personnel. Just the people who are part of the movement were allowed to stay on."

"Movement...as in bowel?" Ben asked.

Lab coat guy was barely able to choke back a retort. His lip was already swelling.

"Our organization," the man replied. "After the eradication of non-members, the remaining staff dwindled significantly. I wasn't even sure who all had been invited to the party until everyone else was gone."

"You mean dead," I said.

"Yes," he replied, defiance flashing in his eyes. "Just like you all will be very soon."

Ben cocked an eyebrow just before he backhanded him again.

"*Party*...that makes it sound rather innocuous," Neil said, his tone thoughtful.

"Which direction is the biohazard unit?" I asked.

"To the right," he said with a slur, turning his head to spit out a broken tooth.

Ben grinned. "By all means, please lead the way, my good man."

We met resistance as we rounded the next corner. Two people – a man and a woman – wore lab coats identical to our captive's. They were also armed as our captive had been previously, but their reflexes were not fast and they were still fumbling for their holstered handguns when our bullets ripped into their bodies.

We dragged them into what looked like a break room and continued.

After witnessing two of his peers disposed of without fanfare, our captive became more accommodating and informed us that we could expect perhaps fifteen or twenty people tucked away in various corners of the maze that was Level 4. Mostly scientist types, he said, as there had been no attacks on the base, nor any internal conflicts, so security had grown lax in the months following Clean Sweep.

We found the next group of five humans in a lab several minutes later. Despite our silenced weapons, the noise of bodies writhing about, slamming against tables and knocking items off counters, created a violent cacophony that seemed loud to my ears. I could only imagine what it sounded like to Grog. If there was anyone in the vicinity, they would be alerted, which decreased our odds of surviving each altercation without injuries or casualties.

Finally, we reached the hazmat area.

"I don't have access to this room. My card won't open it," our captive informed us through swollen lips.

"You could have told us that twenty minutes ago, *douchebag*," Ben said. The man flinched in anticipation of another blow that didn't come.

"Here's the moment of truth," I said as I fished a piece of blue plastic out of my cargo pants pocket. It was one of the two that we'd retrieved from the safe at Ian's loft. The silver one looked identical to our captive's and it had worked for the elevator. Since Ian was a squad leader for the Omegas, he'd most likely been isolated with them in the hazmat area during Clean Sweep, and his blue card should open the door – we hoped.

We were betting the farm, the town, the country and the world on it.

I slid the blue card in the electronic reader next to the metal door. It slid open, revealing a large room with an assortment of computers and scientific equipment, but no people. Another set of glass doors twenty yards ahead would take us into a chamber which would lead to the self-contained hazardous materials area.

That was the good news. The bad news: there was no magnetic card reader at the chamber. Rather, what appeared to be an optical scanner was the method of security used to access the inner sanctum.

"Grog, do you know what this is?" Neil asked.

He shook his head.

Ben shoved our captive to get his attention.

"Any of those scientists have access here?" he asked the man.

"Maybe. I didn't get a good look at who all you killed." The tone wasn't petulant, just matter of fact.

"Okay, let's go get one of them."

"I'll help," I said.

Grog pantomimed checking a watch.

"No, not yet. We need to make sure we can get inside first," I replied.

He nodded in understanding.

"Hold down the fort, people. We'll be right back."

It took another ten minutes to carry the dead scientist our captive had selected back to the hazmat area. At any minute the wrath of the NWO could come crashing down on us.

Ben held her body up to the optical scanner while Neil had the gruesome task of holding her eye open.

Nothing happened.

It took two more trips back to the lab, two additional dead scientists and fifteen minutes before we located the body with the ocular golden ticket.

The chamber door finally slid open.

"Now, Grog," I said to the hybrid. He closed his eyes and became very still.

Chapter 18

Joe took off his backpack and removed a metallic canister. Crushing sadness engulfed me. These would be the last few moments I'd spend with my uncle, and it was even more painful than I'd imagined it would be.

I hugged him for a full minute, somehow managing not to break down. Then everyone took their turn. Monica's embrace was lingering and intimate. Tears slid down Abby's face, silent and unchecked. The time for goodbyes had run out.

"Okay, get outta here. All of you. I got this covered," Joe said.

At any second, the Omegas would be here, summoned by Grog.

We scrambled out of the room, down the

corridor and around the corner – back to the break room we'd found earlier.

The moment after we'd hidden ourselves, an elevator dinged in the distance. My skin crawled at the thought of dozens of Omegas prowling the corridor outside. We heard no footsteps, but I sensed movement, perhaps a displacement of air, as they glided past the room where we hid.

Grog waited for them at the hazmat entry. He had connected with them telepathically, explaining (in whatever alien thought language they used) that another operation similar to Clean Sweep was eminent and they'd been instructed to take cover in the hazmat area as they'd done before. They would be safe there.

If all went according to plan, he would escort them into the contained area where Joe would be waiting. Once all the Omegas were inside, Grog would seal the door from the outside. Then Joe would release the deadly VX nerve gas Neil had brought for the purpose – the same nerve gas Saddam Hussein used on the Kurds in 1988. I have no idea how he got his hands on it. It might not affect their alien physiology, but the damage it would do to the part of them that was human should be enough. Within seconds of exposure, the Omegas would begin to convulse. Next was paralysis, respiratory failure, then death within a few minutes. We knew these creatures had lungs, and it followed that they would be vulnerable to a fast acting agent delivered through the air.

The horrible part was that Joe would suffer along with them. From the beginning when the plan was in its infancy, he had insisted on volunteering for the suicide mission. Of course, he was the perfect candidate – the only candidate, really. The cancer had seen to that.

Now, as I visualized what was happening in that room, I had a panicky urge to run back and save him – we'd figure out another plan. Instead, I counted the minutes on my watch and resolved to make them pay, as painfully as possible.

Finally after what seemed like hours, Grog appeared in the doorway and gave us the thumbs-up signal.

The Omegas were dead and so was my

uncle.

###

It was time for the second part of our mission: getting to Level 6 and freeing any human captives that might have survived Clean Sweep, or were newly-taken prisoners. Having discovered the agenda of the NWO and its Omega mercenaries, we didn't hold much hope for survivors. Most likely the humans who had been abducted in the last few months were dead, but we needed to make sure.

As we approached the elevator for Level 6, an ear-piercing alarm blared and the ceiling lights flashed red. Even though we had anticipated this, it was startling when it happened.

"Stealth mode is over. Remember, shoot everyone and everything on sight," Ben yelled over the jarring sound of the alarm.

The elevator to Level 6 was not accessed by a key card but rather another optic scanner. We were screwed.

Ben grabbed our captive. "You have access to this?"

The man nodded.

"Then do it!"

He placed his non-swollen eye level with the scanner. The metal doors slid open. We piled in while Ben and Neil guarded both ends of the corridor. Neil swept in behind me and as Ben moved to follow, rapid gunfire exploded.

When a bullet struck Ben, it seemed to happen in slow motion and with excruciating clarity. Then suddenly it was over, and the world moved again at a sickening velocity. He fell into the elevator and we pulled his legs inside. Dylan punched the button and the metal doors slid shut. We heard more gunfire and felt the impact on the closed elevator doors.

We headed down the shaft.

Abby tended to Ben on the floor, her movements smooth and calm. I didn't see any blood so allowed the tiniest seedling of hope to take root. His eyes were open and lucid – another good sign.

"Where were you hit?"

"Fuckers got me in the chest," Ben wheezed. Abby unbuttoned his shirt, revealing the Kevlar vest. Three slugs were embedded in the material. Ben probably felt like he'd been horse-kicked in the chest, but other than some sore ribs, he'd be fine once he got his wind back. I sent a silent thank-you to whatever deity claimed responsibility. At this rate, I might just allow those crazy Christians to convert me.

Dylan studied our subdued yet still hostile captive.

"Why do you have access to Level 6?" he asked the man. I recognized that clinical glint in his eye. I followed his gaze to our captive, feeling my fists clench of their own accord.

"I'm a medical doctor as well as a research scientist. I was asked to, uh, treat the patients there from time to time."

Not one person in the elevator believed him.

Abby stood to face him, getting very close when she asked, "Are people still there?"

"I don't know! I haven't been down there in a month or so. That part of the protocol has been put on hold."

"Come on, asshole...fess up. You weren't

treating those people. You were dosing them. Admit it!" Abby had her hands around his throat before anyone could stop her. We allowed a few moments of strangulation before the situation threatened to get out of control. With gentle firmness, Monica pulled her away from the man as he slumped to the floor, gasping for breath.

What a pussy.

I looked at him and asked, "Is that true?"

He nodded.

Abby composed herself and removed the video camera from its case. The elevator doors slid open just as she hit the record button.

The stench of human decomposition hit us – so noxious, I thought I could actually feel a horrific, viscous quality in the air.

Nobody wanted to step into the cavernous room that was Level 6, but we had to. Just as Doyle had described, prison-type cells ran along either side. The walls themselves appeared to be rock of some sort – whatever the mesa itself was made of. The dim lighting added to the oppressive, ghastly feel of the place. The smell of urine and feces underscored the lingering odor of decomposition.

Silence confirmed what the smell implied: there were no living people here. "Let's do a quick sweep, people. Abby, keep the camera rolling...we'll have this guy do the voice over," Neil gestured to our captive. "Then we need to get the hell out of here."

"What happened here?" Abby prompted the man as she panned the camera over the bodies in the first cells then held the camera up to his face. Her voice was so steady, nobody watching the video would have guessed she wept as she spoke.

Off camera, Neil aimed his weapon at the man's head as he'd done earlier. The captive seemed resigned to his fate and began to talk.

"They were put out of their misery," he said simply. "Plans had progressed to the next phase, so they were no longer needed. And we certainly couldn't just release them to tell the world what they'd seen or been subjected to."

"What had they been subjected to?"

"Experiments, of course. I wasn't involved with that part of the operation, so I can't say exactly. My job was just to keep them...manageable. And quiet."

"How many people?"

"Less at the end than when trials were being conducted. Perhaps thirty or forty here now."

"How many people would you say have passed through these cages?"

"Hundreds. Perhaps thousands since the beginning."

"And children? How many children, in your estimation?"

Abby began to waver. We had just about all we needed anyway.

"Children weren't part of the normal protocol, but if I had to guess, I'd say several hundred – since the beginning. I guess they were needed for certain facets of the experiments."

"How were they killed?"

He sighed. He knew his time was near.

"We just made them go to sleep. They never felt any pain...at the end."

Abby swept the camera around the room, slowly, one last time. I could imagine how the video would play to an audience – like a colorized version of the black and white images of Dachau and Buchenwald after the Allied Forces arrived.

"We need this guy for anything else?" Ben said in a voice that told me exactly what was coming.

"Nope," I said.

We left the man on the concrete floor of Level 6.

The next order of business would take place on Level 5. As we took the short ride back up, we began removing the MKI-II grenades from our packs. In the planning stage, we'd decided there wouldn't be time for planting explosive devices in the areas we intended to destroy. Quite possibly we'd be under duress as well, so the lightweight yet effectively destructive characteristics of the MKIIIs would do the job.

When the door opened up on Level 5, or as I'd thought of it ever since our conversation with Doyle the janitor, the home of the Creature from the Black Lagoon, we were caught off guard. Probably we were still emotionally processing what we'd just witnessed. Whatever the reason, when the elevator doors opened, we weren't ready for the firepower that hit us.

It was the same situation the soldiers on Level 1 had found themselves in. We hit the floor but not quickly enough.

Neil had the presence of mind to toss one of the grenades out before the doors closed again. I barely registered the muffled explosion as I looked in horror at the damage in the elevator.

Abby seemed okay. She was pulling out the first aid kit again while frantically tugging at Dylan's shirt, already soaked with blood. Neil was unhurt. Ben held his left bicep and grimaced in pain, but he was able to stand. Monica also had an arm wound but her demeanor indicated it wasn't serious.

Grog appeared physically okay but the expression of utter sadness on his strange features made him look more human than ever before.

I crouched next to Dylan just as Abby got

his shirt opened. The Kevlar had done its job protecting his torso from serious injury, but it didn't extend up to the carotid artery in his neck. Blood pumped rhythmically from the wound. More quickly than I would have thought possible, it saturated the floor.

"Stay with us, Dylan. Don't you dare close your eyes!" Abby sobbed.

He struggled to obey, but the effort of keeping them open was more than he could manage.

"Josh, you'll take care of the gang, right?" he whispered. "The house is yours. It's all been taken care of. That apartment is way too small for them."

"Don't talk like that, Dylan. You're not going anywhere," I hissed through chattering teeth. I was freezing and my brain didn't seem to be registering events properly.

"Josh, just promise me, okay?" Dylan pleaded. "The legal stuff is already taken care of. I'm counting on you, buddy."

What the hell was he talking about? I wondered. *Why was it so damn cold in here?*

SECRETS UNDER THE MESA

Neil slapped my face.

"We don't have time for that, Josh. Snap out of it," he said, then slapped me again for good measure.

After the second slap, he and I both realized there was blood on his hand. Then everything went black.

Chapter 19

Regaining consciousness felt like swimming from the bottom of a dark lake to the bright sunlit surface. The acrid smell of ammonia assaulted my sinuses and a loud explosion brought me fully to the surface.

We were in some kind of dormitory.

"What happened? Where are we?" I sat up quickly, then wished I hadn't. The dizziness made me fall back down to the tiled floor.

"We're on Level 7," Monica replied.

"What are we doing here?" I tried to get my brain to function, but it didn't want to cooperate.

"Who the hell knows? Ask him," Ben gestured to Grog who was removing a MacBook from his pack.

"After you passed out, we went back to Level 1. It was crawling with bad guys, blocking our primary means of escape. Grog insisted we come to this level. We think it's where all the hybrids were kept," Abby said. Her face was blotchy and eyes were red.

Then I remembered what would make her look like that.

"Dylan?" I whispered. She glanced to her right. I followed her gaze and saw my best friend lying on a narrow metal-framed bed...one of the dozens that occupied the space.

"He's gone, Josh," she whispered.

"Josh," Neil said, louder than necessary. "You'll have to grieve for him later. You sustained a head injury, but it seems the bullet just grazed your skull. The impact might have caused a minor concussion. Took a bit of hair and bone with it, but not much. You'll be fine."

I nodded. He was right. I would have to process Dylan's death later, but that didn't stop the crush of agony that rolled over me like a frigid Arctic wave. How would I ever come to terms with the guilt? How would I bear the pain?

"Is everybody else okay?" I said and started to stand. My head swam and my thoughts seemed disjointed, but it was getting better.

"Monica and Ben got hit, but they'll be fine too."

I felt the side of my head where a large bandage covered most of my ear and a good portion of my skull. That's when the pain decided to make an entrance.

"What was the explosion?"

"The elevator," Ben said grimly. "We sent it back up with a grenade. They can't use it to get to us now, but we can't use it to get out either."

"So we're stuck here? You've got to be kidding me."

"It was my idea," Monica said, her voice deadpan.

"Josh, we all agreed," Neil added. "You didn't have a vote because you were unconscious and the decision had to be made. We wouldn't have stood a chance against them in our current state."

"So, we're just going to rot here? Great plan," I said. "I think I'd have taken our chances rather than die in this shit hole."

"We needed to buy time. We also didn't want them getting Grog."

I hadn't considered that. He just might be the last hybrid alive at this point. Hopefully, we'd managed to inflict enough damage to cause some delays for the NWO. I wasn't naïve enough to think we'd foiled their plans completely, but perhaps we'd bought some time.

Grog finished typing and held up notebook so we could read what he'd written.

"Omegas and Zetas live here. In this place. Before. Elevators took us to areas. Outside and other places. One time we no use elevators. One time we crawl through square tunnels. Human bosses called it drill. Took us to outside."

And just like that, we were given a second chance. I could have kissed Grog on that creepy mouth.

"You mean like a ventilation system?" Neil asked.

Grog shrugged. He didn't know the word

ventilation.

"Metal tunnels shaped like a square," Neil pantomimed, "where air goes through."

Grog nodded slowly. *Perhaps.*

Ben smacked him on the back with his good arm and said, "Lead on, my man!"

We gathered up our gear and started to follow Grog toward the far side of the dormitory.

"What about Dylan?" Abby said. "We can't just leave him here."

"That's right," I echoed. "No way are we leaving him here."

"Look guys, there's no way we can carry him crawling through air ducts," Ben said, his voice soft. "Do you think Dylan would want us jeopardizing ourselves just so we could give him a proper burial? You know how he felt about that kind of stuff anyway. He always said he thought funerals were morbid and unnatural."

That was true. And I personally agreed with that sentiment. Still, leaving him here in this terrible place seemed like abandonment. How could I do that to my best friend?

"Josh, he's right. It's not like we're abandoning him." Of course Abby could read my thoughts. "Dylan, *our* Dylan, isn't in there anymore."

All that we'd endured during the last six months – even the loss of Joe – didn't compare to walking away from Dylan.

I would never forgive myself.

"Let's go."

We followed Grog to the far end of the dormitory and turned left down a small corridor. It appeared to be a service area with rooms marked 'Electrical', 'Housekeeping', and finally, 'HVAC'. That's where we were headed.

Inside were several commercial A/C compressors to the left, and large electric heaters on the right. Grog walked up to one of the huge compressor units and motioned for us to help him move it. It was heavy as hell but we managed to slide it several feet from the wall.

Behind it was our escape route – a small square tunnel of metal sheeting. How in the hell would Ben squeeze his massive frame through that?

I could see he was having the same thought.

"Thank goodness it's a commercial system," Neil said. "Normally these ducts are even smaller. It'll be tight, be we can do it."

"I'll go last then," Ben said. "If I get stuck, I don't want to block anybody behind me."

Excellent point. But after leaving Dylan behind, I wouldn't leave Ben to an even worse fate. I'd go second to last.

Grog would lead, followed by Abby, Neil, Monica, myself and Ben. Just as we had decided the order, we heard sounds coming from the corridor – faint but unmistakable.

They were coming after us.

The destroyed elevator still had a shaft which our adversaries were able to utilize. Even now we could hear the screech of metal doors protesting a forced opening.

"Let's move, people!"

We slid a table under the opening of the air duct, which was more than six feet above the floor. Grog leapt onto the table then disappeared into the small square tunnel. The others were quick to follow.

I'm an average sized guy. Entering that closed-in, metallic tube was uncomfortable...I could imagine how difficult it would be for Ben.

"You coming, Benny? I know it's tight but I think you can do it," I said. I craned my neck, struggling to send the flashlight beam behind me. Ben still hadn't entered the tunnel.

"Ben, what's taking you so long?"

His face appeared in the lighted square opening several yards past my feet.

"Josh, think about it. They're coming. Right now I can hear voices - they've made it through. We can't leave the duct exposed like this. It will lead them right to you. I'm pushing the compressor back against the wall. That will buy you all some time."

I felt like I'd been punched in the gut.

"Ben, no. Don't do this, please! I'm coming back!"

"Too late, buddy. We're out of time. You take care of our girl, okay?"

And his face was gone.

I started to scramble backward down the tunnel as I heard the screech of metal on tile. The square light diminished with every second. Ben was strong and I knew he could move it on his own if he was determined enough.

"Ben, please!"

"No can do, Josh. Now get your ass moving."

Seconds later the fluorescent light was gone. The duct opening went dark.

"What's going on, Josh?" Monica hissed from twenty feet ahead. The glow stick held in her mouth cast her features in a gruesome caricature of the normally pretty face.

I couldn't say the words. I couldn't explain what Ben had done. It was too much.

"Just go," I said.

She began to crawl again. I caught up with her boot heels several minutes later. The weird lighting from the combination of glow sticks and flashlights added a feeling of surrealism. In my distraught mental state, I imagined we were a pack of trolls tunneling our way through a mountain – a metal mountain in some alternate universe or distant planet. I was jarred out of my reverie by the sounds of explosions and gunfire. I tried to block thoughts of Ben and focused on staying up with Monica's boots.

Time became impossible to measure. It might have been five minutes or thirty when we reached a 'T' in the tunnel. Grog crawled into the opening on the right. Like the legged sections of a centipede, we followed. Thank goodness for Grog and the drills he'd been subjected to. Anyone who didn't know their way around this aluminum maze would be screwed.

I heard Abby's voice from ten yards ahead.

"Grog says we're more than halfway through!"

It barely registered. All I could think about was that two of the people I loved most in the world wouldn't be emerging into the light with us.

We continued. The duct became more treacherous to navigate as it made vertical turns now too. Through a system of pushing and pulling and more than a few strained muscles, we managed to get

SECRETS UNDER THE MESA

everyone up and through.

I became aware of a change in the air quality. The piquant aroma of mountain juniper now mingled with the smell of metal and decaying bodies. When we made the next left turn, a wondrous sight greeted us – a rectangular shaped grid with daylight on the other side.

The head of the centipede got there first. Grog placed his long hands on the grid and pushed.

Nothing happened.

After several more attempts, it still wouldn't budge. The aluminum tunnel seemed to press in on me now that our forward progress had been thwarted. I could feel the stirrings of panic trying to gain traction in my psyche. I'd never liked closed-in spaces. The one time I'd gone for an MRI for a pinched nerve in my back, I had to take a Valium before I would let them slide my body into that cylindrical coffin.

I take deep breaths.

"You okay, Josh?" Monica asked, her head cranked oddly as she shined a flashlight in my face. The sweat was pouring down my face now – much more than the ambient temperature could account for.

"Yeah, I'm fine."

I heard Ben's voice in my head. *'Don't be a fucking pussy.'*

It had the effect of a glass of cold water tossed in my face. The panic began to subside.

"Grog can't get the cover off," Abby called down the tunnel. We'll have to use an explosive."

I could hear dialogue between Abby and Neil but couldn't make out what they were saying. Then Neil's voice

"Can everyone take off their Kevlar and be ready to put it over your heads? It's the best we can do."

Removing our shirts and then our Kevlar vests in such a cramped space wasn't easy or pleasant, but finally we got it done. Grog would toss the grenade, as he was closest and had the best aim.

"Tell me you're not using an MKIII for this," I heard Monica say to Neil.

"No, I think a 3A2 will do the trick," Neil

replied.

The MK3A2 was a concussion grenade used during close combat situations for minimizing casualties to friendly personnel and, as in this case, for blasting and demolition. We would still be much closer to the blast than we should be, but we'd squirmed another twenty feet or so back down the tunnel to put more air between us and the blast.

I hoped it would be enough.

"Okay, get ready, everyone!" Abby yelled. "On the count of three, Grog will pull the clip and toss. Everyone cover their heads! One...two...THREE!"

Under normal conditions, the explosion of an MK3A2 would be loud. In the tunnel, it damn near blew out our eardrums. I struggled to pull the vest off my head and strained to see through the smoke.

The clear blue sky, unmarred by the metal grid cover was perhaps the loveliest sight I'd ever seen. The centipede began to crawl again.

"Grog is out but he had to crawl up. Don't know what the deal is," Abby yelled back.

"Oh, shit. Now I do."

I could see her head poke through the opening of the tunnel into the blue sky. Abby had said 'shit'. That did not bode well.

"Looks like we're on the side of the mesa. It's a vertical drop of a couple hundred feet to the ground below," she said. "Grog went up but I don't see him now. I don't think we can scramble up it like he did."

I could hear the tremor in her voice. She wasn't bothered by tight, close spaces like me, but she hated heights. I learned this on one of our first dates when I talked her into going to Six Flags and riding the giant roller coaster. She said later she'd only done it because she didn't want to be tedious, but when the ride was over, she'd excused herself and run to the ladies room.

"There are no fucking places to hold on to!" The tremor was gone, replaced with the notes of hysteria.

"Abby, it's okay," I yelled. "Just take deep breaths. We'll figure this out."

"Great," Monica whispered under her breath.

"Josh, you know how I am! I don't think

I can do this!" The panic was gaining momentum now. I wish I could have gotten around Monica and Neil to reach her but it was just too tight. I felt helpless back here at the ass end of the centipede.

"I see Grog's head!" she yelled. "He's got a rope! He's motioning me to climb up! Oh shit, oh shit, oh shit! I don't think I can!"

I remembered what Ben's imagined voice had done for my panic attack. I hated myself for doing it, but I had to.

"God damn it, Abby, quit being a fucking baby! Just do it! People are counting on you!" Even from where I was, I could see the hurt on her face. It didn't last long though. She nodded and reached out into blue nothingness, pulling the rope inside the tunnel.

"Tie it around your waist, Abby," I heard Neil say but Abby was in a dangerous mood.

"I fucking know that, Neil," she snapped.

I smiled. That was a good sign.

"Okay, I'm letting him drag me out!" A moment later she was gone. Neil scrambled forward to take her place.

"She's okay!" he yelled. "The rope is coming back down now. I hope they're strong enough to pull me up," he muttered, almost out of earshot. Soon, he was out of the tunnel. Rocks and dirt fell past the opening. Then as if from a great distance, "I'm up! Sending the rope down again!"

Monica never hesitated. She had the rope around her waist and was out of the tunnel in less than a thirty seconds. The woman had some huevos.

Now that I was able to get to the opening, I could see why Abby had been terrified. I looked down to the pinion and juniper below. They looked like the tiny flora you'd see on a model train set. Abby had miscalculated the drop – it was easily four hundred feet. I was amazed that she'd been able to overcome her fear. Even for someone without a fear of heights, it was a sobering sight. I looked up to see the faces of Grog and Neil above me. The tossed rope fell right in my face. It looked to be about a fifteen foot climb to the top. I was amazed that Grog had been able to scramble up without the benefit of a rope.

Thankfully, I didn't have to.

With the rope securely tied around my waist, I hollered up, "I'm ready!" The rope went taut and pulled me out of the tunnel. Within seconds, my feet dangled four hundred feet above the earth. I grabbed scrub brush and rock outcroppings along the way, clawing and climbing with the upward impetus of the rope, helping to get myself up the cliff face as soon as possible. The wind gusted around me – cold and malevolent, like the exhalations of an angered deity. Ten more feet to go and I would kiss the ground at the top the second I got there.

As I was imagining how happy I'd feel to get off the wall of this mountain, the rope went slack.

I'd just latched onto a large sage bush and my feet had some purchase on a protruding rock, no more than two inches in depth. Otherwise, I'd have been on the ground four hundred feet below, a vaguely Josh-like meat suit full of broken bones.

"Hey!" I managed to yell. "What the hell are you doing up there?"

No response. Then the opposite end of the rope – the one that wasn't tied to me – flew down from above.

Something had gone horribly wrong.

I considered the possibility that armed soldiers from the base had been patrolling the area, or any number of other scenarios which didn't end well for my friends. Then I was forced to consider my own demise on the side of the mesa.

Chapter 20

I thought of Abby. A minute later, I started to climb. I reached for another rock outcropping two feet above the sage brush I'd been holding onto for dear life.

It held. I lifted my left leg up to a root of some desert tree which seemed fairly solid and might bear my weight. I hoisted myself up three more feet.

I had to go slow, but it was killing me. My mind was barely able to focus on the task of climbing. A myriad of scenarios, each worse than the last, flashed through my mind. All of them ended with Abby, dead, on the top of the mesa. A scrub brush I'd grabbed onto suddenly came out of the ground by the roots. I almost lost my balance but clutched onto a piece of rock exposed by the now absent bush.

Five more feet to go.

It took me another long ten minutes, but I did it. As I scrambled over the ledge at the top, the scene that greeted me was not one of the ones I'd contemplated while clambering up the side of the mountain.

Neil and Abby stood with their hands up. Grog was on the ground, unconscious. Monica stood in front of Neil and Abby. Her back was toward me, but I could see she held a gun in her hand which was pointed directly at them. The object she held in her other hand was a Taser. That would explain why Grog was on the ground and I'd heard no gunshots.

"Hey, Josh. Come join the party," Monica said in that level voice which seemed to define her. "I didn't know if you'd make it or not. You surprise me yet again." She didn't take her eyes of Neil while she spoke to me, but the gun was pointed at Abby. She knew that would keep me from making any foolish moves.

"Please make a wide circle around me and come stand next to your friends," she said. "I will shoot her if you make any fast movements. Hands up, please."

I gave her a wide berth and circled back around to stand beside Abby, the rope trailing behind me.

"I was just starting to explain to Neil and Abby who I am and who I work for. I admit to some feelings of camaraderie considering all we've been through together."

"That would be nice," I said, unable to keep the sarcasm out of my voice. "I can't believe you're betraying us like this."

"No, not a betrayal, Josh. That would imply that at some point I had loyalty to you and your little cause. That was never the case. I'm loyal to my employers, who pay me exceedingly well for what I do. And who will pay me an exorbitant sum once I deliver our friend to them." She indicated Grog's unmoving form, but her eyes never left us, and the hand which pointed the gun at Abby's chest was dead steady.

I thought with remorse of the Kevlar vests we'd left behind in the tunnel. They might have given us a fighting chance.

"So, as I was saying, you and Joe were

right about there being another 'player', as he called us. I have to admit, I wasn't entirely faking my fondness for him. He was a special kind of man, your uncle. Too bad we weren't able to recruit him."

"So who are you?" I asked. Of course I was curious, but at that moment, I just wanted to stall for time.

"In a nutshell? We're a multi-national firm which provides military expertise, state of the art equipment and highly trained troops to clients all over the world." Her smile was bland, a competent salesperson.

"Mercenaries," Neil said.

"Oh, Neil. We really hate that word. We're not so different from the defense contractors hired by the US military – although we don't operate with the constraints they do. Most potentates aren't as picky about political correctness as the good old USA.

"Grog, here, will be a feather in my cap," she continued. "I would have loved to have gotten my hands on one of the Omegas, but frankly, wrangling one of them would have been difficult. I think it worked out much better this way. In addition to providing me with such a magnificent trophy, you all helped me accomplish the second half of my mission, which was throwing a wrench in the gears of the NWO." The emotionless smile again. She might have been commenting on the weather.

I thought back on Monica's actions over the last week, but the one that stuck out in my mind was her protective behavior of the child, Lebron, at Doyle's apartment. Either there was a spark of humanity in her or she was the best actress on the planet. It prompted my next question.

"What about your daughter, Monica? Does she know what you do for a living? Quite the example you're setting for her."

A shadow of something – remorse perhaps? – flickered across her face, then was gone. I hoped I'd hit a nerve.

"Who do you think I'm doing this for?" she said. The smile was gone, replaced with that steely look I'd come to know well. "I'd been slogging away at the DPD for years, barely making enough money to support us, when I was approached. It was a no-brainer. I would keep my job with all the so-called benefits," she sneered, "but I would also be a recruiter and Girl Friday for my new employers. I was in a perfect position to provide a variety of services, and I just couldn't say no to that second salary."

"So, as usual, it's all about the money," I said.

Anger flashed in her eyes. "That's easy for you to say, Mister Entitled. You were given a free ride by your parents. Handed everything your entire life. You have no idea what it's like to be the daughter of illegals in this country. The way people look at you...judge you. I want better for my daughter than what I had."

"And you think this is the way to do it?" I taunted. "Betraying good people who are trying to help others? You plan to kill us, I assume? Do you really want your daughter to be successful in the way that you are?"

"No!" she spat. "I want better for her! Can't you see that? Everything I do, I do for her. I don't expect you to understand, and

I really don't give a rat's ass if you do."

Monica still stood with her back toward the edge of the cliff. Twenty feet behind her, a large cluster of sage brush moved in a decidedly un-sage brush-like way. A large figure emerged from behind it and practically flew the twenty feet to where Monica stood. Ben's brawny form smashed into her diminutive body, knocking her to the ground. The gun flew out of her hand.

She held fast to the Taser.

Quick as a ferret, she pressed the black box against his body. The reaction was immediate – Ben jerked and flopped on the ground, helpless and undignified. But, his initial assault had done the trick.

Neil grabbed the gun from the ground before Monica could scramble to it. I leapt the few feet toward her while she struggled to stand. Stomping down, I pinned the Taser-wielding forearm to the ground. I could feel the delicate bones break beneath my boot.

She cried out in pain and released the Taser, but I didn't stop. I grinded the sole of my boot into her broken arm, waiting for her to beg me to quit. When she finally did, I took another long minute of pleasure in her agony. Finally, I realized hurting Monica wasn't going to bring Dylan back. I made myself stop.

"Stay down, Monica. Don't move a fucking muscle or I will shoot you. That's a promise." She remained on the ground, beaten and diminished. She was actually crying now. I wished I could say I felt sorry for her, or worried about what might happen to her daughter now, but I didn't give a rat's ass about either one of them.

Ben still twitched, but he managed to sit up. The goofy smile on his face turned into a ghastly caricature every time his facial muscles convulsed.

"Good to see you, Benny," I said with a grin as goofy albeit less twitchy than his.

"Thanks for the breadcrumbs, Josh. I'd still be crawling around inside that ant farm if it weren't for you."

Seeing the glow stick in Monica's mouth had given me the idea. I had half a dozen wedged in a pocket and used every last one of them to lead Ben out of the air duct maze. I hadn't allowed any real hope that he would ever see them.

Neil held the gun on Monica while Abby tied the detective's hands behind her back. I think my sweet Abby enjoyed the pain she caused.

At that moment, Grog sat up. The dazed expression he wore was so comical, I almost laughed. But I didn't – we owed him our lives. The last thing I would do is make light of his confusion.

Abby squatted next to him and explained what had transpired during the last few minutes. The confused expression diminished and was soon replaced with the bewitched one he wore when looking at Abby. That boy had it bad.

I turned my attention back to Monica. What the hell were we going to do with her? I was pondering the issue when we heard a shout in the distance.

Neil promptly hollered back. "Over here!"

"Who is that?"

"That's our ride."

"What are you talking about, Neil

Young?" Ben asked. The twitches were coming less frequently now.

"I think you call her Loretta," he said with a tired grin. "This way."

Ben and I pulled Monica to her feet, none too gently.

After several minutes of tromping through cacti and scrub brush, we came upon a dirt road similar to the one on which we'd arrived just a few hours ago. It seemed like a lifetime ago. I felt the absence of Dylan and Joe more poignantly now than ever. It was wrong, so wrong, that they weren't here to enjoy this modicum of victory.

Two black Suburbans (of course) were parked fifty yards up the road. A passenger side door opened and Loretta emerged.

I'd forgotten how attractive she was. The simpering, lecherous drunk was long gone, not that she'd ever really existed at all. In her place was a confident woman with keen eyes that missed no detail, and a smile which hinted at a wicked sense of humor.

"Well done, Neil. I have to say, I honestly

didn't think you'd make it. Any of you," her gesture included all of us. "Two are missing? Am I to assume the worst?"

The uncomfortable silence was answer enough. "I apologize for your loss." Loretta managed to sound sincere while still exuding the charming, businesslike demeanor. "And this one is not a team player, I'm guessing?" she indicated Monica who squirmed under the scrutiny.

Neil nodded.

"Jonathon, please take her to the other vehicle. Make sure she is secure, of course." The man was compact, but his physique implied countless hours at the gym. He escorted Monica to the second SUV.

I never saw her again.

"So, this is Grog," she continued. To my surprise, she walked toward him and extended her hand. "It's a pleasure to meet you finally." He took her fragile-looking hand in his strong grasp. She winced the tiniest bit but the smile never wavered. Her delight at meeting was undeniably genuine.

"Let me guess," Ben said to Neil. "You have a tracker. What, some kind of implant?"

Neil nodded, and slid his shirt sleeve up to his elbow, exposing a small, pink scar on his forearm.

Ben showed his approval with a wallop to Neil's back.

"Neil, we'll be expecting a full briefing within the hour," Loretta said. "Please, everyone into the car and we'll eventually get you back to your own vehicles. For now, though, we have some matters to discuss."

Chapter 21

Our tired and diminished group piled into the Suburban. The driver gave us a cursory nod but otherwise didn't seem inclined to converse. Once we were all situated, Loretta continued from the front passenger seat.

"We're going to one of our secure locations back in Dulce. It's safe and private. We can have a nice chat."

We didn't talk much on the drive back to town. What Loretta wanted to discuss with us was anyone's guess. All that was on my mind at the moment were the people who weren't with us.

Thirty minutes later, we pulled into the parking lot of an Ace Hardware store designated For Employees Only. The building looked like it had been there for fifty years. It, like much of Dulce, was in need of paint and repairs. We entered through the employee entrance door after the driver manipulated a series of rusty-looking locks. We were only slightly surprised to see the difference between the rundown exterior and the upscale, modern interior.

Of course Loretta wouldn't work in a dump.

"We're going down. The bulk of the facility is underground."

Just like everything else. All the important stuff in Dulce happened below ground.

The elevator stopped at the third level, according to the flashing number above the doors. We emerged into a hallway with plush carpeting, expensive-looking artwork on the walls and soft lighting. People dressed in what my office would have called 'business casual' passed us from both directions, their demeanors were friendly but businesslike. Most of them smiled and nodded to us in greeting. A few ogled us in our bloody, tattered paramilitary clothing, and Grog drew a few stares, but most never missed a beat.

"This way, please." Loretta guided us down a smaller corridor off to the right and ushered us into a large conference room with several doors leading to who knew where. Water, coffee and donuts waited for us on a side table.

Ben didn't hesitate.

"Please, help yourself," she said in a wry tone. "Use the restroom facilities if you need to," she gestured to one of the doors. "I'll be back in a few moments. Neil, come with me, please." They left through a door at the farthest corner of the room.

We were situated at the table when she returned twenty minutes later.

"I have a business proposal for you. All three of you. After what you've seen and experienced, you would be valuable assets to our organization. I know this is a lot to throw at you right now after what you've been through, but I want to get everything on the table as quickly as possible. I wonder if you even have jobs to go back to in Dallas? Especially Ms. Montgomery here."

Good point.

"You need answers and information before you can consider our offer, of course, but a brief overview will serve us best at the moment."

She had our undivided attention.

"As I mentioned before to Josh, we're a sort of watchdog organization. We've been keeping our finger on the pulse of the NWO for a very long time, as well as the other people and groups whose agenda was to acquire extraterrestrial DNA. Let me be very clear – we rarely intervene. Outfitting Neil with the equipment you requested and providing his services to you was against protocol. I'm taking some heat for it too, though I don't regret it. According to Neil's report, you were quite effective in derailing the plans of that rather diabolical group – at least for now. So, well done." She smiled, allowing us a moment to bask in whatever glory we felt the situation called for.

"Still, our prime directive is and always will be one of passive observation. Monitor what mankind does with the tools it was given back in ancient Sumer, as well as how it uses the gift left here in the underground caverns of New Mexico.

"You've seen wondrous sights, and perhaps disturbing sights as well. We're on the brink of a major turning point in our evolution. The first one, which occurred all those thousands of years ago, was not of our choosing. This next one will be, if we take that path. As you have witnessed, the results of genetic engineering can go very wrong or, as in Grog's case, very right. It is not our mission to determine mankind's path. If you choose to make public the video taken at the base, we will not interfere. You are given free will in this as in everything. Frankly, I would be quite interested in seeing the public reaction, but I'm not convinced that option would be in the best interests of our country or our planet. I'm no fan of the NWO, and I admit it would give me great satisfaction to see them exposed. However, most likely, the video would be discredited as a hoax and your personal reputations would be massacred. That's how they operate.

"Now, back to our mission here. We are

observers, but even more importantly, we are ambassadors. We are the go-between, as it were, between our race on earth and those who orchestrated our existence."

She paused to gauge our reaction. Something told me we were about to be blown away. Was she saying what I think she was saying?

"You mean the Anunaki? The ancient aliens who altered us are still around?" I asked. Even as I said the words, I couldn't believe how absurd it sounded. I looked at Grog, who sat next to Abby, happy and tranquil.

Maybe it wasn't so absurd.

Loretta smiled. "They never left, Josh – not all of them. They're concerned about the recent events, but as always, will not interfere. They are utterly resolved to allowing mankind to command its own destiny. We are part of a galactic experiment that has been ongoing for thousands of years. They anticipated that our species would eventually unlock our own genetic code and that manipulation was bound to follow. They were dismayed that their essence would be utilized in the form of such creatures as the Omegas, but some good came from those experiments as well, as Grog's presence here can attest."

Her attention focused on him, like two benevolent blue lasers. The human side of Grog squirmed in his chair.

"Would you like to meet one of the patriarchs of your family, Grog?" She didn't wait for his response, but walked to the door which she'd gone through previously.

When she emerged again, she was followed by something that made Grog look completely human.

Its huge black eyes encompassed the upper half of its face. The slit of a mouth was wide and became wider when it saw Grog. Its features, if taken individually, should have been monstrous.

But somehow they weren't. The enormous eyes projected kindness, and when it placed its long gray hands on Grog's shoulders, the gesture was unquestionably one of affection.

Loretta's smile was dazzling, but it paled in comparison to Grog's.

at the same time. Clearly, Joe did not share my opinion.

"We'll camp out on your sofa, Abs. You're not spending the night alone."

"Don't be silly. I have two guest bedrooms all ready for you."

Of course she did. I knew she was secretly delighted that her Laura Ashley bedding would finally have some company.

The rest of the night passed without incident. The only kidnappings, covert attacks and alien encounters that took place for the next six hours occurred within the confines of my dreams.

of him, think about what they'd be willing to do to us. They've already proven they're willing to kidnap and kill."

"Ben's right," I said. "I don't think it's wise to tip our hands quite yet. We don't know who we can trust."

Dylan looked exasperated. "Fine," he said. "I'm beat. I'm heading home to see what Loretta's crew did to my house while I've been gone. I need to pick up the animals at the clinic too." "You want me to come with?" Ben asked him. "I could bunk at your place tonight. Save me the trouble of driving back home." I knew Ben's offer wasn't self-serving. He wanted to make sure Dylan wasn't alone in case there was a repeat of what had happened the night before.

"I think that's my cue to depart as well," Ian said as he stood. After some over-the-top flowery compliments about Abby's cooking, a suave kiss of her hand and a firm handshake for rest of us, he left. I still hated him for his cool accent and the debonair manner in which he pulled off the hand-kissing, but I couldn't help liking him

Chapter 22

"Loretta, we know there are more of the Omegas because Grog can still hear them. What the hell are we gonna do about it?"

"Joshua, the question isn't what *we* will be doing but rather what *you* will be doing. As you know, it is not part of our directive to get involved. If you decide to strike out on your own, you will be in the same situation that Neil was when he came to you. We will be forced to cut ties with you until such a time that you are no longer actively involved in pursuit. You'll have the same deal as before: access to state of the art weaponry and electronics, but no further help or communication."

I had her on speaker phone so Ben and Abby could hear. I locked eyes with Ben as he nodded. My gaze moved to Abby, who was also nodding.

"Deal, but I want one more thing."

A dramatic sigh. "What then?"

I glanced at Grog who was watching me over the screen of his MacBook, an interested gleam in his eyes.

"I want Grog."

"No can do, Joshua. He is not part of the deal."

Loretta had more to say, but we never heard what it was because Grog moved toward my cell phone with the quickness of a jungle cat, and hung up on her.

His long fingers flew over the keyboard of the Mac then he turned the screen o face us.

"Time for a donut run, yes Ben? I get shotgun!"

Excerpt from Troop of Shadows

The Troop of Shadows Chronicles is my most popular books. The following is an excerpt from Book 1 of the Troop of Shadows Chronicles. Enjoy!

***

EXCERPT FROM THE TROOP OF SHADOWS CHRONICLES:
Dani cursed the weight of her backpack. The final two items from the ransacked Walgreens, crammed in as an afterthought

ten minutes ago, might cost her everything. After surviving the last twelve months of hell only to be thwarted now by a can of Similac and a twelve-pack of Zest soap, would be sadly anticlimactic. Despite running at a full sprint down a dark suburban street, dodging overflowing garbage cans while eluding three men who would steal her hard-won tubes of Neosporin and likely rape and kill her in the process, she snorted at the thought of a fictional headline: *Young Woman's Life Ends Tragically but Zestfully Clean.*

****

Damn it, she would ditch the backpack. She could come back tomorrow night for it, but right now staying alive outweighed any future benefit its contents might provide. As her pursuers rounded the corner behind her, she darted across the front lawn of a house and leaped over a cluster of dead juniper shrubs. A year ago, those shrubs had been green, manicured, and providing curb appeal to the upscale neighborhood; they functioned now as a hurdle component in the obstacle course Dani navigated on most nights.

She angled toward the side of the house and around the corner, only to come to an abrupt stop next to a six-foot barricade. Residents of these sprawling bedroom communities situated between Dallas and Fort Worth clung to their privacy fences as fiercely as their rural counterparts did to their firearms. Why all those day-trading dads and cheerleader moms required such secrecy was beyond Dani. She didn't care. All that mattered was how difficult they made her nightly forages. Only idiots or people with a death wish traveled alone on the streets anymore. The clever ones navigated through backyards and drainage ditches, shadowed easements and alleyways, avoiding open spaces and other humans.

Especially humans traveling in groups.

Stealth and caution were second nature to her now, and she was pissed at herself for loading up the backpack with more weight than she could easily carry at a full run.

Rookie mistake.

She flung the pack into the undergrowth of a once meticulous garden, making a mental note of the enormous red tip photinia which camouflaged the bundle in a leafy shroud. She hoped to be alive the next day to retrieve it.

She clambered up the fence, finding a toehold on a warped plank, and squirmed over the top. A silver fingernail of a moon did little to illuminate the backyard. Weak starlight reflected off the inky surface of a half-empty, kidney-shaped swimming pool. Her Nikes gripped the concrete deck as she skirted the murky water and made a beeline for the back of the yard that was, of course, separated from its neighbor by a privacy fence. It was a tall one too — a full ten feet. There were no bushes or trees to use for leverage either. She scanned the area for anything that might serve as a step ladder.

Of all the yards she could have chosen for her escape, she'd picked one with a damn ten-foot fence.

Her heart raced from the sprint, but not from panic. Gone was the young woman from a year ago, the full-time floundering college dropout and part-time surly Starbucks barista who spent too much time reading books and not enough time looking for a job that would allow her to move out of her parents' house. She was too smart for her own good, everyone had told her. She should have taken that secretarial position in North Dallas, but she would have lost her sanity in that environment. The tedious filing, the ringing phones, the office politics — in other words, hell on earth for a girl with an IQ over a hundred and fifty.

Despite the recent horrors, she'd come into her own at last, after twenty-one years of meandering through life unfocused and unchallenged. The extra twenty pounds she'd been carrying courtesy of Freddy's cheeseburgers and Taco Bell burritos were gone, thanks to her newfound self-discipline and endless hours of Krav Maga training with Sam. Not only had she transformed her body, she'd elevated and strengthened her mind as well. Before the power had gone out, she'd watched countless tutorials on T'ai Chi, Qigong, and Buddhist meditation. During that same window — when people were beginning to get sick, but before most of them had died — she'd combed book stores and libraries within a fifteen-mile radius. When the country went dark and people realized that life-saving information was no longer available with a few keystrokes, Dani had amassed reference material on subjects as diverse as hydroponics and combat first aid, ancient meat drying techniques and bomb making. Between martial arts lessons with Sam, she spent every spare minute absorbing the printed esoteric knowledge like a greedy lizard on a sun-drenched rock.

Knowledge was survival.

When the first of the men slithered over the fence into the backyard, she hadn't found anything to use as a foothold. Another figure followed behind him. She closed her eyes, took a deep breath and released it from her lungs, slow and measured, then took off at a full run toward them. While she ran, fingers slid down to a leather sheath secured to her belt. Two seconds before she reached the first of her would-be assailants, a Ka-Bar — the grandaddy of tactical knives — was in her hand.

Dani used momentum and every ounce of her one-hundred-twenty pound frame to slam the first man into the second, knocking both assailants off-balance and unprepared for her next move: a vicious stab to the groin of the first. He collapsed to his knees. She followed with a backhand movement, opening up the throat of his companion. A similar gesture to the man with the injured groin silenced his moaning.

June (Sixteen months earlier) Archaeological site, Ancient Sumerian city of Uruk30 km east of As-Samawah, Iraq

"This is big, Harry." The American anthropologist spoke to Dr. Harold Clarke, key council member of the British Institute for the Study of Iraq, whose connections were responsible for funding the current multi-national excavation project.

"Indeed, it would seem so, Thomas."

The clay tablet was still embedded in the rock that lined the floor of the ancient Sumerian cave. The previous artefacts found in the area in recent months dated from

3200-3000 BCE, but this new find appeared to be much older. The scratches were difficult to decipher in situ, but were certainly cuneiform. Still, these were somehow different. Harold and the American, who was also an expert in ancient logophonetic languages as was Harold himself, knew it instantly. After delicate brushes had whisked away the last grains of sand and the first photographs taken, a hasty charcoal rubbing revealed something that startled both men and left Harold with an uneasy feeling in his stomach. Although crude in its rendering, next to the wedge-shaped Sumerian symbol for 'god being,' was a detailed representation of the double helix.

SECRETS UNDER THE MESA

Liberty, Kansas
September,(Thirteen months earlier)

"Steven, will you please drag yourself away from the kitchen and mow the front yard? The neighbors are beginning to grumble. I saw them gathering up torches and pitchforks this morning. Better hurry."

The man sighed, irritated but amused. He glanced up at the woman carrying an overflowing basket of clothes to the laundry room. Even after fifteen years of marriage, she still took his breath away. How had a socially awkward nerd straddled with debt courtesy of dual master's degrees in mechanical and electrical engineering, gotten so lucky?

"Clever girl. Your nag-to-funny ratio is flawless, as usual."

She blew him a kiss and began stuffing clothes into the ancient Kenmore. Steven lifted the last of the mason jars from the pressure canner using rubberized tongs designed for the task, then placed the hot jars on the kitchen table. The contents, cubed chicken and broth, still boiled inside the glass. Seconds later the lids began to pop, indicating a vacuum seal. He knew it was silly, but the sound always made him smile. It said, *"You did it right, Stevie Boy! Good job! Now your family won't starve during the zombie apocalypse!"*

Except for his wife Laura, he kept those thoughts to himself. As far as his son knew, the whole 'prepping' thing was just his dad's quirky hobby. But Steven knew better than most how vulnerable the country's power grid actually was. Detonating a nuke twenty-five miles above the earth would spawn an electromagnetic pulse and devastate the grid, setting the country's technology back more than a hundred years. What terrorist group or enemy rogue nation doesn't have wet dreams about crippling the United States? An EMP would be an effective, relatively easy way to do it. All electrical devices stop working and everything goes dark. Supply chains are broken, food becomes scarce, and the fabric of society unravels quickly and violently. Steven could picture the bastards salivating at the thought as they crouched in some Afghani cave.

Those who prepared now might survive if they were sensible, cautious, and discreet. He'd never shared his obsession with his friends nor his co-workers at Kansas Electric — not that he had many friends, and his co-workers tended to avoid his eccentric behavior — so discretion came easily.

He'd filled up the root cellar with first dozens and then hundreds of canned vegetables and concentrated soups, tuna fish, and Spam. The canned items segued to rice, sugar, salt, pasta, and a large variety of beans stored in Mylar bags and food-grade buckets. He'd discovered the shelf life of peanut butter was surprisingly short, so he purchased a powdered version in bulk. High-acid foods like tomatoes and fruit degraded their metal containers, so he learned to can them himself in mason jars. Commercially canned meat was cost prohibitive, which led to buying a pressure canner at the Goodwill store in Salina and educating himself on methods for preserving poultry, pork, and beef. When done correctly and stored under optimal conditions, his food would last for years — decades even, despite the assertions of the FDA and the *Ball Blue Book Guide to Preserving*.

He'd built the cellar himself with the help of his oldest son, Jeffrey, whose stringy thirteen-year-old muscles and quiet tenacity had proven invaluable. They'd completed the job over a weekend six months before, and it was almost filled to capacity. He eyeballed the pint jars still bubbling on the kitchen table, considered Laura's reaction to the idea of a second cellar, and decided that battle would be more easily won with the leverage of a tidy yard. She didn't embrace this business of planning for the end of the world, but she did tolerate it. Barely. And for that, he loved her even more.

He kissed her cheek, squeezed her backside, and headed out the door to the shed where the lawn tools were stored. On the way, he noted the newly installed wind turbine fifty yards from the house near the back fence line. The three propeller-like blades spun with an eerie robotic grace, conjuring electricity from the movement of air with silent efficiency. When he received his annual bonus, he intended to add solar as a back-up for those times when Mother Nature's bluster didn't cooperate. For now, the turbine powered only the well pump; they still relied on Kansas Electric for everything else and would continue doing so until Steven could work out the glitches with his off-grid system. He experienced moments of anxiety when he thought of all that still needed to be done. If his family were to remain safe in a world suddenly turned upside down, he better get cracking.

Starting with mowing the lawn.

It was an important chore only in terms of his marriage — and therefore immensely important — but his mind had already leapt ahead to the next project. He estimated the yard work would take him until lunchtime, which meant a good five hours of daylight left to start on the new root cellar. He could put a big dent in it if Laura didn't have other chores lined up for him, assuming she green-lighted the plan in the first place.

As he pondered the best angle from which to approach that marital-landmine-riddled task, his cell phone vibrated in his jeans pocket. The display showed an image of a smiling woman with dark hair and more than a passing resemblance to Steven.

"Hey, sis. Long time no hear. What's new in the sexy world of molecular genetics? Have you discovered the gene responsible for penis length yet? I'm asking for a friend."

"Hey, little brother. What's happening in the steamy world of mechanical engineering? Did you finish the schematics for that female sex bot? You're destined to be rich, you know."

He could hear the smile in her voice but also something else. Fatigue? Worry?

"Not as rich as you if you get that penis thing nailed down. What's up, Julia Petulia? How's Stan?" He knew she despised the pet name, especially now that she was a big-shot scientist with diplomas covering the walls of her office and the letters 'Ph.D.'

printed on her business cards.

"Stan's fine. Still no sign of the cancer, thank god. He's dealing with the normal bullshit at the firm."

"You doing okay? You sound tired."

"I'm exhausted. Work has been kicking my ass. Which is why I'm worried that I may be overreacting..."

Steven didn't know much about her current project, just that she'd been studying the phenotype of a particular gene in order to determine its mutation characteristics...the usual stuff. He was a smart guy, but the human genome didn't hold any great interest for him, so he usually zoned out when Julia rambled on about her work. She probably did the same during their conversations about his work, although recently she'd asked about disaster preparedness, which had struck him as odd.

"Overreacting how?"

"The behavior of the molecule I've been working with is like nothing we've ever seen before. And not in a good way."

She had his full attention now. "What do you mean? Not good how?"

"The way in which it's expressing is unprecedented. It's been dormant until now. We knew its nature was developmental, meaning it would become active at a certain stage of its lifespan, versus how a 'tissue specific' DNA molecule can make hair fall out because it's located in the scalp."

His attention began to wane. Julia sensed it and hurried on.

"This gene has suddenly self-actuated in most of the samples we've collected. This is crazy behavior — DNA is highly individual — but this gene is acting identically in almost all of the samples, at nearly the same time...like a collective consciousness thing."

"I'm with you so far I think, but where's the bad news in this? What's it doing that has you guys at Stanford so nervous?"

Silence on the other end while she formulated a response. Seconds ticked by. Steven was beginning to wonder if the connection had been dropped when she finally spoke.

"In layman's terms, it seems to be telling all the cells in the body to self-destruct, which should be impossible, yet it's happening before our eyes. If we're right about this..."

"What? What does it mean?"

"Steven, if we're right about this, it would mean the end of humanity as we know it."

He suddenly found himself sitting on the overgrown lawn.

Press conference given by the Centers for Disease Control
Atlanta Georgia
November,(Eleven months earlier)

"It's not airborne. We know that for sure. But it's not clear how the disease is spreading." The man behind the makeshift podium spoke into more than a dozen microphones representing a huge variety of national and world news affiliates. His face was pale and haggard, suggesting days of sleep deprivation, but his carefully prepared speech and quiet, self-assured demeanor conveyed confidence. The scientific community would prevail over this dire threat — that was the message he intended to project.

"It's neither bacterial nor viral. Its characteristics are similar to autoimmune diseases such as rheumatoid arthritis or lupus in that certain cells of the body attack other cells. Specifically, it works in the vascular system and is analogous to SNV — systemic necrotizing vasculitis — but the onset occurs over hours rather than months or years.

"We are working around the clock to get a handle on this. We understand that people are afraid, but panic only makes the situation worse."

He pointed to a female reporter from Reuters.

"Will the PSI be raised?" she asked.

"That's up to Health and Human Services. Since this isn't influenza, the protocol is different. However, I expect the Pandemic Severity Index to be upgraded to level 4 within the day so that additional federal and state resources may be utilized."

He nodded to a dark-skinned man from Al Jazeera News.

"Is it spreading as rapidly in other countries as it is in the United States? Is there a demographic it favors?"

"We believe the event is happening worldwide at the same frequency and diffusion as it is here. There is no evidence to indicate that any segment of the populace is at higher risk than any other. It appears to be an equal opportunity illness and is presenting in all ages, all ethnicities, and both sexes without bias."

"Director Frieden!" A young man from CNN didn't wait to be called upon. "What is the mortality rate?"

He'd been dreading this question. Facts and candor would adversely affect a society already exhibiting hysteria, and the White House had issued a mandate two hours ago that panic must be contained even at the price of the truth. He'd withheld most of what they knew about the disease to everyone except his fellow scientists at the CDC, and of course the group from Stanford who had initially tipped them off about the gene mutation.

"It's still relatively low," he lied. "But we haven't been able to determine accurate numbers at this point."

If people knew the mortality rate, it would spark the immediate breakdown of social order and more people would die as a result of the pandemonium. This was the balm with which he soothed his conscience. Withholding the truth now would be saving lives.

At least for a while longer.

Even though every person on the planet possessed the DNA molecule responsible for the widespread deaths, not everyone's were self-actuating...yet. Those in whom it had, were dead within a day or two.

When it happened, it was quick and catastrophic. The vascular system became inflamed and blood flow to vital organs grew restricted. Death from suffocation or kidney failure occurred mere hours after the first sign of chills and fatigue. The speed with which the body responded to the directive given by the gene was unprecedented, and any therapies they might develop to battle it would take months or years. Director Frieden knew from his research that at the rate the illness was occurring in the population, they would never beat it in time. Fate had placed him at the helm of the Centers for Disease Control during the most significant event in human history.

Its demise.

****

The series is available on Amazon: https://www.amazon.com/dp/B01E4KAD8U

Your Opinion?

What Did You Think of Secrets Under the Mesa?

If you didn't like the book, please tell me... if you did like the book, please tell everyone. My email address is: nicki@nickihuntsmansmith.com.

If you liked the book, please leave a review. Studies have shown that most readers say reviews (both the number of reviews as well as the rating) are an important factor in their buying decision. Please take 2-3 minutes to leave a review.

Here's a ink to Amazons review page for Secrets Under the Mesa.

https://www.amazon.com/review/creat

e-review?&asin=B00O3EL09Y

You can follow me on Facebook at:

https://www.facebook.com/AuthorNickiHuntsmanSmith/

You can signup for my newsletter at:

https://nickihuntsmansmith.com/webs. My subscribers are the first to know of a new release.

I look forward to hearing from you!

Nicki Huntsman Smith

Books by Nicki Huntsman Smith

All my books are enrolled in the Amazon Kindle Unlimited program. So if you are a Kindle Unlimited subscriber, like me, you can read all of my books for free.

DEMON CHASE- Book 1 in A Monstrous Dread SeriesA nail-biting, supernatural suspense horror series begins with DEMON CHASE.

TROUBLED SPIRITS – Book 2 in A Monstrous Dread Series – The thrills continue in Wyoming

A DIFFERENT KIND OF MONSTER – Book 3 in A Monstrous Dread Series – Not all monsters are demons…(Estimated publication date is February, 2024)

SUBLIME SEVEN Time Travel with a Transcendent TwistFollow the evolution of a soul as told through seven incarnations on earth and beyond.

TROOP OF SHADOWS – Book 1 in the Troop of Shadows ChroniclesA riveting, multi-character post-apocalyptic journey starts here with Book One.

BEAUTY AND DREAD – Book 2 in the Troop of Shadows Chronicles SeriesThe second installment in the Troop of Shadows Chronicles follows the characters you loved (and hated) in Book One.

MOVING WITH THE SUN – Book 3 in the Troop of Shadows Chronicles SeriesThe third installment in the series takes place in Florida and introduces a new cast of characters, along with some old favorites.

WHAT BEFALLS THE CHILDREN – Book 4 in the Troop of Shadows Chronicles SeriesThe fourth installment in the series takes place in Appalachia and introduces new characters to love and hate, along with an old favorite.

THOSE WHO COME THE LAST – Book 5 in the Troop of Shadows Chronicles SeriesThe fifth book in the series returns to Whitaker Holler where two adversarial clans finally determine the fate of their people once and for all.

DEAD LEAVES, DARK CORNERS – A collection of short storiesAn eclectic assortment of nail-biting short stories and one spine-tingling novelette.

SECRETS UNDER THE MESAA pinch of "X-Files" and a dash of "Stranger Things".
PERCEPTIONS A short story.

Report Typos and Errors Here

Thank you for helping make my books error free. I have tried to make it a s simple as possible to report any type of error you might have found.

If you click on the link below, you will be taken to my website where I have a form specifically designed to capture the error information.

If you are on on a Kindle or any other type of ereader you can just click on the link. If you are reading a paperback, you will need to type in the URL.

Report all errors here:
https://nickihuntsmansmith.com/errata